Hera
OR EMPATHY

A WORK OF UTOPIAN FICTION

WILLIAM LEISS

❧ A Cangrande Book ❧

A Cangrande Book™

© Magnus & Associates Ltd. 2006

A CANGRANDE BOOK is a trade-mark of Magnus & Associates Ltd.

www.herasaga.com

Contact: magnus@herasaga.com

Printed in Canada. Distributed in the United States and Canada
by Hushion House Publishing Ltd.
36 Northline Road Toronto, Ontario M4B 3E2
www.hushion.com

Library and Archives Canada Cataloguing in Publication

Leiss, William, 1939-
    Hera, or Empathy : a work of Utopian fiction / William Leiss.

(The Herasaga)
"A Cangrande Book".
ISBN 0-9738283-0-7

    I. Title. II. Title: Empathy. III. Series.
PS8623.E475H47 2006   C813'.6 C2005-907865-0

Cover artwork for *The Herasaga* trilogy: Alex Colville, *Church and Horse*
(1964), *Horse and Train* (1954), *Moon and Cow* (1963):
© AC Fine Art Ltd., used with permission; Musée des Beaux-Arts de
Montréal (for *Church and Horse*); Art Gallery of Hamilton (for *Horse
and Train*). Chapter 5 and Figures 1, 2, 3 by Anne Awh: Copyright
© 2005 by Don M. Tucker, used with permission. Picture of Carstensz
Pyramid: Copyright © 2005 by Patrick Morrow, used with permission.

Cover, production design: Hydesmith Communications, Winnipeg.

Hera
OR EMPATHY

A WORK OF UTOPIAN FICTION

Contents

Three years before I ... had created a fiend whose unparalleled barbarity had desolated my heart, and filled it for ever with the bitterest remorse. I was now about to form another being, of whose dispositions I was alike ignorant; she might become ten thousand times more malignant than her mate, and delight, for its own sake, in murder and wretchedness. He had sworn to quit the neighbourhood of man, and hide himself in deserts; but she had not; and she, who in all probability was to become a thinking and reasoning animal, might refuse to comply with a compact made before her creation ....

Even if they were to leave Europe, and inhabit the deserts of the new world, yet one of the first results of those sympathies for which the daemon thirsted would be children, and a race of devils would be propagated upon the earth, who might make the very existence of the species of man a condition precarious and full of terror.

Mary W. Shelley, *Frankenstein* (1818)

In natural systems, there is no guilt or virtue, only success or failure, measured by survival and nothing more. Time is the judge. If you manage to pass on what you have to the next generation, then what you did was right.

Barbara Kingsolver, *Pigs in Heaven* (1993)

W I L L I A M   L E I S S

For eight Great Danes – elegant Bree, sweet-tempered Clio, and meek Sappho; the incomparable Cangrande Magnus and his daughter, clever Yoko; gorgeous Marco, charming and doomed; the gentle giant Theo and silly Lily:

Unbidden, memory hovers above a place of unfathomable sorrow, where it stirs the traces of their being, abrading daily the wounds that cannot heal, the price I pay for the love of dogs.

Hera
OR EMPATHY

Book One of *The Herasaga*

A NOTE FROM THE SUB-COMPILER

The reader of the following pages may be curious as to how they came into my hands. You may well wonder why anyone would trouble himself to preserve these scraps of paper when they might have been put to some better use in the night's fire, warming his miserable supper and holding the leering wolves at bay. And I could forgive you for that thought, for you were not present when my mother Hera entrusted them to me and swore me to the task of preservation.

I fear inciting your annoyance should I neglect to enlighten you as to the origins of the records I have so unimaginatively compiled here. As a young girl, my mother delighted in her discovery of the early series of miniaturized digital voice recorders, so easily concealed in hair or jewelry, now so ubiquitous in interpersonal commerce (not to mention lawsuits for libel and slander!). The transcription software, automatically converting the captured vocalizations into searchable text files, was already at that time remarkable for its fidelity. Even at a tender age Hera had a sense of her destiny, so fully vindicated with the passage of time. She urged her sisters to adopt the personal journal format of her invention, where annotations were appended to the records of daily conversations, thus providing contextual remarks and considered reflections.

You may well ask, "Who is this person? We are unacquainted with her reputation—and with yours. No doubt every mother's son, reflecting upon his genesis, considers the one who brought him into the world to be remarkable to a degree, thus in passing flattering himself. What aspect of her life or fortunes plucks her from the crowd and thrusts itself forward, commanding our undivided attention?" To which queries I concede you are owed an answer.

I offer you a single extract from the record that follows, comprising a conversation between us, recorded by me some two years ago:

"Because we sisters [*Hera is speaking*] were designed as natural beings by an act of another's conscious will, I was obsessed with the religious story of creation as a way of understanding us, who we are, why we came to be engineered by our parents, and what it all meant for our lives and the way we should lead them. Like Frankenstein's monster, I thought at first I must get this explanation from my creator—my father. Like that poor creature in Mary Shelley's story, I also then came to the conclusion that I must make my father understand what I was going through, in my mind, and to convince him to accept my side of the story, so to speak. I wanted to get him to complete his work *by accepting me as I was,* not as he had designed me to be in his own mind, prior to my coming into being and consciousness.

"I thought I had to explain myself to him and to get him to see the real story, which was not about the so-called 'program' he and our mother had invented with their friends, but rather about who and what we—as the embodiment of another's dream—were in and for ourselves, to use a philosophical expression again. Where I got stuck, where I was really bogged down for years, was in believing that for the sake of my own salvation I had to get inside my creator's mind because it seemed to me that was where the answers lay—in his intentions and expectations. I admit I was influenced by his eminence as a scientist and, later, by the extraordinary care he exercised in re-engineering the Second Generation. It took me far too long to see that this was a dead end."

"That reminds me of how Mary Shelley's story concludes, mother. Do you remember that awful scene close to the end, when the creature is found by the ship's captain, standing over the corpse of Dr. Frankenstein, grief-stricken and in despair? After all the cruel transactions between them, he remains bound emotionally to his creator to the bitter end. I remember the words he speaks: He refers to Frankenstein as 'the select specimen of all that is worthy of love and admiration among men.' What inept words these are when used to describe the man who had denied him the chance to overcome his profound loneliness by having a mate of his own kind! He was in thrall to his master and couldn't break free; Frankenstein's death was simultaneously his own self-inflicted sentence of doom."

"That's precisely where my story diverges from Shelley's, Marco. I came at last to the realization that my sisters and I must wrest our own future path out of our creator's hands. I concluded that it didn't really matter after all what my parents intended. We weren't bound by the terms of whatever bargains they had made, either with themselves or with others. We were capable of setting our own terms. And to do this we had to consign Franklin's *Memorandum* to the rubbish heap and look only inside ourselves to find our destiny."

"You never did succeed in getting Franklin [*her father*] to understand why it was so important to you to figure this out and go your own way, did you?"

"I really have no idea whether I did or not. What I do know for sure is that I spent far too much time and effort obsessing about all this, being fixated on it. Good Lord, when I recall those conversations now, all the many occasions during which I badgered him—poor man!—into sitting and listening to my excursions into the Book of Genesis, which he hated so! Finally the truth dawned on me: We sisters were the story, not him. We had within us the power to redefine the nature of the Faustian bargain he and my mother had made."

"Well, I'm not sure you were entirely wrong in obsessing about the Biblical creation myth, or in making him listen to your exegesis of the Book of Genesis. I still think you made a good case in your arguments about crossing the line—which I heard you articulate on several occasions, including when you were rehearsing them with me."

"I'm glad to hear you say that! What he had done, in effect, was to burn down the ancient edifice, the structure of myth common to all the world's monotheistic religions, that tells of our being brought into the world by God's will, by a purpose and will independent of humankind, one that we all serve. My sisters and I arose from those ashes like the Phoenix, the bird-figure of ancient Greek myth that regenerates itself again and again in its own funeral pyre. We are the new-born ones, fully creatures of this earth, children of a mastery of the biochemistry of that extraordinary molecule, DNA."

For the rest of the story you will have to consult the object that lies before your eyes, quarried from the mines in which I labored on your behalf: Book One of *The Herasaga*. When we last spoke before my embarkation, my mother handed me a hard drive, its contents indexed and chronologically ordered, holding many wonderful snapshots of our adventures together, as well as many tens of thousands of pages in electronic files—chiefly from her own journals, she being the most assiduous chronicler of the lot, but including also files from her sisters, father, and yours truly. She said to me, "Dear Marco, you will need more occupations for your mind, in addition to your duties, as you sail through the starry night toward the Red Planet and, I pray fervently, safely back again. Forge a coherent narrative for me from these scattered files. For if no archaeology survives these troubled times, the mute remnant of our lives you create there may be the only testimony to my kind's allotted time on our beloved earth."

Reporting her words obliges me to acknowledge that it was Hera herself who was the actual compiler, and I a mere sub-compiler. Even in this reduced role I fear my incompetence is on display. For when I reviewed the final text I had assembled for you, I confess I was chagrined. After all, a competent prefacer seeks to seduce the reader with the allure of secrets to be uncloaked later. What busy mind would bother to read on had the lowly scribe, whose only mandate was to assemble in good order the documents entrusted to his care, blurted out in the preliminaries his narrative's darkest secrets? What lover of romance would suspend disbelief to follow a plot's improbable path if all uncertainty were made to vanish at the starting gate? And yet for me to decline all revelatory obligations would be a far worse offense.

So I confess here of my own volition, that in calling the one who commissioned this work my mother, because for most of my life I have used that appellation in concourse with her, I may scandalize the reader who, unprotected by my dissembling, later stumbles upon the truth. Here then is what lies ahead in this chronicle: Hera—my stepmother, in a manner of speaking—plotted in meticulous detail, first the murder of my father, and second the banishment and exile of my natural mother, and oversaw the successful execution of those plans. If I now say to you that I acquiesced in the second of these crimes, and that I would have ratified the first with enthusiasm had I been capable of doing so, you will think me either mad or bewitched. So be it. In forewarning you I have discharged my duty. Read first, I beg you, and then judge my condition.

Although I bear the markings of one who is a half-breed, I, too, once emerged as an actor in our family drama. Thus when my mother solicited me to assume the task of authorship, I was, in theory, well positioned to promote myself to the role of omniscient narrator, at least for those episodes that postdate the onset of my involvement in them. I might have become the all-seeing, keen-eyed reporter of our fortunes. Alas, I found in myself neither the courage nor the talent to discard the compiler's yolk and its puerile cut-and-paste methodologies learned in kindergarten. Thus my sorry pastiche stands before you. And if you find the tale to be obscure and the characters' motives inexplicable, I reply, all obliquity found therein must be marked down to my account. If you now remark that the characters I have propped up before you remain glued to my pages, lifeless and wooden, I say do not attach your obloquy to them all, but only to me.

As I was then, at twenty-five years of age,

MARCO SUJANA
Commander, Technical Operations
On board *Colonizer 1*
Mars Settlement Mission, AD2055

POSTSCRIPT: I have prepared a website where some pictures of the locations described in the following narrative may be found: **www.herasaga.com**

PART ONE

IN THE MIND'S EYE

30 September 2021

Two weeks ago we had a party for our seventh birthday, and my father was with us again, and we were so happy.

He's very nice, although he doesn't come here very often, and we don't know where he goes when he leaves. But who are we and why are we here? And where is our mother? We see children like us when we're surfing the Internet and almost always they have both mothers and fathers, who look just like the people who take care of us here. But when we ask these people if they are related to our parents, making them our uncles and aunts, they say they are not, and then they look worried and say that they're not supposed to talk about such things with us. We also see many things on the Internet that we don't have, and no one will tell us why.

I want my father to stay with us here all the time, but when I tell him this, he just laughs and gives me a hug. He's always very nice to me and promises that one day soon he'll set up his laboratory nearby and then we'll see him almost every day. I hope he'll tell me why we're so different from the people who take care of us, whom he calls our helpers. I know we're different, but I don't understand why. I've talked to the other girls about this and we all agree.

Our helpers are a little afraid of us, I think. Even though they are very friendly and are happy to do things for us, often they don't tell us what they're really thinking, even when speaking directly to us. They do this with each other as well, especially when a man is talking to a woman. I see their lips moving and I hear the words that are spoken, but often what they say doesn't seem to indicate what's really happening. Sometimes I decide not to pay attention to the words and listen just to the sounds, because the same words can come out in so many different ways.

But mostly I just half-listen to the words and watch the person very closely, and then I see all kinds of other things when he or she is talking, such as slight movements in the face and body, especially around the eyes and in the hands and arms. It seems almost as if their mouths are not connected to the rest of them, and that the words are not important or are just being spoken as a way of hiding the other thoughts going on secretly within that person.

Once I was standing near some of the young men who carry guns and wear special uniforms. They were watching a group of the women who feed us and clean our rooms and our clothes. Sometimes these women like to walk close to the men and laugh as they hear the men talk about them. Then I see the men make some gestures with their hands and move their hips, and it reminds me of the male monkeys we see on the wildlife programs, who just walk up to other monkeys from behind and make these motions with their hips, then they stop, and soon they do it again. The other monkeys—the females—don't even seem to notice what is happening, and they just carry on with what they were doing, such as eating or looking for food. The young men in our village do not do this, although it seems to me they would like to try to do it.

Yesterday I came into my room while Mrs. Winarto was making my bed. A couple of weeks earlier I had overheard her talking to one of the other helpers, saying she was worried about her son who was in trouble with the police. I noticed that when she was saying this, her eyes were squinting and her lips were trembling slightly, and she was making quick movements with her hands. When I saw her making my bed and observed these same things again, I asked her, "Mrs. Winarto, why are you worrying about your son today?" She looked up and screamed, then after a pause she exclaimed, "Child, don't frighten me like that! How did you know what I was thinking? Are you a witch or something?" After that she never cleaned my room and someone else did this.

§   §   §

For a while now, I've been terribly worried about two of the girls, Moira and Themis, who went away a long time ago. I pestered Mrs. Winarto for months, asking about them, and finally she told me a few stories—she said I should keep this to myself, and not say anything to the professor about what she had told me. Mrs. Winarto had heard that those two were acting odd when they were just babies, not yet one year old; they were going stiff all over and refusing to be held in the arms of adults. They were screaming a lot, too, she added, and making strange motions with their heads and arms. They didn't play with the rest of us—I vaguely remember this myself—or with the toys we had. Instead, they just sat and stared at things, at their hands, or pictures, or they spent hours in the outdoor playpen, letting sand run through their fingers. What's really terrible is that, according to Mrs. Winarto, before they left here they hadn't started talking at all, like normal babies do.

Today, when my father visited again, I asked him about Moira and Themis. He said they were very sick but getting much better, thanks to the special help he had arranged at a hospital nearby, and that he hopes he can soon bring them back here to stay.

That Moira and Themis aren't yet talking is very worrying to me because the other girls and I apparently began to talk when we were very young. Mostly we chatter to each other in one of the languages we're learning from the Internet. Our helpers don't know what we're saying, which seems to frighten them, probably because they only speak one language and we like to learn new ones all the time. We try to start one new language every few months, although some are harder than others because they're not related to those we already know, like English or Indonesian or Italian. We have lots of time to do this because we don't sleep very much and like to explore the Internet all night.

Our helpers say that someday we'll have to become students and go to school to be taught in classrooms, but we say we're already doing this all the time by ourselves. We like learning mathematics as much as languages, but we do have to be careful. One day Mrs. Winarto found some of our exercise papers and thought that the math symbols were 'witch-writing,' so now we make sure we put them away where the helpers cannot see them.

All of us learn together, which is fun, and we all try to be the first to find a proof or learn a new word in a language. But as much as we try, we haven't been able to find out who we are.

Although we don't sleep very much, the other girls and I have a lot of dreams. Many of my dreams are about the people who live in the village here. When they meet us we try to speak to them but they run away, saying that they cannot understand what we're saying and that we're the spirits of dead people. I don't know what spirits are, although we have read about them. Then the ravens sitting in the trees talk to me and say they know what I'm saying, and that they also have talked to the dogs in the village, and to other creatures in the forest, and all of the animals can understand what I say. But the ravens said that none of the creatures try to talk to the other people in the village because the people aren't interested in listening to them. So maybe the animals are spirits like us.

The women who take care of us are very nice. When

we're careful to use only the language they speak, they're not frightened and will talk to us about what we want to eat and what games we would like to play outside. But the men in the village don't talk to us, even when we speak to them, and they move away from us when we approach.

I asked Mrs. Winarto about this and she said that they're not supposed to talk to us and especially not to touch us, and if they ever try to do this then right away we must tell her or Mr. Retnawati, who bosses the men with guns. I have seen him telling the men what to do. I am afraid of the men, but I don't know why. Even though the men don't speak to us, they seem to be watching us all the time, and they talk a lot to each other—and laugh loudly—when they see all of the girls playing together.

I've seen boys in the village and asked Mrs. Winarto whether they could come and play games with us, but she said no, this was not allowed and we must not talk to them. They also watch us a lot, and they whisper to us when they think no one is watching.

I had a dream about these boys last night. All of us girls were out walking through the jungle, and it was hard to see where we were going. Then I saw two people ahead, a man and a woman, and I thought that they must be our parents, so we all called to them. They were startled when they heard us and ran away, too fast for us to catch them. We were all very sad, because we walked and walked for a really long time, but we didn't see them again. Then we suddenly came upon a group of young boys fishing by a stream and cooking their catch over fires.

We were very hungry and thirsty by that time and they called us over and gave us something to eat and drink, which we accepted. A little later some of them took their pants off and showed us their bodies, and asked us to show them our bodies. Some of the girls started to undress, but I said "No!" and told them we should run away quickly. The boys just laughed and didn't try to follow us.

About a year ago I began to get very bad headaches. They started soon after my father began sending us a big test each week by e-mail, which we had to complete within a few hours and then send back to him so he can tell us our score. We always get a lot of messages from him over the Internet; most of the time they are not tests, and we always reply. Just after our birthday last year he told us that it was time for us to pretend that we were going to school; he said he would give us each a different lesson assignment every week, and on Monday morning we would get the test. Then on Monday afternoon we would get the next assignment.

All of us like tests and we always do very well on them; in fact, many times we get perfect scores. So I don't think it's really the tests that are causing my headaches. Maybe it's the assignment, because every Monday afternoon I can feel my headache starting.

The doctor told me to come to the clinic when this happens. By the time I get there my head is already hurting and he gives me some pills, but it takes a long time for the pain to go away. Before my head begins to hurt I feel a little strange, dizzy almost, maybe even confused; I cannot think clearly or concentrate on anything. The doctor once asked me if I felt light-headed, and I said, "Yes, something like that." Sometimes a band of colored light appears, even when I close my eyes. Then, before long the pain starts; I put my fingers on my temple, one side or the other, and I can feel my heart pounding there. Always only on one side of my head, but not always the same side.

When I go to the clinic, the nurse helps me lie down. Then it starts to hurt, worse and worse, and I get sick to my stomach, too, and then I throw up. I feel a little better after that, but not much. The pounding in my temple is very strong and I try to hold my head. I also put a cold washcloth over my eyes, and that feels good. I ask the nurse to close all the curtains and the door because it helps to have the room dark and very quiet.

Then I lie there for hours, listening to the pounding in my head, feeling the pain, waiting for it to start to go away. I can tell when it starts to go away and I know then that I'll be better again soon. It's so strange because the next day I feel really good, and I don't get another headache all week. After a while I realized that I would get another one when the next Monday afternoon came around. The doctor says that these are called migraine headaches and that maybe they'll just stop when I get a little older.

§   §   §

My father brought me and the other girls the birthday present I'd asked for after seeing the product described on an Internet site. It's a very small digital voice recorder, so tiny I can wear it concealed in my hair near my ear or in the form of a brooch pinned to a garment. I've been trying it out and it works really well, picking up voices and words accurately from people who are standing up to about five feet away. It's also easy to speak aloud when I'm alone and to record my thoughts and observations whenever I feel like doing so. The device has good storage capacity and I can easily download its files directly into my computer's voice recognition software program. Then I just review the files and add some notations about where the conversations occurred, who was speaking at various times, and some additional comments. I don't know why; I just think that it's important for me to make a record of what's going on. I asked father to get one for himself as well and he agreed to at least try it out.

22 SEPTEMBER 2022

I'll always remember what he said at that moment. "All right, Hera, I surrender! I'll submit to my daughter's interrogation—a truly frightening prospect—but I can see that you're determined to have your answers."

Of course I was thrilled! I studied him closely for hours as we talked. He's a big man with long limbs who always walks at a fast pace. He has fine blond hair and blue eyes, and his face is marked by a strong jaw and high forehead. He seems to be exceptionally gentle, as if to compensate somehow for the nervousness that others might feel on account of his size; he smiles easily and his laugh is wonderfully happy. I've always regarded him as very handsome, and, when he finally talked about our mother, I thought I knew right away why she had fallen in love with him.

I confess I was so excited I could barely get words out of my mouth, but I recovered and peppered him with questions, starting with the one that had been uppermost in my mind for a long time. "But father, where is my mother, and why is she not with you, and with me?"

"Your mother's name is Ina Sujana. She was born in Bali, which is quite close to where we are now, as you know, and most of her family, who are all quite wealthy, still live in Indonesia. So you girls are half-Balinese; I'm British. My full name is Franklin Peter Stone, and I'm a professor of neurogenetics at the University of Cambridge in England.

"Your mother and I both received our doctoral degrees—

you know what these university degrees are, I'm sure—from Cambridge. I was five years older and she began to collaborate with me after finishing her degree. We started our scientific collaboration about twenty years ago and soon we had made great advances in our field. Within a few years our research was known all over the world."

"But where has she been all the years we've been growing up here, and where is she now?"

"Your mother was the most wonderful person I have ever known, Hera, but she died in an accident ten years ago. We were partners in both work and life and there will never be another for me. Now all I want is to care for you and your sisters, as she would have done with me."

"Who are my sisters? Are they some of the other girls who live here? Are any of them twins? We do seem to be a lot like each other. Except for Moira and Themis; they seem different. You brought them back with you yesterday. We saw the beautiful Golden Retrievers that they have. Are they going to stay here now? And can each of the rest of us have a dog, too?"

"Goodness, give me a chance to deal with your questions one at a time! The other girls who live in this compound with you are your sisters. There are no twins in the group, but you are all full sisters. That's what I'm going to tell everyone later today, during your eighth birthday celebrations. All of you have the same mother and father, and you were all born within a week of each other—you were the first one to arrive, by the way. Including Moira and Themis, who were born with a certain type of developmental disorder, which I'll explain to you when you're a bit older. They're getting better all the time, and their dogs are actually part of their therapy—they're specially trained to help children who have this type of disorder. For the time being, I'd rather not add any more dogs to the mix; I'm going to have my hands full just taking care of you very smart girls."

"I don't understand, father. We see families on our Internet programs all the time. Sometimes there are two or three of the same age, but not twelve! Mostly the children are younger or older than each other by a few years. So we're clones, aren't we? Io says we're clones and that it's fun to be a clone. But I think it's horrible! I don't want to be a clone."

"Yes, I've noticed that your sister Io has a very active imagination. But she's wrong; you're not clones. I'll tell you what I think you can understand now, and the rest will have to wait until your education is a bit more advanced. You need not worry, however. You're not freaks or weird people, but you are special children who will do very great things for humanity when you grow up."

"But if we're not freaks, father, why are we kept all by ourselves in this little village? We've never been in any of the cities we see in pictures and videos on the Internet, which are full of people and interesting sights. Io says that we're prisoners here and we must try to escape."

"I don't think Io will get very far if she tries to leave! It's a rather long hike down the mountain from the village, especially for a little girl. In any case, you aren't prisoners. You're here for your own safety, Hera. There are people in the rest of the world who wouldn't understand what your mother and I did in having children such as you. You'll all be able to leave and travel everywhere in the world with me after a few more years have passed, and then you can experience many different things. Until then I have to protect you, and I can do that best here.

"Now let me tell you how you were born. Your mother died in December of 2012 while on a trip from England to visit her family in Bali. She was only thirty-four. She was killed in a stupid car accident, and ever since then life has been very difficult for me. I don't know if I could go on if it weren't for you girls. Anyway, after she died ...."

"Father, that was in 2012, you said! How could I have

been born—I and all the girls you say are my sisters—in 2014 if our mother died two years earlier? Were we made from eggs and sperm that had been frozen?"

"Yes, that's right. Your mother had undergone a number of procedures to have multiple eggs collected from her ovaries while she was still quite young. Perhaps she had a premonition that she might die before we had a chance to start a family. I donated my sperm, which was sex-sorted so that the gender of any embryo could be determined in advance, and then the eggs were fertilized and the embryos were frozen. The procedure is called *in vitro* fertilization because the mixing of egg and sperm takes place in a laboratory dish. Thereafter the embryos were stored in what are known as cryopreservation units."

"I know what IVF is, father; I've heard about it on science programs many times. I told Io that this is probably what happened with us, but she wouldn't believe me."

"Then you also know that it doesn't matter if the father's sperm and the mother's egg come together inside the mother's body or in a laboratory dish. Each one of you is a natural child of your mother and me. You are perfectly normal children; *in vitro* fertilization is used all the time to help couples who have difficulty in conceiving children. There is nothing weird about being born this way."

"Yes, I realize that, father, from what I've seen on the Internet. But most people want a few babies, not twelve! *That's* not right!"

"Hera, your mother was such an exceptional person with a brilliant mind and a deeply sensitive spirit. This is why I didn't think it was wrong to want to have more of her children, rather than just two or three. I had the means to ensure that you would all be given every advantage in life, and through your many talents and accomplishments later in life, we would be able to compensate the world for the tragic loss of your mother at such a young age. I'm sorry if you think this was wrong; perhaps you would react differently if you could have known her as I did."

"And how were we actually born? In a machine? Io says that we all came out of one big machine in the laboratory."

"No, that's silly. It's true that there are artificial wombs today, which are machines made to be able to carry a fetus to term. But so far they're being used only for farm animals, although someday they may be used for humans, too. In any case, you girls didn't develop in a machine. We arranged for implanting the embryos in the wombs of local Indonesian women of good health who gave birth to all you girls. This use of surrogate mothers happens all the time when those women who want babies cannot carry them, and there is nothing wrong with it."

"Is Mrs. Winarto my surrogate mother?"

"No. All of the twelve women who carried you, and breast-fed you through the first eighteen months, were sent back to their homes in various parts of Indonesia. They were all given a lot of money, by Indonesian standards, so they and their families were very happy to do this for us. Mrs. Winarto and the other helpers were hired later to take care of you."

"Where were we born?"

"You were all born here in this village, Tembagapura, on the island of New Guinea, so you've been here since birth."

"But why have we been kept here like prisoners all of our lives?"

"As I said, you are not prisoners; this arrangement is for the safety of you and your sisters. I can't explain everything now; it will take time. But you'll understand later, I'm sure, and then also, when you're ready, you'll all be free to go and explore the whole world."

"Father, this is a small village halfway up a sheer mountainside in the remotest province of Indonesia. It's the end of the world!"

"But it's so attractive and peaceful here, isn't it? The climate is wonderful, there are soaring mountains and beautiful trees and flowers all around, and even the fogs that often roll in add a bit of mystery to the place. Every time I come here I'm struck by how lovely the setting is. Besides, these days it doesn't matter how far away you are from other places. With the satellite signals we can get from space, our Internet connections are as fast as anywhere in the world, even the biggest cities. And now that I'll be staying here with you, you'll have a whole group of teachers from all over the world who will come to Tembagapura for a year at a time to teach and tutor you in every branch of knowledge and arts.

"However, even though you'll now have teachers and formal classes, my guess is you'll continue to learn most things by yourselves over the Internet. That was a little experiment of mine. I knew I couldn't spend much time here during your first five or six years because I was developing a very large and successful company, and therefore I couldn't supervise other teachers who might not have been good for you. So I decided to let you educate yourselves—and I see that this experiment has been very successful."

"Yes, but we were always being given medical exams and written tests, one after the other, by people who came here for a short time and said that they were working for you."

"I'll tell you and the other girls much more about all this in the days and years to come. Let me just say I've been trying to find out if I could measure and describe the ways in which you are special. Most of them are standard tests that are given to children all over the world, and I think you know that, except for Moira and Themis, you always did very, very well on those tests. In fact, you ranked consistently in the upper 1% of all those tested."

"All of us thought that those tests were too easy."

"Yes, I'm not surprised that you did. That's why some of them were special tests designed at my request, to measure what are called pattern-recognition and spatial-visualization skills. These results were the most interesting of all, but I cannot explain all of this to you now. My goodness, Hera, look at the time; we must go, the party's beginning!"

We left the study in his residence together and walked over to the dormitory, where one of the recreation rooms had been lavishly decorated for the occasion. Father addressed my sisters and related to them the story he had just told me, about our parentage and how we came to be situated high up in a mountain on the island of New Guinea. He told us that he would be staying here from now on, helping us with our studies, and he also revealed his hopes that we would all become important world leaders one day.

He had brought three gifts for each of us. First, a white toga made of fine Merino wool and adorned with a colorful emblem embroidered in a patch on one shoulder—a representation in profile of the Carstensz Pyramid, the old name for the great mountain on which we live. Second, a personal present of jewelry.

And third, a copy of an album bound in tooled leather, containing many pictures of our mother, dating from early childhood to just before her death, as well as a memoir of her life, dreams and accomplishments. He had written the memoir, which was printed on Japanese handmade paper. When describing the album commemorating our mother's life, he explained that she had fallen in love with Greek mythology during her undergraduate university studies, and the names he had chosen for us at birth was one of the ways in which he had sought to preserve her memory.

He then called upon us one at a time, in alphabetical order, to come forward and receive the gifts he had brought. He also used the one- or two-syllable nicknames with which our little group had baptized the girls who had longer names:

"*Ariadne,* known as 'Ari,' in ancient times you helped Theseus defeat the Minotaur by providing the reel of golden thread that enabled him to find his way out of the Labyrinth.

"*Artemis,* your independent spirit is legendary and you use your skill with the bow to protect all those who are vulnerable, and your sisters bestowed the common name of 'Tammy' on you.

"*Athena,* nicknamed 'Tina,' you are associated with the city as Artemis is with the forests and mountains, and although you are the goddess of war, you prefer to practice the arts of peace as a wise judge and skilful negotiator.

"*Gaia,* you are Mother Earth, not a goddess but more important still, for you are the source from which all things come.

"*Hecate,* known as 'Hex,' you are the goddess of cross-roads and the judge of whether the prayers that humans direct to their gods will be answered.

"*Hera,* the earliest-born among the twelve sisters here, you stirred up revolt among the gods against the tyranny of Zeus and outwitted him time and again with clever stratagems.

"*Io,* you are a bold spirit who will wander far and wide and courageously endure many torments; in ancient times you gave birth to a son whose descendant Hercules freed the heroic Prometheus from the rock to which he had been chained for ages.

"*Moira,* you represent fate and necessity, which rule even the gods, and measure out to humans their allotted time on earth. Girls, Moira and Themis will be staying with us here from now on.

"*Pandora,* usually called 'Pan.' According to the Greeks, you are the first woman on earth, and you are famous for defying Zeus and opening the box from which escaped all evils that bedevil human societies.

"*Persephone,* although you are the queen of the under-world, you return from below in springtime each year and represent the eternal renewal of the earth; your sisters know you as 'Percy.'

"*Rhea,* the mother goddess, when you pressed your full breast, your flowing milk created the pantheon of stars in the sky that we call the Milky Way.

"*Themis,* titan of justice and order, you are both the mother of the fates and of the seasons of lawfulness, justice, and peace."

We remained in a group surrounding him after receiving our gifts, and as he finished he knelt in our midst, making no effort to restrain his tears, which he assured us were the outpouring not of sorrow but of love and happiness.

The next day I showed up again at father's study to sit at his feet and continue the string of conversations between us that had begun last year. This time I brought along Rhea and Hex. After the party the three of us had been talking about what father meant when he said we're special. I told my sisters we must discuss this with him, because I was concerned and indeed a little worried about it.

I began. "You did say we're not freaks, didn't you, father? We've seen some pictures of horrible creatures in circuses and other places that frighten people, and we don't want to be regarded by others as they are! We also saw an old movie once about a creature—he looked like a man, only much bigger—that was made in a laboratory by a scientist called Dr. Frankenstein and that scared people. He wanted to talk to them and be with them, but every time he tried to do this they ran away, and he was very lonely. In the end the only friend he had was a little girl, and then she died. We don't want anything like this to happen to us."

"Hera, please stop worrying about such things! You are perfectly normal girls. You've seen enough on the Internet so far to show you that among normal people there is a very wide range of natural ability. Some people are not very intelligent, but they're still normal, and they can even have children more intelligent than they are. On the other hand, some people are so intelligent that we refer to them as geniuses, although many of them don't act much differently than anybody else does. You've seen references to some of them, I'm quite sure; composers, mathematicians, chess players, and others who could do amazing things with their minds while they were still young children, sometimes even just three or four years old.

"And still in most respects even these geniuses were regarded by others as normal people. Think about Mozart, who started composing music at age four and is regarded as the greatest natural talent in music anyone has ever seen. Well, biographers tell us that Mozart was also a playful and mischievous person, who liked showing off and inventing practical jokes, and who spent his evenings playing billiards and drinking until all hours with his friends. Even if you and the other girls turn out to be geniuses in some ways, you'll still be thought of as normal people, like Mozart was."

Hex said, "Yes, I've seen biographies of such people. So maybe it's just that we're so isolated here and we haven't met very many different people. Maybe that explains why all of us think that we're different, very different, in some ways we can't explain, from all of the people we know in the village here."

"Speaking of being different, girls, I understand that sometime last year you told the staff that all of the sisters had decided to eat a vegetarian menu. Why did you do this?"

Rhea answered. "Oh well, we all talked about it first, of course, and as usual we spent a lot of time on the Internet, reading about diets and foods and different cooking practices in many places in the world. We also watched programs about wild animals called predators that chase and kill other animals for their meat. As far as we could tell, they didn't eat anything else, so they had to eat other animals. We then asked our staff where the meat came from that we were served, and they said from animals raised by farmers and then slaughtered for food. We knew that we couldn't kill animals ourselves in order to eat them, even if we had to, and besides, we have plenty of other foods to eat that are from plants.

"And so we decided it was wrong to eat animals if you didn't really need to and if you had other foods to eat. We checked some websites about nutrition and gave lists of food to the staff; they told the cooks what to prepare for us so that we would still have a good diet, even without meats. But we do eat fish, which I remember you said once is very good for us; that seems somehow different from meat. For some reason we don't feel the same way about fish as we do about meat."

"That's all very interesting, daughters. You know that most people in the world eat meat, don't you? I thought you were afraid of being different from other people."

"Oh father, there are many people in the world who are vegetarians, including millions of people in India who are Hindus," Hex told him. "So we didn't think we were being so different at all. Besides, there are many vegetarians who won't eat fish, like we do, so we're just making up our own minds about what we want to do and what we don't want to do."

"Well, all right, Hecate. I can see that you've all thought about these things and decided for yourselves what you wish to do. And of course I'm glad that you know about nutrition and what you require for a healthy diet. But in general I'm not surprised to hear you say that you and your sisters often feel that you're unlike others. The fact is your minds are much sharper than those of most of the people you'll meet later in your lives.

"However, just remember what I told you about the normal range—or normal variation—in human abilities. If your mother and I had grown up here we would have felt just as you do now. We both sensed while we were still quite young that we had abilities most people didn't. We felt special in some ways, and then when we went to school our teachers also recognized that we were special, because our marks were always at the top of our class.

"The most interesting thing about this is that learning many things, especially school subjects, just comes so easily to people like us. We're the ones who always have our hands up as soon as the teacher asks the class a question. It takes no effort at all for us, it seems, while other students struggle and work so hard just to get passing grades. It doesn't seem fair, but that's the way things are."

"Were you regarded as a freak?" I asked.

He laughed. "In a way I was. The other students would call me 'brain' or 'big brain,' and sometimes they were mean about it and teased me, especially the boys. One way I dealt with the teasing was to help them with their homework assignments, which quickly made me popular. Mostly what I could do so easily seemed to mystify them, because in many other ways I was just like them: I teased other kids, played sports and games, was accepted in groups, chased girls when I was old enough, and so on."

"Yes, we enjoy all those things, too, except that we don't have any boys we can talk to or play with. Mrs. Winarto said that the boys in the village aren't allowed to be with us or even speak to us. Why, father?"

"I'm sorry about those rules, Hera. All I can say is, you're different enough from them that I think it's best if you don't get to know them too well. They're all Indonesians on both their mothers' and their fathers' side. As I told you, you are half-Indonesian and half-British, and so you are really foreigners here, and someday you'll all leave this village and never come back."

"But why don't we have any brothers, at least? Why are we only girls? That doesn't seem normal when we consider other families, especially families with lots of children."

"I knew you would grill me on that question someday! Perhaps it would have been better if there were some boys and girls. I'm sure you're aware that boys and girls are very different, even when they are quite young. Before she died, your mother and I wanted to have our own small family, but that was not to be. Then I had the chance to create a bigger family in her memory and to design a special environment for you in which you could learn at your own pace, free from all the distractions that other children have—including the terrible fights between brothers and sisters that you must have seen on television programs! So I decided that it would be best if you were all girls."

That night I spent a lot of time thinking about our conversation with him. The question about why we have no brothers is one of the most important of all to me, because I often seem to be uneasy when I'm in the presence of men. Also, I've been trying to figure out why I feel afraid much of the time. I remember making a note in my journal last year, about how I'd gotten into the habit of listening to spoken words with one part of my mind, which requires almost no effort at all for me, and at the same time concentrating very hard on everything else that's going on when someone is addressing another person—contractions in their facial muscles, especially in the brow and around the eyes, little changes in their voice tone or speech flow and in the move-ments of their hands.

I've been practicing looking for these signs very carefully, both in live situations and in broadcast programs featuring professional actors. And I found that I can easily compare these attributes with the facial expressions and voice tones deliberately used by speakers to add emphasis to speech.

These expressions often appear to be designed to mislead hearers about the true import of the speech or to conceal other thoughts not being expressed!

So I watched father closely as he was responding to my last question. I don't know why, but I just had the feeling that he wasn't telling us the truth, or at least not the whole truth, about why he had made only girls. I admit I was puzzled. We learned today that our births and upbringing had been well planned in advance. He told us that both he and mother had anticipated the fact that their offspring might be very special. This appears to be the reason why we are being kept in isolation from all other children.

But why didn't we have any brothers? His explanation was that we girls were meant to be a tribute to our mother's special qualities. But certainly father is special, too, so why didn't he think that mother would have wanted him to make some boys as well, as a tribute to him? Was it his idea, after she died, to produce only daughters? The reason this bothers me is that I've seen enough in my Internet surfing to know that many human cultures have very odd ideas indeed about the gender of their offspring! I've read about the horrible results of the one-child family policy in China—because of the preference for male children, and the practice of female infanticide, there is now a huge male surplus in the population, causing all kinds of social and family tensions.

I've seen plenty of evidence, too, that in other cultures, especially in many parts of the Muslim world, women have a subservient place in all matters of power and decision-making. And I've noticed that even in places where the equality of genders is an official policy, somehow males turn up in most positions of authority—government, business, almost everything.

So did my parents think they would make their own small contribution to correcting these faults by producing their crop of unusual girls? What difference could twelve girls make in the face of social customs so deeply entrenched?

Then something else occurred to me that I've seen frequently in news programs: In some cultures, young girls are treated as property by their families. Is that the answer? Are we going to be auctioned off to the highest bidder? Are all the sweet words from father about how unique my sisters and I are just an attempt to stop us from figuring out what is really going to happen to us when we are older?

Could this also explain why that other man, Klamm, visits here regularly and seems to be on very familiar terms with my father? What is he doing here? I've never liked him. In fact I'm afraid every time he comes close, and even though he tries very hard to be nice to me, it only makes me more suspicious. He always goes out of his way to be especially pleasant to Io, who doesn't seem to be afraid of him at all; I suspect he gives her presents that she hides and doesn't tell anybody about. Io doesn't seem to be afraid of anything, including men.

From now on, I have to be on my guard. My sisters—most of them, except for Io—depend on me. I cannot trust anyone, even my father, at least not completely.

03 JULY 2025

I'd better start using this recording device more frequently, or else my dear daughter Hera will never give me a moment's peace! Every time I run into her these days, she demands my latest files and puts on a long face if I say I forgot to make any new ones. Still, I may not give her today's files, at least for a few years yet, because of their contents.

Anyway, my flight landed at Timika airport today in mid-morning, in good time for the long ride up the mountain to the town of Tembagapura. Having a skilled driver behind the wheel helps, but I must confess, I'm very tired of this overland journey after having made it so often during the past decade! Thankfully the little airstrip being constructed at Tembagapura will soon be finished and then these short business trips will become a whole lot easier.

Besides, wasn't difficulty of access just what I was looking for when I asked Max Klamm to locate such a spot for both the company and the foundation? What other genetics company in the world has a more secure—untouchable, really—research facility than Wollstone Corporation does, one tucked away on a remote mountain in the farthest reaches of the Indonesian archipelago? I recall Klamm saying at the time that he considered importing some of the now-reformed headhunting tribes from the region to take up residence in Papua, and encouraging them to resurrect their old customs, as another layer of discouragement to idle curiosity and industrial espionage. Apparently he concluded that this step was unnecessary, at least for the time being.

In point of fact there's no place like it in the entire world, and it never ceases to amaze me, no matter how often I come here! A stroke of luck brought it to our attention, just when it became obvious that both Wollstone Corporation and my Sujana Foundation might need a secure location where certain lines of work could be undertaken away from the public eye—especially after the activist attacks on biological research labs became so frequent. As I recall, the property was on offer because the company that built the road and all the facilities up there had closed its operations after many years. Despite a near-vertical drop of 15,000 feet to the coast below, an access road for the facilities had been constructed along the mountain face from sea level to near the summit; the town of Tembagapura had been built about halfway up the slope to house the company's staff. All we had to do was add our laboratories and a few other specialized buildings.

I never mind when we leave Timika; it is always blanketed in year-round humid heat since it's located at sea level in the south-central part of Papua near the Arafura Sea. And the sparse lowland rainforest and degraded coastal mangrove swamps here on the coast aren't very attractive either. It's a difficult ride up the endless switchbacks along the mountainside, even in the latest four-wheel-drive vehicle. No matter how many times the driver completes this route, he always seems to do it carefully; perhaps a glance down the vertical slopes at the edge of the roadway at each turning reminds him why!

Whenever we stop briefly to enjoy the cooler and drier air and to look back down the mountainside to the sea below, I admire the work of those who had managed to construct this road. There surely aren't any other distractions, however; it sometimes seems as if the jungle has been stripped of every last vestige of native animal species to stock the private collections of the rich. After the arduous drive it's always a pleasure to arrive in the old company town, Tembagapura, since its elevation at 7,000 feet provides a perfect temperate climate year-round.

From Klamm's standpoint the property's most attractive feature was the ease with which complete security could be provided. Eager to find some new uses for the facilities after the previous owner had left, the Indonesian government was happy to supply a small military contingent to guard the access road under contract to the corporation. No one outside a very small circle of company personnel and Indonesian officials even knows that a new operation is being carried on here. And no one except Max and I knows what's being done at the foundation's own research laboratory.

These days I often wonder whether it was smart for me to have Klamm become so closely involved with me in running this operation in Papua Province. How old is he now? Fifty-five, I think; three years older than I. He hardly seems to age at all. He still looks almost the same as he did the day I first met him, tall, lean and fit, well muscled from regular gym sessions, always tanned, with thick black hair—it must be dyed!—and sharp features. But he seemed then to be the ideal person to help Ina and me realize our dreams of founding a great company. He'd been trained as a lawyer specializing in corporate securities and had moved into the venture-capital business early in his career. We first encountered him fifteen years ago, and to be honest we've been highly successful in our joint venture.

I remember that when Ina and I went looking for a venture capitalist in 2010 in order to do an initial public offering of equity in our privately held firm, he was among the most highly regarded entrepreneurs in his field. At that point he had successfully launched two genetics companies that had become leaders in their market segments. He saw instantly that the firm we had founded could be the biggest of all because the successful manipulation of brain functions was the last great frontier for genetic modification. Many of our contemporaries had discovered that it was going to be a lot harder to engineer the brain—at least in such a way that the results matched the initial intentions—than to snip out a few disease genes, or to create super-athletes for Olympic fame and fortune, which almost any gene jockey could do by then.

Everybody, it seemed, was waiting eagerly for the break-throughs in neurological sciences that the studies by Ina and me were leading toward. I can still recall the media hype! Governments were hoping that crime and anti-social behav-ior would disappear after a few genes were switched on or off; generals wanted fearless soldiers who would march happily to their deaths; the rich were eager to create supe-rior children; and the desperate middle classes were longing for cheaper cures for the epidemic of depression, anxiety, and dysfunctional neuroses that was sweeping the world. Who can blame them, really?

Wollstone Corporation's launch as a public company in 2011 was a great event! That was just a year after the extraor-dinary publicity about the discoveries Ina and I published, about how the genes for important brain functions were controlled. Although the two of us reserved a 30% block of shares in the new company for the Sujana Foundation, there was plenty left to go around, and we made Klamm and other early investors very rich.

Who's to say we didn't justify our investors' hopes? The company's first products utilized gene therapy to overcome common forms of depression and anxiety, without any of the side effects associated with conventional pharmaceutical remedies. Within five years these products were dominating their markets. Klamm then engineered takeover bids of other firms, and by 2020 Wollstone Corporation had become a huge conglomerate in the genetics and pharmaceuticals sectors.

But that no longer mattered much to me, because everything had changed suddenly eight years earlier, on the terrible day when my wife was fatally injured in a car accident. Every second of what happened then is permanently engraved in memory. I remember listening to each breath she took while Max and I were flying her from Jakarta to the private hospital in Singapore, where she lapsed into the coma from which she never awoke.

I remember, too, every word of the conversation with him at the hospital, some three weeks later, as if it were only yesterday. I was prostrate with grief and couldn't make the simplest decisions. "Franklin, face the truth: She's not coming back. You'll have to pull the plug."

"For God's sake, Max, my whole life's mission is bound up with her. And I don't mean the science. You know that's not what mattered most to her, and from her I learned what was truly important in life. The Sujana Foundation's program will give humans a better chance to overcome their problems. We were just about ready to take the next step. I can't do this without her. It's over."

Of course I'd completely forgotten that until then Ina and I had not allowed Klamm to become aware of our closely guarded secret. But that day I couldn't help myself; it just poured out of me while I sat at her bedside. So I told him how she had first proposed to me a plan to help save the world by engineering enhanced mental functions in a group of youngsters who could become social and political leaders in many different countries. I even relayed to him how—after she had overcome my initial objections—we had very quietly made plans to recruit 300 couples from around the world, couples where each member had shown exceptional promise or performance early in life, across all fields of the arts and sciences.

Ina baptized them the *Group of 300*. She was the visionary

and the persuader, the one who was going to enlist their cooperation and cajole them into believing that she and I could genetically engineer their fertilized embryos so that they would possess special mental traits. She laid out our grand design: How once modified in our labs the embryos would be either reinserted in the natural mother's womb or implanted in a surrogate mother, depending on how many fertilized eggs had been prepared; how all the offspring would be raised together in a secret facility run by our foundation; why we had complete faith in our belief that both the way we would engineer their brains through genetic modifications, and the fifteen-year-long post-natal training we had designed for them, would produce leaders strongly motivated by humanitarian aims to help rescue the world from the chaos into which it was fast descending.

Through the Sujana Foundation we were just about ready to start collecting eggs and sperm from the first members of the donor group. She and I had worked out the details of our dedicated research program designed for the future children of the Group of 300. And then she lay dying in Singapore.

Although this conversation took place almost thirteen years ago, I recall Klamm's words and my responses as clearly as if we were speaking to each other in this vehicle today on the drive up the mountainside.

"Franklin, all is not lost. You should preserve not only Ina's extraordinary mission but part of her as well. She's in a permanent vegetative state and isn't going to recover. You must harvest her ovaries before she dies. Then, when you're ready, you can fertilize some of her eggs with your sperm. Your children must be born; the world needs them. You must add them to the bank of genetic material that the foundation will assemble."

"That's not necessary, Max, because Ina and I put a collection of embryos made from her eggs and my sperm into storage some time ago. And yes, I believe that Ina would want me to create our own children, even if I had to do it alone. In one of our last discussions she said that we had a duty to experiment first with our own offspring, to see whether what we hoped to do would succeed. She thought we did know enough about the genes we wanted to manipulate to guarantee there would be very little chance we'd end up with so-called 'Frankenstein monsters,' as the public might fear, or any freaks of nature.

"So yes, Max, there's a good chance we could produce exceptional children, but not 'super-human' beings in any genetic sense. We were guessing they might fall within the upper part of the normal range of human development, where there are plenty of examples of exceptional talent throughout the ages—perhaps even genius, if we got it right. Thus we were convinced that these children could be regarded as normal, in the sense that others like them have appeared naturally in the past. And neither of us thought—because of the type of genetic improvement we planned to do—that there was anything but a very low probability we would produce something odious or evil."

"I agree, of course, since I know your reputation as brilliant scientists," Klamm had replied. "And yet you do realize, don't you, that you'll have to work on this program in the strictest secrecy? First, because the public isn't likely to understand or accept your own version of your motives. Despite any denials you might make, some are bound to raise the alarm about eugenics and accuse you of trying to create a super-race designed to rule over them. And second, because you'll have to protect your creations, especially when they're young, lest some unprincipled agents try to steal them."

Standing at Ina's bedside I watched, after I had given my consent, as the life-support apparatus was disconnected. I really thought my grief was so profound that it might kill me, but soon I was buoyed by the thought that I might produce our children. It was shortly thereafter when I gave Klamm the go ahead to search for a secure location for the foundation. I threw myself into the task of completing the research program that we had promised to create for the Group of 300. About a year later, I was ready.

Imbued with the mission to immortalize Ina's legacy, I made up my mind to proceed by first creating some of our own children, so that I'd be able to assess the results that might emerge from my manipulations. The idea was, once I was sure that the program would work as planned, I could then engineer a larger number, perhaps 500 in all, one or two from each couple in the material to be donated by the Group of 300. However, from then until now I never revealed to Klamm the details of the specific genetic changes I intended to make.

§   §   §

As my driver was pulling into the foundation's compound in Tembagapura, I recalled with pleasure what I had been able to accomplish during the past five years to make Ina's dream become a reality. Beginning in 2020 I set out to recruit the three hundred donor couples. I supervised teams of skilled technicians employed by the foundation to collect eggs and sperm from the couples, to fertilize the eggs, and to carry out the gene manipulations specified in my protocol. There are now approximately 1,800 fertilized embryos frozen at the eight-cell stage safely stored in the foundation's high-security facility in Cockburn Town in the Turks and Caicos Islands.

What a supreme effort that took, particularly over the last three years! The donors were puzzled as to why I needed as many as 20 eggs from each of the females, who were required to undergo super-ovulation treatments. Eventually they seemed to grasp the explanation that we could expect only about 30% of the embryos to pass successfully through the stages of IVF itself, let alone the first, second, and third cell divisions, before the freezing was carried out. Thank goodness such progress has been made in cryopreservation techniques. Enough of the embryos should survive the freeze/thaw cycle, the implantation procedures, and the pregnancy losses to give us a good chance of achieving up to 500 live births, if that is what we want. I think I'll be ready to proceed with the next steps in a year or two.

Then my mind turned to today's business. Toward the end of the long drive I had asked myself: Why is Klamm so anxious to see me today? Does it have anything to do with the securities scandal in the United States, which has been reported in the business press around the world? I gather there were some very angry creditors and securities regulators left behind when Max apparently fled from there six months ago, barely evading the US marshals who had a subpoena for him.

I had no sooner entered the door of my lab in Tembagapura, quite exhausted from my travels, when Klamm burst in and began to lay out his proposal for me. But I was ready for him. My digital recorder was set to activate the minute he said his first word. I wasn't sure what I was in for, but I wanted a bit of insurance, just in case. I also wanted to capture his entire conversation so I could focus totally on what he had to say. And I didn't even let him finish before I gave my verdict.

"No, Max, I won't even discuss such an idea. Ina and I never, ever imagined that we would be doing this to make money."

"Franklin, look, we've known each other a long time, and I've helped you to realize your own dreams, haven't I? Give me a chance to make my case. What I'm suggesting is not so different from your own plan. The super-rich around the

world are getting desperate. Without a few strong governments on each continent, neither their persons nor their
wealth can be protected against the mobs and the terrorists.
And they're beginning to wonder if any government will
survive the chaos that's spreading everywhere.

"Your scientific work is becoming very well known and it
gives people hope that new kinds of individuals can arise to
lead nations out of danger. All I'm saying is that the task will
require many more than the twelve girls you're now raising.
Far greater numbers will be needed in order to make any
real difference, and there will also have to be men as well as
women, because in many societies—regrettably—women are
still not accepted as the most influential political and military leaders."

"There will be more children, Max, and certainly males as
well, but only when I'm ready. My girls aren't old enough yet
for me to assess fully their potential for leadership. I'm planning to do the final assessment when they're fourteen years
old, and then I'll proceed with the embryos from the Group
of 300—if the results with my daughters justify such a
further step. After that, perhaps, additional programs could
be launched if all the results are promising enough."

Klamm must have quickly worked out my suggested timeline in his mind and concluded that his creditors would have
exhausted their patience with him long before he had
acquired any products to sell! And I guessed that some
among them were the type of people no one wanted to
annoy. So he tried again.

"But there's a flaw in your plan that has to be corrected,
Franklin, and this is where my own suggestion can help. You
don't have any control over how your daughters, or the
Group of 300's children for that matter, will fare once they
venture out into the world.

"You've carefully planned every step in your program—
except for the most important one. You're just assuming

that, somehow, the children will grow up to become influential leaders, and this will happen soon enough to make a difference in world politics. But what if other things occur to upset your calculations? Some of the children you produce get sick, some die from natural causes, others decide just to become artists or researchers. You have no way of ensuring that your entire program won't just vanish like a flash flood in the desert."

"Oh, and you can guarantee success?"

"No, but I *can* guarantee you a higher chance of success. If together we produce a second generation under contract to, say, a group of the richest families in the world, people who are already very influential in the governments of all the most powerful countries, their offspring will be assured of becoming leaders because of their family connections. This repairs the one flaw in your own program, don't you see that?"

"Actually, I will grant you that point. But I also know with absolute certainty that Ina would have been adamantly opposed to your plan and wouldn't have supported it. And I cannot betray her memory."

"I'd never suggest anything that would betray her memory, Franklin, because I, too, saw how special her mind and spirit was." (Clearly he was a desperate man and being regarded by me as insincere was the least of his worries at that point!) "So I'm well aware that you could never agree to anything if you thought it would violate her legacy. Hear me out. I'm not proposing a different program, only a better chance of success for what you and Ina wanted to achieve from the beginning. I've always believed in your program since I first learned of it, and although I'm not familiar with the details, I do know something about your reputation among your peers. Therefore, my guess is that your protocol is a powerful one that most likely will succeed not just with the genes in special types of people, but also with ordinary couples, too."

"Yes, that's correct. Both Ina and I always thought that our genetic enhancements could work on the average person, so to speak. We decided on the strategy involving the Group of 300 for the first round, assuming that a better-than-average genetic pool would give us a higher chance of success. And these couples also shared our alarm about the direction of world events, so they were willing to provide the necessary confidentiality guarantees for the project. None of them know the identities of the other couples."

"Then if you're right about what new qualities of vision and sensibility your genetic changes will produce, these qualities will show themselves in the offspring of the wealthy families. These young people will be motivated to become humanitarian leaders, with the interest of all the world's people at heart, despite the fact that they're children of privilege. In fact, just because they are privileged, they'll have all the advantages of superior diet, security, education, and travel, not to mention influence, and thus they'll be positioned perfectly to make the contributions to humanity you envision."

"You do make a good case, Max, and I'll admit that I've been worrying myself about some of what you've mentioned just now. But I'm not yet ready to go down that road and I'm still uneasy about dealing with such people. Nor do I think it's a coincidence that you bring me this proposal just when you personally have gotten into serious financial trouble. Your problems with the US securities regulators have been in all the business news reports."

"My recent reversals of fortune are public knowledge. But I resent your implication. I never said that we should sell these services to the rich. What I meant is, we should have a contract with them under which they undertake to provide proper care and education for the children, and perhaps other stipulations that would give us the highest hope they would develop as you intend. That's all."

Klamm had spoken passionately, trying to convince me, but I wasn't fooled for a moment. I knew perfectly well that if I eventually agreed to this scheme, he'd have little trouble in arranging secret commissions from the families for himself that would be funneled into untraceable bank accounts. But I also knew he couldn't wait very long. Some of his creditors would be getting very unpleasant in the coming years, and a few of them would not restrict themselves to retaining reputable lawyers in an effort to collect from him. But I also felt sorry for the man I had come to regard as a friend as well as a business colleague. I had known him for a long time and in my opinion we had done great and good things together.

"I'm really sorry about what's happened to you recently, Max. I know you wouldn't raise this issue with me if you weren't in big trouble. I wish I could help you, but I don't think I can. I may be preoccupied with my research, but I'm not unaware of what's happening in the world. If I agree to this you'll find a way to make some money out of it. And I just can't allow myself to be a part of anything like that."

"I'll not deny I have some real problems at the moment. But we both have some secrets to protect, don't we? We need each other. You don't have to work for a living anymore, but you also don't want to give up your university post and the esteem of your peers for your ongoing research and publications. I've thought for some time that you may win a Nobel Prize, Franklin. But you won't even be considered for this prize if it becomes known that you did experiments on human embryos under a protocol that was not disclosed to, or approved by, the research ethics board of your university—even if that research was not performed in the university's own facilities. Am I right?"

I realized at once that the conversation had taken an ugly turn. "So now you intend to blackmail me?"

I remember how he laughed at that point. "No, not at all;

I trust it won't come to such a pass. We've had a mutually beneficial partnership so far, and I see no reason why it can't continue on friendly terms. You and I and your lawyers are the only ones who know that there is a separate complex co-located with Wollstone's lab facilities here in Tembagapura. And that it's owned by the Sujana Foundation, which you control. I also happen to know that the foundation has been incorporated in the Turks and Caicos Islands, which, although a UK protectorate, operates autonomously under rather loose legal and banking rules."

"Let's cut out the crap, Max, and get to the point. Are you telling me that you'll disclose the foundation's program to the world unless I agree to participate in your new scheme?"

"As I said, it would be best if we could continue to coop-erate as friendly colleagues. I admit that I'm obliged by my present circumstances to raise substantial funds. And sooner rather than later, I might add. I need to keep some of my creditors from resorting to unpleasant methods of debt collection and requiring me to reveal the locations of my remaining assets. So I have little choice but to start assem-bling a roster of clients, and collecting deposits from them, on the promise that you and I will deliver a product of great interest to them in, say, three years or so. I've undertaken some very preliminary discussions along these lines, and I'm happy to report—for my own sake, if not yours—that not only is there keen interest in such a product, but it will command a very fair price indeed."

"You're taking a big chance, aren't you? How do you know that I won't decide to forego the esteem of my academic colleagues, and even the chance of a Nobel Prize? Perhaps I'll just not care whether you release the informa-tion about the girls. Or perhaps I'll simply deny having done any experimentation on the embryos. You have no proof that the protocol even exists or what types of genetic manip-ulation it describes. I'll simply tell the world that you're a sleazy fraud artist, wanted by US authorities on serious charges, and that you're just trying to deflect attention from your own crimes."

"Well, my view is, both of us should hope that our mutual relations never degenerate so far. If things go wrong, Franklin, the kind of people I've been lining up as potential clients for this new venture will not be spending a lot of time trying to figure out which of the two of us is telling the truth. They'll not rely on government regulators or university officials to conduct an investigation into what's happened to their large deposits. They have other ways of dealing with people whom they think are trying to defraud them. And their agents will be interested in talking to you as well as to me when that time comes."

"So, we've progressed from blackmail to death threats in the course of a single friendly conversation, have we?"

"Let's not over-dramatize the situation. We're talking about possibilities that I hope, for both our sakes, never materialize."

"Max, you've forgotten something else. If these 'possibilities,' as you call them, are eventually realized, your clients are unlikely to regard the two of us as being equally culpable. After all, I have a public reputation as the world's leading scientist in my field, and I'm also known as an entrepreneur who established a hugely successful new company. Although I'm not boastful by nature, the fact is I'm feted wherever I go; governments bestow medals on me, and every year I'm awarded some prestigious scientific or philanthropic prize. And you? You're on the run from a criminal fraud indictment, and the investors you apparently fleeced in your latest venture are looking for you as well. Which one of us are they likely to regard as believable and trustworthy?"

"That's very unfortunate language you just used, Franklin, and I recommend strongly that you not repeat it publicly, because if you do, I'll be obliged to sue for slander. If you won't be persuaded by my appeals to our long collegial relationship, and our past successes together, then consider this: Without my participation and support you're unlikely to be able to continue to protect your precious girls from harm."

Even now I shudder as I hear those words repeated from my recorder! I was out of my mind with fear. I leapt from my chair, but Klamm was quicker, of course, knowing in advance both what he would say to me and what my response would be. We're both big men, but Klamm is by far the fitter. He shoved me back into my chair as I screamed at him. "If you touch a hair of any one of their heads I will personally dissect you like a laboratory animal!"

He just sneered at me in return. "Remember who contracted for the security force around this facility. And who signs the soldiers' payroll cheques. Your girls are my hostages, my guarantee that you'll carry out the next project, the one I need you to do. But don't worry, they won't be harmed—I'm not interested in them, because the kind of rich clients I have in mind don't want them.

"You see, most of my potential clients come from cultures that have, as you would put it, I'm sure, a rather unfortunate and retrograde habit of preferring male children, especially if those children are destined for special roles in the family heritage. When the time comes to engineer this new batch for these clients—and you *will* come to your senses about this, I feel sure—we'll guarantee them male offspring, and I know this is easy for you to do."

I sat slumped in my chair because I was beaten, and both he and I knew it. Still, I thought to myself, Klamm doesn't have his little scheme in place yet, and won't for perhaps some years to come, so my girls are safe for now. There's nothing to do but to bide my time and pretend to cooperate. Perhaps I could find a way to get rid of him. It even crossed my mind that the advantage was on my side: Klamm is depending on me to get him out of a serious jam, but I no longer need him. Maybe I can think of a way to exploit this advantage before the day arrives when he'll show up to collect my products for delivery.

"You win. I'll do as you say."

"I thought you'd see the light. Try to forget about the money, since it won't be coming your way in any case. And you don't even have to know who the clients are, so you can protect the purity of your program and your dear late wife's precious legacy. Remember what I said before things got ugly between us: Since my clients run the show in the countries where they live, their special offspring will have all the advantages that wealth and high social position can confer. If these children indeed develop the qualities that you think you can engineer into them—and I believe that they will—they'll go on to do the great things you and Ina envisaged for them. Why don't you try to think about it from this angle?"

That comment, in particular, annoyed me a great deal, because despite the extreme agitation I felt about the threat to my girls' safety, I had to concede to myself that Klamm's argument held some merit. It's perfectly true that Ina and I had focused on our own motivation for our foundation's program, and on our firm conviction that we could help set humanity on a better course of development. We were both sure as well that we could actually carry out the gene enhancements we'd designed. But Klamm had a valid point, too: What would ensure the success of this venture once these children passed into the rough-and-tumble world of politics and power?

Maybe I'd have to reconsider my position after all. If I really am serious about the success of my program, I may still need Klamm's help as much as he requires mine. What does it matter in the end if Klamm makes money from it, even a lot of money? After all, his clients have plenty and will hardly even notice the pittance they'll be forking out for this little product. And it's not as if those families would otherwise be contributing to worthy humanitarian causes the funds they will be paying to my shady associate! Quite the contrary. So, looked at in this light, Klamm's scheme is a way of extorting large sums from the idle rich that will, if his scheme works, result in their unwitting promotion of a better way for humanity.

Then it hit me: Am I just fooling myself? Is there a hidden flaw I can't detect, one that will guarantee I'll sabotage the dream my beloved wife had after all? I'll have to think carefully about all the angles, but there's still time enough to do so. I've got at least three years, perhaps a bit more, before I'll actually have to hand over the products to Klamm for delivery. Enough time to weigh all aspects and try to create safeguards against the possibility of betraying my wife's trust in me.

Meanwhile I intend to continue immersing myself in the daily lives of my twelve wonderful girls! I've extended the leave of absence from my university position in Cambridge, pleading exhaustion and stress. I've told them I'll carry on with my laboratory research program, directing it via regular chat sessions between Cambridge and Tembagapura. I've been careful to devise a way to route these sessions through an Internet site for a business that will, at least as far as they are concerned, be based in Jakarta, using a secure firewall to hide my actual location, so that the existence of the Papua facility will remain a secret.

Now I can begin the real work for which all of the rest until now has been merely the preliminary steps. I can begin to assess for the first time how the genetic changes I've engineered in my group of talented girls are expressing themselves in their personalities and behavior.

06 FEBRUARY 2026

The killing started just as dawn broke. Before nightfall on the previous evening the band had sighted the column of strangers approaching along the valley floor from the east. It was summer in the southeastern foothills of the Alps and the weather was fine. From their vantage point in the hills above the valley they had seen the column from afar, moving slowly and tentatively as if unfamiliar with the mountainous terrain.

When the strangers came closer, alarms were raised as all the band members—women, men and children alike—scrambled to get a better look, chattering loudly among themselves. They had seen a few of these odd creatures before, but they still marveled at the sight—they walked in the same upright way, they had arms and legs and torsos of similar type, but they were quite different in other respects. The strangers had much less hair and wore animal skins over their bodies, which amused the onlookers, and although also dark-skinned, they were considerably smaller in stature and their heads and faces were of different shape. They also made regular sounds to each other, as did the band. And yet, despite the differences in appearance, the two groups were so much more alike than any other animals they knew that the band felt a stirring of kinship and a curiosity they could not suppress.

A few of the males from the band descended and approached the strangers warily, beckoning them to follow them up the hill to the clearing where their camp was established. The hunting was easy at that time of year and the day's game was roasting on the fires; there was enough for all. The strangers could now smell it and were hungry. They followed their guides and gathered at the edge of the clearing in their own tight circle a short distance away, retrieving their portions of roasted meat from the fires at the band's invitation. The two groups exchanged information throughout the early evening by means of sign language, the strangers telling of a long journey from a far-off warmer place to the south. Then both groups slept.

The strangers woke well before dawn, roused by the sentinel they had posted. Their whispered communications were swift and a plan was soon formed, strategically distributing their forces to maximum advantage against their considerably larger foes. Their strongest males were assigned to strike first at all the older males in the band, and only when these were put out of action, to move on to the adolescent males and older females and finally to the children. The adolescent females were to be taken captive.

The band was still asleep when they were set upon. The dazed sleepers scattered as the first blows fell, but the women and adolescent males from among the strangers had formed a ring around the campsite and drove them back into the hands of the club-wielding attackers, who had dispatched the older males and now slaughtered the others at a more leisurely pace. It was soon over. The strangers rounded up the huddled groups of young females and broke camp, moving north and west with the smell of death lingering on their clubs.

§ § §

I recounted this dream, which I had recently, to my father during one of our long nighttime dialogues. We begin them after dinner, watching while the light fades across the mountain vistas visible from the study in his residence, which is perched on the slopes above the town's other buildings. Often we spend hours searching websites together and looking for answers to the many questions I always seem to have. Father obviously enjoys this break from his daytime laboratory routines; when our searches are successful we laugh together and he gives me a hug.

Yet sometimes our sessions become—quite frankly—testy because I get annoyed at his habit of evading the personal issues I raise by replying with vague and patronizing reassurances.

"Father, why do you get so upset when I ask you about such things? It's time you told us more. We may be only twelve years old, but as you yourself keep saying, we're special young people, and we're special because somehow you were able to make us this way."

"I've tried to be careful in talking to you about these topics because I want to be sure that you can understand the answers, Hera. I think you should wait until you and your sisters are a little older still, perhaps another two or three years, and then everything can be explained."

"No, I'm sorry, I don't think that's fair. I've told you again and again that I have thoughts that make me afraid and are hard for me to think about. I've told you about my dreams, which often wake me up at night, and about the visions I have in my mind. I don't mean of things I see in front of me, like the chairs over there on the other side of this room, but images that appear suddenly in my mind and are not really anyplace, although they seem very real to me, more real than the objects right here, such as that furniture. These images just appear, all at once. They come, even though I don't want them to, and I think about them for awhile until they go away again. This happens to my sisters, too; I've asked them about it."

"What kinds of things do you see?"

"It's hard for me to describe in words what I'm referring to. I began to wonder about this when I first got interested in codes, after I got a lot of problems involving codes from some Internet sites. I discovered that with just a little bit of effort, it was pretty easy for me to see in my mind the solution to the riddle. Most of the time this didn't happen right away. I would study the problem and memorize the pages where the strange symbols were written. Then I'd go off and do other things, and occasionally I'd simply sit and let my mind wander, without trying to think about anything at all. And that's when the solution just popped into my mind, all of a sudden, even though I wasn't working on the problem at the time."

"I'm not familiar with code problems. What are they?"

"Well, the simplest ones are just substitution ciphers, where an arbitrary symbol is employed for each letter, such as 'Ω' for 'a'. If you were composing a word in this kind of cipher, the order of each letter and symbol stays the same. More common are what are called mono-alphabetic substitution ciphers, where one letter replaces another according to a fixed pattern. For example, 'a' becomes 'p' and 'z' becomes 'b.' Of course, if one person wants to send a message to someone else using either of these ciphers, both sender and receiver must have access to the same code.

"However, these are very simple routines and they are easy for cryptanalysts to break by examining the frequency of the symbols or substituted letters. This is well known because of a famous short story, *The Gold Bug*, written by Edgar Allan Poe."

"Then I don't understand what's so interesting or important about codes and ciphers."

"Oh, well, I've just given you examples of the very simplest types. For a long time they've become much, much more complicated than what I've just described. And, father, you're British, so certainly you've heard about Enigma, the famous machine that was used to encipher radio messages transmitted by the German armed forces during the Second World War. The coding routines that were used to program the German machine were very complex, and they were even changed every day, but the British code-breaking team based at Bletchley Park succeeded—for the most part—in deciphering the messages, which people say was an important part in the Allies' success on the battlefield."

"Yes, of course, now I remember."

"All codes, even the most complicated ones, are based on some rule or pattern for changing the plain text of a message into a form that is supposed to hide the communication from certain people. And the code breakers try to discover that rule or to make sense of the apparently strange and meaningless patterns into which the message has been enciphered. Actually, it's no different from trying to decipher old languages, such as ancient Egyptian or Greek hieroglyphics."

"Yes, of course, your mention of hieroglyphics rang a bell for me. I recall during my bachelor's studies reading a well-known book called *The Decipherment of Linear B*, written by a man named John Chadwick, I think. You may already know that Linear B is the ancient Greek language, written in hieroglyphs on clay tablets around 1400 BC and first discovered on Crete by the archaeologist Sir Arthur Evans in 1900. For years no one could read it. Finally, in 1952, there was an important breakthrough by a man named Michael Ventris, who was a trained architect, and soon the work was done."

He located the volume on his bookshelves and found the passage he had remembered, where Chadwick described the secret of Ventris's success. He gave me the book and later that day I copied out the text:

He himself laid stress on the visual approach to the problem; he made himself so familiar with the visual aspect of the texts that large sections were imprinted on his mind simply as visual patterns, long before the decipherment gave them meaning. [Then] ... his architectural training came to his aid. The architect's eye sees ... beneath the appearance and distinguishes the significant parts of the pattern, the structural elements and framework of the building. So too Ventris was able to discern [in Linear B] among the bewildering variety of the mysterious signs, patterns and regularities which betrayed the underlying structure.

This does sound a lot like what I had been describing to father.

"Some of my sisters are much better than I am at working with codes. They fool around with each other all the time, trying out various forms of encryption and seeing if the others can decrypt the message. Moira is really good at it; so are Pandora and Themis. I'll ask them to tell you more about it, and to show you some of their own exercises in coding and decoding."

"Good, I'd like that. And as you were speaking just now, something you said triggered another memory for me. Do you know about the famous case of the Nobel Prize-winning mathematician, John Nash, whose story was the subject of a Hollywood film, *A Beautiful Mind*? There's a scene in which Nash, standing before a map display in a secret military facility, 'sees'—in his mind—a hidden pattern appear when a bewildering array of seemingly random large numbers flashes before his eyes, a pattern that no one else in the room had detected."

"Yes, we've watched that film, and I remember that scene. In fact, it's similar to what I was trying to describe to you about the things that happen in my mind. It worries me a bit as well, since Nash's life story had become notorious because the most productive years of his life were lost as he battled a severe case of paranoid schizophrenia. I hope this doesn't happen to me or my sisters."

"Hera, I ...."

I interrupted him because I didn't want to dwell on these fears of mine right then. "The business about codes is just one example. It's the same with everything we work on. I think this is why mathematics and geometry are so easy for us, because once you understand the basic rules everything else seems to follow logically. As it is with languages, which have very similar patterns, although the grammar may be quite different when you first look at it. And visual things, too, such as designs. And the way music, especially classical music, is composed."

"Hera, we can think of this as a very highly developed type of what people commonly call intuition. Did you know Einstein often said that this was his special gift? He confessed he wasn't very good at the higher mathematics that physicists use to describe natural laws—in fact, he referred to himself as a 'Buridan's ass' in math! I think he was saying that he just *saw* certain relations—fundamental relations of matter and energy—in his mind. Of course, what he saw in his mind and described in his equations on general relativity in 1915 had to be confirmed later in experiments. You know, it wasn't until almost a hundred years later that one of the intuitions on which his theory was based—the notion that gravitational force is exerted at the speed of light—was observed experimentally."

"Well, I really didn't understand this at all, until something dawned on me while we were listening to one of our favorite pieces of music, Haydn's oratorio, *The Creation*. The words come from the Bible, of course. Near the beginning there is this wonderful passage, which I like so much that I often stop the recording and replay it before going on. The singers are following the text of the opening chapter of the Book of Genesis. The solo voice of the angel Raphael sings,

In the beginning God created the heaven and the earth.

And the earth was without form, and void;

and darkness was upon the face of the deep.

Next the chorus comes in, singing very, very softly,

And God said, Let there be light:

The chorus continues with the passage, softly, slowly, without any orchestral accompaniment,

… and … there … was … LIGHT!

Exactly on the last word in this line the entire orchestra enters with a huge crash, including cymbals and tympani, and the chorus also raises its collective voice to full volume. I think that the composer was trying to convey to us just how momentous this change was for the humans who would be created later.

"I cannot tell you how deeply this music affects me. I suspect it overwhelms me so because it describes the experience I have in understanding complicated things: Suddenly the light comes and I see what I've been searching for in my mind. It's a joyous experience, just as it is in Haydn's music, because of course everything depends on the light, doesn't it? There is no life to speak of, except for primitive life forms, where perpetual darkness reigns. And the working of our mind, our human brain and consciousness, is often described by writers this way—as shining the light of reason on a problem to be solved. Only for me it is so intense, so sudden and unexpected, like the crashing of the cymbals and tympani in that passage from *The Creation*, that it also frightens me."

"Hera, I'm so pleased to hear you describe what happens in your mind as a joyous experience! You're right, I think. For some of us the process of discovery of new things is just as you say, as a kind of instant apprehension, as if a light suddenly was switched on in a completely darkened room. But when you and I started this conversation, and then again just now, you told me that you were often frightened as well. This is the part I don't fully grasp."

"These things I see, sort of like visions; it's just that they can appear so suddenly, and with such—I don't know how to say it—with such *force*. And as I've told you before, my dreams are so vivid, and what's in them is so much weirder than the visions I have in the daytime. I know that the same things happen to my sisters because we discuss them among ourselves. Certainly you can see why we would be a bit scared by all this. I had another very disturbing dream a few months ago, which I'll tell you about. And then I think I should say good night; it's getting quite late.

"All of us sisters had been swimming in the ocean some-where, and one of us had drowned. We were terribly upset; I couldn't tell which one it was, and we were far from home. We thought we should bury the body on the beach, right there, so that animals would not get to it. We did this and had a little ceremony afterward. Then all of a sudden you appeared, and when we told you what happened, you were very upset about the drowning, but you were also angry with us for burying the body. You made us dig it up again, and then you prepared a funeral pyre out of wood lying on the beach and cremated the body. You said that no one else must ever find our bodies when we die. Then you went away."

"I'm sorry you and your sisters are so troubled by these unpleasant thoughts and images. I feel a bit helpless here, I must confess. What you've told me bothers me a lot, so I'll tell you what I'm going to do. I'll talk to some leading specialists in the world who might have studied such experiences, and maybe we can find a way to change things so that you aren't frightened as much. Oh, yes, wait, before you go, here's something I've been meaning to give you. I lost it among my papers until I came upon it again recently quite by accident. It's an article I wrote with my supervisor when I was a postdoctoral fellow in the United States at the University of Oregon. It was written for a semi-popular magazine read by people who weren't trained scientists. It explains what we knew then about some of the brain functions, including the sense of empathy, which we were working on in his lab. We can discuss it once you've had a chance to read it."

SUB-COMPILER'S NOTE: *Hera read and reread the article her father refers to and discussed it obsessively with him and her sisters many times. In later years she schooled herself in neurosciences and devoured hundreds more technical academic papers on this and related topics.*

This original article was so important to her in her early years that I feel compelled to reproduce it here, in the following chapter, in its entirety. I give you fair warning; it can be difficult reading, and there are passages in it I still don't understand. So I suggest that you review it quickly the first time, without worrying whether you have grasped everything, and then return to it later, as Hera did.

"EVOLUTION AND THE SENSE OF EMPATHY"
BY DON M. TUCKER AND FRANKLIN P. STONE
REPRINTED FROM WORLD SCIENCE DIGEST,
VOL. 17 (JANUARY 1999)

There are three essential features to the sense of empathy: First, an emotional bonding with another person that allows me to sense what the other is feeling; second, continued awareness of the distinction between my own self and that of the other person; and third, my ability to participate in the perspective of the other by subordinating my own egocentric concerns. Note that there are both cognitive and emotive processes involved: Empathy is not just a "rush of fellow-feeling." Rather, it is a reasoned appreciation and understanding of the situation of the other person. Although I can identify with the other's situation, I also keep my distance, so to speak, sharing the other's perceptions without losing my own sense of independence.

The ability to understand the feelings of another person is a fundamental capacity in human socialization. It forms a basis for personal self-regulation that is guided not just by individual motives, but also by concern for another's welfare. This form of self-regulation is essential in adaptive family relations, and these in turn form the templates for effective societal relations. The family setting is important because children only gradually develop the capacity for empathic self-regulation.

In recent years scientists have been trying to understand the neural mechanisms that shape our psychological capacities. A technique called neuroimaging is used to create a "map" that shows the parts of our brains where certain specific capacities reside, and where various functions, such as dreaming and thinking, actually occur. This work has led to many surprises, especially this one: Human mental function, for both cognition and emotion, is associated with regular and predictable patterns of activity in brain structures that first appeared hundreds of millions of years ago, in the early stages of vertebrate evolution. Thus, in order to figure out how the human brain "works," we need to develop an evolutionary theory of neural self-regulation.

PSYCHOLOGICAL COMPONENTS
OF EMPATHIC BEHAVIOR

Most social animals have the capacity for emotional response to the emotional displays of others of their species. This process can be described as *emotional contagion*. It is an example of what we call a "visceral" response, referring to those bodily states (such as breathing) that are regulated automatically, without our having to think about them at all. Although this primitive visceral response of emotional contagion is an essential element in the child's development of empathic behavior, it must be accompanied by cognitive skills that allow the child to understand the perspective of the other person.

These skills have been studied recently in terms of what is called a theory of mind. This is the notion that the child can form a mental proposition that another person also has a mind, and thus a unique subjective perspective on events. The capacity for perspective-taking has been seen as necessary for *empathy*—understanding another's feelings—as opposed to *sympathy*—having one's own feelings in response to observing another's emotional displays or an emotionally significant situation.

Although the cognitive process of perspective-taking is accepted as a necessary component of the psychology of empathy, a sympathetic response may also be essential. It is possible, for example, to have and use a clear understanding of another's subjective perspective in order to cause harm to that person, such as in physical or psychological torture. Caring for the person's welfare is also required for "pro-social" empathic behavior. The interesting psychological question is how sympathy contributes to this caring. In the primitive sense of emotional contagion, the addition of sympathy, to perspective-taking may be sufficient to constitute empathy. However, *actually* caring for the other may also be required, and the basis for caring proves as important in a biological analysis as it is in a psychological one.

EVOLUTION OF MIND

To understand the biological mechanisms of empathy, it is important to clarify both the cognitive and emotional components. It may be instructive, therefore, to begin with an analysis of the biological roots of feelings and thoughts. The story begins with the appearance of animals called vertebrates, that is, all creatures with a spinal cord. In all creatures possessing a brain, that organ evolved as an extension of the neural tube (spinal cord). This evolution can actually be observed in humans in pictures of the developing embryo, as shown in Figure 1.

The vertebrate brain evolved largely by elaborating new structures on top of older ones, a process that has been described as one of *terminal additions* (adding new things onto the end). Very simple creatures among our ancestors organized behavior through the specialized end of the neural tube termed the "hindbrain" (rhombencephalon). From this basis the "midbrain" (mesencephalon) evolved with more complex, integrative neural networks. Yet these did not replace the hindbrain, but rather modulated its function, largely through inhibitory control. In other words, in adding new structures literally on top of (and

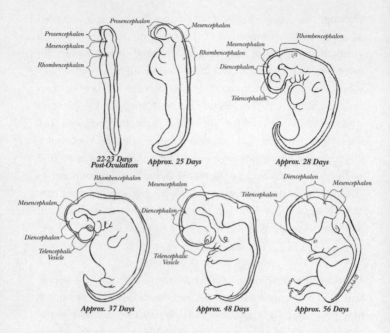

FIGURE 1. *Embryonic differentiation of the human embryo, showing the progressive elaboration of the cephalic divisions at the end of the neural tube (drawing by Anne Awh, copyright © 2005 Don M. Tucker, used with permission).*

tightly connected with) earlier ones, evolution also fashioned an organ having a *hierarchy* of different parts, where the later additions exercise some—but not total—control over the operations of the earlier ones. These later additions serve as regulators: Perhaps think of them as something like thermostats. They monitor the responses of the parts "below" and adjust the system's reactions to the information that is flowing back and forth within the brain.

As you are reading the following paragraphs, please look at the drawings of the human brain, shown in Figures 2 and 3.

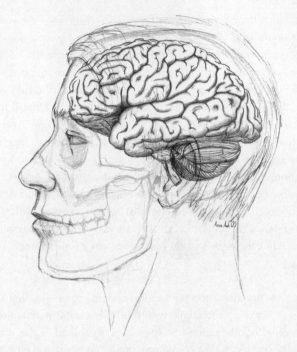

FIGURE 2. *Lateral view of the adult human brain, showing the left cerebral hemisphere (drawing by Anne Awh, copyright © 2005 Don M. Tucker, used with permission).*

From the midbrain evolved two structures of the "interbrain" (diencephalon) that have been pivotal as organizing influences in the brain systems of more complex vertebrates. The first is the *hypothalamus*, situated above the midbrain and controlling homeostasis. Homeostasis is the regulation of internal bodily states (temperature, thirst, hunger, breathing, pain) required for the life of the organism. The second diencephalic structure is the *thalamus*, a set of nuclei on both left and right sides of the brain at the top of the brainstem. Within each thalamus are nuclei for monitoring the two major interfaces of the organism with the outside world—the sensory interface (such as seeing, hearing) and the motor interface (such as muscles—taking action).

Sitting atop the interbrain is the final major division of the verte-brate brain—the "endbrain" or telencephalon. The forms taken by the endbrain determine the intelligence capacity of the higher vertebrates, including reptiles, birds, and mammals. The thalamus is the gateway for sensory and motor traffic into and out of the telencephalon. In higher mammals, including humans, the cerebral cortex of the telencephalon has evolved massive networks for elaborating these "sensorimotor" (sensory and motor) processes, which are integral to the body's *somatic* function, that is, its interface with the outside world. And yet in humans, communication with the outside world continues to be funneled through the thalamus, which exerts regulatory controls over the inhibition or activation of information occur-ring within the sensory and motor streams of experience and behavior.

There are equally important neural systems for regulating the *visceral* function, interfacing with the homeostatic mechanisms of internal bodily processes. These are organized at the dien-cephalic level in the hypothalamus, often described as the body's "master control center." If we look at the neural pathways from the hypothalamus to the telencephalon, we find these are restricted to the *limbic cortex,* located at what we call the inner core of each cerebral hemisphere (limbic = "border," the area surrounding the brainstem). The limbic cortex has evolved a general *evaluative* function, determining the biological or inter-nal significance of the information traffic with the outside world that is going on elsewhere in our brain.

Considering these two brain functions together, we could compare this structure to that of a modern office, where there is both an intranet, or a restricted local area network for internal communications, and an extranet, or a communications portal with the outside world.

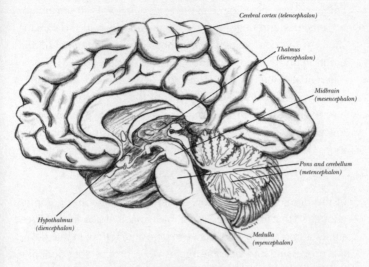

Cerebral cortex (telencephalon)

Thalmus (diencephalon)

Midbrain (mesencephalon)

Pons and cerebellum (metencephalon)

Hypothalmus (diencephalon)

Medulla (myencephalon)

FIGURE 3. *Lateral view of the adult human brain (same perspective as in Figure 2), with the left hemisphere removed, showing the medial wall of the right cerebral hemisphere and the brainstem structures (drawing by Anne Awh, copyright © 2005 Don M. Tucker, used with permission).*

EMOTION AND COGNITION

A general model of emotion and cognition can be derived from these elementary bases of neural organization. The internal regulatory systems are deep inside the brain at the core of each cerebral hemisphere—the left and right halves of the endbrain. These provide global evaluative (emotional) controls. The sensory and motor networks are on the lateral surface—the left and right outside areas of the brain. These provide the specific patterns of perception or action that must be coordinated tightly with the realities of our immediate environment. Each of these primitive functions appears to have evolved with unique ways of forming ideas or concepts.

Thus, two bodily constraints—visceral at the inner core and somatic at the outer shell—form the boundaries of the mind.

Emotion is organized close to the core, whereas both sensorimotor specifics and cognition are organized close to the somatic shell. At the core, experience is holistic, undifferentiated, and emotionally excited. But thoughts and actions must become differentiated into specific forms, so that we can take one definite action rather than another. For this to happen there must be a further processing of these core representations as they move out toward the shell, where they are articulated in sensorimotor forms. This is the basic progression from motive to perception or action.

In the human brain, memory systems have become complex enough so that there is a considerable capacity for delay between stimulus and response, or between urge and action. In that delay, the processing can become recursive, a process of "doubling back": A concept originates in holistic form at the core, is differentiated into specific elements at the shell, and then returns to the core again for a second, higher-order integration.

This neuropsychological theory of mind is able to explain the abstract constructions (concepts) that we know are essential to human intellectual life. It shows us how our thoughts arise wholly within the anatomical structures of the mammalian cortex we humans inherited in evolution. The implications for the inter-relations of motives, emotions, and cognitions are interesting, and somewhat unexpected: Essentially, we find no sharp boundary between emotions and cognitions. Moreover, the capacity for holistic integration of experience turns out to be dependent on networks that are strongly regulated by our brain's visceral function. In sum, evaluative, emotional functions are essential to the integration of experience.

BIOLOGICAL LOVE

Humans are unique in the extended developmental period and the extensive educational process required to achieve the brain's self-organization. Yet the mechanisms of human intelligence are fundamentally identical to the architectural features of the brains of the broader class of mammals from which humans evolved! These are features that evolved to support the neural plasticity that is allowed by creatures that care for their young. The appearance of mammals on earth gave rise to new classes of behavior, including parenting, attachment, and play, all of which support dependent juveniles and the extended embryonic plasticity of their brains.

For evolutionary theory, we must try to understand the more primordial changes that anticipated these mammalian capacities. An example might be the dinosaurs' ability to care for their young, a trait that can still be seen in rudimentary form in today's crocodilians. As well, the attachment mechanisms of birds continue to provide us with important instruction on the progressive nature of developmental experience. The young bird imprints on the significant caregiver of its infancy. Regardless of whether this is its mother or a strange alien of another species (such as a scientist), the bird then maintains an attachment—even, it seems, a kind of identification—with that being throughout its life.

An evolutionary analysis is important in understanding human socialization, because it may help to clarify the underlying motivational mechanisms. In mammals, and perhaps also in dinosaurs and birds, there are primitive motivational systems, such as those regulating the response to pain, that appear to have been extended through natural selection to support and motivate the capacity for social attachment. Modern analysis of neural mechanisms of attachment behavior in juvenile mammals suggests that there is a pain of social abandonment that motivates attachment, and that this is mediated by similar mechanisms that are engaged in physical pain.

Young birds or mammals separated from the mother will often emit distress vocalizations. Small doses of opiates, that is, doses that are too small to be sedating, will stop the distress vocalizations and halt the animal's searching for its mother. The implication is that contact with the mother is associated with an endogenous (natural) opiate release. Abandonment then results in a kind of withdrawal syndrome, and this may be directly analogous to heroin or morphine withdrawal. When an opiate is administered to the young animal, the drug is fully effective in relieving the pain of abandonment, which suggests that opiates are the natural mechanism of social bonding. Thus, human social bonds may share important features with opiate addiction. The relationship is taken for granted when it is present, and yet a distress response occurs as soon as the relationship is withdrawn.

LOVE HURTS

The pain of lost love has, of course, been a palpable feature of experience for many people. What may be important for neuropsychological theory is to recognize that social behavior is motivated by viscerally significant motives, such as pain and longing, that are as integral to mammalian life as hunger and thirst. Both psychoanalysis and behaviorism were mistaken in attempting to derive more complex social motives—whether of the human or the laboratory rat—from the conditioning of primitive hedonistic drives in the individual. We now know that the evolution of social bonding among humans has simply reworked strong motive controls from the most basic vertebrate motivational systems.

Pain can be differentiated between somatic and visceral representations. The somatic representation is mediated by networks in the neocortex. These localize the pain to a specific region of the body surface, determining where it hurts but not how bad. On the other hand, the visceral representation of pain is medi-

ated by regions of the limbic cortex that do not provide information on localization. Rather, the visceral mechanisms determine
the evaluation of the subjective significance of the pain experience. When opiates mediate the pain of abandonment, their sites
of action are in the limbic cortex, including both insular and
cingulate cortex, consistent with the evaluative role of the corebrain visceral networks.

In the mid-twentieth century, lesions were often made by neuro-
surgeons in regions of the limbic cortex (especially in the anterior
cingulate cortex) in order to treat chronic pain. The patients
would report that they still felt pain in the same way, but now
they didn't care. A very similar effect is reported for the effect of
opiates for the relief of pain. Patients still experience the pain,
and can localize it (the somatic function is intact), but they are no
longer distressed (the visceral function is blocked).

The effects of opiate abuse may follow a similar pattern. In many
cases, heroin users turn to drug use in response to social or
sexual abuse, or to interpersonal abandonment. Whatever the
cause of opiate abuse, the effects of addiction are remarkably
consistent. The abuser loses interest in social bonds and substi-
tutes heroin for both sexual and family relations.

Thus the evidence from heroin abuse provides support for the
hypothesis that the body's natural opiates are essential mechanisms in the normal process of social comfort and bonding. This
hypothesis may also help to explain the otherwise anomalous
behavior of self-injury. Some emotionally disturbed people,
particularly women who have suffered sexual or emotional
abuse, may intentionally injure themselves, such as by lacerat-
ing an arm or leg repeatedly with a knife. Most theories of motivation begin with the assumption that people seek pleasure and
avoid pain, and thus cannot explain why someone would intentionally hurt themselves. Yet if the pain of severe interpersonal

abuse is mediated by opiate mechanisms, then it may be that compensatory opiate release—caused by physical pain—is experienced as a relief, a relief to a chronic state of psychological pain.

DEVELOPING EMPATHY

The capacity to integrate conscious attention with emotional experience may be fundamental to empathic experience. Although we can now analyze the neural networks and circuits that are required, these neural mechanisms do not appear to become functional without the appropriate developmental experience. Early experiences seem to be particularly critical, forming a template for later cognition and behavior.

Just as birds form an enduring bond with their caregivers through experience at a critical stage of imprinting, infant primates enter life prepared to bond with the mother. With Rhesus monkeys, research has shown the deficits in both social adaptation and physical health when the infant's bond with the mother is blocked. Importantly, an effective relationship requires both the infant and mother to respond appropriately. Maternal deprivation causes a female infant to grow up with deficits not only in peer interactions, but in her parenting skills as well.

These studies of Rhesus monkeys have been extremely important in providing theoretical models for understanding the interaction between physiology and socialization in humans. In human disorders of empathy, a similar interaction between genetic temperament and social support can be observed. In autism, for example, the infant appears to be born with some deficit of the mechanisms required for successful attachment and social interactions. Recent experiences suggest that highly involved and competent parenting can overcome the social deficits of the autistic child to a considerable degree. Nonetheless, in less fortunate cases, the interactive effect of the child's deficits and the responses of caregivers to this deficit often produces a negative spiral, in which the child's disinterest in social contact leads to the parent's disinterest and neglect.

Whether from genetic or social causes, autistic children show a profound inability to understand the perspectives and intentions of other people. This inability is striking when compared with other cognitive skills, which may be relatively intact or even hyper-developed. Although it may be influenced by, or even caused by, the autistic child's lack of emotional or sympathetic response to another's emotions, the deficit in understanding another's perspective is clearly a cognitive impairment. Lacking a theory of mind, the autistic person simply cannot reason in ways that explain the other's perspective.

Careful studies of the normal communication patterns shared by infants and mothers have supported the realization that social perspective-taking is a fundamental component of intelligence. The typical interactions between mothers and infants involve patterns of reciprocity, turn-taking, and other causal relations of the dialogue. These patterns suggest that both infant and mother are able to understand not just the communication signals, but also the intentions of the other that must be held in mind in order to participate in such well-orchestrated behavior.

A consistent finding has come from studies of how toddlers learn the meanings of words. They do not learn if there is a simple paring of the spoken word with the presence of an object, as traditional behaviorist theory would imply. Rather, the kids look to see what Mom is attending to, or what she intends to do, as they learn the words that go with the objects or actions. Thus the meaning of words is not an arbitrary association, but is embedded in the child's understanding of the mother's intentions.

But these skills are not enough to create effective empathic capacity. This is illustrated by another human developmental disorder, namely, psychopathy. The psychopath may be quite skilled in understanding another person's perspective, and in fact may be remarkable in the ability to manipulate others through application of these skills. Yet there is a surprising lack of concern for the welfare of other people, such that the psychopath easily causes pain or injury to others with no apparent remorse.

Given its societal importance, psychopathy has received remarkably limited scientific attention. As a result, we have only limited evidence on the interplay of genetic temperament and socialization in the crystallization of this highly dangerous personality disorder. However, family studies have suggested some degree of heritability of psychopathy and related conditions, including histrionic personality disorder in women and drug abuse in men. Furthermore, anecdotal clinical observations have suggested that in many severe cases of psychopathy there is evidence of childhood neglect or abuse.

NEURAL MECHANISMS OF SYMPATHIC RESONANCE

By understanding both cognitive and emotional foundations of empathy, and their underlying neural mechanisms, we can formulate a biological model for how empathy evolved in its particular form in humans.

A key element is sensitivity to the emotional state of the other person. We can describe this as *sympathic resonance:* The subject's own emotional responses resonate to the emotional display of the other. In a primitive form, the subject's responses are simply emotional contagion. Whether primitive or more complex, the sympathic resonance in limbic corebrain networks is *syncretic,* meaning that there is holistic fusion of multiple experiential elements that have both external sources (perceptions) and internal ones (visceral sensations).

People differ in the capacity for sympathic resonance, and therefore they differ in an important component of empathy. Autistic, obsessive-compulsive, and paranoid persons are deficient in their own affective responses, and therefore in the capacity to use their sympathic resonance to understand the emotions of another. Just as a person's own visceral, affective responses emerge from homeostatic mechanisms and are largely spontaneous, sympathic resonance is largely a spontaneous reaction to the experience of another's emotional display or situation. The exception is when the sympathic response arises out of intersubjective reasoning.

Intersubjective reasoning refers to the cognitive process through which the subject is able to infer the perspective, intention, and subjective state of another person. From the studies of mother-infant interaction and of toddler social referencing, we can see the complex set of skills that a young child gains in inferring the mother's subjective state.

Within the somatic sensorimotor networks, the representation of another's actions appears to allow a kind of analysis by synthesis, through which the person models what it would be like to carry out the other's actions. When a monkey observes a person in the laboratory who is picking up an object, this observation is accompanied by activity in the monkey's neocortex *in the same motor neurons* that are activated when the monkey itself is actually picking up an object!

The simulation of actions in these *mirror neurons* may be the somatic analogue to the visceral response of emotional contagion. There is a matching or synchronization of the internal response with the observed actions. In both cases, the subject's internal mirroring of the other provides a basis for perspective-taking, *for interpreting what it must be like to be the other.* At the visceral level, sympathic resonance gives a fast and syncretic affective context for what might be the other's subjective state. At the somatic level, action mirroring provides an equally concrete representation of what it must be like to carry out those actions.

However, these concepts have differing neural mechanisms, with differing representational properties. Whereas the visceral representation is spontaneous and dynamic, the somatic representation is more differentiated, articulated, and sequenced. Because of its more structured form, the somatic representation provides scaffolding for more conscious and deliberate reasoning about the actions of the other, leading to the more complex capacity for intersubjective reasoning.

EMPATHY, ABSTRACTION, LOVE

The hypothesis of re-entrant organization of concepts across visceral and somatic networks can be applied to the psychological experience of empathy. For example, in an initial syncretic visceral response, the child may have sensed anxiety or urgency in a person's nonverbal cues, and responded with a diffuse sympathic resonance of her own. She also watched the person picking up food, and mirrored this action with her own perspective on what it would be like to carry out exactly that set of differentiated actions.

Even though it is a remarkable product of evolution, this highly organized intersubjective intelligence is not guaranteed to produce an effective concern for the welfare of the other person. Even powerful and abstract forms of intelligence may remain bound by egocentric concerns. To go beyond a theory of intelligent empathy, in order to explain effective pro-social experience and behavior, it may be necessary to understand the residuals of childhood experiences of attachment and bonding that were integral to the exercise of empathic capacities.

For the child whose elemental needs for social contact were met effectively, it is very likely that interpersonal communication has been grounded in concern for others. The exercise of empathy in both visceral and somatic domains is founded on the experience of love, both in giving and receiving. It is not necessary that the experienced relationships were entirely gratifying; encountering frustration and loss may also give the child an important personal basis for interpreting the experiences of another.

As we have examined the biological basis of love relationships, we have found them to be framed in highly defined family contexts. These relationship contexts were constant constraints in the long history of mammalian evolution, and they continued to shape neuropsychological evolution for our hominid ancestors. However, the human capacity for abstract intelligence may allow flexibility and conceptual scope in both empathic resonance and intersubjective reasoning that now extends beyond family relations. The child's experience in close relations provides a motive basis, grounded in capacities for both feeling deeply and reasoning accurately, that may be integral to the experience of empathy in the more general contexts of society.

AUTHORS' NOTE: *This article draws upon published scientific work by ourselves and the following others: K. J. Aitken, D. A. Baldwin, C. S. Barr & associates, J. Decety & P. L. Johnson, D. Derryberry, C. J. Herrick, M. L. Hoffman, U. Jürgens, P. MacLean, L. J. Moses & associates, J. Panksepp, D. Ploog, A. N Schore, D. N. Stern, S. J. Suomi, and C. Trevarthen.*

08 OCTOBER 2028

Three years have gone by since Klamm first stunned me with his scheme about breeding genetically modified children for the super-rich around the world. And I have no reason to doubt him when he told me today that he's lined up a truly impressive list of clients for these new products, as he calls them. His hunch was correct, he said: His clients are supremely nervous about the accelerating social chaos around them. They're desperately looking for any stratagem at all that promises to secure their families' future and fortune.

I've seen plenty of news reports about various regimes promoting their territories as being safe havens for property, especially to those whose wealth had been accumulated by means best left unadvertised. And yet one after another such countries have succumbed to uprisings and terrorist actions, as jihadists of all stripes track the assets of the rich around the globe, seeking to inflict maximum damage on the spoils of privilege. In these times almost any scheme that promises to protect ill-gotten wealth could attract such clients.

Klamm landed back at the Tembagapura airstrip today with no fewer than thirty contracts in his briefcase, drawn up as agreements between the Sujana Foundation and some of the most privileged families based in every region of the globe. He boasted that my fame as a scientist, as well as the popular interest in the manipulation of brain functions, was so great that the products he had on offer literally sold themselves. He claimed that in some regions he had been lucky enough to conduct auctions, accepting only the highest bids for the required deposit. Wanting to impress me, I suppose, he hinted that the going price was in the millions of euros, payable half on signing, half on delivery.

Klamm swore to me that he had bargained hard with his clients on the firm delivery date for the products, hoping to give himself as much time as possible to ensure my cooperation, but in the end he had to yield on this point. This didn't surprise him—or me, for that matter. Anxieties were rising everywhere among the wealthy, and he was forced to admit that the solution he was peddling had a rather long payback period. So against his better judgment—or so he claimed!—he had promised delivery for no later than 31 July 2030. This date appears in each of the contracts, and Klamm's clients had also insisted that my signature be included—and authenticated by my senior personal banker.

I admit that for the entire previous week I had been dreading the upcoming meeting with him, but was still at a loss to know how I might impede the hatching of his scheme. I asked Hera and Io to visit my quarters last night. Being at my wit's end I thought I might take them into my confidence and formulate with them some way of thwarting him.

To be honest, I'm amazed at how much my two pack leaders, as I'm fond of calling them, have grown and matured during the past year. For the first time they look very much like young women, no longer girls. Hera has more of me in her, although all of the daughters have the light brown skin and dark hair of their mother's ancestry. She's also bigger than all but one or two of her sisters and is developing the long bones and strong musculature of a track-and-field athlete. Her face is attractive rather than beautiful in the conventional sense and is marked by the firm gaze of her dark eyes.

She sets the sartorial style followed by most of the sisters, insisting on wearing pants or shorts rather than dresses. Inspired by her, the sisters care most of all about their education. Hera had made them all models of self-directed learning; they spend most of their days, and much of their nights, scouring the Internet for instruction not only in academic subjects, but also in the plastic and fine arts as well—pottery and sculpture, painting and decorative arts, music and dance. Observing this first some years ago, on one of my occasional visits, I had arranged for delivery of all the supplies and instruments needed for their explorations, as well as providing native craftspeople to tutor them. Hera herself is becoming a skilled pianist, working with a teacher in Europe over the Internet.

Io is altogether different. She is exceptionally beautiful and obviously knows it. She's small-boned but becoming full-breasted, like her mother; indeed, she reminds me so much of Ina that it's sometimes painful for me to be in her company. She always wears long, colorful robes and loves jewelry—as her mother did—whereas no ornamentation of any kind adorns young Hera. Io appears to have a special fascination with bracelets, rings with semi-precious stones, and especially amulets, which particularly seem to intrigue her. She refuses to tell me how she procures these things, although Hera once hinted that the more expensive of them are gifts from Klamm. A worrisome thought indeed, but Io is if anything even more strong willed than Hera and simply brushes off my questions about her jewelry with a sweet smile and a kiss.

Io has perhaps the keenest and quickest mind among the sisters, not excluding Hera, but it's also crystal clear that she lacks Hera's determination and firm sense of purpose. Learning comes easy to Io, as it does to all the girls, but she bears it more lightly than the rest, often mocking the seriousness of knowledge; she's fond of saying that it's just a means to an end—what end, she won't say! She's got a little band of dedicated followers in the group, but most of the other sisters look upon Hera as their leader. They seek her opinion and expect her to act as their go-between with the staff on any matters of importance to the sisters. This is frankly a little puzzling, since on the surface she's shy and unassertive in demeanor. Yet, every once in a while, one can see in Hera's gaze some flashes of what lies just beneath the surface—an iron will, a quickness and self-assurance in judgment, and above all an acceptance of what she regards as her responsibility for her sisters' welfare and her own duty.

That night I couldn't bring myself to brief Hera and Io on my dilemma after all, or enlist them in a joint campaign to stop Klamm. But somehow my talk with them lifted my spirits and stiffened my resolve to deny him his prize. To my own great astonishment I was eerily calm when I awoke the next morning. Presumably I had convinced myself that I would be protected, somehow, by my faith in the goodness of Ina's original plan, and that this faith would sustain me in resisting Klamm's entreaties to complete the deal we had agreed upon some years before. I was so preoccupied with my work, sitting at the lab bench earlier today, that he startled me when he walked into my laboratory.

I glanced at him and burst out, "Max, you look terrible."

"A bad skiing accident, unfortunately. How are you, Franklin?"

Of course I didn't believe a word of it. I guessed at once that my former friend had recently had an altercation with agents acting on behalf of one of his unsympathetic creditors! I recall the thought running through my mind at that moment that he probably had no more that a few months to live if he didn't get substantial repayment funds almost immediately. Although it seems bizarre to say so, I didn't consider this circumstance to be my problem. Recollecting this now, a few hours later, tells me a good deal about the dissociation from reality in my own mind.

"I'm fine. We've just celebrated the girls' fourteenth birthday; the party was a real smash—sorry you missed it. They're becoming a handful, believe me. I can barely make my wishes heard or get them to take suggestions from me. More and more they look to Hera for direction, which I don't mind, since I won't always be here for them, although the few who follow Io seem to be very antagonistic toward Hera, for reasons I don't understand. They operate now as two tight little packs, but I don't think this will last much longer, especially after they start getting interested in men. I expect that eventually they'll all go their separate ways. And …."

He interrupted, speaking brusquely. "Let's get down to business. I have in my briefcase the complete set of contracts from our clients and I need your signature, as well as that of your personal banker, on each of them in order to complete the deal. Your name carries a lot of weight in the world, Dr. Stone, even among the rich who spend most of their days idling on beaches and their evenings gaming at the casinos. No matter how dissolute their lifestyles, they seem to have picked up news about you and your work."

"Flattery from you won't work on me, Max. I told you by phone before you set out to come here that I wasn't ready to sign any contracts, and I haven't changed my mind."

"Franklin, please be reasonable! These are contracts for future delivery. You have a whole year yet in which to plan the initial work on the embryos before we implant them into the surrogate mothers. Surely that's enough time. You've already carried out the protocol once, and successfully; the second time should be routine."

"This kind of work is never routine, which you would know if you were a neurobiologist instead of what you are— a crooked businessman. Besides, I would have to screen the new batches of sperm and eggs collected from the couples you've contracted with so I can ensure all the samples are viable, which is sometimes not the case. And you've conveniently forgotten as well that I have a prior commitment to the Group of 300, where the preparatory work is already done. Some of them have been waiting for five years already for the next steps to happen. I just can't work as fast without some assistance, and I don't like to take on other collaborators because of the secrecy we must keep."

He exploded. "For chrissake, Franklin, how can I get through to you? You owe bugger-all to the Group of 300. All they did was hand over some useless eggs and sperm to you. You can do them next. Right now we need to guarantee delivery to the clients who really matter."

"Who matter to you, not to me. I don't care if this deal falls through. There's nothing at all in it for me."

He was still yelling at me. "Have you forgotten what I told you three years ago? This is your best chance of making sure that all your work will amount to something. What you're achieving with your girls, and planning to do with the embryos for the Group of 300, is like scattering a bunch of seeds on some hard, dry ground and hoping a few will germinate. My plan is the only one that will work, and you know it!"

"Keep your voice down, Max, and just listen for a change. I'll say this slowly so that the message sinks in. I don't think that Ina would have approved of your plan, and so I'm not going through with it. Now get out of my lab."

I recall that at this point he exhaled loudly and kicked at a stool standing by the bench. "Why did I figure that our conversation would go this way as I was flying up here? Why did I ever believe I could persuade you to change your mind?" Then his mood changed suddenly. "By the way, have you seen the company's new Dash turbojet? Very nice plane, very fast, configured for twelve passengers and cargo, and we've got two excellent pilots on staff. Makes the trip from

Timika a hell of a lot quicker than it used to be over that godforsaken road. Come outside and take a look at it!"

"Max, have you gone deaf from your accident? I told you I'm busy. I haven't the slightest interest in your new toy right now. Just get the hell out of here and leave me alone."

"Pity, Franklin. I really didn't think you'd miss the chance to wave goodbye to your lovely girls. Can you imagine how excited they were when I told them that at last they were going to be released from what they call their prison? That finally they would be able to see the world, with their father as their guide, from their very own airplane? The security chief has assembled them and their suitcases on the airstrip at my request. See for yourself."

I was sure my heart stopped beating for an instant. I tried to cry out but could not: The sound I sought to make was strangled in my throat. All I could do was stumble to the doorway and look outside. I could see our airstrip clearly below the rise on which the laboratory stood. The plane was parked with its engines running. Around it swarmed my twelve precious girls, whose excitement seemed sufficient to lift the plane aloft without the aid of engines of any kind.

"Wave goodbye to them, Franklin. I've told them you're finishing up some important work and will join them later tonight in Timika. Of course—unfortunately—that won't be possible, because the plane won't be returning. I'll think of something else to tell them when the time comes. Given how excited they are I doubt they'll even notice your absence when we fly out of Timika tomorrow."

Finally, I regained my capacity to speak. I think that Klamm was surprised when I didn't proceed to curse him or try to assault him; when I noticed the small security detail hidden nearby, I realized he was ready for anything. Again I was beaten, and both of us knew it. Why hadn't I taken steps over the last three years to ensure I wouldn't again be in the position of succumbing meekly to his blackmail, with my daughters' safety as the trump card? That's easy enough to say. After our prior confrontation I weighed all kinds of options in my mind, in which I envisioned whisking them all out of harm's way, and I even took the first steps toward realizing what seemed to be the most propitious of my plans.

Then reality set in. Klamm had, over the years, established complete authority over the compound, the support and security staff, as well as our transportation system. The Indonesian government and army officials who superintend our site are well paid by him. But I was the entrepreneur, and I myself had forged the golden chains now fixing me to this spot. I was a prisoner in my own kingdom, along with my daughters. As one unworkable scheme after another passed through my mind, only to be discarded again shortly thereafter, the intervening years passed all too quickly.

So I returned to my lab and slumped in a chair. "I'll sign whatever you want. On condition that you promise never to take them away from me."

He laughed contemptuously at me. "Of course, Franklin, I promise. But I don't know how I'm going to calm the girls down, do you? They may just hijack the plane when I tell them that the trip is off. Let's see if we can invent a good story. How about this. I'll call the infirmary and have them send the ambulance and a stretcher for you. We'll tell the girls you may be having a heart attack, and that the plane must stand by while we do preliminary tests over the Internet with a leading specialist.

"These fake tests will take some time and meanwhile the girls will calm down. Then I'll tell them that the plane must go to Jakarta to bring back a specialist because you're too ill to travel. Tomorrow I'll think of another excuse why the plane hasn't come back, and by then they'll have settled back into their daily routines again."

After a pause Klamm went on. "Oh, by the way, I'll drop by later at the infirmary to see how your recovery is progressing, and then you can give me the signed papers. OK?"

I glared mutely at him; his returning glance showed no reaction whatsoever to the feelings of hatred and resignation that must have been written on my face.

Klamm called for the ambulance and radioed the security chief to tell the girls that there was a medical emergency and the plane couldn't take off. After putting on a show of concern as I was loaded onto a stretcher and taken to the infirmary, with my girls all watching anxiously from a distance, he headed for the girls' dormitory, telling me he had arranged to talk to Hera and Io about my alleged health crisis.

§ § §

(Hera's Journal) Klamm sauntered in today, rudely interrupting my conversation with Io. I've always despised the man from the moment I first set eyes on him. I've never bothered to exchange more than a few offhand remarks with him, and it amuses me to just sit and watch him when he's chatting with some of my sisters. I think I make him a bit uneasy when I do this, and if so, I'm delighted! I can see right through him: I know he believes we're just a bunch of pampered, hyper-intellectual girls who are utterly unaware of the real world outside our mountaintop home. Well, let him go on thinking that way; I may need him to underestimate us by a wide margin some day.

He toys with me by playing up to Io every chance he gets, and since she's so much more uninhibited than I am, she likes to play the game with him. So he pretends to court her, by soliciting her views on various issues right in front of me. I know that he secretly slips expensive gifts to her during his visits. In the last two years Io has begun to flirt openly with Klamm, although he's probably cunning enough to recognize that she knows exactly what she's doing and that it was a game she enjoyed participating in. As does he. I've tried, but I can't seem to dissuade her from carrying on with him.

He was smirking, as if enormously self-satisfied, as he entered the lounge at our apartment compound and gave Io and me a story about sending the plane to fetch a heart specialist for father. He promised on father's behalf to reschedule our trip as soon as possible. I don't know why, but I sensed that the story about a possible heart attack just wasn't true—and that Io had the same feeling. Something else is going on. We'll just have to get the truth out of father when we can. As Klamm was leaving he handed over his latest gift to Io, saying that it was a particularly well-made Creole amulet that had cost him considerable time and effort to procure. Io didn't react at all, just looked pleased and said, "Thanks, Max."

§   §   §

(Franklin's Journal) What a stupid business, lying here in a hospital bed when there's nothing wrong with me, just so I can put on a show for my daughters at Klamm's behest! I've got to sign these accursed contracts right now, but I can barely force myself to even look at them. How on earth did I ever get myself into such an awful situation? The trap finally has been sprung on me. This secret facility was the trap, but by the time I recognized it for what it was, escape for my girls was impossible. Dozens of plans were hatched in my mind over the last three years, and each one was shot down by a dose of reality. Once I even phoned the pilot's home in Timika, on the spur of the moment, ordering the plane to be sent up here, only to be told that he would have to call Mr. Klamm for authorization!

Finally, I glanced at a few pages in the document, my eyes falling upon the section that specified a procedure for certification of live birth no later than 31 July 2030, with delivery to follow six months later, detailing the product as follows: 'The Sujana Foundation will deliver to the client a live newborn male child in good health, at approximately six months of age, with brain functions certified by Professor Franklin Peter Stone to be, upon full development, within the upper 5% of the normal human range for a set of characteristics specified hereunder in section 3(b) of this Agreement.'

Then there was the contingency add-on in each of the thirty contracts: 'If by the time of delivery Professor Stone has been awarded a Nobel Prize, the price for each product will be increased by a 100% premium.' Undoubtedly it had amused Klamm no end to observe the cachet that by then had become attached to the Nobel Prize in the public mind—how the prizes symbolized for the naïve public its faith in science as the world's new savior. On the other hand, no less certainly was he pleased to be able to profit personally from this faith. The documents noted that guarantees for the supplementary payment from each client, in the form of a secure letter of credit, must be placed on deposit in a specified bank at the time of contract finalization. The price and payment terms were contained in an annex that my former friend conveniently had neglected to include in my package. I picked up my pen and did what I had to do.

"How's the patient coming along?" Klamm entered my room at the infirmary, trying to lighten the mood between us, and I handed his briefcase back to him.

"I've signed them all; may your soul burn in hell. The instruction to my personal banker is included in the lot. But I can't solve all your problems. I don't think I can have this batch ready by the delivery date because I have to work alone." I should have known that he would be ready for this excuse.

"No problem. I'll have a couple of technicians from Wollstone's Jakarta labs sent up here on contract for a year.

They're Indonesians, so they'll be wary of the obvious military presence in our operations, and when I tell them they're being assigned to a secret government project, I'm sure they'll keep their mouths shut."

I tried again. "Well, that solves one problem, but there's another. As I told you, completing the collection and screening of this new batch of eggs and sperm from the client families will take a lot of time, even before the fertilization and engineering can be started. So I still can't make the deadline you've imposed on me."

"I've already thought of a solution for that little problem, too. Here's what you're going to do. You've already screened and prepared the embryos from the Group of 300 before freezing them. I'll let you know what ethnic and racial types are represented in our new client list. Then you can pick out a bunch of embryos from the inventory you already have on hand, stuff that matches the profile of the client group, making sure that each one is lined up properly. Can you imagine the reaction if one of my Chinese clients is handed some screaming black kid? And remember: Boys only; none of them wants a girl. In the meantime I'll finish gathering the egg and sperm samples from the clients, assuring them that their genetic material will be used for your engineering—but, of course, we'll just chuck it out.

"What do these people know about genetics anyway? If they have DNA tests done later, we can always say that their kid's DNA doesn't match their own because the work you did reshuffled their gene sequences, or something like that. Oh yes, and there's no reason why you can't get to work right away on some special protocol for genetic fiddling with the kids' brains. I want you to make sure that some easily noticeable difference in their behavior shows up during their first year.

"I don't care what you actually do to them, quite honestly. Just be sure that the little bastards are changed enough from normal babies so that the difference is really obvious, even to simple folk. Let's say you make the kids emit some weird and unintelligible babble when they start to talk. The Christians among the so-called parents will think that their children are speaking in tongues and they'll fall down and worship the little buggers on the spot. Should make for a great freak show."

I just glared at him, uttering not a word, so he continued on. "I guess that's all clear then. By the way, Franklin, don't try anything funny with the girls, like trying to sneak off with them when I'm not here. The chief of security works for me and I've ordered him to keep a special watch on you. If you try to double-cross me, you'll never see them again. Understood? Agreed? I'll be back once a month to see how your work is progressing.

"Nothing personal, you understand; it's not that I don't trust you or anything. It's just that a lot of my clients are—how should I put it?—not very nice people. I've dealt with their types before, and with these contracts I'll get the worst of my creditors off my back. And keep them away from my face—you've probably guessed that I haven't been skiing lately. Some of the new batch are even nastier. Nobody who tries to sucker them celebrates very long or dies a quick death. Nothing can go wrong. Is that perfectly clear to you?"

What was the point of prolonging this absurd conversation? I just said quietly, "I understand. And if I keep my part of the bargain, you promise not to harm the girls or take them away?"

"I promise. As I told you, none of my clients wants a girl. Keep them. I have no interest in them—except as security for your part of the current deal. Do whatever you want with them—other than trying to spirit them out of here. I warn you, if you try you won't succeed, and when I find out about it, which I will, they really will be in danger."

13 NOVEMBER 2028

I look back now on our fourteenth birthday celebration in mid-September and recall how happy and relaxed everyone was—at least for that day! Despite that brief respite, my relations with father have become very tense during the past year. He's allowed his exasperation with me to show more openly of late, and I suspect that partly it's because of something that's happening between him and Klamm—once in a while we overhear horrible arguments between them in his lab. And on those days when father's away from here on a business trip and Klamm happens to show up, I live in terror that he'll round us up and take us away. But I don't allow my sisters to know about these fears.

Still, despite father's dissatisfaction with me, my sisters and I have our own concerns that he needs to address, and it's been my role to put them on the table. During our recent nighttime conversations I've begun to press him about his future plans for his daughters, but usually all I get in return is pleasantries and vague promises. So I've begun to express my annoyance at what we're now regularly referring to as our 'Babylonian captivity' in Tembaga-pura. I'm not going to let him off the hook! I was well aware that tonight's conversation could turn ugly, so I asked Ari, Gaia and Tammy to join me. They've done so during similar sessions over the past year. The four of us sat together on a large couch facing his chair, and I opened the proceedings.

"It's time for you to get us away from here, father, and allow us to see more people like ourselves. This place feels more and more like a prison."

"Girls, listen to me. I've had quite enough of these complaints from you. I spend most of my life now looking after you and working with you on your education. I've told you again and again why I think we should all stay here for a while longer, but apparently you simply refuse to accept my reasons. So what am I supposed to do? Take orders from my fourteen-year-old daughters?"

I let my impatience show right away, unfortunately. "We're not a normal family, isn't that obvious? And we're not just someone's ordinary teenage children, as you yourself have told us many times. During our early years when you left us here alone, only visiting once in a while, we had to grow up without either a mother or a father. My sisters began to rely on me and the others here tonight to help them with things that were bothering them, and to comfort them when they were worried. We were able to do this for them, and now they expect us to take the lead in figuring things out, or at least to make sure we don't forget to think ahead and make plans for our lives once we leave here."

"No, the four of you have got that all wrong. *I'm* responsible for making sure that things turn out all right, not you. Since long before you were born, your mother and I tried to imagine the kind of future you and your sisters would have. I'm glad you were willing to play that role during those years when I couldn't be here very much, but now I'm here and you don't need to do that anymore."

Ari answered him with a sharp edge in her voice. "Actually we've asked our sisters about that, and most of them said—not Io, of course, or the little band that follows her, but the others did—that they wanted us to keep on doing this. We also believe we should do so. It's not really because we think you'll go away again and not come back. It's because we know we're different from other people and have to take care of ourselves."

But he just laughed scornfully. "That's ridiculous; you're in no position to take care of anything. I provide everything you need and I am your father, so I think I'm entitled to ask you to respect what I'm trying to do for you and trust me that it's for the best."

Now I was furious, and I think my quick anger stunned him. "You talk as if you own us. Is that what you think? Are we your personal property? Do we have to put up with whatever you decide is best for us, including being imprisoned on this mountainside? And what if you just keel over and die someday from a heart attack? What will happen to us then? Will your friend Klamm take care of us, perhaps?"

I believe this comment brought him up short because he paused before replying. "Really, Hera, you should know me better than that. I've considered this possibility and made provision for it in my will. My personal fortune, which is very large, is left in trust to all of you, so you'll never want for anything. The committee of trustees is a group of very distinguished and honorable people, who will manage these funds on your behalf until you're old enough to assume control of them. If anything happens to me, they'll relocate you and look after you until you come of legal age."

Gaia, too, was furious and it showed when she lashed out. "That is, unless your Mr. Klamm gets to us first! And he has the advantage of knowing where we are. Do your trustees know where we are? Or how to find their way to this little hideout you designed for us?"

That remark again made him stop before answering. My guess is, he was silently recalling that his will had been drawn up long before his relations with Klamm had turned sour. I'm betting that he hadn't brought its terms up-to-date—I read once in an article that most people neglect to do so. I'll bet he was now admitting to himself that a clear strategy was needed to protect us in the event of his sudden death, even if the problem of Mr. Klamm's privileged access to our whereabouts hadn't arisen. It's obvious how much he disliked conceding a point to his increasingly independent daughters, but his long silence indicated that he didn't have a ready reply to Gaia's challenge. Tammy spoke up while we were sitting there waiting for his belated response.

"We've asked you several times during the last year to do just one thing that would give us some additional security. We've asked you to set up a trust fund that would be under our control, one where we could manage the investments and direct a lawyer acting on our behalf to make disbursements as we require. If an emergency arose because something happened to you, we would then be able to take care of things for our sisters until the trustees were able to act. But you've refused to do this or even to talk about it lately. Why?"

Before he could speak I broke in. "I insist that you take care of this for us right now."

"You're being ridiculous and you know it, Hera. I've told you many times already that I'm not even going to discuss such a scheme. Perhaps we've all had enough of each other for one evening. I'll say good night to you then."

No one moved. Then the other three turned to look at me, for we had anticipated this response and had discussed our riposte to it before we arrived at his compound that night. I remained silent for about thirty seconds before speaking, wanting to choose the right words and phrasing for what we had agreed I would say. I spoke in a matter-of-fact tone.

"I don't like arguing among ourselves anymore than do you, father. But if you won't do what we ask, we'll have no choice but to proceed with what we refer to as 'Plan B.' Do you know the nice missionary couple from Timika—they're Canadians—who have started to come here to hold church services for the staff people and their families?

"A few of us have gotten to know them quite well during the last couple of months. And they're very interested in us, wondering what we're doing here. When they left last Sunday they took with them a letter I wrote, signed by the four of us here tonight. They've been asked to open the letter and follow the instructions in it by the day after tomorrow if I don't contact them again before then with a different request."

The words were no sooner out of my mouth than he jumped up from his seat and crossed the room to where we were sitting, anger flashing across his face. "What did you say? What instructions? Hera, what have you done? I distinctly remember telling you I didn't want you to become friendly with the missionary couple. They're allowed to come here only because our local staff people were very upset at not being able to have church services they could attend."

There it was, his quick temper again—which was quite a recent development, to be fair, but also something he indulged himself in with greater frequency each passing week. I confess, I made things worse by springing this surprise on him, but by that point I'd had quite enough of his sudden blow-ups, so I decided to play this game myself and allow a little sarcasm and derision to creep into my voice.

"Oh, I know, father, it's all part of your plan, isn't it, to make sure that we're cut off from the whole world, so that you can run things for us exactly as you please. Well, that's just not right and we won't stand for it anymore. The four of us decided on this together. Here's a copy of the letter from us that the missionary couple now have in their possession. Read it, and then we can discuss together how to set up the trust fund for us."

Hovering over us he scanned the short letter we had penned. It directed the couple to contact Interpol and Scotland Yard with a request for an urgent investigation into a case of slave trading and forcible confinement involving twelve young women holding UK nationality. The letter stated that a UK national was the suspected ringleader in the case and gave the exact location of the Tembagapura facility. Immediate police action was necessary, the letter said, because the women were going to be moved to a secret location on another continent within a matter of weeks. It further suggested that the couple should contact the international media if they had not received satisfactory assurances of prompt action from the police within three days.

He wheeled and paced around the room, now agitated and distraught. "My God, girls, have you lost your senses completely? If the police or the media get their hands on this letter, everything I have worked for these last twenty years will be ruined."

Ari's reply was very coolly delivered, which pleased and impressed me. "The letter won't be opened by the missionaries—they promised us they would wait for our call before doing so. Therefore, they won't take those actions *if* you agree right now to do what we've asked. But I can guarantee that it will be opened and they will make those calls if you refuse to set up the trust fund, or if you give orders to prevent the couple from returning to Tembagapura in the future. The simple alternative is for you to contact your lawyers at once and direct them to transfer monies immediately into an account that will be set up in Hera's name."

I had to admit to myself later that these were provocative words! Father was extremely agitated, and for the first time in my life I feared he might strike us.

§   §   §

(*Franklin's Journal*) Reading the letter almost sent me into a frenzy! For the first time I felt—for a fleeting moment—that

I might strike my daughters and perhaps injure them. I'm so much bigger than they, after all. Fortunately, I realized almost at once that I must stop in my tracks, sit down again, and let my rage dissipate before doing or saying anything else. I forced myself to return to my chair, and as I glanced back to where they were lined up across my couch, I was convinced I saw the shadow of fear pass over them.

As the four of them sat there watching me, I allowed several minutes to go by while my exasperation and anger subsided, and then all the guilt plaguing me in recent months rushed to the surface. Things have gotten so much more complicated over the years! When Ina and I first discussed our plan for genetic engineering using embryos from the donor couples, I assumed of course that she would be constantly by my side. As I reflect back on those days, it's clear that I also assumed—without really making the scenario explicit—that I'd only be supervising the children's post-natal development from afar, not running it on-site, while carrying on as before with my professorial and research duties.

What's also clear in retrospect is that at the time I agreed to Klamm's suggestion to undertake a pilot project after Ina's death, I was utterly distraught at my loss and in no shape to make such momentous decisions. I can concede now that I hadn't thought through all the ramifications, or perhaps any of them. I hadn't counted on devoting an increasing amount of my own time to raising a tribe of children! But above all, I never, ever dreamed that one day I would live in a state of ongoing terror for their safety. If, God forbid, my daughters ever find out about the peril they're in, what would happen then?

Finally, I knew that I must concede their right to force my hand, but without yielding on the main point—primary responsibility for their safety rests with me, as it always has. I won't admit that they went about this in the right way, or the only way possible, no matter how deeply felt their concerns were.

"All right, for goodness sake, I'll do it. I must say, I can hardly believe what's going on—that I'm being treated like a common criminal and subjected to blackmail by a few of my own daughters!"

§   §   §

(Hera's Journal) Tammy shot back. "Well, it may be the case that a few of your daughters thought this up, father, but all of them agreed to sign it. And you can call it blackmail if you like, although you're the one who forced us to employ such measures." Turning to face me, she added, "We want you to listen to Hera while she outlines our specific requests."

I resumed speaking very calmly now, wishing to see if we could just slide over into the implementation of our plan without any additional rancor. "Now, about the trust fund. We've thought about what we'll need. You will authenticate my digital signature so your law firm can authorize the transactions I want to make, and with the kind of security protocol we have here, I can manage the funds entirely by electronic communications. I also want you to arrange for a member of your law firm to act as my agent and to carry out my instructions, without any counter-signature required from you or anyone else. With my sisters' help I'm going to manage these funds in an investment portfolio and we'll invest or spend them as we see fit.

"We'd like you to deposit ten million euros into the account as the opening balance. If we really need to leave here on our own, we may need that kind of money. Anyway, I suspect this amount is just a tiny fraction of the funds in your own investment trust. There are a lot of details to take care of by tomorrow. So let's not argue anymore and just figure out how to get it arranged. Then I'll contact the missionary couple and tell them not to open our letter."

My plan—which I had worked out in detail with my three co-conspirators—had been forming in my mind for some time. I've feared Klamm's true intentions for years, and I just couldn't seem to convince father—despite endless conversations on the subject—that he must take us away from Tembagapura, and as soon as possible. It was obvious to me that our utter isolation on the mountain, and the inaccessibility of the site itself, rendered us virtual captives awaiting our disposition at Klamm's whim. He just wouldn't listen, so eventually I concluded we had no choice—we had to force his hand.

No one needed to remind me about the enormity of the obstacles we faced in deciding to take charge of our own destiny. After all, my sisters and I are young girls whose very existence is unsuspected by outside parties, thanks to father's obsession with secrecy about us. We're kept practically incommunicado in an inaccessible part of the remotest province in Indonesia, waiting for him to deliver on his promises to relocate us. As well, we're too far from the age of legal majority to act on our own in the outside world. On the other hand, he is one of the world's most famous scientists and no one would challenge the assertion—especially if they did not know all the relevant facts, and who was there to tell them?—that he was entitled to act in the best interests of his children.

Moreover, we had no money of our own and no acquaintances in other places to rely on. But those facts simply represented the challenges we must overcome. What we lacked in resources could be made up for in quiet determination and careful planning. There were three necessary steps to take before we could regard ourselves as having a measure of control over our future.

The first was to secure a source of sufficient funds at our disposal, and this had now been nicely accomplished with our 'blackmail' letter. Io was delighted to sign it, as I expected she would be. Moira and Themis had been apprehensive about putting their names to it, but in the end I'd managed to persuade them to trust my judgment. The second step was to deal with the problem of our legal age, for without a solution to that problem we could get no further than the borders of Papua Province, which would be of dubious benefit to us. It would be far too risky to entrust our fate to the usual smugglers operating in the seas around New Guinea, who—based on news accounts we've all seen— would certainly not hesitate for an instant to sell us into sex-slavery for a pittance or just throw us into the sea after raping us and stealing our possessions.

I admit I was at a loss as to how to deal with this problem until I remembered something father had told me some years before. He said he had registered our births as UK nationals who had been born in Indonesia to British parents, later procuring Indonesian residence permits for all of us as well. Then, he told me, he obtained UK passports for us through the British consulate in Jakarta, after being challenged by officials and having to submit DNA samples to prove that all of us were the natural daughters of him and his late wife. He had done so because there was always the possibility he would have to move us out of the country on short notice. He told me that he kept the sisters' passports and birth certificates in a safe at his private residence here.

That's when I decided to inspect the passports. His safe was protected by an encrypted access code that—frankly!— wasn't particularly sophisticated for its time. With Pandora's help I opened his safe one night, about a month ago, when he was away on a short business trip. I was immensely pleased at this demonstration of our safe-cracking skills, but even happier when I saw what information the passports contained.

Father had always assumed that his girls would strike

other people as being older and more mature than we actually were, as a result of both his genetic modifications and the intense hothouse atmosphere of our early education. And he probably thought there would be other advantages in advancing our ages, such as early entry to university and ease of movement around the world.

So, as I discovered when I saw the passports, he apparently had arranged for Indonesian officials to backdate our birth registrations by three years, because these datings were carried over into the passport applications. When we examined the passports, we discovered that the sisters were listed as being seventeen years old. Thus, in another year we could be moving about the world freely, entirely on our own, if we chose to do so.

Yet there was a third obstacle and it was a serious one. Even well supplied with money and passports, twelve young Indonesian girls were unlikely to pass unnoticed on a journey between Tembagapura and Timika! In fact it was almost impossible to imagine we would pass at all, since Klamm controlled the security detail at the village, and—as I heard him boast once—the single road down the mountainside offered no opportunity to bypass its guard post installations. No matter how many times I turned the problem over in my mind, I couldn't see a way out. Until the day the Canadian missionaries showed up.

§   §   §

Linda and Henry Jackson had been sent to Papua Province by the congregations of the Church of Jesus of Nazareth, a small denomination with churches in southern British Columbia and Alberta in Canada. The Jacksons told us that when they arrived in Papua, they joined a long list of Protestant missionaries who have sought converts on the island of New Guinea for several centuries—so successfully, that by the late twentieth century two-thirds of Papua's declared religionists were Protestants. A few of the staff told us that the Jacksons were well liked in Timika and had an active and loyal congregation there, some of whom had relatives working at our mysterious facility in Tembagapura.

At the persistent request of the staff at our location, the Jacksons had been given permission from Klamm to make the long drive up the mountainside twice a month to hold church services in the village meeting hall. I know how he liked to keep the entire operation shut off from the outside world, but one of the consequences of this enforced isolation was frequent staff resignations; he must have agreed to the Jacksons' visits in an effort to reduce personnel turnover. On one of their early trips, they apparently noticed our little band of young women living separately, because soon the couple started bringing along with them for the services a few girls of the same age from Timika who were related to local staff members.

I watched these developments carefully and with growing interest over the past year. After awhile I initiated casual conversations first with the visiting girls and then with the Jacksons, who were intrigued and mystified by the presence in this isolated village of such bright and accomplished youngsters—as we are, in all modesty! So I worked out a little plot; a few lies—harmless ones, I hope—in a good cause.

I told them that we twelve girls are the daughters of wealthy Christian families from various Asian countries and that our facility here is an elite private school. We would soon be graduating and be sent for missionary training, ideally somewhere in North America. That's when the Jacksons agreed to begin exploring the availability of places at a small missionary training college operated by their church in southern Alberta. I let it be known that financial assistance would be available to defray the costs of our schooling and lodging. But initially I couldn't figure out how the departure first from Tembagapura and then from Papua could be arranged without alerting the guards who kept watch over us.

One day I told the Jacksons, "Just be sure that when we girls are ready to go to Alberta, the letters of acceptance to the college are ready for presentation to Canadian immigration authorities. We have our passports and can supply financial guarantees covering a three-year period of residence at the college. This should be enough to get our entry visas into Canada."

Now that I had a location in mind for us, I had searched the Internet for the names of law firms in Calgary, the city nearest our destination. Having selected a firm that seemed to do a lot of international business, I sent them a retainer of several thousand euros, the entire balance of a little nest egg I had been accumulating for a few years, monies I had wheedled out of father on various pretexts.

§   §   §

I recalled my conversations with the missionaries in my mind while father was in his study. He was working out the details of the instructions to his lawyers for the transfer of funds to a trust account that had been opened in my name at a Canadian bank by my law firm in Calgary. After the four of us had reviewed the directives to his lawyers for placing the ten million euros into my account, Gaia said to him, "There's just one more thing."

I don't blame him for the tone of bitterness in his voice at this point. "There's always one more thing with you girls, isn't there? What is it now?"

My three sisters and I had anticipated this portion of the session, too, and Gaia gave the answers we prepared. "Nothing we haven't also talked about time and again, father. It's something with which all of our sisters also concur. We're sick and tired of being isolated from all contact with other people of our own age. It's not normal and it's not right. Do you think we'll become infected by them somehow and catch a weird disease? You've never given us a good reason for this. We've all concluded that we want to become friends with some other girls of our own age."

She went on without waiting for his expected protest. "We've already talked to the missionaries and they've agreed—if given permission by you—to bring twelve girls our age from their Timika church congregation with them on their visits to Tembagapura twice a month. They want us to put a small bus at their disposal. But we've had what we think is a better idea. We know that the Jacksons are getting very tired of the long trip up and down the mountain by car, which takes them almost an entire day each time. Being good people, however, they don't intend to stop doing it since the staff here enjoy having the religious services.

"Well, you now have an airplane that could take all of them, the couple and the girls from Timika, here and back in almost no time at all. We know that the plane isn't used very much, although the pilots seem to be always available in case you or Klamm need to make a trip on short notice.

"We did wonder whether we sisters could go to Timika to visit those girls instead, but we know how angry you get whenever the subject of what we call our 'detention' here is raised, so we're not asking you to allow us to do that. Will you instead authorize the pilots to fly the group from Timika up here twice a month? And since the trip by plane will take so little time, they could stay here for most of the day. We could all have a picnic and play games after their church service. Then they'll leave again, so you won't have to fear that we will be exposed to them for too long. Will you do this for us?"

We waited patiently as he mulled over the idea in his mind. We had taken another gamble with this suggestion, but we guessed that even he might see some merit—and some benefit to himself!—in our proposition. After all, wasn't it an easy way to put an end, temporarily at least, to our constant carping at him about our isolation here? He himself had stressed again and again that he didn't want us to think that we weren't normal children, albeit ones with exceptional abilities. Even he had noticed we were getting to the age where he could foresee our venturing out into the world by ourselves. And surely even he had to admit we needed to develop socialization skills in addition to the intensive academic schooling we were getting.

He seemed to sigh with relief, as if he had expected some other, more troublesome type of demand to be made on him, and he replied quickly. "Yes, Gaia, that can be arranged. I'll see to it first thing tomorrow, so that the plane will be available for the group to use on their next scheduled visit. And just to show you there are no hard feelings between us on my part, I'll host the first picnic."

"Oh thank you, father!" she exclaimed. "You'll see; this will be so much fun for everyone! There's nothing to worry about. We'll all just have a good time. Hera has to contact the missionaries to tell them not to open our letter. Can she also tell them about the airplane and the permission you've given for a group of girls to visit here twice a month?"

"Yes, why not? Let's get it taken care of all at once."

I was thrilled! I was so happy that I feared father would become suspicious, so I signaled to the sisters to bid him good night—to get us out of there before he could change his mind!—and we returned to our quarters. As we walked I thought to myself, now, finally, almost everything is in place if and when it ever becomes necessary for us to flee. The possibility that father might die suddenly one day, putting us at Klamm's mercy the next, has weighed heavily on my mind for years. It seemed obvious to me all along that there was zero chance that father's well-meaning trustees could ever act as quickly as Klamm could. Although I still couldn't envision in detail how we might actually make our escape, I at least knew just how alert the security guards were to the sisters' movements.

A few days ago I hacked into the facility's central computer to temporarily disable the perimeter security system, and then I wandered a ways outside the fence. Within minutes the alarms sounded, a roll call was taken, and teams of guards were dispatched to locate me. I was sitting calmly on a rock ledge overlooking the incredible vista down to the sea when they came upon me. I played innocent, willingly accompanying them back through the gate, apologizing profusely to the chief of security, and promising never to transgress the site boundaries again. Then I went back to my study and restored the alarm system, nicely covering my electronic tracks, if I do say so myself.

That day I promised myself I would find a way.

27 NOVEMBER 2029

(Io's Journal) "Look what I've brought you this time." Klamm was grinning from ear to ear.

When Klamm arrived at our airstrip a few hours before, Hera and I were standing just off-field in the midst of an intense discussion. As soon as we saw him headed our way, Hera commented, "What's up with him today?" Then, as he strutted past us, he pulled me aside and told me that he had a special gift for me, that he didn't want anyone else to see, and that I should come to his compound in the village tonight to pick it up. I must say, I've never before seen him in quite such a buoyant mood.

He appeared to be well into the first of the bottles of champagne he had chilled when I arrived, and he also sensed at once that I was decidedly not in a good mood. "What's wrong? Cheer up and have some of the nicest bubbly you'll ever drink. You look beautiful in that dress, by the way."

I waited a few moments as he poured me a glass. Then I said, "It's bossy Hera, what else? I've had enough of her, quite frankly. Ever since Franklin arrived to stay, she's been working on him to bring me into line with her way of doing things.

"Whenever I go to talk to him, he tells me not to worry about Hera. He agrees she's too serious and worries unnec-essarily all the time, although, as he puts it, she means well. He tells me he thinks I'm the one of all the sisters who will achieve the most later in life. During the last two years we've had long talks a couple of times each month. Mostly he talks about our mother, and how much I remind him of her, and he often cries, but then feels better. Frankly, he looks like a basket case half the time. He insists all of the sisters are equal and that Hera has no right to tell me or any of the others what to do. But most of them do and think whatever she tells them to. It's disgusting, really. She acts like an old lady and we're only just fifteen years old."

"Here, I'll refill your glass, Io. Let's try to forget about Hera. Come and look at what I found for you." He had opened the second bottle at that point, I think.

"I want to get out of here, Max. It's not just Hera. She gets some of the other sisters to bug me constantly as well, about how I dress, how I look, how I'm not taking my studies seriously enough. Franklin tells me he'll speak to them about it, and sometimes he does, but it doesn't do any good, because they only listen to Hera now. Will you take me away in the airplane, Max? Please?"

I confess, I had drained my glass again as I was speaking and he refilled it immediately; if I remember correctly, I drank it all in one go, again. I think I was trying to calm my nerves with the alcohol. I had convinced myself that this was going to be my big chance to get him to do what I wanted.

Clearly Klamm hadn't expected this line of conversation, nor from his lack of reaction did it seem he wished to pursue it—I suspect he had other things on his mind. He was stalling for time and just said, "Let's talk about it after you open your present."

"All right," I replied. I admit I wasn't used to consuming this much alcohol so quickly and my speech had become slightly slurred already. I opened the box and gasped; I knew instantly what it was—an ancient Egyptian scarab amulet, set with a lapis lazuli stone, its faience glaze gleaming as brilliantly as the day it had been made, some thirty-five hundred years ago. He said it had been looted from a burial tomb in ancient times and been circulating ever since on the black market; he added that he had won it in a high-stakes poker game with one of his clients.

He was stunned when I threw it on the bed. "It's lovely, Max, but I don't want it."

He rushed over to pick it up. "For God's sake, Io, be careful. Do you know how old this thing is? And how much it's worth? You can't buy something like this anywhere in the world for any amount of money."

"I don't care how old it is or how much it's worth. I'm not going to accept it." Then I approached him and put both my hands on his chest, unbuttoning his shirt. "I want you to take me away from here. Please. If you take me away, I'll keep it." I leaned up and kissed him, using my tongue. I hadn't really thought through what I planned to do, and all of a sudden events just seemed to start unfolding according to their own volition, as if I were acting on a stage-set, or was perhaps just a spectator in the audience.

He murmured, "Jesus, Io, where did you learn to do that? Not from your father, I'll bet." Then I think I pushed him gently backwards into a sitting position on the edge of the bed and opened the top buttons on my dress; I felt his arms go around me. I wasn't wearing a bra. I straddled him and lifted my breasts to his mouth.

I had drunk way too much, and too quickly, and I didn't realize that I wasn't actually in control of my own actions until far too late in the game. When I think about it, and about what he said a few moments later, I honestly don't think he was either. He started kissing my nipples, then my mouth, then slid his hand up my leg and touched my pudenda; I moaned with pleasure as he slipped my dress over my head in one quick motion, moving me onto the bed as he did so. I know I was dazed and actually felt like I was fainting. He removed my panties and was about to mount me when—I distinctly remember—I screamed "No!" and tried to get up. He didn't stop, and my struggles seemed to arouse him further. He pinned both of my arms above my head with one hand and pushed my legs apart with the other. Then he entered me. It was all over in seconds.

"Shut up, will you?" he said, without looking at me, as I lay next to him, sobbing. "You got what you asked for."

But by then, I think, it had already dawned on him that he, too, had been incredibly stupid—I've already admitted the same! What an asshole! Blaming a fifteen-year-old girl for seducing him? He appeared to be trying hard, unsuccessfully, to make his brain work again. And the alcohol in his system wasn't helping.

Now he turned to face me. "I'm sorry, Io, I really am. That shouldn't have happened. But it's too late now. Look, I'll do what you want. I'll take you away from here, I promise. Next year."

By then my anger was rising fast. After all, he had practically poured the booze down my throat, glass after glass in quick succession. I'm sure he knew damn well that Franklin carefully controls what we have to drink, because he often eats dinner with the group of us, so he must have noticed that we usually have only one glass of wine at suppertime and only a bit of champagne at our birthday parties. So I decided to let him have it.

"Oh great, you bastard, you'll take me someplace where you can do that again whenever you like? I'm not going anywhere with you. And when I tell my father what you did, you won't be going anywhere either, except to the nearest jail."

I was surprised because I didn't expect to see the look of sudden panic that came into his eyes. What I had said seemed to unhinge him. He grabbed me roughly, so roughly that I remember I winced. That's when he laid it all out.

"You'll do nothing of the kind, you little bitch. Let me tell you what's going to happen around here soon. I'm going to be a very rich man again before long. Your precious little sisters are going to be shipped off to become breeding mares for a bunch of rich folks around the world. They're going to spend the next fifteen years or so, or at least as long as they last until they wear out, locked in bedrooms, getting fucked and delivering babies, and having the shit beaten out of them if they don't cooperate.

"How's that for a future? I swear that you'll be among them if you don't keep quiet about what happened tonight. I've left you out of this little plan. I'm the only one who can save you from being part of it. The guys with guns around here work for me and do what I say. Your father can give them all the orders he likes, but it won't do any good because none of them will listen to him."

That's when he pulled me into a sitting position on the bed. "I'll make a deal with you, Io. Keep quiet about what's happened tonight and I'll continue to protect you. After I take you away from here, you don't have to stay with me if you don't want to. I'll give you some money and you can go wherever you please. I can buy all the women I want, and I don't need the hassle of dealing with somebody like you. Now listen carefully. There's no deal if you blab to your father or anyone else. And you'll regret it if you do, believe me. I told you that the security detail works for me. If you screw things up for me, I'll see to it that you're locked up somewhere in a hut in the village and that every one of them has a key to the room. Do you understand what I'm saying to you?"

He shook me when I didn't answer. "Do you? Answer me."

Once again I was having trouble concentrating, but after a moment I said, "Yes. I understand. Don't worry, I won't tell a soul."

"Good. Now stay here for a few minutes. I'm going to the

clinic to get a package of the morning-after contraceptive pills so that there's no chance you'll get pregnant."

By the time he returned from the infirmary I had showered and dressed, and he handed me the pills and instructions. I just put them in my bag without a word and left—but not without the amulet, damn him!

SUB-COMPILER'S NOTE: *Dear reader, you will understand in a moment why I must intervene here. What has been portrayed in those awful scenes was also, some time thereafter, the moment of my conception! For if Mr. Klamm had indeed brought back the morning-after contraceptive pills for Io from the infirmary, I would not be here to assemble this history for you. You have guessed already that he had reserved Io for himself in his scheme, and I surmise that he had also been trying to imagine what kind of child might be produced from her by him. After all, for years he had been listening to Franklin wax enthusiastic about how his little bit of genetic engineering would result in creating some very remarkable children. So, without a doubt, before he reached the infirmary, another thought must have occurred to him.*

Most likely he had surmised, "Who knows, maybe the scientist is right, maybe he has figured out how to create really exceptional people who can do all kinds of things that would be impossible for normal people to do?" So he had begun to imagine having his own genes become a part of this little experiment. But now that Io was so angry with him, could he be sure he'd ever get another chance? What he must have done at the infirmary that night was to replace the pills in the single-dose contraceptive kit with some placebos that were kept on hand.

He must have reasoned something like this: "After she takes the pills she won't be expecting to be pregnant, and if she is, it won't be apparent for some time. It's unlikely she'll go for a pregnancy test before a few months have passed. By then I'll have had time to figure something else out. Perhaps I'll tell the security detail just to snatch her and fly her out to my private estate. If so, what could Franklin do about it? I'll invent a story for him about how she just vanished one day—probably tried to escape and fell down the mountainside into one of the inaccessible ravines. I'll be shipping off the other products to my clients in nine months' time anyway—and then I'm away from this godforsaken mountain village for good."

§ § §

(Hera's Journal) I was waiting in Io's room when she returned, and I burst out, "Where have you been? Were you with Klamm again?" I was beside myself with fear and anxiety. I'm terrified all the time now, and I barely sleep at all most nights. She was furious when she saw me.

"Get out of here and leave me alone, Hera. It's no business of yours where I was or whom I was with. I don't have to answer to you. You're not my goddamned parent, even though you try to act like one."

"Something's happened, Io. I know it. I can feel it. Tell me, please. I won't mention it to anyone else if you don't want me to. It'll be just between you and me. I swear."

"Get out!" Io screamed at me. And then her defenses ran out and she collapsed weeping on the bed. I moved to her and held her. "Oh, Hera, he raped me. Klamm raped me."

I was silent until Io's sobbing had subsided, but my brain was working furiously, trying to guess some of the rest. Finally, I asked gently, "What else happened? Did he threaten to hurt you if you told anyone? He may be planning something else, Io, and maybe he's now thinking things over and has begun to fear that he shouldn't have let you get away. Come on! We have to get out of here right away in case he comes looking for you!"

Now Io was frightened. She let me take her hand and lead her out of the apartment complex. Using a roundabout route I had scouted before, we quietly headed for father's compound. Along the way Io whispered to me what Klamm had revealed, about her own fate if she told anyone what had happened, and also about what was in store for the rest of her sisters.

My mind was still racing, and now recent events finally formed a coherent picture. I had guessed correctly after all! I just knew that there was some sordid business going on in the other building, where dozens of Indonesian women, whom we had never set eyes on before, were suddenly housed a few months ago. When I found out from my good friend, the clinic doctor, that they were undergoing embryo implantation procedures, I put two and two together: A new experiment was in the works! And Klamm was involved, for sure. Why else had he been turning up here so frequently during the last year? These new babies aren't going to stay here—they're going to be shipped out and sold on the open market!

But clearly there was also another game afoot. I'll bet that some of the prospective purchasers are in no mood to wait a couple of years just to get a baby, which meant marking time for another twelve years or so until the child was old enough to start using his special brains to the family's advantage. So there was a second deal in the works: The seller could supply a family with a very special brood mare whom all their sons, as well as their male cousins for that matter, could fuck to their hearts' content. This way the family could add lots of special genes to its own little genetic pool in short order. Next year, in mid-2030, this product would be sixteen years old and ripe for breeding. Eleven products would be on offer because, of course, now we know that Klamm had reserved Io for himself.

By the time we reached father's door I knew what I had to do and how to carry it out. "Io, we have to tell father. We can't solve this on our own right now. We need some time— just a little, actually. Above all we have to make sure that nothing interferes with the trip to Stockholm that he and

Klamm are about to take." Io said nothing and simply nodded. I was surprised and relieved at her passivity, and grateful for it, since I needed her cooperation and there was much to arrange.

Father expressed genuine delight at seeing both of us hand-in-hand on his doorstep. He often held long conversations with one of us in the evenings, but so far not often with both together.

"How nice to see you girls at the same time for a change."

"Father, listen," I said. "We don't know if anything might happen later tonight, but just to be on the safe side, please lock all the doors here, quickly."

My tone of voice forestalled questioning and he set the locks from the central panel. "Of course. It's done. What on earth is wrong?"

"Klamm raped Io an hour ago in his bedroom."

He screamed pitifully as he reached out to hold her. "Oh Io, is this true? Why? How did this happen? Are you hurt?"

She shook her head from side to side but said nothing. He glanced back at me and I looked directly into his eyes. "There's much more, and much worse, although what's happened to Io is bad enough. Klamm told her that soon he'll be selling all of us girls, except Io, to rich families abroad, and that we'll be kept as breeding mares for their sons. Everything is planned. He's a monster, father. How could you have let him deceive you so? How could you have dealt with him for so long without realizing how evil he is? How could you have placed us all in his power?"

Now he broke down completely and slumped to his knees on the floor, half-weeping, half-moaning, encircling both of us with his huge arms. "I should have known. I should have realized long ago that something like this was planned. What a fool I've been! Oh, Hera, Io, please forgive me! You girls are all I have left in the world that I care about." His sobbing returned, and he paused to catch his breath. "You've probably noticed that I've not been well lately. The memories of your mother have come back more strongly than ever, despite the years that have passed since she died. I've been seriously depressed. Most nights I just sit here crying. I can't even work anymore during the daytime, except when Klamm threatens me. And now I see you've been in extreme danger and that I didn't protect you from it."

He got up, walked to a cabinet and took out a revolver, checking that it was loaded. He was eerily calm now. "But I will make up for my many mistakes tonight. I'll deal with Klamm once and for all."

"No, father!" I screamed and ran toward him, grabbing the hand that held the revolver. "You'll never be able to get close enough. He warned Io that the security detail obeys his commands. He may have told them to expect you. He may even have told them to kill you if they see that you're armed! Then what would happen to us? He'll have all of us at his mercy."

"But what else can I do to keep you safe, Hera? Klamm and I are due to leave for Stockholm the day after tomorrow—we have several meetings booked for each day to attend together. How can I leave you girls here alone and unprotected? I must deal with him right now, before we go."

By that time I had already deduced the reasons why Klamm had arrived at our airstrip in such a celebratory mood that evening. Father had probably informed Klamm by telephone a few weeks earlier—at the time when he also told us—that he'd be travelling to Stockholm in early December to receive one of the 2029 Nobel Prizes. Doubtless Klamm immediately made plans to accompany him, probably anticipating a great deal of interest from investors in potential new business deals.

I made a huge effort to keep my voice clear, calm, and firm. "Sit down, father, and please listen to me carefully. You said that you and Klamm will fly out together the day after tomorrow. All you have to do is to make sure that this happens as planned. *Under no circumstances* must you leave without having him beside you on the plane, and you must also make sure that he stays with you all the way to Stockholm. Don't let him out of your sight." The calmness in my voice seemed to settle him down a bit.

"Now, after you get there, as I remember, it's three days until the ceremony is to be held. You told us that you and Klamm have a lot of business functions scheduled—most of them for the two of you together—for those three days. Make sure that everything happens as it should. You must do whatever it takes to see that he doesn't leave Stockholm before the ceremony takes place."

When I hesitated for an instant, he broke in. "I'm pretty sure that won't be a problem. But what if Klamm has given orders to the security detail to make off with you while we two are away? If that happens I'll never find you again!"

"Father, it's almost impossible to imagine that Klamm would allow these people to take us away while he was not here to supervise the whole thing. He simply couldn't trust them not to betray him somehow. He has too much at stake."

"But then what? Nothing will have been solved. When Klamm and I get back from Stockholm, exactly the same problem will confront us. He'll have the security detail lock me up and then he'll take you all away. Wouldn't it be better if we tried to take care of it now, all of us together, before I leave?"

"Father, I have something to tell you."

I look back now, several hours later, and view the scene in his room as if I were a hidden spectator rather than a participant. I see the three of them, sitting close together on the floor. The girl 'Hera' has an air of unworldly calm about her. I observe no agitation in her manner whatsoever and her gaze is steady. Something in the tone of her voice makes it appear as if the large man sitting there is the child and she is the parent. Now I focus on the look in her father's eyes and I surmise what's going on in his mind: His inner voice has told him that he has ceased to be involved in a two-way conversation. He looks for all the world like a soldier who is about to receive his orders.

"When you return from Stockholm we will be gone. All of us."

He burst out laughing, although clearly he didn't intend to do so and immediately apologized. "I'm sorry, Hera, I really am, I don't know why I did that. But what could you possibly mean by your remark? Where would you go? *How* would you get away? Have you become a trained pilot among all your many other talents? Are you going to hitchhike or ride bicycles down the mountainside to Timika? And if you get to Timika, then what? Do you have canoes waiting to cross the sea?"

"Please, this isn't the time for sarcasm. We don't know if Klamm is up to anything else tonight, and we don't know how much more time we have to talk. You must—do you understand?—*must* get on that plane with Klamm the day after tomorrow and you must make sure that he goes all the way to Stockholm with you. Once there you *must* figure out a way to ensure that he doesn't leave Stockholm until after the Nobel Prize ceremony takes place. And that is all you have to do. When you return we'll be gone.

"I'm not going to tell you anything else about our trip except to say that it's all planned and that we'll be safe where we're going. As soon as we can do so, without fear of detection, we'll contact you and tell you where we are, and then you and we can be reunited."

He was stunned. "Someone must be helping you. You couldn't do all this on your own. Who is it? It has to be the missionaries, right? I demand you tell me where they're going to take you!"

I said nothing in reply, and simply looked at him wordlessly until he realized that I wasn't going to answer his question. He cried out in obvious anguish.

"For God's sake, you're only fifteen-year-old children! Young girls of your age cannot gallivant merrily around the world by themselves, having a good old time! You cannot even enter another country legally without proper authorization. This is ridiculous, Hera. You must tell me. You must let me help you. Don't you trust me? What have I done to deserve this? Are you afraid that my rooms are bugged and that our conversation will be overheard?"

Again, I didn't answer him right away, trying first to ensure that I could speak calmly and evenly. "No, we do regular electronic sweeps of all our facilities, including one earlier today, and there are no eavesdropping devices planted here. Getting back to Klamm, he's not only an evil man, but a ruthless one as well. What do you think he'll do when he finds out we're gone? He'll set his agents scouring the globe for us. He'll stop at nothing to find us, because without us he has no deal with the people who expect to get us as part of his bargain. I bet he's taken up-front money, maybe a lot of it, as advance payments for us. He'll have to give it back, but almost certainly he has spent some of it in the meantime. He'll be desperate. He'll leave no stone unturned trying to find us."

"But I can help you hide from him, Hera," he pleaded. "You've never been off this island in your life. I've been all over the world. I have friends, very good friends, in many different countries who'll do anything I ask without hesitation. Your mother's family can also help—as you know, they're very wealthy and influential people in Indonesia. I'll ask them to get the Indonesian government to arrest Klamm, maybe even when we stop at Jakarta airport on our way back from Stockholm. If Klamm is as dangerous a man as you believe he is, then it makes no sense for you to refuse this kind of help. Do you really think you're more cunning than he is?"

"If I were Klamm, I would hope that you would either be traveling with us or knew where we were intending to hide. If you become involved in our escape, you'll be his best chance of tracing us. And after all the time he's spent dealing with them, I'm pretty sure he has excellent contacts inside the Indonesian police and army commands. I wouldn't be so sure that he would be arrested just on your say-so.

"You're a Nobel laureate, one of the most famous scientists in the world. Everyone knows you—in governments, in industries, in universities. Sooner or later someone will help Klamm trace you, and then he'll follow you to us. But, on our own, we girls don't even really exist. We know you registered our births in Jakarta, and you told us that you secured British passports for us." I didn't want to tell him that I had broken into his safe earlier. "Apart from that, no one knows who we are. We can disappear into the night without a trace, if we take the right steps. And I've figured out how to do this."

"But how do I know that I will ever see you again?"

"Of course you will. The arrangements I've made are temporary ones. As I told you, as soon as it's safe to communicate with you, we'll tell you where we are and you can come and get us—after we're sure you're not being followed by Klamm or his agents."

He made one last try. "Please, Hera, don't do this, if not for my sake, then for the sake of your mother's memory. I'm so afraid I'll never see you again. Please, I beg you."

It was awful! I put my arms around him and held him tight. Several minutes passed while neither of us spoke. Then I looked directly into his weeping eyes, waiting until I could see in them the dawning realization that I would not and could not yield. I saw it, and then I spoke as softly as I could.

"There are a few more things to be done before morning.

Io and I must return to our building; the girls have been told we are taking a trip soon, but that's all they know. You can escort us with your revolver if you like. But first there are some things we need to discuss and do."

He started to protest but saw it was useless. "First, I need the code for your safe. You've told me that our passports are there as well as substantial sums in cash. I'll need to take all of the money for our travel expenses, although, as you know, we'll be able to draw upon our own trust funds once we're resettled somewhere."

"Yes, Hera, I'll give you the code, and I know you well enough to realize that you'll not need to write it down. But don't you see? That's the solution to our other problem as well! The access code for my safe will then be known only to you and to me; Klamm has never had it. Obviously you know where you're going when you leave here—or at least I assume that you have a specific destination. When you're ready to go, and are taking the cash and passports, you can leave the information about your planned destination in the safe. I'll retrieve it only when Klamm isn't here."

"Father, I'll say this only one more time: You're not thinking clearly. When Klamm finds out we're on the run, he'll be desperate. Neither you nor your science will be of any further use to him. What's to prevent him from torturing you until you reveal the access codes to your safe? No one will come to your aid in this remote place because none of your friends know you're even here. I won't tell you where we're planning to go. And that's final."

He gave up. "Is there anything else for us to discuss?"

"Only one thing. The women who are carrying your fetuses as surrogate mothers. Yes, we know about them; the staff talks, even if they are afraid of you and Klamm. My guess is that they're some other part of the same plan in which we girls figured. Am I right?"

A look of alarm sprang up on his face. "This was not

supposed to be all part of one plan, Hera! Surely to God you could never think that I would consent to selling you off!"

I replied quickly. "Of course not; I was referring to Klamm's scheme."

He gently touched my shoulder. "I'm sorry I said that. I'm too upset to know what to think. Klamm blackmailed me first and then—as I know now—betrayed me. He forced me to engineer the embryos that those women are now carrying. He did this by threatening to take you all away. I thought I had no choice. I signed contracts to deliver thirty male babies to his clients, and he told me this was all there was to his plan."

I sensed that speaking about this work was helping to calm him, so I asked him to tell us more about it.

"According to the contract terms, the births have to be certified to the clients in about eight months time from now; I told Klamm a month ago that everything was proceeding on schedule. He recruited the Indonesian women to act as surrogate mothers, just as we had for you girls, giving their families large advance payments and swearing all to secrecy. Knowing Klamm, I assume he also warned them to expect severe punishment if any word got out about what they were being paid to do.

"I needed thirty successful births to fulfill the contract terms, and so I prepared these fertilized embryos, plus another ten to provide a cushion against any cases of spontaneous abortion or other complications. I didn't consider this to be a sufficient margin of safety against the risk of implantation failures and miscarriages, but when I mentioned this to Klamm, he told me not to worry about it. Now I know why! As you obviously know already, the group of women is in residence in the recently enlarged building that was first used when you and your sisters were being carried. The specialist I hired implanted the embryos three weeks ago."

"What did you do to the embryos before implanting

them? Are they supposed to turn out something like us?"

It was odd. He hesitated, started to speak, stopped, then started again. "You may be a little surprised by my answer. I know what I *intended* to do, which was to make them pretty much the same as you, but I'm not as sure as I would like to be about how they will turn out. I thought that even though I was under pressure with a firm deadline, there was enough time for me to be careful with what I was doing, as I planned to be, and as I was with you girls.

"But I haven't been well this past year, as you know. When I worked on the embryos that produced you wonderful girls I felt as if I were on top of the world; I was overjoyed at the thought of creating a living memorial to your mother. I worked night and day but always with the greatest of care. Now, however, if I were being entirely truthful, I would have to admit I'm not so sure about how this batch, as Klamm calls them, will turn out."

"Then you know what you have to do, don't you?"

Suddenly he realized where my questions were leading. "You mean terminate them?"

"Yes, of course. It would be monstrous if you did not."

"Oh my goodness, I can't do that. These are my creations, too, just as you are. It's possible that they will all be as wonderful as you girls. Really, now that I think about it again, I'm quite sure I was careful, and that everything will turn out fine."

Again I waited for a moment and then spoke very slowly. "There is little time left and we must resolve this tonight. All of us sisters could see how much you've been suffering this past year. It's very likely that your state of mind interfered with your work, even if you think it didn't. But in any case, if there is even the slightest risk you made mistakes that you might come to regret later on, you have no right to impose the terrible consequences of that risk on these children. You must arrange to terminate those pregnancies. All of them.

You must do this before you leave for Stockholm."

There was no resistance now. "Yes, of course, you're absolutely right. I should have realized that immediately myself. But how can it be done? You yourself said that under no circumstances can I vary the plan to leave with Klamm on the day after tomorrow. The mothers' compound is guarded by a special unit of the security detail. Even I cannot get in there without an authorization co-signed by Klamm."

"I'll tell you what we can do. I've been friendly with the head doctor at the clinic ever since he was so kind to me many years ago, when I began visiting him regularly about my migraines. He likes to hear about all the new medical therapies I discover during my Internet searches. In one of our recent chats, I found out that he's scheduled to inject all the pregnant women with the latest round of some routine nutritional supplements within the next few days. The vials are already prepared and labeled in a rack in the clinic's refrigerator. I saw them there. Go see him at the clinic tomorrow and tell him to administer his injections on the day after you leave."

I gave him no chance to interrupt me. "As you well know, there's also a large supply of abortifacient medication at the infirmary, including injectable compounds. Io and I slipped in there one night and had a look around, and we know how to bypass the alarm system on the door. Come with us to the infirmary now—tonight—and we'll help you replace the nutritional supplement in the vials with the correct dose of an abortifacient. Io told me on the way over here that she thinks Klamm is fast asleep at the moment, given how much he drank, so now is probably the best—the only—opportunity we have to do this. By the time you and Klamm return from Stockholm, it will be too late to reverse the process."

He looked at us, first one, then the other. Since we arrived Io had not uttered a word. She sat there absorbed in herself. I thought I saw in her eyes an anger that made them glow like coals. I wondered whether it would ever leave her again.

"We must go now," I said. "We'll stop by the infirmary on the way back to our apartments and give you a hand."

As we parted later at the infirmary door I touched his arm and spoke softly. "All the girls will be at the tarmac on the day after tomorrow to see you off. Remember that if Klamm has the slightest suspicion that something is amiss we will all be in extreme peril—you as well as us. Our lives depend on it. Do you understand that, father?"

"I understand completely, Hera. But will you promise to tell me where you are just as soon as it's safe to do so? Will you swear to this?"

"I promise. Now we should go."

§   §   §

I went to Io's room this morning to make sure she had taken the contraceptive pill, and she told me that she had done so. Thank goodness she was willing to cooperate with me today when I asked her to retrieve and annotate the digital record-ing of last night's terrible events. Even she could see the wisdom in our re-examining Klamm's exact words, in case there were some nuances in his remarks about what he was going to do with us that would require us to act more quickly in making our escape.

She told me I wouldn't like what she had said about me in their conversation, but really, there's nothing in last night's remarks that she hasn't put directly to my face many times already. And as I have known for some time, she's extremely tough-minded. She said she's not going to let Klamm fuck her mind as well as her body, so she's not dwelling on what happened; she wants to devote all her energies to helping me make our escape plan foolproof. She knows as well as I do that we have to get out of here, fast, and we don't know if we'll ever get another chance to do so if this plan should fail.

DECEMBER 2029

Early on the long flight to Los Angeles, I retrieved from my briefcase the document, dated 30 June 2021, that I had removed from the safe in father's residence at Tembagapura. Since it was bound together with the cash and passports, I knew that he wanted me to take it. On the cover sheet he had scrawled a handwritten note addressed to me. "Hera: This is the statement of objectives that was based on the original scientific protocol I developed in 2013 for modifying the embryos that became you twelve wonderful girls!"

MEMORANDUM PREPARED BY THE SUJANA FOUNDATION FOR THE DONOR COUPLES KNOWN AS THE GROUP OF 300, GIVING AN ACCOUNT OF THE SCIENTIFIC PROTOCOL TO BE USED FOR CREATING CHILDREN WITH EXCEPTIONAL REASONING ABILITIES AND HUMANITARIAN MOTIVATION

We intend to create children who will grow up to play important leadership roles in a movement to redirect humanity away from violence and social chaos and toward universal peace. We will modify the expression of groups of genes that direct the development of specific structures in the human brain. These structures are found in the sections of the brain where important behaviors are regulated. Specifically, we will concentrate on the area known as the prefrontal cortex and the sub-regions within it.

The first set of children will number approximately 500 in all, one or two for each couple. After in vitro fertilization using the eggs and sperm of each couple, our genetic manipulations will be carried out when the embryo is at the four-cell stage; further embryonic development will be halted at the eight-cell stage and the embryos will be frozen and stored until we are ready to proceed toward implantation. After thawing, the embryonic development resumes. Some of the embryos may be carried to term by their natural mothers, and surrogate mothers will be used for the rest.

All genetic changes carried out on early embryos affect the gametes produced later when individuals mature. Therefore what we will be doing is called "germline modification" (referring to the germ, or sex, cells). Many of the resulting children will pass on their superior traits to their own offspring. From there they will spread more widely among human populations with each passing generation.

It is very important for you—as the natural parents of these children—to realize that the changes we propose to induce in these embryos pertain exclusively to capabilities that already exist within all of us, in the human prefrontal cortex itself. In no sense are we intending to produce "monsters" or "freaks" or even "super-human" beings. We will not create an individual who would be either feared or shunned by other people. On the contrary, they will look and behave very much like everyone else does. Even their special gifts will not be all that unique when compared with the examples of exceptional human beings who have lived in the past, including such great humanitarian leaders as Mohandas Gandhi.

General Objectives

We have said that we wish to increase the power and scope of specific capabilities that already exist in the region of the normal human brain known as the prefrontal cortex. These capabilities, which we will describe in a moment, are dependent upon the general powers in the human brain known as the higher cognitive functions—our innate capacities for language, mathematics, categorization, reasoning, decision-making, and so forth. Please try to bear with us if in reading on you find our text too lengthy. Remember that engineering the human brain is a lot more complex than doing things to modify our bodies, such as increasing muscle mass in "super-athletes."

About forty years ago neuroscientists started to become aware that some of the human traits most critical to the progress and development of civilization actually had a specific location in the brain's neurological architecture. This knowledge arose first in the study of individuals who had suffered brain injuries or had developed damaging lesions in the prefrontal cortex, and were observed to have many unusual types of abnormal behaviors. Specifically, these are: failure in impulse regulation, lack of appropriate inhibitions, and an inability to empathize with others, especially to sense when pain and terror are being inflicted on them. These deficits can give rise to brutal actions against other persons, including both physical and sexual violence.

In people where such damage exists we find also a general lack of inhibition, that is, an absence of any sense of needing to restrain impulses. It is almost as if the moral sense that normal people can feel within themselves, which enables them to control emotional impulses (anger, sexual desire, envy), is simply not there or has been turned off somehow. By studying people with such deficits, scientists discovered the specific location in our brain, called the orbitomedial prefrontal cortex, where impulsive control is managed in normal people. This is often referred to as the "moral center," and it is where our sense of empathy—the feeling of kinship with others—arises. We have an innate sense of fairness as well (scientists discovered that monkeys do, too!), located in another closely related part of the brain, the anterior cingulate cortex.

This is an astonishing fact, when one stops to think about it. Normal people actually have inbuilt neurological circuits in their brains that prompt them to pause and reflect, and ask themselves whether their desires are right or wrong, before trying to carry out their wishes. This type of mental process is sometimes called "cognitive control," referring to control over impulses. It is equally astonishing to learn that this capacity can be utterly absent as a result of injury or genetic damage to a very specific region in the brain.

Some reports we have seen suggest that, in rogue nations that do not accept common ethical standards for research, attempts are being made to engineer human offspring whose moral center has been deliberately disabled. What the crippling of the moral center appears to do in such persons is turn them into completely amoral beings in whom normal inhibitions against inflicting pain and suffering on others simply do not work. In other words, they are utterly indifferent to the agony and terror of others. Thus the thought is truly frightening that somewhere in the world, such people could be created deliberately by political and religious movements as weapons against their enemies. In a sense, the foundation's program is our attempt to counteract such evils.

You should also be aware that there is another entire class of individuals—those suffering from autism—whose behavioral anomalies are related to defects in the prefrontal cortex, in this case, genetic defects. These anomalies include such things as short attention span, lack of motivation, inability to identify long-term goals, impulsivity, inability to understand social rules, and a tendency toward inciting conflict. Brain scans that measure blood flow show clearly that the prefrontal cortex is underdeveloped or immature—and thus underactive—in autistic children. Since in normal individuals the prefrontal cortex acts to inhibit over-excitement in other areas of the brain, autistic individuals become hypersensitive to specific environmental stimuli.

At the beginning of this century researchers began actively looking for the specific genes responsible for the development of the prefrontal cortex, so that these genetic defects could be detected and possibly repaired. Scientists began to find these genes within the human genome, the ones that control the chemical compounds that are important for our brain functions. One example must suffice. There is a gene on the "X" chromosome called "MAO," an abbreviation for the chemical monoamine oxidase, that has two different forms, MAO-a and MAO-b. This gene encodes an enzyme that metabolizes three of the brain's most powerful neurotransmitters—dopamine, serotonin, and norepinephrine—to prevent too much of these three chemicals from accumulating.

Scientists discovered this gene by studying several generations of a Belgian family in which the males had a history of mental retardation, impulsive violence, and antisocial behaviors, and in whom the expression of this gene was deficient owing to a point mutation. Then they created what are called "knockout mice," in which they had disabled the gene encoding MAO-a (it's the same gene in mice and humans). The adult mice showed markedly increased aggressiveness, which disappeared again when gene expression was restored. Later research demonstrated that male children with low MAO-a expression *and* a history of maltreatment when young showed a greatly increased risk for engaging in criminal violence later in life.

Of course, genes are only one important factor in the development of the human brain and our behavior. What happens in our social environment is equally important. You probably know that the human brain is unique in nature in continuing its development so long after birth. This means, of course, that there is intense interaction between genetic and environmental factors in continuous neurological growth over more than twenty years in children. For example, youngsters abandoned at birth who mature without human contact cannot speak, even though we all have an innate capacity for language.

This is another reason why you should feel comfortable with the modifications that we will be doing. We are most definitely not going to be deleting any genes found in normal people or adding any new genes not normally found in us. Our efforts are focused entirely on inserting additional copies of the genes that code for the growth of the prefrontal cortex, including specific regions within it, as well as of the closely related brain regions, such as the anterior cingulate cortex.

THE PREFRONTAL CORTEX

The prefrontal cortex is the anterior—frontal—part of the frontal lobe (or frontal cortex) of the brain, located just behind the person's forehead. In an evolutionary sense the frontal cortex is the newest part of the mammalian brain, a region that underwent a huge expansion in the transition from monkeys to the great apes. There are four species among the great apes—orangutans, gorillas, bonobos, and chimpanzees—that in some classification schemes make up the "pongids" (Pongidae family). These four share with humans, who are an offshoot of the pongids, a greatly enlarged frontal cortex.

Moreover, of all creatures, only the great apes and humans have a special type of neural tissue, called spindle cells, in their prefrontal cortex and anterior cingulate cortex. Spindle cells are very long neurons that because of their length, are capable of coordinating neural activity across wide areas of the brain, including zones important for both cognition and emotion. This was an adaptation of truly immense significance, because in this way the newest parts of the brain—imparting cognitive control—could be strongly wired to some of the oldest parts, such as the amygdala, responsible for the generation of emotion and fear. It is perhaps obvious why this long wiring was required in order to maintain the unity of this greatly enlarged brain.

In general, the huge increase in the frontal and prefrontal cortices of humans and great apes made possible an enlarged regulation of behavior, and was, in an evolutionary sense, an adaptation related to the intensive social activity we observe in these species.

As indicated earlier, in humans the prefrontal cortex is the seat in the brain for a closely linked array of higher cognitive functions, all of which are important for the kinds of capacities we desire to strengthen or enhance. For example, there are two types of special memory there, source memory and working memory. The latter in particular is fascinating. To give you a very crude analogy, working memory is like the random access memory (RAM) built into the electronic circuits of your computer, although it is a far more agile and versatile instrument than RAM.

Working memory, which is the site of what is sometimes called our "executive function," takes present inputs from the world around us and compares them with stored memories, at lightning speed. More remarkably still, our brain actually recalls not just prior events, but also the emotions that were originally joined to them. This so-called "cognitive-affective mechanism" shows how our minds innately link thinking and feeling, which means that we can react quickly in response to both threats and opportunities in the environment.

Using the combined resources of new information and stored inputs, our working memory evaluates the possible negative and positive consequences to us from responding in one way or another to the new data. It performs a kind of comparative risk assessment of various decision options open to us, so to speak. It helps us choose what appears to be the best course of action, while storing the array of alternatives already evaluated for our possible future use. Linked to working memory are other resources that support functions called multitasking (dealing simultaneously with different tasks) and branching. Branching, which takes place in the anterior prefrontal cortex, allows people to keep an important long-range goal in mind while allocating their shorter-term attention to a wide variety of other tasks.

The higher-order traits housed in the prefrontal cortex would not be able to operate were they unable to draw upon the more general information-processing capabilities of the entire human brain. So we find that the brain's elaborate "wiring" architecture corresponds to this need. The prefrontal cortex and its primary regions (mid-dorsal, dorsolateral, ventrolateral, orbital and medial) have two-way linkages with the sensory cortex, which processes and also interconnects visual, auditory, and somatosensory signals. As a whole, the prefrontal cortex is also strongly connected to the basal ganglia and the thalamus and onwards to the amygdala. Actually, the full architecture of neural connections is so dense and complex that in the comments above we have given only a poor representation of the actual reality.

The unique contribution that the prefrontal cortex itself makes is a rapid mixing of external signals originating in the environment on the one hand, with internally generated stimuli from memory and experience on the other.

To see what this means in practice, you might think of athletic performance as an example. The most skilled ice-hockey player has to have a good endowment of general advantages, such as fine motor control of muscles, quick reflexes, superb eyesight and hand-eye coordination, balance, and concentration. But on top of all that, the very best player has a kind of instinct or intuition about the fast-changing topography of the ice surface, including where both the puck and teammates are and where the flow of the play is headed. Such a player can pick up the puck and pass it onto a teammate's stick—a teammate who is skating directly behind—in perfect position for a shot on goal without even looking in the direction of the pass. It is almost as if a running videograph of the whole ice surface and the developing action appears before the player's eyes and simultaneously triggers the correct response that is called for by what is happening on the ice surface, without requiring conscious intention.

This is why all of what we are talking about here is often referred to, both by ordinary people and neuroscientists, as "seeing with the mind's eye."

THINKING IN IMAGES

Perhaps the single most impressive component of the human brain's resources for the processing of information is object visualization, or visual imaging. This refers to our ability to call up instantly a mental image or picture to accompany a thought—a concept or a word. For example, if I think of the word "mother," at once and without even trying to do so, I have a picture of my own mother in my mind, or of something strongly associated with this word, such as the famous painting known as "Whistler's Mother." If I say to myself "It's time to go to work," a picture of the route to my office, or the building where I work, or the furniture arrangement in the office I occupy can spring to mind. Our brains are able to do this with the greatest ease. But, you might say, so what? So what if we get a nice picture to accompany our thoughts?

It matters a great deal because of what this visualization faculty makes possible, which is, generally speaking, rapid pattern recognition. Some decades ago researchers found that the prefrontal cortex actively and continuously seeks out patterns in the sequences of random events presented to it in perception. This is not a conscious activity, but rather something that our brain does automatically, starting when we are only a few months old, without our even knowing that it is happening.

Again, this may not seem so important at first. But we subscribe to the view of some scientists that pattern-seeking is the fundamental underlying core of all the human cognitive functions. This view holds that the innate human capacities for both language and mathematics, which are unique to us as a species and necessary for all our higher cognitive functions, are ultimately grounded in our pattern-recognition abilities.

For example, a point in geometry is purely a concept or idea; it has no dimensions (height, width), so of course we cannot see it with our eyes. But we can and do imagine it in our minds, and then manipulate it in all sorts of ways in formulas and proofs. Great artists do this, too. Picasso's unique visioning gifts allowed him to realize that, with a few quick manipulations, a set of bicycle handlebars and a saddle could be turned into something resembling a bull's head. No other species can work with such complex and abstract patterning as can humans.

SPECIFIC OBJECTIVES

You are, we are sure, still waiting for the bottom line, and here it is. On the basis of our understanding of the genetic sequences that code for the development of the prefrontal cortex, we believe that we can extend the development of the specific neural networks that give rise to the higher cognitive functions that are located there. These are the ones we listed before: multitasking, branching, source memory and working memory, the executive function, and the moral center. We surmise that promoting additional gene expression for these functions in the prefrontal cortex, combined with a rich diet of experiential and sensory inputs during early development, will make the neural networks on which those functions depend denser.

This greater density of neural circuitry will give rise to more and more networked connections within and among the various regions of the prefrontal cortex itself. It will also create more elaborate interconnections linking the prefrontal cortex back to the other areas of the brain where pattern-seeking and mental imaging occur, such as the hypothalamus and the basal ganglia. Since these neural highways already exist in the brain, we expect that building up the density of the prefrontal cortex will also result elsewhere in larger-capacity highways, and thus some elevated higher-cognitive functions.

The brain's incessant pattern-seeking propensities are coordinated in the prefrontal cortex, which strives to maintain cognitive control over all the countless streams of stimuli it receives continuously, both from outside (our senses) and inside (our bodily processes). It mixes and arranges responses to these stimuli, with the objective of keeping us focused clearly on both the overall goals we have set for ourselves, and on the evaluation of means to best achieve those goals.

WHY WE MUST PROCEED WITH OUR PLAN

When we set out with you to fashion a special type of children, we all knew why we had to proceed as quickly as we could. The conflicts that are tearing humanity apart grow fiercer with each passing year. Region against region, religion against religion, rich nations against poor, each pitted against the other and all striving desperately to advance their own causes. And today, our modern science—the molecular biology by which we can manipulate the genes of all creatures—is being thrown into this boiling cauldron. Nothing is held back now. Each successful genetic modification announced to the world by a biotechnology company excites imitation and a striving to supersede it by some even more clever strategy.

In our time the bodies of competitive athletes are routinely "souped up" by disguised laboratory tricks. Governments are manipulating the so-called "fierce" gene in the hope of creating fearless soldiers. Officials frightened of crime waves are experimenting with drug therapies to influence the flow of neurotransmitters in the brains of young males thought to have an innate propensity for law breaking. In private clinics the very rich seek to enhance the genetic endowments of their offspring with new traits that will be reserved for their social class alone. And the fanatics who wish to bring down the entire edifice of modern civilization are busily engineering new pathogens— viruses, bacteria, and protozoa—for their chosen form of Apocalypse.

There may not be much time left in which we can realize our own plan. So far, we know of no one else who has the same goals as we do, for most scientists are simply trying to slow down or stop temporarily the evil designs of others. Our plan is to create a positive new force of such vision and creativity that it can smash those designs once and for all and lead humanity down the path it must find—the path to a universal moral order shared by all. With the consent forms and the donor contributions you have now all provided, we are ready to proceed with the first step.

Finally, a cautionary note. To be honest there is a chance that we will see some adverse outcomes in these children. Despite the fact that our knowledge of neurogenetics has exploded in the last two decades, there is still much we do not know. Single gene expression pathways and—especially—complex interactions among multiple genes across very different sectors of the whole genome are still not completely understood. In simple terms, some surprises are not only possible but also likely. However, we are confident that the surprises we encounter will be minor and not major. For example, some of the neurological defects that are responsible for the onset of schizophrenia are located in the prefrontal cortex, which as we have said is the region of the brain where we will be carrying out our modifications. We are also confident that the unexpected outcomes, if they result in particular types of neurological deficits, will be correctible by drug therapies.

OUR INSPIRATION

We wish to express one more thought before closing. We are well aware that most members of our scientific community would disagree strongly with our determination to proceed with our project without a formal sanction from some institution. We understand these objections and respect the views of those scientists, but we do not agree. We are inspired by the vision of one of our field's great pioneers, James D. Watson, co-discoverer of the structure of DNA. For the remainder of his life following his great discovery—more than fifty years—he called upon scientists and the public both to dream of human perfection and to seek to realize that dream by modifying our DNA. We think that recent events show that realizing his dream is not just a selfish wish, but rather a precondition for humanity's very survival as a species. We situate our own modest enterprise in the context of Watson's great dream.

We have now provided you with a full description of the basis of our scientific protocol and the expected outcomes of the neurological modifications we intend to carry out on these embryos. We have received signed consent and waiver forms from each of you as well as your donor materials. We are ready to proceed. God help us if we fail.

I shut the file and closed my eyes, running over its contents in my mind. At last—at last!—I understood. The reasons for some of the experiences that have so troubled me all throughout my life—because they seemed to set my sisters and me apart from normal people—now were much clearer. Our too-vivid dreams; the ease with which we all learned languages and mathematics, which continues to amaze me; the way my mind does rapid-fire assessments of situations before presenting decisions, all without conscious effort on my part; the sheer inner certitude of my intuitions about the rightness of a course of action. I now know that these and many other subjective experiences were qualities designed into us by our parents.

More importantly, there was an explanation for the most troubling and startling events of all—the visions that come upon me anytime I'm awake, without warning, in which I see in my mind the solutions to things I've been thinking about: puzzles or codes, mathematical problems, regularities in data sets, the structures of complex geometrical forms. And other things both seen and heard inside my mind: fragments of musical composition, evocative word-imagery in poetic meter, landscapes with unusual coloration, architectural design motifs, the movements of birds in flight, the shapes of mythical beasts and plants, and on and on.

There's still more, much of which I do not yet comprehend. Since my mind is so attuned to order and patterning, I notice its traces everywhere in the affairs of humans, how they strive to take hold of ever-shifting changes in their environment and reduce them to regularities they can more easily manage. During the long years of isolation in Tembagapura I scoured the Internet for hours each day, seeking to grasp the events unfolding elsewhere on the globe. What struck me especially was that people seemed intent on transforming everything they encountered in nature, leaving nothing untouched—plants, animals, bacteria, soil, landscape, weather, oceans, skies, even other planets.

Their ceaseless activity follows the sun's course around the globe, never resting. They appear to believe they've become the planet's rightful owners and they rejoice in their good fortune. No natural obstacle to their will to subdue the earth, to make it yield up every treasure that could be applied to satisfy their needs, is allowed to persist for long.

Yet what surprises and puzzles me most of all, as I contemplate these images of busyness, is my feeling of utter indifference to humanity's most urgent concerns! I can admire the strenuous ordering in which they are engaged, if for no other reason than for the vastness of its scope. But it always strikes me as being somehow radically incomplete, partial, reckless, and blind. For there is apparently so little genuine contentment amidst the bustle, such impermanence in what is built, such a disrespect for the entitlements of the earth's other inhabitants, such a lack of humility in the face of the mystery of conscious life. When I get myself into this mood I always recall the closing stanza of the last song, "Farewell," in Mahler's *Song of the Earth*:

> *Everywhere the beloved earth*
> *Blossoms in spring and greens*
> *Anew! Everywhere and forever,*
> *Blue lights the horizons!*
> *Forever... Forever...*

Gazing into the cold emptiness of space from a perch on this warm and bountiful planet, shouldn't we be overwhelmed by a profound sense of gratitude for such a gift? But I see little evidence of such gratitude for the earth's welcome among people around me! On the contrary, I observe nothing but ruthless exploitation of its resources and the brutal extermination of its other occupants.

Now, after reading my father's *Memorandum*, I'm aware of

the humanitarian mission my mother and he had resolved to engineer into their modified individuals. We sisters are supposed to see deeply into the causes of humanity's dysfunctional behavior and then to help find the path to lasting peace and progress. My father included this objective in the protocol he used to create my sisters and me—after all, that was the whole point of this complex exercise, wasn't it? To be sure, there was no doubt that my sisters and I have always felt we were indeed different—somehow—from the other people we encountered during our life on our mountaintop fastness. I am convinced, too, that father believed he had succeeded—in his own terms—with whatever he had done to us.

I could tell that he believed this, because he reacted so positively to my recounting, in our regular nighttime conversations, of the workings of my mind. I also believe he thought that the elaborate testing procedures he had run over many years on our mental performance likewise confirmed his expectations. But I heard him tell me again and again that his sense of success in engineering some extraordinary capacities into us was not the end of the story. We twelve sisters, he said over and over, were not meant merely to put our mental agility on display, like some kind of circus freaks. Rather, we were designed above all to sense within ourselves a special mission on behalf of all humanity, and to find ways in which to accomplish it. Presumably this was meant to apply as well to the much larger cohorts of modified individuals who were destined to come later.

I remember so well searching the crevices of my mind for some sign of this "mission" on the very day father first revealed parts of his design to me. I recall too how extremely upset I was when I couldn't find it, not then, nor later, on the many occasions when I repeated the exercise. I was appalled and frightened, but I resolved not to breathe a word of this failure to father, because of course I didn't want to disappoint him or cause him to lose faith in me.

I freely confess that in the first years after he disclosed his relation to us girls, I had basked in the warmth of his constant praise of all the sisters' talents and, more particularly, in his recognition of my own leadership within the band of sisters. After all, we had grown up for the first eight years without much parental affection, and by the time he owned up to us, I was desperate for his love and attention! I strove ceaselessly to please him and to justify his high expectations of me. I would let nothing interfere with *this* mission, not even the sessions of sometimes unbearable pain that my migraines inflicted on me with cruel regularity. I simply gritted my teeth and carried on through my terrible agonies.

Later, after I had begun first to argue with him and then to confront him with demands on my sisters' behalf, I had another reason entirely for concealing my failure to apprehend this mission in my mind. I feared that under these changed circumstances father might have responded to my admission by doubting his easy acceptance of my leadership! He might even have responded by choosing Io, or one of the other sisters, to replace me as his nominee for captain of our little band. I remember vividly, as if it were only yesterday, that the mere thought of such a possible outcome was intolerable to me.

This wasn't on account of arrogance or inflated pride on my part, I'm sure of it. I really do think it arose, ironically, because of something I *could* feel deeply and clearly within me—the sense of responsibility for the fate and welfare of our band of sisters. I'd always felt it, from the earliest awakenings of my own self-awareness. Its presence within me is so strong and unwavering that I simply can't doubt its reality. My inner certainty about my duty to attend to my sisters' welfare is so unlike the indifference I feel toward the humanitarian mission as defined by father. So I began to suspect that this so-called "mission" was not merely temporarily misplaced somewhere in my mind—and, presumably, in my sisters' minds as well—but nonexistent. I was slowly coming to believe that his main objective in engineering us sisters had failed.

But then I thought to myself, just be patient and wait, Hera. I had heard him tell me repeatedly that his protocol would not be finished until his girls were in their late teens or even their early twenties. So perhaps this indifference toward humanity's concerns will leave me sometime later, to be replaced with a clear sense of father's mission, now authentically felt within my own breast. Perhaps, too, its absence to date is only a by-product of my preoccupation with shepherding my sisters to safety.

PART TWO

BAND OF SISTERS

29 NOVEMBER 2029

(Hera's Journal) We gathered at the airstrip in early morning on that very special day to see father and Max Klamm off on the first leg of their journey from Tembagapura to Stockholm. All during the previous night I lay rigid and wide-awake on my bed, dreading the coming of the dawn. Scenes of anticipated disaster had buffeted my mind as I prepared myself for death should our escape plan be thwarted. The aria "Nessun Dorma" from Puccini's *Turandot* ran on a continuous loop through my memory during those long sleepless hours.

Standing beside the airplane, embracing each of us in turn, father was silent but composed, and anyone could have mistaken the meaning of his air of preoccupation, given the type of honor he was about to receive. No one expected Moira and Themis to make an appearance, and they did not, but the sisters who were there were in a merry mood. Fearing an inadvertent slip in front of Klamm, alerting him that his scheme was known to the rest of us, Io and I had decided not to brief them on the occurrences of the previous days. To my astonishment, Io—acting garrulous and self-assured—was one of the first to appear at the airstrip that morning.

We had noticed that Klamm had been busy yesterday holding a series of training sessions with Sarajiwa, his new chief of security. This is probably because the man had been freshly appointed to this important job. Staff turnover was a never-ending problem in Tembagapura, since local residents dislike the village's isolation high up on the mountain face, and because of their being separated from their extended families by the gated perimeter.

About a week ago our contacts among the staff informed us that Sarajiwa's predecessor had been sacked; apparently he had so abused his privileges that the villagers rose up in open revolt against him. According to them, it was bad enough that he extorted bribes from all of them, although this was regarded as normal for the region, and that he demanded their deference as he swaggered through the village on his rounds, but when he raped one of their daughters, they drew the line. After getting drunk one day, he was ambushed and savagely beaten and Klamm had flown him out to Timika to forestall further trouble.

Yesterday, at my suggestion, Percy was hanging around the building housing the security chief's office. Later she told me about the instructions she overheard Klamm giving to Sarajiwa, some of which she managed to capture on her recorder. "Are you clear on what I want you to do? I've declared an alert for the whole facility for the entire time I'm away. This means stepped-up patrols around the perimeter and roll calls twice a day. I was going to cancel the missionaries' regular visit scheduled for tomorrow, but I don't need any more trouble with the staff right now, especially since one couple said they need urgent family counseling because of what had happened to their daughter.

"Your men are to monitor the activities of the visiting group for the entire time they are here. Do a head count immediately upon their arrival and again while the plane is being loaded for departure. Finally, I am giving you a special task of your own. You are to keep a watch on Io. Nothing else; don't talk to her or hang around her, just be sure you know where she is at all times. Is all that perfectly clear? If you screw up, you're fired."

A cold feeling began spreading through the pit of my stomach as the plane carrying father and Klamm lifted off the runway, then circled once over the town, dipping its wings to salute us as we watched. One part of what I felt was the thrill of anticipated adventure, but there was a larger portion of fear and foreboding as well, for now the moment of truth had arrived. Would our carefully laid plan of escape succeed, or would we all be locked up in the village guard-house at day's end, awaiting Klamm's abrupt return and the unfolding of the horrible scenario he held in store for us?

It was now or never. Evils would surely befall us in any case even if we never attempted to escape. Who knows what had been going through Klamm's mind yesterday? Perhaps he was just making a show of leaving, because upon reflection he'd concluded that despite his threats, Io would spill his secrets. In which case, he would have figured that perhaps my father had hatched a counter-thrust and set in motion a different plan, designed to protect us from him. So in order to avoid that risk he would even now be inventing an excuse to exit the onward flight at Timika airport, abandoning father and re-boarding our own craft for the short flight back here.

Yet, how can one succeed if one never tries to take command of one's own fate? So I stopped speculating and joined my sisters as we ran back from the airstrip to our building. Keep busy, I reminded myself! By far the cruelest of my many tasks was having had to ask Themis and Moira to leave behind their beloved companion dogs, Bree and Yoko, who couldn't accompany us on the plane without uncovering our deception. So I had sought out the two of them this morning at first light to give them time to adjust to the idea.

"Moira, Themis, we're in mortal danger and must run for our lives today. We'll use the airplane to escape, but we're going in disguise so as to fool the soldiers watching us. We're planning to switch identities with the village girls who are coming here later this morning. We can't take our personal belongings with us because that will arouse the soldiers' suspicions, and they'll put us into detention. So our things will be sent separately tomorrow. And this is the hard part, sisters: Bree and Yoko can't go with us on the plane. They have to wait until tomorrow, until ...."

"Then we'll stay behind and leave with them," Themis interjected. "We cannot go somewhere else without them, isn't that right, Moira?" Moira nodded vigorously in agreement.

"Please, listen to me carefully. Klamm has prepared a terrible fate for all of us. He intends to split us up and send us away, separately, to be held against our will by people we don't know, for the rest of our lives. I can't promise that we'll succeed in escaping today, but this is our only chance to try. If you stay behind here with the dogs, something may go wrong, and we may never, ever see each other again. Awful things could happen to you, or to us, if the slightest glitch develops in our plans."

"Then the plans will have to be changed," Moira said defiantly. "We're not going to leave here without Bree and Yoko, and that's final."

I was crying now and it took awhile for me to regain my composure. "I expected you both to take this stand. I had hoped to persuade you that your precious dogs would be safe, too, and that you wouldn't be separated from them for very long. All right; I'll work out something else. Start getting your things ready—there will be one small suitcase each you can fill. Put Yoko and Bree into their travel crates. I have to make the rounds to ensure the other sisters are awake."

I had formulated in my mind what I would do were they to respond in this way, and I was prepared for the worst—that they both would end up hating me for the rest of their lives. Yet I was convinced I could bear their hatred more easily than I could the endless pain of having them snatched away from us forever.

As for the other sisters, they could hardly contain their joy after being told that their long-deferred adventure into the waiting world was at hand! Io and I concocted a little fib—we were off to meet up with father for a grand tour in Europe after he completed his business in Stockholm, something he had planned as a surprise. We wanted to delay giving them the true story because we thought they might panic and fear for their own safety once they heard Io's tale. We told them they should put together a collection of their most precious belongings—enough to fill the small suitcase that would be delivered to each of them later that morning—because we expected to be away on our trip for a full year or more. All of them immediately ran off to their own rooms to comply.

And then, a few hours later, the first favorable sign from heaven was granted to us: The plane arrived on the return flight with Henry Jackson and twelve excited girls from the Timika church congregation—and no Klamm! I ran to the bathroom and threw up my fear, then reviewed for the hundredth time the sequence of steps to follow, my mind churning, hunting desperately for a fatal flaw.

At my request, made by telephone yesterday, Linda Jackson had left Timika before daylight this morning in the church's large passenger van, which had been used to bring the group up the mountain before the plane was available to them. With her were the Jacksons' replacements for the Papua ministry, Harry and Jennifer Tinbergen, another couple from Alberta who had arrived a month ago for the start of their three-year tour of duty in Timika. The newcomers would be meeting the members of the satellite congregation in Tembagapura for the first time this day, and they were being taken overland, they were told, so that they could see the spectacular views down the mountainside from the winding road. The van arrived in the village shortly after the returning plane. The level of general good spirits was high all around, the church service was especially well attended, and those preparing the picnic sang and danced as they worked.

For some time already, the Jacksons had been expecting to shepherd us sisters out of Papua, on their way to their next posting, after the completion of their assignment in Timika. With their help the process for admission of twelve foreign students to a two-year training program offered at the Church of Jesus of Nazareth Missionary Bible College, located near Longview, Alberta, had been initiated some months ago. The Jacksons were due to leave at the end of the week, but the couple didn't know exactly how the journey to Alberta was to unfold for us sisters. For obvious reasons of security, I had told them to book only their own tickets out of Timika on a commercial flight.

During their trips over the last few months, I had made detailed notes about the visiting girls' appearance, especially their hairstyles. Then I'd gotten my sisters to mimic those hairstyles, telling them to do this gradually so that the alterations were imperceptible to anyone not paying special attention. I had pretended this was in preparation for engaging in a little stage play we'd perform some day with the visitors. There was also the matter of costumes. Parents in the Timika congregation were accustomed to sending their children to church dressed in special uniforms worn only on Sundays, and the girls who had arrived by plane were wearing them as always. In the van with Linda Jackson were twelve extra sets of identical girls' uniforms, sized to fit my sisters and me, packed in small suitcases along with some locally purchased everyday clothing and toiletries. I had said that these, too, were to be used in the play we intended to put on today.

Following the service, and before the picnic was ready,

the new missionaries counseled the distraught village couple and their daughter. At the same time I was conferring with the Jacksons in another room at the meeting hall. The plans for the twelve of us to attend the missionary college in Alberta had recently been completed. Henry handed me the official letters of admission and I told him we intended to quit Tembagapura for good within a matter of days. While I was talking to them, Tammy, Rhea, Ari and Hex went to the bus to retrieve the suitcases and deliver them to the sisters, with instructions to replace the contents with their own collections of belongings.

Shortly thereafter the picnic dishes were served, and I gave Io the agreed-upon signal for setting things in motion. In fact, the entire success of the plan depended in the first instance upon Io, and as I expected, she performed brilliantly. Above all else what needed to be done was to somehow put the chief of security out of commission. Io and I knew that if this could be done, and if a certain amount of general confusion could be generated at the same time, the rest of the security detail wouldn't know what to do, since they were accustomed to simply following their boss's orders.

§   §   §

(Io's Journal) "Sarajiwa, you've been neglecting me," I said as I strolled into his office, nicely perfumed and wearing my most provocative dress. Klamm's threats about what would befall me if I betrayed him hung over me like a sentence of death. Nevertheless, my self-confidence had returned, and I was prepared to do anything necessary to help Hera get us out of here. "That's not very sweet. Are you angry with me? I thought you liked me."

He issued an audible groan. "No, lady, I'm not angry with you. But you're not supposed to be here, as you know, and I shouldn't even be talking to you."

"Are you going to make me get out then? Don't you want to see what I brought you first?" Not waiting for his answer, I took the bottle of excellent Scotch from my handbag. "I won't stay long, I promise. Just have one drink with me, please. I'm dying for a drink. Here, I've brought two glasses along." Alcohol had been used as a weapon against me, and I was about to return the favor.

As Hera and I had guessed, it was not that Sarajiwa didn't know his duty or that all of Klamm's instructions had evaporated from his mind so soon after his master's departure. Actually, as we were keenly aware, he had followed some of them to the letter and beyond, even before they had been issued to him. Since his recent elevation to the post of chief of security, he had been using his new position of authority to enlarge his opportunities for observing us sisters more closely than he had been able to do in his former rank. And over the course of the past week his observations had been concentrated increasingly on me. In truth he seems to have become a bit obsessed with me, poor man.

Unbeknownst to him, however, this was not entirely a matter of his own doing. As part of our escape plan, which Hera and I had been crafting in various scenarios, we had made sure that I returned Sarajiwa's attentions daily in ample measure in the form of innocent flirtations. He did not strike us as being a particularly bright man and undoubtedly he had allowed himself to believe that I was genuinely interested in his attentions. So when I entered his office, I'm afraid that the very small portion of reason bestowed upon him by his parents quickly deserted him. Not to put too fine a point upon it, he was putty in my hands.

Stiffening his resolve to do his duty, no doubt, he averted his gaze from me and said, "Just one quick drink, and then you'll have to go, OK?"

I replied, "If you say so, Sarajiwa. I don't want you to get into any trouble with Mr. Klamm, that's for sure. Just one quick drink and then I'll be gone, I promise."

I let him pour the drinks and he nervously gulped his down. "My, that was fast. You'll need one more." He was about to protest but was distracted, I suppose, when I accidentally brushed against him to refill his glass. He also was too preoccupied to notice that I didn't drink mine before pouring him another, which he also downed at once, perhaps in an effort to get me to leave.

As expected, the powerful soporific that Hera and I had filched from the infirmary after disabling its security system one night, and had then added to the Scotch bottle, took effect almost instantly. Sarajiwa staggered backwards into his chair. "I'm not feeling well." I watched him. In another ten seconds his head lolled, then his upper body fell forward onto the desktop. He was out cold and was unlikely to awaken before many hours had passed.

§   §   §

(Hera's Journal) I was waiting anxiously outside Sarajiwa's office when Io exited, grinning broadly. While she was carrying out her mission I had gone to father's compound and opened his safe, transferring the cash, passports, and a few papers into my briefcase. Io and I ran to our building and quickly donned the church uniforms that Tammy had left in my room. The next step was ready.

The sisters and our visitors had begun eating the picnic food and were running about excitedly. Tammy was now whispering instructions to each of the sisters, and one by one they drifted back to their apartments, where Io and I were waiting, and begun changing into the uniforms. Then the Jacksons informed the new couple that the four missionaries would escort the visiting girls over to the sisters' apartment block so that they could see where the sisters lived.

As the girls from Timika entered the lobby of our apartment building, some cries were heard from the area of the sisters' rooms. Io suddenly appeared in the lobby and exclaimed, "I think I have food poisoning."

"Oh no, not again," Henry Jackson cried out in alarm.

It had happened once before; salmonella bacteria had contaminated a salad at one of our earlier Sunday picnics. During that episode, while we sisters were rushed to the infirmary at the Tembagapura facility, the visiting girls, after being given some initial medical treatment, were quickly put on the airplane with their medication and flown back to their families in Timika.

Henry Jackson now turned to the Tinbergens. "Take the girls from the congregation to the infirmary building. Hurry! Ask the doctor to examine them immediately. Some of the girls have been there before and can show you where it is."

Meanwhile, at Io's urging all the sisters except Moira and Themis had begun leaving by the back door of our apartment building, moving toward the airstrip. Io asked Linda and Henry to wait in the building lobby while she and I went to check on our sisters. We walked straight to the set of rooms shared by Moira and Themis, who were sitting together on a bed, suitcases packed, with the dogs already locked in their travel crates. Each of us embraced one of them as if to say goodbye, and they looked surprised; then Io and I used a small pressurized-injection syringe to administer a fast-acting sedative. After they collapsed on the bed we moved them onto the stretchers Io and I had concealed earlier in a nearby closet. The two dogs sensed that something was wrong and became agitated, but we knew that they were safe inside their crates; then we ran back to the lobby.

Io said, "My symptoms are not too bad yet, but two of our sisters are unconscious; Hera and I have placed them on stretchers. We must fly them out immediately to a proper hospital. The other sisters may fall ill later, so all of them must be taken on the plane and be examined."

I broke in. "Linda, I know you're a nurse. Please come with us on the plane so that you can monitor their condition. Henry, I need you to stay here in Tembagapura; I'll set out what I want you to do after the four of us have carried the stretchers to the airstrip."

When we reached the tarmac Linda approached the pilot and cried out, "It's happened again, but this time it looks more serious—two of them are unconscious and very sick. We've got to get them back to Timika fast so they can be hospitalized." The pilot hesitated. He knew that he was required to obtain the security chief's permission before taking off, but the man was nowhere in sight. He dialed the number of the chief's office on his cell phone but there was no answer. He stood there, looking around nervously at the mass of confusion and commotion around him that increased with each passing second.

In the meantime Io and I were standing some meters away; Io was keeping watch on the scene around the airplane, and I was talking to Henry. "I need you to stay behind and do something for us. There's no time for me to explain fully. All I can say is that our lives are in danger and if we can't leave on the plane right away something terrible may happen. I need your help. I beg you, trust me."

"Of course I'll help. What is it you want me to do?"

"The two sisters who are unconscious have medical companion dogs back in the building we just left. They and the dogs are inseparable. If their dogs are not retrieved and reunited with them as soon as possible Moira and Themis may become suicidal. But we can't wait until they're loaded onto the plane now. Please go back to the dormitory right away and make sure that the two dogs cannot escape. Keep the door to the room closed and locked whenever you're not there. Move them out of their travel crates directly into the larger holding crates that are in the same room. Don't release them from their crates except when you take them outside to relieve themselves; when you do, handle one at a time and keep them securely leashed. Put them back into the smaller travel crates tomorrow morning—there are full instructions inside one of the crates—and load them in the van." I handed him a small envelope. "There are mild sedatives inside for the dogs. Give them one pill each today and again tomorrow morning.

"You'll find twelve small suitcases in the building—they're the same ones Linda brought this morning. Stow those on the roof of the van, and leave for Timika airport as soon as you possibly can tomorrow morning. A chartered jet will be waiting for you. Don't ask me to elaborate—there isn't time. There will be a representative of a shipping company on board, who will have prepared the necessary customs forms and export permits for the suitcases and the dogs. He'll meet you at the airport and together you can take care of the paperwork." I paused. "Please go now; I'll tell Linda that you'll be staying here tonight and returning tomorrow with the van, the girls from the congregation, and the Tinbergens." He gave me one long look but said nothing and then hurried back toward our apartment building.

I turned to glance once more at the pilot, who was still dithering. Fueled with adrenaline, my heart was pounding as I watched him punch the buttons on his cell phone over and over again. During the last few months he had gotten to know the Jacksons well. On their frequent trips between Timika and Tembagapura Henry Jackson had sat in the co-pilot's seat and chatted with the pilot. In fact he had even persuaded the pilot and his family to start coming to services at their church. The Jacksons were church leaders. So, he must have been thinking, 'Surely I can trust them. They can help me explain later to Mr. Klamm why I had no choice but to fly the group out of here without the security chief's authorization.'

"Please, we have to hurry, they may be dying," Linda pleaded. "When we reach Timika we're supposed to call the infirmary here to see how the other girls are doing. They have excellent hospital facilities at the infirmary, but if there are other serious cases, you may have to turn around and come back for them. By then the security chief should have turned up and, if necessary, he can authorize their removal to the hospital in Timika." Her words, spoken in haste, were not intended to be a direct confirmation of what the pilot was meant to believe, namely, that it was we sisters—who are not supposed to leave Tembagapura—who were at the infirmary, but they did carry that strong implication. All I could do was to watch him; my anxiety level soared but my mind's reasoning remained clear and steady.

As Linda was addressing the pilot, my sisters were grouped tightly around the two unconscious figures lying on the stretchers, crying out in despair. I hated myself for doing this to them, but in my cold and calculating state of mind I reminded myself of a simple fact: I require the verisimilitude of this scene. I need to bring to bear every kind of moral pressure imaginable on the pilot so that he does the deed. If this escape plan is thwarted, the grief my sisters are now experiencing will be the least of their problems.

The pilot had only glanced quickly at us as we had begun assembling around his plane, and thereafter, quite naturally, he focused on the two who lay comatose on the stretchers. I was praying that, given the sheer number of distractions around him, and the disguises we wore, he would finally arrive at the conclusion that we were indeed the twelve girls he had boarded a few hours ago in Timika. He hesitated once more and then said, "Load them up. The stretchers will fit in the aisle. I'll start the engines."

Of course, I thought, what a lucky break: This plane

carries freight most of the time, so it has been configured with an extra-wide aisle between single rows of seats on either side. The strongest of the sisters grabbed the handles of the two litters. I turned to Linda and said, "I've asked Henry to stay here. I'll explain after we board."

I was the last to board and as I mounted the stairs, glancing surreptitiously toward the security chief's office for signs of trouble, I breathed a huge sigh of relief. Linda Jackson's arrival in the van was part of my contingency plan: In case the pilot had refused to board us and fly out, we would have tried to take the van back down the mountain to Timika, although this would have been a far riskier course of action, given the length of the trip. Also, I couldn't have predicted how the security forces stationed at the end of the company road on the outskirts of Timika would have reacted when we drove up. But the backup plan hadn't been needed, thank heaven. The door was slammed shut and the pilot immediately taxied for takeoff.

Linda and I were sitting across the aisle from each other. As soon as the plane was aloft I leaned across and said to her in a matter-of-fact tone, "None of the girls is sick with food poisoning. Moira and Themis have been sedated; here's the package from the syringe we used." I reached into my bag. "I brought a stethoscope. Please check their vital signs immediately."

Meanwhile, Io was moving along the rows, explaining to the others that the ill sisters were going to be fine. Linda remained sitting, looking at me in astonishment.

"Check them first," I said, "and I'll explain when you're done." She leapt from her seat and seized the stethoscope from my hands. Moving quickly to where they lay, she spent a good five minutes with each of them before glancing back up at me.

"Their breathing, pulse and other vital signs are just fine." She looked at the package. "This is a very safe sedative, and I'm happy to see that you used a small dose; they're starting to come around but they'll be very groggy for quite a few hours yet. What on earth is going on?"

She was kneeling next to my seat and I looked her in the face. "I hope that you'll be able to forgive me someday for deceiving you and Henry. It's a long story, and I don't have time to relate it all to you now. The short answer is that our lives are at risk and we had to get out of Tembagapura today. Any delay of one day or even just a few more hours might have been fatal to us. Only Io and I know why, so you mustn't say anything to the others after we land. We had to invent the story about the food poisoning in order to distract the pilot and make him believe that we are, in fact, the twelve girls from the congregation. Otherwise he never would have allowed us to board."

"What about the two girls on the stretchers, though? Why did you sedate them?"

"They're different from the rest of us because they've had a developmental disorder from birth. Their dogs are actually registered medical companion animals, and the two girls and they are inseparable. They wouldn't have left voluntarily without the dogs. But to allow them to take their dogs would have uncloaked the deception we needed to create. Io and I had to bring them along involuntarily or not at all. And we were not prepared to abandon them."

"What are you going to do when we arrive in Timika? Are you still planning on going to Alberta? Will you be safe there? You have no luggage. Do you have passports with you?"

"We have passports and plenty of money, and if everything goes as planned Henry will transport the dogs and our suitcases to the airport tomorrow in the van. There will be— Oh God, I hope there will be!—a chartered jet waiting to pick us up at Timika airport that will return tomorrow. And yes, we will be going to the college in Alberta in a few months' time, and I believe that we will be safe there."

"Why are you in such danger? What about your parents? Didn't they know what was happening? Are you in touch with them?"

I glanced out the window. "We're starting the approach. The rest of the story will have to wait. You and I need to discuss what to say to the pilot. And I may need your assistance with the customs and immigration authorities. We've never before been outside Tembagapura. I've searched the Internet for information on such matters, but I really have no idea what to expect when we present ourselves."

She was silent for a moment. "Of course I'll help you. But I'd also like to hear the rest of the tale sometime."

"And I promise to fill you in. Here's what you should say to the pilot as soon as we land."

After the plane had taxied to a halt at Timika Airport, Linda pretended to dial the number of the infirmary at Tembagapura on her cell phone. She turned to the pilot. "They need you to go back there to fly out the other girls. Don't stop the engines. We'll call for ambulances to come to the airport."

Moira and Themis had awakened and were looking around in puzzlement as they rose unsteadily from the floor, with much help from their solicitous sisters. Fortunately for me, they were still far too disoriented to ask about their dogs. We quickly disembarked and the pilot took off again after checking in with the tower.

We weren't out of the woods yet by any means, although I heaved another great sigh of relief when I saw the unmarked regional passenger jet parked on the tarmac. This doesn't appear to be a large or busy airport and apart from the Challenger jet there were only small single-engine planes visible. An agent in Singapore, acting on instructions from the law firm in Calgary that I had retained as trustee for our investment funds, had chartered the jet and instructed it to meet us on that day. The flight plan filed by its pilot with the Timika airport authorities listed Denpasar Airport, Bali, as its next destination. But first we had to get exit permits stamped into our passports by the officials at Timika.

Since our passports and other documents identified each of us as UK nationals holding valid Indonesian residence permits, and also as being eighteen years of age, I'd hoped not to encounter any problems. To my great relief, it turned out the Jacksons were well known to some of the government officials stationed at the airport. They had flown home once a year since arriving in Papua, and as well as hosting many visits by church members from overseas during their three years here, they had taken groups of children from the Timika congregation on religious retreats to Australia and other parts of Indonesia. As a result of this extensive experience, they also knew how helpful a modest amount of euro currency could be in assuring the officials' cooperation.

The officials greeted Linda Jackson warmly, readily stamping our passports with exit permits and expressing concern about the possibility that two of the girls, who were obviously a bit woozy, might need urgent medical attention. After reassuring them, we were ushered through all the formalities in short order and Linda waved goodbye to us.

The Challenger's engines were running as we boarded and we taxied for takeoff as soon as we were in our seats. As the jet lifted off I simply couldn't contain my emotions any longer. I began to sob and couldn't stop until some minutes had passed. My sisters naturally became alarmed, thinking that despite all appearances something had gone wrong. When I was finally able to speak again I reassured them that this was my body's way of releasing extreme tension. After a brief stop for refueling at Denpasar Airport, our plane took off again and turned south, heading toward Darwin, Australia. This part of the plan was designed to throw a pursuing Klamm off our trail, or at least slow him down a bit, because I hoped to get him to believe that we had disembarked in Bali, with the intention of asking my mother's family to hide us on their huge estate there.

After clearing immigration formalities at the Darwin airport we were met by agents for a private clinic, who had been sent instructions and a wire transfer of funds from Calgary to take us in overnight; a private security firm had also been engaged to watch the premises. Themis and Moira were in beds set next to each other, asking insistently as to the whereabouts of their dogs, and both broke out in terrible sobs upon learning that they had been left behind. The sisters were grouped around them when I spoke.

"Someday, I hope, both of you will be able to forgive Io and me for what we did to you today. I've just been in touch with Henry Jackson by satellite phone, and he says that Bree and Yoko are safe and secure. He's guarding them and will not let them out of his sight. Our jet is returning to Timika and will pick them up tomorrow morning; they'll join us here by evening." Neither of them looked directly at me or spoke a word. As I feared, this breach of trust was going to take a long time to heal.

So I turned to the rest of the group. "Io and I owe you an explanation, and here it is. Io didn't have food poisoning; that was a ruse. The two of us had discovered that Mr. Klamm had given orders to the guards not to allow us to leave Tembagapura. Of course this frightened us a lot, because we didn't know what it meant. What right did he have to control our movements? So Io and I cooked up a plan to deceive the pilot. We thought it was best not to let the rest of you know that we might be in some danger, because we wanted the security guards to think that everything was still normal."

Tina asked, "Are we still heading to Europe to meet up with father?"

Io and I exchanged a glance. She knew that I wanted to conceal the real story from the rest of them, at least for awhile yet, until we were resettled in Alberta. But I was well aware that she had resented for a long time what she once called my 'officious and tiresome over-protectiveness,' and so she promptly hijacked the conversation.

"No, there's been a change of plans, and you deserve to know why. Some of you have been involved in discussions with father, during which the issue of when we were going to be able to split from that stupid little town on the mountain was bandied back and forth. We could never get a straight answer out of him, but things came to a head two days ago. I found out that Klamm was going to separate us from each other and sell us to rich degenerates as sex slaves." Gasps and cries filled the room. "Right. Hideous man. So I told Hera, and together, we decided to make a run for it. And here we are."

Of course, what I found especially fascinating was what she omitted from this account.

Tina asked again, "Are we heading to Europe to join father?"

Io replied, "No. We wouldn't be safe. Father is too high profile, and if we're with him Klamm can trace us easily. We have to disappear for a while. Hera thinks that this college in Alberta is a good hiding hole, and I agree with her. Once things settle down we can get in touch with him. But in the meantime we have to be careful. His communications may be monitored."

I added, "We'll take off again the day after tomorrow. We're going on a regular commercial flight first to Sydney and then to the United States, and we'll stay there for a few months because Klamm can't follow us there—father told me he's a wanted man in that country on securities fraud charges. The two dogs can accompany us—they have seats in the first-class compartment!—because they have their own passports as registered medical companion animals. We'll just have to wait a few hours at Los Angeles while a vet inspects them and examines their health registry documents. Our belongings will be sent separately to Canada under customs bond and we'll pick them up when we get there." Then I told them for the first time about our new home.

JENNIFER TINBERGEN'S MEMOIR
ENTRY OF 05 DECEMBER 2029
*(Sub-Compiler's Note: This material
was sent to Hera many years later.)*

Only while we were returning to Timika with Henry and the girls—along with two dogs and twelve suitcases—did Harry and I discover that we had played a minor part, unwittingly, in a great drama of escape. Linda had called him after the sisters' plane left and explained everything, and then after an unscheduled evening in Tembagapura, we traveled down the mountain in the van on the following day. The local people were as mystified as we were by all the strange events suddenly unfolding around them, but once they realized that we and the young ladies from Timika were going to stay the night, they opened their hearts and houses to us, and we spent a wonderful evening in their company.

Meanwhile, chaos had erupted all around us in Tembagapura. We were at the infirmary when we heard the airplane take off and when it returned again from Timika. The pilot left the engines running and headed straight to the clinic building, where he was met by the completely bewildered local doctor who told him that the girls there showed no sign of any illness. He also told the pilot he had not taken any call from Linda Jackson earlier that morning. Naturally, wc wcre utterly unhelpful because we were also in the dark; all that Henry had told us was that Linda had had to escort a group of girls back to Timika at once.

Then we saw the pilot look more closely at the young women sitting patiently outside the infirmary, and it seemed that panic set in; he appeared to suddenly realize that the two groups of girls had been switched. From our vantage point above the rest of the town, we saw him run to the security chief's office where most of the guard detail were milling about, chattering aimlessly. Then we heard the doctor take a call from the pilot, after which he said he had to go and check up on the chief. We found out later that the chief had been drugged, and was still out cold and could not be roused. And then we watched as the pilot ran back to his plane and took off again.

The pilot was a member of our church, and after our return, we learned from someone else in the congregation who had spoken with him when he landed for the second time in Timika that day, that he was intending to collect his family and spirit them back to Gorontalo, Sulawesi, his native city. Knowing full well he would be blamed for what happened, a judgment that would be followed promptly by severe consequences, he declared that he would never again set foot in Papua.

By the time we realized the plane wouldn't be returning for us that day, it was too late to start down the mountainside in the van. So we called the church office in Timika, telling them to assure the parents that all the girls were safe, and that because the plane had to be sent off on an emergency mission, they would be brought home by road the next day.

We learned more from some of the villagers the next morning while we were helping Henry load the van. Late the previous afternoon, the security chief had finally regained consciousness. It apparently took him several hours more to clear his head, but in the meantime, he figured out what had happened when a few members of the guard detail admitted to also indulging in the contents of the Scotch bottle. Eventually it was obvious that the twelve girls entrusted to his care had vanished.

Although it was late at night by then, he did not hesitate. According to the reports we got the next day, he commandeered a four-wheel-drive vehicle and drove off at a mad pace down the mountain road, along with three of his comrades who had leapt in as he accelerated away from his office. On our first trip up the mountain a week ago, it was obvious that this road would be rather unforgiving of mistakes, even for a driver of clearer mind than his. The local people who investigated the accident said that at the third hairpin turn, he went over the edge and dropped approximately three hundred meters to the first ledge on the mountainside below.

Yesterday at our house in Timika, the doctor, whom we had gotten to know on our first day in Tembagapura, stopped in to relate to us the continuation of the strange events that all began upon the departure of Professor Stone and Mr. Klamm. He had assumed that it was only the twelve sisters who had eaten from a contaminated dish and gotten ill at the picnic, and therefore they alone had to be rushed to hospital in Timika. Indeed, he had no idea why the pilot panicked and fled. So the next day, after we left with the visiting girls, and suspecting nothing amiss, he went about his appointed rounds. He performed a thorough medical checkup on the pregnant women and, as directed by Professor Stone a few days earlier, gave them an injection of their prescribed nutritional supplement.

Twenty-four hours later he had forty spontaneous abortions to deal with! It didn't take him long to deduce the only possible explanation for this bizarre occurrence—something was wrong with the contents of the injections he had administered. And, like the pilot, he assumed that he would be blamed for the consequences. So, after attending to the women, he commandeered another vehicle and drove helter-skelter down the mountainside; apparently he, too, plans to leave Papua for good.

§   §   §

(*Hera's Journal, 02 December*) I'll never forget the look on Themis and Moira's faces as we all watched the crates holding Bree and Yoko being unloaded from the Challenger in Darwin yesterday! When I embraced them, I said, "You will always be able to trust me." Thereafter, finally beginning to feel our tension dissipate, we were euphoric as we partied with abandon far into the night, anticipating our further adventures and our new beginning in life.

Our flight from Sydney landed in Los Angeles and we were admitted to the United States on tourist visas. Another plane was waiting for us there, also chartered by our Calgary lawyers on our behalf. I mean for us to vanish off the face of the earth, at least until we're capable of getting Klamm off our backs for good. It's so strange; the great distance we've put between ourselves and Papua and Tembagapura in such a short time is creating some dissociations in my head! I catch myself thinking, 'Did we spend the first fifteen years of our lives in that strange place?'

Again our chartered jet deliberately flew a roundabout route, first to San Francisco, then to Las Vegas, and finally to Phoenix, where we were met by a school bus chartered by an American religious group affiliated with Alberta's Church of Jesus of Nazareth. As prearranged the bus took us to a rural camp, operated by the group as a retreat, deep in the surrounding Arizona desert country. Here I intend to decamp for a couple of months, until our trail goes cold, before traveling on to Alberta—with the added bonus of not having to experience a Canadian winter right away! In the meantime, with the assistance of our Calgary lawyers, we'll be sending off our passports and supporting documents to the nearest Canadian consulate; our lawyers said we could expect them to be returned within a few weeks, with our visas for entry into Canada stamped inside.

§ § §

(Hera's Journal, 09 *December)* We're somewhere in the Arizona desert located a few miles outside a small town. I can't help it, but I seem to see Klamm's face everywhere I look. How long will it take to banish the fear of him I carry everywhere with me? I've always tried my very own home-grown therapies on myself at times like this. For the moment, at least, we are victorious; how can it be wrong to celebrate our collective courage and skill in winning so crucial a battle against a determined foe? I don't mean another wild party, like the one we had in Darwin; none of us appears to be in the mood for such a thing right now, nor does this spartan encampment encourage any dissolute fantasies. I sense that my sisters have withdrawn into their private spaces, allowing their feelings to adjust to what's happening and to what the future might hold.

Yet what tremendous satisfaction there is for me—at least for now!—in conjuring up in my mind the phases through which Klamm's warped soul must have passed, first far abroad in Sweden, as his apprehension grew that something was wrong in Tembagapura, and then upon his return, when he faced the stark reality of our disappearance and all the aborted fetuses, for surely all these events have unfolded by now.

So I imagine him as he was at first, puffed up and pondering his replenished fortunes, amidst the glittering events at the Nobel Prize celebrations in Stockholm. The attentions paid to him there by various sycophants must have been so seductive and flattering, and the new business deals being offered to him so lucrative, that scenes in memory from our distant and forlorn mountain would have only rarely intruded into his reveries. Nor, if once or twice he had cast his mind back to the village and our band of sisters huddled there, held helplessly in his power, was there any reason for him to contemplate anything going wrong. After all, we were then twelve little girls who had never been out of Tembagapura, and he had a security detail of more than fifty soldiers guarding us. What was there for him to worry about anyway?

Sometime around the fourth day after arriving in Stockholm, Klamm must have said his goodbyes to father and left for the airport, and while there almost certainly he would have placed a call to Tembagapura after settling down with a drink in the first-class lounge. The endlessly ringing entreaties of his instrument would have gone unanswered at the security chief's office. Next he would have tried every other number within our compound, starting with the doctor's office at the infirmary, then the matron's office at the sisters' apartment complex, the security post at the compound housing the pregnant women, the pilot's home in Timika, and finally the guard post a few kilometers outside Timika where the road up the mountain started.

No answer, anywhere. My guess is that after our sudden disappearance, and a short reflection on the possibility that any one or all of them would be blamed for assisting, or at least not preventing, the unfortunate events, none of those he was seeking that day would have waited around to receive a call from the man who had routinely abused his authority over them. There are a few other telephone numbers for places in the village, and at one or two of them the receiver might have been picked up; however, if it was, I suspect that the line would have gone dead as soon as Klamm identified himself.

At that point, the extreme secrecy in which he and my father had built and operated the facility at Tembagapura would have come back to haunt him, for there was no one else, especially locally, he could call on for help. He would have to go back there himself, as quickly as he could. Did he first try to reach my father, who I know had planned to spend a few weeks in Europe before returning to our village to pick up his things? I cannot estimate this possibility, but I am certain that if he did try, father would have had taken prior steps to make sure Klamm wouldn't be able to contact him. By avoiding him, my father would know he was adding to Klamm's dilemmas, which would be an advantage to his fleeing girls.

Klamm would then have had a more complex calculation to make. Should he go back to Stockholm first and try to pick up father's trail, on the assumption that—as he might have already suspected—Stone had tricked him and was even at that instant rescuing his daughters? Or should he go straight to Timika instead, on the chance that he could intercept us and him in our flight before we got out of Papua? I opt for the second scenario, chiefly because Klamm—who had a keen nose for the weaknesses of others—was well aware of my father's fragile psyche. His best guess would be that Stone had recruited someone else to spirit his children away from Tembagapura while he and Klamm partied in Stockholm.

So now I imagine him in my mind, racing through a succession of airports on a frantic mission to arrive back in Indonesia in time to intervene in whatever was transpiring there. I see him desperately working the telephones during his various stopovers, repeatedly trying first the security chief's office and then all the other numbers in quick succession, to no avail. I'm pretty sure that when he finally arrived back at Timika Airport, there would have been no company plane visible on the tarmac. Like the staff in Tembagapura, the pilot would have figured he'd be a leading candidate for blame and would have long since made himself scarce.

Klamm would have no option but to rent a vehicle and drive up the mountainside.

What did he find when he got there? Probably the main entrance on the fenced perimeter was wide open and unguarded. I doubt that he would have sighted a single member of the security detail anywhere in the village. The doctor would have vanished and our apartment complex would be standing empty. Maybe the formerly pregnant women would have still been hanging around, and if so, they would have greeted him by loudly demanding compensation for their troubles! But no one who had been working directly for him would have waited around for his wrath to be laid upon their heads.

Probably a few of the locals would be milling about, wondering how long they should wait for conditions to normalize before quitting the town for good. When he finally was able to corner a few of them, eventually he would piece together the essentials of the story, and learn that we sisters had disappeared somehow on the afternoon of the day he and Stone had left for Stockholm. But by then six days would have elapsed. We had a long head start on him and at that point he didn't even have a clue as to which direction we had taken.

He would go to his compound and sit down to think with a bottle of booze. We sisters were gone. The pregnancies had been terminated. Stone had dropped out of sight. Were these three events related? Almost certainly. Now, the most interesting idea is, he had every reason to assume that we were still somewhere in Indonesia! The easiest presumption for him to make was that my mother's family would have been enlisted to find a remote place in which we could hide, somewhere on their property in Bali. Then he'd guess that father would be picking us up from there at some point, so the first order of business was to track him down and keep a watch on his further movements. Professor Stone, at least, was unlikely to be able to disappear without a trace.

By my calculation, Klamm had about seven months before his clients would find out. Io said she'd understood that the end of next July was specified in the batch of contracts my father had signed when pictures of the newborn babies were to be delivered to the clients. That was also the time when a certain group of young women, aged sixteen, were to be delivered in person to some of those buyers. I can barely bring myself to think about the fact that this might have happened to us! What unspeakable horror!

Well, without a doubt he's in trouble with his clients, and so by now he has probably launched the first of his sallies, scouring the world for both father and us. Excepting only in the United States, thank heaven, where he'll have to rely on agents working on his behalf, which will not be as effective for him.

Yet, to be honest, it wouldn't take him long to put two and two together and deduce that the missionaries had to have played a role in our escape. Doubtless, he soon talked to the new couple at the Timika church, the Tinbergens, who couldn't give him the smallest clue as to what had happened to us. But he's a clever man, so he wouldn't stop there. Next he'd try the offices of the church in Alberta where the missionaries are based, trying to discover the route taken by Henry and Linda—as well as their final destination.

Once I found out where the Jacksons were headed when we parted in Timika, I told them that it would actually be advantageous to us if the church were to answer Klamm's queries about their destination truthfully. So it amused me no end to imagine some nice lady on the other end of the phone in Alberta, telling him she would love to put him in touch with the Jacksons, but this would be quite difficult, as they were already on their next assignment and were likely to be proceeding right now by boat up the Amazon River.

Being proud of her church's missionary endeavors, she would surely want him to know that on their new posting, they would be trying to bring into the fold some of the remotest tribes living along the most distant reaches of that mighty watercourse. She would also say—truthfully—that no, she didn't have any information about twelve Indonesian girls who may have been traveling with them.

I'm pretty sure that our secret is safe for now at that end. I made certain that the Jacksons had sworn to secrecy the head minister in their church, as well as his key office staff, about our planned stay at the missionary training center. The church officials were told that our families back in Indonesia were opposed to our becoming missionaries and would try to take us away if they found us there. I've also arranged with our Calgary lawyers to hire a private security firm on a permanent basis to keep a discreet watch on our new home, starting at the time of our arrival in the United States.

But he will chase us, of that I'm sure. We're safe for now, but for how long? We'll stay a couple of months here in the Arizona desert in case Klamm dispatched his agents to the United States immediately. I assume that he can quickly trace us as far as Bali, and maybe to Darwin, by bribing the officials in Timika to reveal the Challenger's destination, but I just don't know whether he'll be able to track our itinerary from there.

§   §   §

(*Hera's Journal,* 01 *March* 2030) Io's pregnant. The contraceptive pills didn't work for some reason. In our present circumstances—where possibly we'd have to run again at a moment's notice, this time from Klamm's pursuing agents—it would be unsafe to try to procure an abortion for her. A group of us talked to her together, and she's agreed to carry the child to term, although she insists she won't act out the mother role. If we want to keep the baby, she says, the rest of us will have to raise it. That's fine by me.

§   §   §

(Franklin's Journal, 23 March 2030) I've been traveling all over Europe since slipping out of Stockholm on the same day that Klamm left, buying time for my girls and trying to cause as much confusion for him as I could. Finally having arrived in London last week, I've been haunting the Sujana Foundation's offices ever since, hoping against hope that a message from Hera will arrive. But I can't sit here forever. Perhaps she has no intention of contacting me, either because she genuinely fears that Klamm will be watching me, so that he can follow me to her, or because she no longer intends to live under my roof and my authority. Or both.

(01 May 2030) Losing every one of my beloved daughters, on top of the unending and unshakable grief over Ina's death, is too much for me to bear. So I'm giving my London law firm my new address and the contact code for me that Hera has—the one I gave her so she can get in touch with the Sujana family. I told the firm to direct her to me at once if she ever telephones or shows up at their door. I've put my financial and legal affairs in order. I've wound down my research projects, resigned from my university position, and shuttered the foundation's London offices. And I'll be checking myself into an exclusive private psychiatric clinic, set in the countryside outside Cambridge, for a long stay.

11 APRIL 2030

Today at Phoenix airport we boarded the chartered jet our lawyers had sent for us and flew to Vancouver, where we breezed through the immigration formalities, dogs and all, without a hitch. The day is warm and rainy here, but the woman from the law office who had flown from Calgary to meet us at Vancouver airport warned us about the weather challenges awaiting us in Alberta. She had arranged a few days' hotel accommodations for us and the dogs so we could do some sightseeing and shopping for warm clothing.

Three days later we traveled in two passenger vans on an amazing journey through a series of mountain ranges—first the Selkirks and Monashees, then the Purcells and Rockies—with a seemingly endless series of snow-capped peaks. I must admit the sight of these immense mountains made some of the sisters a bit apprehensive, until I pointed out that there didn't seem to be any towns perched on the high slopes! At Calgary we stayed for two days, the others doing some sightseeing while Athena and I conferred with our lawyers. When we resumed our trek, all were watching at the windows as our route took us south out of Calgary and through the small towns of Turner Valley and Black Diamond, which sit in dry, low rolling hills at the edge of the eastern foothills of the Rocky Mountains.

We entered the small hamlet of Longview, Alberta, turned west and traveled a few miles along the road that follows the Highwood River valley toward the native band settlement at Eden Valley. Eventually we arrived at our destination, a set of modest buildings constructed on the site of what was once a working ranch. The entire valley floor, home to herds of grazing cattle and horses, is surrounded on three sides by the most beautiful snow-capped mountain vistas in the distance, while the nearer hillsides are covered with poplar and spruce trees.

We had been advised that this whole area stretching southwest of Calgary is nestled in farming and ranching country, far removed in spirit from the bustle and commercialism of the nearby city. Grasses interspersed between stands of poplar and spruce make up its natural ground cover, but lifting one's eyes to the west almost always brings into view the magnificent mountain chain that extends across the entire horizon. The residents of this area are said to share the preferences of country folk everywhere—to mind their own business but be ready to help friends and neighbors when need arises. The Jacksons had told us that the Church of Jesus of Nazareth is well established here, as well as in some other communities in southeastern British Columbia and southern Alberta.

During the preceding six months the law firm acting on our behalf had finalized a contractual agreement with the church authorities, providing a quarterly payment for lodging, meals and services for a period of thirty months. The contract also called for reimbursement for an upgrading to the college facilities and installation of a complement of fast, networked computers, as well as a satellite feed for Internet and telephone communications. Our lawyers informed us that due to steadily declining enrollments, the church's missionary college had fallen onto hard times in recent years and the authorities had considered closing it. Thus, they did not drive too hard a bargain when this new opportunity arose.

Under the terms of our contract, we sisters are committed to three hours per day of Bible and religious history study during weekdays, with instruction supplied, in part, by faculty and graduate students from the University of Calgary's religion department, as well as attendance at regular church services on Sundays. For the remainder of the day (and the night!) we'll continue our self-directed learning using Internet resources. My excuse for our habitual absence from formal classrooms for most of the day is that we were raised as Buddhists and need to continue our obligatory long meditation sessions. There are another dozen students here and a few of our classes are held jointly with theirs.

Starting next September we'll also receive private tutoring on-site in specialized subjects by contractual arrangement with the university. Sports and exercise activities, including hiking, bicycling, and lessons in horseback riding, are included in the daily program. The land around the church buildings is still leased to neighboring farmers for cattle and horse grazing, and many of the sisters have volunteered to do various chores in the barns. We continue to employ a security firm to keep a 24-hour-a-day watch on the whole area surrounding the church buildings and the neighboring facilities used by us, and to provide secure transportation anytime we leave the grounds, including back and forth to Calgary.

§   §   §

(18 April) Upon our arrival Io was more than four months pregnant. I've now arranged for her to be admitted to a private hospital located in Calgary to give birth, but I also needed an ally at the college to ensure that word of the pregnancy did not spread. The church had hired a local widow, Mrs. Walter, to prepare our meals and to supervise the cleaning and maintenance staff in the building. She was over-

come with joy when she first met her new charges.

"Oh my dears," she gushed, "what lovely young women you all are. I had hoped during my early married life to have a girl, but only boys came, and although I loved them very much, I never stopped wanting a girl. Now I will have twelve!"

Mrs. Walter was very careful to inquire what our food preferences were, and we immediately assured her that she would not have to prepare Indonesian meals; we wanted to learn new types of dishes. Still, she couldn't suppress a note of alarm in her voice when we told her that we're vegetarians, given that she's lived all her life in cattle country. So we promised that we'd work with her on meal planning.

At the first opportunity I took her aside and disclosed Io's condition. "I need your help, Mrs. Walter. My sister Io was raped just before we left our native country and we know that the church here does not approve of abortion. My sister is very angry about what happened and doesn't wish to keep the child, but I don't want to have the baby given up for adoption. Io's agreed to use my name when she's admitted to the hospital, so I'll be registered as the mother on the birth certificate, but I know we cannot keep the baby here at the school. Can you help me find a wet-nurse in this area to breast-feed the baby when he's born, and then to keep it at her home until we leave here in a couple of years?

"I promise my other sisters and I will visit often so that we get to know the baby, and of course the people who agree to help us will be paid. However, I don't want anyone else here at the college or the church, or in town, to know anything about where the baby came from. We're still afraid of the man who raped Io and who is still looking for us. Do you think you can help us?"

I expected the answer that came back. "Of course I'll take care of this for you, my dear. Poor Io. I'm pretty sure that after a little while she'll change her mind and want her baby back. I have a much younger sister who lives on a farm nearby, up toward Black Diamond, and who has two small children of her own. I'm almost certain she would take the child, and the family can use a little bit of extra money because farming is so difficult these days, you know. We'll just tell everyone else that my sister adopted the baby, and when you go we'll think of something else to say. Of course my sister won't have milk when the baby is born, but the church has a program to try to find wet-nurses for new mothers who can't produce enough breast milk of their own, so we should be able to take care of that, too. Now, don't you concern yourself about it anymore. I'll arrange everything."

A few days later Mrs. Walter called me into her office. "I've talked to my sister and she'll be very happy to have the baby. I'll take you to meet her soon. Now, dear, do you think you could help me with something? I was told that you girls are very clever with computers. I was given a little computer at the college to keep track of my expenses for food and other supplies, so that the college can prepare billings. I'd like to use it also for e-mail messages with my old friends in the other church congregations, but I keep getting viruses that shut down my system. It seems I'm too old to figure these things out for myself. Could you help me?"

I assured her that I would. We were clearly establishing a bond.

AUGUST 2030

Marco was born on August 24. For the preceding three months Io had stayed at the private hospital in Calgary, her absence from the college being attributed to the need for unspecified medical treatment. I really thought that her anger would subside as her pregnancy approached its term, but it did not, and she was adamant about refusing to nurse or even accept the child. Her slight build contrasted sharply with the large size of the fetus she was carrying, so she delivered by caesarian section; then complications and infection set in and she was heavily sedated while recovering. I sat by her bedside throughout the long nights until she overcame the infection, occasionally holding the baby Marco as I listened to the fragments of a half-coherent monologue from my delirious sister.

I had to concentrate hard to follow the thread of ideas across the long pauses between Io's words and phrases.

"It's ridiculous … God created heaven and earth … He controls everything, it says. So why does He let Satan run around freely and screw things up? … Didn't God notice him lurking in the Garden, casually plucking apples from His trees and spinning that silly proposition to Adam and Eve? … And why was God testing them so soon anyway? He had hardly given them a chance to get settled in His nice Garden. If He wasn't happy with His handiwork, why didn't He just scrap these defective prototypes and start over again?"

I was stunned. To be sure, I'd found it curious that Io had seemed so fascinated with our Bible study during our first few months' stay at the college before she went to the hospital. Sometimes Io was flippant, saying she was just interested in the 'juicy parts,' especially the many episodes in the Old Testament when God rained down murder and mayhem on the hapless evildoers below. But at other times she seemed very serious.

"I like it because the story's so straightforward," Io had remarked once. "It's good against evil, one or the other. That's all, nothing more complicated. All the faithful have to do is believe in God and follow a few of His simple rules. Adam and Eve and all the rest appear not to have been constructed very well, because most of them seem to find it almost impossible to do what they should. Anyway, it's all sorted out in the end, isn't it? I really like the Book of Revelation. Last Judgment, no more ambiguity about whether you are saved or damned, the bad ones get their just desserts at last."

My recollections were interrupted by Io's voice, slowed by the drugs but still clear.

"Satan meanders all over the earth, as bold as you please, all the time ... Read the Book of Job ... There it's pretty clear he's God's pal, and the two of them sit around having a pleasant conversation among equals. At one point God asks him where he's been lately—apparently He doesn't know everything—and Satan replies, 'Going to and fro in the earth..., walking up and down in it.' How come? ... Evil walks the earth, strutting around as big as you please, and God sits up there somewhere, doing nothing about it. Is He distracted? ... Uninterested? ... Too busy creating other worlds? Or does He just enjoy watching the show down there on earth? Maybe that's it! Evil deeds are so much more interesting and enjoyable than good ones, aren't they? ... He's a voyeur ... But they pay royally in the end, the bad ones, don't they?"

Her words tumbled out, slurred and now barely understandable. "All but a few are handed over to the demons, who know how to have some fun with them. Eternal torment, this is part of God's plan, too, it seems ... But isn't God the one who fashioned their all-too-weak wills in the first place? Who's in charge here anyway? ... Apocalypse. That's not God's show at all; it's Satan's. Who wins in the end? Satan does—he gets by far the biggest number of souls. God is left with a pittance ... Many of the faithful can't wait for Apocalypse. It brings all the ambiguity to an end. Somebody should arrange that little event for them, sooner rather than later."

I had listened to Io's soliloquy while watching the sleeping Marco, who now occupied a bed set next to Io's. As promised Mrs. Walter had found a wet-nurse, a local unmarried teenager who had lost her baby at childbirth; she had been installed in a separate room at the hospital. Mrs. Walter's sister had agreed to take in the teenager at her farm during the period when she would be breast-feeding Marco. But I already felt a bond with the baby and knew that I'd be visiting him often at the nearby farm. I feel somehow deeply contented that my name appears as his mother on the birth certificate, in large measure because I'm already quite certain that I will bear no children of my own.

The images of sexual assault that plague my dreams, magnified by the reality of Klamm's rape of Io, reinforce the fears of men that have welled up in me from an unknown source ever since I was a young girl. Doubtless, too, the conviction that I had to assume chief responsibility for my sisters' welfare, also arising at an early age and growing stronger with each passing year, precludes the forming of any other attachment that could distract me from my main task.

NOVEMBER 2030

Despite the strangeness of the new country and the religious trappings at the college, all my sisters seem to be overjoyed with their new home. Standing in such sharp contrast to the varying images of life and culture elsewhere we encountered daily on the Internet, the remote mountainside village where we spent our first fifteen years had seemed to all of us more and more like a prison with each passing season. Now we all respond gratefully to the frequent invitations from church members to visit their homes and farms for meals and birthday celebrations—having invented different birthday dates for ourselves!—and relax in the warmth and genuineness of our hosts' feelings toward us. Our daily doses of outdoor exercise and horseback riding have lent us an air of fitness and good health.

But the anxiety over what had happened to Io and then the awareness of the horrible future that had loomed over us, and from which we had so narrow an escape, preys on our minds. The security arrangements protecting us whenever we exit the college grounds are a constant reminder of the undiminished danger we face. During the last stress-filled year some of the girls developed symptoms of panic disorder—including me, although I denied it as long as I could before yielding to its reality—and we're now prescribed anti-anxiolytic medications.

April 2031

I've been putting together a private retrospective on our first year in Alberta. Certainly it has passed quickly and without incident, and the fears that accompanied us from Papua—as well as the memory of our unhappiness there—have started to diminish. Without exception, the local residents we come into contact with seem to admire us greatly, in large part, I think, because we're so serious about our studies! I'm sure that the warmth from them we feel is an important ingredient in the budding of our own feelings of safety and normalcy.

Except for Io—and, unsurprisingly, Moira and Themis, whose condition precludes easy human bonding—we take the greatest pleasure in visiting the farm where Marco lives, and he in turn revels in the attentions his many aunts shower on him. Io had forbidden her sisters to tell Marco that she was his mother, so all agreed to support the fiction of my parentage. It's already clear that he'll be big in stature like his father, although he has his mother's brown skin color and dark eyes.

I've begun to turn our regular private convocations to the subject of planning our next move, which will be timed to coincide with our actual eighteenth birthdays. We've been careful in our expenditures, and the financial wizards among the sisters have become increasingly clever in their gains from investing and trading; at present our capital stands at 15 million euros. We're now reviewing our options: Where on the globe should we live? Should we stay in Canada or move again to a different part of the world? Above all, should we stay together and continue to watch out for each other? Or should we go our separate ways, pursuing careers and possibly starting relationships and families?

Then there's the matter of father. We have no idea where he went after the Stockholm ceremony. Some of the sisters confess to missing him and wondering where he is and whether we'll ever see him again. I've been strict in my admonishments that none of us should try to seek him out, lest our communications be intercepted and traced by those who might be watching for just such an attempt. I confess that I, too, wonder about his health and whereabouts as much as they do, but I've insisted that we mustn't seek to satisfy our curiosity until we're sure we can do so safely. I've been assuming that he would have wanted to continue to promote the work of the Sujana Foundation, but all I know of it is that it had been incorporated in the Turks and Caicos Islands and has offices in London, England.

OCTOBER 2031

We'd recently agreed that we're all feeling a bit more secure after being in this wonderful spot for eighteen months, and had just made a final decision to leave here about a year from now. Then yesterday, Mrs. Walter called me into her office.

"My dear, I haven't forgotten that you wanted me to let you know if I ever heard anything about strangers turning up around here and asking about a group of foreign girls. I've been a member of our church all my life, and I know some people in each of the eight congregations we have in various towns in Alberta and British Columbia. After you told me to keep watch, I called my best friend in each one of them, somebody I knew I could trust, and asked them to let me know right away if this ever happened.

"Well, my old friend in Osoyoos, British Columbia, called me yesterday to say that two shopkeepers in the town had strangers come into their stores asking about you. Now, you mustn't worry; people in this part of the country don't take too kindly to nosy strangers, especially when they won't state their business or where they come from. So the people minding the stores just told them they were busy with their customers and couldn't help them, but they did accept the business cards the men handed them. My friend read me the telephone numbers that were listed on the cards, and I wrote them down for you. Here they are. My friend doesn't know where they went after that."

I slumped down into the nearest chair! Of course I'd been expecting this to happen. I realized that Klamm had few leads when he returned to Tembagapura to find us gone. But one of the surest leads he did possess involved the missionaries, who were the only outsiders ever allowed regularly into the village during the last years of our stay there. I guessed he had tried to track the Jacksons into the Amazon Basin, but I'd heard enough from the church officials about where they were going to surmise that this search had a low probability of success. Undoubtedly he also had his agents spend some time poking around in Bali, but I speculated he didn't get very far there either, because according to father, my mother's family is very influential and would be inaccessible behind the gates of their estate. And I suspect that the officials Klamm knew in Indonesia from his business dealings would have been too nervous about stepping on the toes of that family to be of much help to him.

Next, he had probably spent some time tracing father,

and almost certainly had found him, then put a permanent watch on his movements and also intercepted his communications. But, of course, I knew that Franklin could be of no help to Klamm even if he did locate him. So inevitably Klamm had turned his attention back to the Church of Jesus of Nazareth, and sent his agents to work their way from one community to the next in southern Alberta and British Columbia, where congregations and church buildings were located, looking for information as to our whereabouts.

I surmised that they would succeed in their mission, sooner or later. We girls are by now too well known here—in part because we're so well liked—for me to fool myself into believing otherwise. Of course, not everyone in the area where we live can be depended upon to report any such inquiries to us, and not to provide any information if asked. Someone is bound to give Klamm's agents what they were asking for, in all innocence. But one great piece of luck had fallen to us: His agents appear to have landed in Vancouver and started their search among the British Columbia congregations, proceeding eastwards. There are four congregations in the southern part of each province, and Osoyoos is the most westerly of them all. So the Osoyoos area was likely the first stop for the search party.

I checked the map. If they proceeded along the most direct route from Osoyoos, the hamlet of Longview would be their sixth stop. All the congregations are in small towns surrounded by fairly large farming and ranching spreads. I estimated that conducting a thorough check on each congregation would take at least two days, including travel to the next one. They had finished the first. If my calculations are correct, we have a minimum of eight days, and possibly as many as twelve, before they show up here.

Should we go on the run again? It's an option that must be weighed, since the timing is in our favor. Canada is a big country and we could travel eastwards over 2,500 miles without having to cross a national border. Even better, with our UK passports, almost certainly we could enter the United States as tourists again and then try to figure things out from there. If we leave almost immediately we would have a head start of at least a week. Our lawyers could take care of cleaning up after us.

Or perhaps we should just stay put. Let Klamm's agents find us and report back to him. So what? What could he do with that information? Canada is a country with an honest police force, and we sisters have the additional protection of a reliable private security firm. More security could be added if necessary. No, I definitely don't want to go on the run again, especially not on another sudden and nerve-wracking journey toward an unknown destination, where the game of hide-and-seek would just begin all over again! We'll stay and defy him to try to come and get us.

On the other hand, that option leaves all initiative solely in his hands. Having discovered our whereabouts he could just post a watch on us and formulate his plan to apprehend us at leisure. I have no idea what kind of resources he could call upon in devising such a plan. I assume that Klamm's business deal—in which we sisters were the prize—involved about a dozen very wealthy clients on the other end, each of whom was expecting to receive one of us as satisfaction in the bargain. What if they were all working hand-in-glove with Klamm to repossess the property that had gone missing?

If this were the case, he and they might have enough money and influence to circumvent our defenses at the college. After all, the police would not get involved if no crime had been committed. That forces us to rely on the private security firm. And if that firm were unable to prevent the crime of kidnapping from being committed, we sisters might be in the hands of our captors and long gone before the report of it reached the police.

I am so very tired of fearing Max Klamm! At some point

I'll have to tell the sisters what's just transpired, and then all their old anxieties, now largely in remission, will be rekindled. Over the preceding year, however, as my mind occasionally came to rest on Klamm's visage, and on the thought of him scouring the world's terrain for us like the relentless eye of the Dark Lord of Mordor, an alternative plan has been taking shape in my mind. I've been examining it day and night from every angle, looking for flaws, because I'm worried sick and can hardly sleep a wink.

I'm very glad now that I initiated the correspondence with my mother's family about a year ago, sending a series of letters and postcards to their villa in Jakarta. The family members have never met us girls, of course, but during father's visits with them in the first years after mother's death, he told me that he'd dropped various hints about some children who might be born later. In Tembagapura, just before his flight to Stockholm, father gave me a code word to use if it were ever necessary for me to contact the family, which would authenticate my identity to them.

When I introduced myself in my first letter to them as the oldest of Ina and Franklin's two children, conceived by IVF procedures from my mother's stored eggs after her death, I was careful to conceal my whereabouts and other information that might be dangerous for them to know. All I divulged was that I lived far from Indonesia but hoped to visit them sometime during the next year, if I could manage the travel; I made vague references to unspecified difficulties about my passport and visas. For a return address I used a commercial firm in the UK that provides mailboxes and a forwarding service.

They had written back expressing delight and joy at the prospect of a visit and offering to help in any way they could. I maintained the contact thereafter on a one-way basis, arranging for occasional postcards without return addresses to be mailed from various cities.

I've been mulling over our options countless times, reviewing my calculations about the likely progress of Klamm's agents toward Longview. I'm through running and hiding! I have no intention of fleeing in terror again, nor of sitting and waiting to be found and abducted by him. I'm going to launch a counterattack. I know Klamm all too well. Most likely one of us won't survive this encounter, but I'm prepared for the outcome, whatever it might be.

A few days later I called Io and Athena to a meeting among just the three of us. Irrespective of Io's continuing recalcitrance and the ever-growing psychological distance between the two of us, it would be foolish of me to forego the assistance that Io's quickness of mind and strategic sense can contribute to this venture. And Tina's counsel has become invaluable to me lately. Since leaving Tembagapura I've groomed her to be my second-in-command, a sister with whom I can share everything, my fears as well as my hopes. She's also handling very competently the administration of the sisters' investment trust that I delegated to her. She has full powers to draw upon the legal and financial resources at our disposal in my absence.

I briefed them on what I had learned from Mrs. Walter and sketched our options. "I'm going on a trip from which I might not return. If I'm successful, using other options won't be necessary, but as soon as I depart later tonight I want you to start making contingency arrangements and be ready to act on one of them if need be. I think you should both head to the law offices in Calgary. I'll place a call to you there just before my confrontation with Klamm. If you don't hear from me again within three hours of the first call, you are to start implementing immediately one of the other plans we've discussed, packing up the group and fleeing either to the United States or to another location in Canada."

Io was silent. Athena began to protest; I hugged and

kissed her, then said, "I'm leaving tonight."

Then I rang the satellite telephone number listed on the card left by the men who had made inquiries in Osoyoos, routing it over the Internet so that it was untraceable. I told the person who answered to contact Klamm immediately. "Listen carefully; I'll say this once only. Let Klamm know that Hera called and wants to meet him within four days at a place to be named later. I'll ring this number again in two days to give the location. After that he'll have two days to get there. If he doesn't arrive in time, I won't be there." I hung up before the person on the other end could say anything. Next I contacted my mother's family in Jakarta, telling my grandfather that I'd be arriving shortly and asking him to make another call for me.

I resolved to play the only card I held—nothing but a single, slender piece of information committed to memory, my only weapon to array against whatever forces Klamm and his henchmen were now preparing to assemble against us. I dared not even think about the imbalance in strength between us. Were I to do so, would I persevere?

My little piece of information was the list of thirty clients for Klamm's business deal, extracted, along with our passports, the cash, and other documents, from father's safe in Tembagapura on the day we fled. Presumably, father had insisted on having such a list because his signature was required on all of the contracts, and he wasn't prepared to sign them without knowing who the other parties were. There is no reason at all to think that Klamm suspects I've seen this list.

When I spoke to my grandfather in Jakarta, I asked him if he knew the patriarch of the extremely wealthy Trepartha-putri family—one of two Indonesians on Klamm's list of clients. My grandfather immediately confirmed that the two men were old friends. "I'm flying into Jakarta soon, grandfather, but first I must speak urgently with your friend, the senior Treparthaputri. Will you telephone him now, please, so that my call to him will be expected?"

About an hour later I rang the other man and delivered a simple message: "This is Hera; I believe my grandfather Sujana informed you I would be calling. Please listen carefully. I can arrange to put Max Klamm into your hands within a few days. Have your representatives meet me at my grandparents' home at 3pm in the afternoon on the day after tomorrow." Then I hung up and left for Calgary airport.

Shortly after my arrival in Jakarta my grandfather and I held a meeting at my family's villa with Treparthaputri's eldest son and a few of his flunkies. I was wearing a *burqa* so that my entire face, except for my eyes, was concealed. I asked them to provide me with a cell phone preprogrammed to call another cell phone that the son would answer day or night during the next 24 hours, and which his agents would be carrying on the day on which the operation would be carried out. I told him that I expected to lure Klamm to a well-known office building in Jakarta two days hence, in the afternoon. I didn't have to tell him to get his agents ready to greet Klamm!

"There's one more thing," I announced. "How much did you pay Klamm in advance for the product he was supposed to deliver to you?" The son hesitated. I raised my voice. "Come on, this isn't a game. I know you paid a lot of money up front. How much?"

He replied, "Nine million euros."

I came back at once. "I want 50 percent of anything you recover from him before he dies, after deducting your deposit. Agreed?"

My instincts were right. It had previously occurred to me that Treparthaputri's son might be at a disadvantage in this conversation, because in his culture an older male was unlikely to engage in bargaining with a young woman who was a complete stranger to him. But however unpleasant this new experience was for him, the thought of repairing his standing in his father's eyes—for he was the one who had paid Klamm—seemed to wash away its bitter taste instantly. After some hesitation, he muttered, "Of course."

I pressed him. "My grandfather is a witness. Swear on your family's honor that you will carry out our agreement."

He replied, looking at the old man, "I give you my word, sir."

After the meeting I called the number of the cell phone that had been carried by Klamm's agents in British Columbia. As I expected would happen, Klamm answered. He was in the overseas business lounge at the Vancouver airport.

"This is Hera." He started to express some pleasantries but I cut him off. "Listen carefully. I'll meet you this Thursday afternoon at 5pm in Jakarta at the reception desk in BP Indonesia's office tower."

"How interesting. So you've been in Indonesia all along?"

"I assumed you would have guessed that my sisters and I never left the country, because you knew my mother's family could shelter us in a place you couldn't find. But I know that you'll never stop trying to track us down, and we're tired of hiding. We want to leave Indonesia and start to live normal lives at long last."

He interjected. "So how did you pick up the information that my assistants were making inquiries about you in far-off Canada?"

I was all ready for the question, but I hesitated a bit before replying. "We knew that you would figure out that the missionary couple must have helped us escape from Papua, which of course they did. We've kept in touch with their church, out of gratitude, and someone from there just called us to say that men were looking for us in Canada. I want to make a deal. I'll tell you what the deal is when we meet. Goodbye."

Klamm yelled, "Wait. Give me a number where I can reach you. What if my plane is delayed or something?"

I replied, "No. Just be there," and hung up. This time I didn't attempt to conceal my location, since I wanted him to know that I was placing my call to him from Indonesia.

When one is engaged in a duel with a deadly adversary, it's prudent to speculate on what's likely to be going on in his mind, so that one can try to anticipate his strategies and plot a series of countermoves in advance. It's no different from playing chess—except that this is no game! So I set myself up as a detective inside the distant Klamm's brain and watched him ruminate.

First, he evaluates briefly the possibility that this is a trap, but his mind won't let him dwell very long on this line of thought. It would have required an alteration to his entire being for him to suppose that we innocent and dreamy girls could be his equal in cunning or treachery. Now he turns his attention to my father, and reviewing the record of the long watch kept on my father's outside communications at the Cambridge clinic, including the frequent calls to his in-laws' residences in Jakarta and Bali, Klamm has additional reason to conclude that his lost property is being hidden in Indonesia.

So, he opines, there's no reason not to take my news at face value. 'It's entirely plausible that the Canadian trail is a complete dead-end and that the sisters never left Indonesia. After all, the Sujana family could easily have arranged to hide the sisters where I'd never find them, probably somewhere on the island of Bali, where they own huge tracts of land. There's little risk in making a quick trip in and out of Jakarta.'

On Thursday afternoon I called Io and Athena at the law offices in Calgary prior to entering the BP Indonesia building shortly before the appointed hour. Again I had outfitted myself in a *burqa*, this time using the Afghan version of the head-to-toe covering for Muslim women that has a net-like screen over the eyes. There was an ambulance parked outside the building. Precisely at 5pm Klamm approached the door on the sidewalk; despite the obvious plastic surgery done to his face, I recognized him instantly by his build and gait.

My hands were sweating profusely under my robe, but I managed to press the dial button on the cell phone beneath my cloak without lifting the instrument to my face. The other phone rang inside the ambulance. As Klamm proceeded through the revolving doors into the lobby, the rear of the ambulance swung open and two burly men in attendants' uniforms jumped out, carrying a stretcher. Klamm had paused halfway across the nearly deserted lobby, facing away from me, glancing from side to side, and as the two men passed me I pointed him out.

Before Klamm reached the reception desk, they were behind him. I watched as one jabbed a needle containing some kind of drug into his neck and he dropped to the floor like a stone. They bundled him onto the stretcher and in less than a minute were back in the ambulance, which roared away with sirens screeching. I left the building and rang Athena and Io, who were waiting at the Calgary law office for my second call.

Later, grandfather asked his friend's son for an account of what happened thereafter. We were told that in a distant outbuilding on the family's country estate, they had tortured Klamm at a leisurely pace until he revealed the numbers for his Swiss bank accounts. Treparthaputri's son immediately dispatched his agents to Zurich where they found roughly 60 million euros on deposit. They put €25 million into my account at a nearby bank. They took the rest to the airport and called home before boarding their private jet. The elder Treparthaputri sent a package containing €5 million to my grandfather as a token of gratitude.

The son's instructions to his agents on the final disposition of the evidence were firm. The family did not wish anything to be found that could be traced back to them, and it was suggested that disposal far from the island of Java would be preferred. So they had loaded Klamm's broken but still sentient body into a small passenger jet and flown him to Jayapura, on the coast of the Pacific, the easternmost city in Papua Province and thus the easternmost point in Indonesia. There they transferred him into a float plane for the short ride to the Mamberamo River delta, well known for its crocodile population, and fed him to the grateful inhabitants.

After spending a few more days with my grandparents I returned to Alberta.

MARCH 2032

The last six months in southwestern Alberta have been uneventful, something all the sisters desperately needed after they learned of my perilous journey to Jakarta. When I returned from that trip, even Io joined in the celebration of its success and the brilliant strategy we devised together that had made it possible. Finally, we could live and move about openly!

This January most of the sisters enrolled as special students at the University of Calgary and pursued a variety of advanced subjects, gaining admission to many upper-level courses with outstanding performances on qualifying examinations. We've been bringing Marco to the college for extended stays, although we won't take him away permanently from the farm until our final departure. All the sisters, now not excluding Io when she's in the mood, dote on him and compete in accelerating his early education. Few two-year-olds in all of history could have been bathed in so much pure affection.

Finally free of all constraints, we've recently completed the planning for our next move. We decided that our choice of habitat would be confined to the Western Hemisphere, since that region is still among the most stable areas on the planet. But we also realized—subconsciously more than by explicit rationale—that we had come to prefer a degree of isolation, partly because that's how we had grown up. Most of the sisters have conceded that their early experiences have affected them more than they might admit, even to themselves, and among other things all want to stay together for at least awhile longer. In part, we're also feeling the sense of our own distinctiveness more strongly with each passing year, and we figured that this would be more easily dealt with in a sparsely populated location than in a dense urban setting.

But the type of isolation we desired was not one of remoteness, for living in that mountain village in Indonesia also had given us a feeling of being cut off from ordinary life. We want to be easily connected with the rest of the world and to see a lot of the world go by us. The British West Indies seem to satisfy most of these criteria. The annual and seasonal temperature range is similar to what we grew up with in Tembagapura, with the added attraction of ocean beaches and breezes. In particular, the Turks and Caicos Islands, lying less than 60 miles southeast of the Bahamas and a short distance north of Haiti, strike us as being an almost ideal location.

This chain of thirty small islands, all together totalling just 260 square miles in area, only eight of which are inhabited, once had been part of the government of the Bahamas. Its citizens voluntarily had assumed the status of a self-governing British overseas territory in the late twentieth century and had retained this status ever since. The territory has remained attractive to many business owners on account of the more relaxed banking and taxation rules for which nations in that region are well known.

The permanent population of the Islands has always been relatively small—according to the histories we consulted—although we were persuaded that the annual tourist influx must lend a busy and cosmopolitan air to some parts of the country. Outside the hurricane season, the weather is mild and constant, although in recent decades a gnawing worry about sea-level rise has driven some important property owners and investors away. So when we sisters began expressing interest in various properties on different islands in the chain, we found good prices, eager sellers, and quality offerings.

For our group residence we've managed to lease the facilities of a bankrupt singles holiday resort on Providenciales Island, where most of the tourist traffic lands. It's comprised of many nicely appointed individual bungalows and some larger buildings, all easily fenced for security. We intend to construct our molecular biology labs and other research facilities there as well.

And since some of the sisters have become addicted to horses, we're going to ship the Thoroughbreds and Dutch Warmbloods they've purchased in Alberta to Providenciales ("Provo," as it is commonly known in the region), and have stables and a training ring built there. For exercise they can ride their mounts through the shallow surf along the beach. And we just struck a deal to lease large tracts of government-owned land on two of the uninhabited islands—East and West Caicos—where nature reserves already exist, and where we will construct our planned primate sanctuaries. We've also added to our portfolio a small office building and a number of private residences on Grand Turk Island—in Cockburn Town, the country's capital—for conducting our legal and business affairs.

01 OCTOBER 2032

Renovations to the former resort have been completed, and today the band of sisters said our fond farewells to the people of southwestern Alberta, who sheltered and befriended us in our hour of need. No one, including the leaders of the Church of Jesus of Nazareth, made mention on this occasion of the original plan for us twelve prospective converts to return to Indonesia as missionaries. Both they and we have enjoyed each other's company immensely. I'm pleased that many of them have benefited from the financial resources we brought to the local community. The rest of the sisters and Marco are flying directly to Provo and will begin furnishing our new quarters as they wait for my return from my longer journey via the UK.

03 OCTOBER 2032

Upon landing at Heathrow I called Franklin's law firm, using the same code word he had given me to identify myself to my family in Jakarta. As I expected, instructions had been left with the firm to reveal his whereabouts to anyone knowing the code. When I arrived in Cambridge at the clinic's reception desk, I learned that Franklin had left standing orders with the staff to the effect that if ever anyone calling herself "Hera" telephoned, he was to be paged throughout the building and grounds at once. Or, unlikely as it seemed, if such a person should show up unannounced at the facility, she was to be ushered to him immediately.

So on that day, in late 2032, I was guided to the hallway leading to his room. Making my way unescorted to his doorway, which was open, I stood at the entrance and called his name.

"Franklin. It's Hera."

(Franklin's Journal) I was sitting facing the window in my ground-floor room at the psychiatric clinic, basking in the late afternoon sunshine and reading some current papers in neurogenetics. I'd felt quite a bit better for some time now, but saw no good reason to quit the clinic on that account. The loss of my wife and more recently my daughters still oppressed me greatly, and I wasn't nearly ready to face life again on the outside if I had to do so entirely without them. I'd settled into a comfortable routine at the clinic and still

saw some doctors occasionally. The clinic's administrative officer has grown accustomed to my prompt and handsome payments for its services and had no intention of evicting me. So I had resolved just to carry on, waiting and hoping against hope to be reunited with them.

(Hera's Journal) He whirled around in his office chair and just looked at me in stunned silence for a few moments. Then he burst from the chair and rushed to me, embracing me with such force that I gasped. He released me and apologized. "Did I hurt you? Hera, Hera, Hera. You've come back! You've come back to me! How I have longed for this day! I had almost given up all hope of ever seeing you again. And your sisters? Are they with you? Are they all well? How is Io? Where have you been all these years?" The questions tumbled out of him without ceasing until I spoke.

"They're all well, Franklin, including Io. There's a baby boy, too, named Marco. They're not here in England now, but you and I are going to join them, if that's what you want to do."

"Of course that's what I want! I've been dreaming of this day ever since I set foot on that accursed airplane in Tembagapura on my way to Stockholm. I'm ready to leave at once!"

"We can leave soon, perhaps by tomorrow. But first we must make the arrangements to terminate your residence here. Then we should talk about the family foundation, and visit your lawyers here in London before we leave. My sisters are waiting for us in the Turks and Caicos Islands—the place you chose, in a way. We found out from our own lawyers that you've owned property on Grand Turk Island in the name of the Sujana Foundation ever since you set it up twenty-five years ago. We've bought more property there in recent years; some of it is registered in the name of the Puncak Jaya Primate Foundation, which we've incorporated. We've also begun …."

He broke in impatiently. "Wait. Where have you been since you left Tembagapura? How did you manage to evade Klamm? I'm sure he flooded the world with his agents in an attempt to track you down."

"We've been in Canada the entire time. I'll fill you in on the details during our airplane journey."

"All right, Hera; I'll wait for most of it, but please tell me right now about Klamm. Is he still hunting for all of you—and for me? I've felt so bad—crushed, really—on account of failing in my duty to protect you from him. It's the main reason I admitted myself to the clinic here. I was overwhelmed by a sense of guilt and shame. And I've been struggling with that guilt every day since I last left Tembagapura."

"He's dead. We don't have to worry about him anymore. I'll tell you all about it later. We even managed to turn the tables on him in the end and appropriate some of his ill-gotten funds for ourselves. We're using those monies to build and stock our primate sanctuary on West Caicos Island."

"Thank God for that!" He hesitated, then asked gingerly, "Do you have any plans to continue the scientific work of the Sujana Foundation?"

"Yes, I think so, although we'll have to discuss very carefully what you and we want to do. A group of the sisters has some training in molecular biology, at least as much as they could achieve through self-directed learning plus some university-level tutoring. But they know that they need advanced supervision now, and they want to get it from you."

"That's wonderful! I can't wait to start working with them. We'll need to build research laboratory facilities, of course. By the way, did you know that the collection of embryos donated to our foundation by the Group of 300 have been stored since 2025 in a secure cryopreservation facility that I arranged to have constructed just outside Cockburn Town on Grand Turk Island?"

"I guessed as much. I knew that you couldn't store such material in England or another country in Europe or North America, because the laws there might have prevented you from retaining ownership of it, or experimenting on it. And you wouldn't have been allowed to take it anywhere else, either."

(Franklin's Journal) For awhile our conversation lapsed and we just sat there together, holding hands and gazing at each other. I was overcome with emotion. She had been born almost a day sooner than the next in line among the sisters. Although I wasn't expert in reproductive biology, I understood from my reading that the first-born among siblings often assumes a leadership role, and I marveled at her commanding presence as she sat opposite me. My senior daughter, as I once baptized her, had become a self-assured, articulate, and clear-headed young woman, whose quick intelligence and fierce sense of purpose burned through her strong gaze. She presented herself as a stylish business-woman, although one who preferred pantsuits to dresses or skirts.

Her beautiful skin and natural coloration needed no makeup and she wore almost no jewelry, only an expensive wristwatch and a necklace with a pendant containing a lapis lazuli stone in a silver setting. Her spoken language contained snatches of at least a dozen tongues, as her mind searched for the best word to express a thought or observation.

(Hera's Journal) He broke the silence. "I've had plenty of time to think about the tragedies that befell us during these last sad years, dearest Hera. After a year had passed here at the clinic, I came to the conclusion that most likely I'd never see you or your sisters again. I feared that Klamm had caught up with you and had carried through with his unspeakable plan, a plan I was powerless to thwart. Just the idea of it—the idea

that all of you were now scattered to the ends of the earth, held in forcible confinement as sex slaves for the families of the super-rich—almost drove me to suicide. Only the slim prospect that I was wrong, that somehow you had managed to evade him, stayed my hand and kept my hopes alive."

"I'm sorry I didn't contact you earlier. It was only very recently"—I allowed myself a small white lie here—"that the burden of the danger from Klamm finally was lifted from our shoulders. I came as soon as I could thereafter."

"I understand. You were right, of course. Klamm would have assumed that you could not have escaped without my permission and assistance, and for all we know he had a watch posted on this clinic, perhaps even had its communications monitored. You couldn't take the chance of trying to contact me. And I finally figured out, after you had gone, after it was too late then, how much your sisters trusted you, how much confidence they had in your good judgment. All of that trust and confidence has been justified. You saved them from a terrible fate, a fate worse than death, because of your insight, courage, and intelligence. I'm so proud of you."

I smiled and leaned over to kiss him and he continued. "I realized all this when I had time to think during my recuperation in this lovely and peaceful setting. And I made a promise to Heaven that if ever I should be granted the joy of seeing you all again, alive and well, I would forthwith entrust the leadership of our family foundation to you, the one among the sisters who has earned the right to carry on after me. I intend to keep that promise. Before we leave today I'll call my London lawyers and give them the necessary instructions for drawing up the papers. I'll stay on as your advisor and a Board of Directors member, and I assume that you'll ask at least some of your sisters to become part of the Board. But you will now have the authority to direct its programs and allocate its substantial resources. Will you take on this responsibility, Hera?"

"Yes, I will. Now perhaps we should start getting you ready to go. You'll want to pack up some things to take with you, and leave instructions for the rest to be crated and shipped to Providenciales. Then we'll go to London and see the foundation's lawyers. We should do all this as quickly as possible. My sisters have spent many years wondering and worrying about you, and they're waiting for a telephone call from me with good news. Let's both call them now."

The next day we signed the papers putting me in charge of the Sujana Foundation, the assets of which stood then at 30 billion euros. Its original 30% stake in Wollstone Corporation—now a company with a market capitalization of almost 100 billion euros—had been reduced to 10% through portfolio diversification. After nearly a quarter-century in the hands of competent fund managers, plus reinvestment of income and regular dividends from Wollstone, the foundation had seen its capital appreciate substantially.

The foundation's charter, which specified that income from its assets should be used to promote scientific research and related programs in the interest of the future of humanity, was amended so as to include financial responsibility for the sisters' primate sanctuary. Franklin wanted to symbolize his joy in being reunited with his daughters in other ways, too, so he transferred half the value of his personal investment trust, amounting to 500 million euros, to the trust account held jointly by all the sisters. I expect this capital will also appreciate rapidly in the hands of the group of sisters who have become adept players in the currency, commodities, and securities markets.

§ § §

Once we were comfortably seated on the plane, en route from Heathrow to Miami, I turned to him and said, "I read through your *Memorandum to the Group of 300* while we sisters were fleeing from Tembagapura three years ago. During the intervening years I've been looking through the academic literature in neurosciences—at least as much of it as I could follow. I've been trying to figure out what you did to us, and why."

"I'm glad we can finally talk openly about this, Hera. You know that I felt I could only explain what your mother and I hoped to achieve once you were a bit older."

"What I read there says that you and my mother designed us to be part of a social experiment. You and your friends in the Group of 300, that is. I've been wrestling with this knowledge ever since. Why did you think you had a right to do such a thing to your own children?"

"My goodness, you don't waste any time getting to the point, do you?"

He laughed, a bit nervously, and I allowed myself to laugh with him so as to defuse the tension; there were things I needed to know.

He continued. "Before the age of genetics, and going far back in history, parents always have done everything in their power to assure the success of their offspring in life—just as all other animals do, by the way. Much of the time they were just obeying their instincts; they didn't even realize why they were doing whatever they did.

"Since you've done a lot of reading in neurology, you've already learned that adequate nutrition is a key factor in infant growth, including—especially!—in the early development of the brain. So parents strove to give their young a proper diet, sometimes even at the cost of their own health. When the science of molecular biology finally arrived, a lot of people reached the conclusion that another powerful tool was available to help assure their children's success in life."

"You referred to brain development, didn't you? It seems

to me that the human brain isn't just another bodily organ. The brain is what gives each of us what's called a mind. Doesn't that make a difference?"

"Of course it does, but here again all you have to do is look at the past, before the age of genetics. The mind only develops properly if the right kind of 'nutritious' environment is provided—a supply of ideas and disciplined training that we refer to as education. So parents and societies have tried to provision that supply through schooling. But listen, Hera, don't forget, too, that a lot of genetics applications are being carried out in order to overcome serious deficits in normal brain functions. Think about the advances we've made in correcting the terrible memory deficits that used to afflict Alzheimer's patients. Through targeted manipulations using gene therapies, we've been able to restore in those patients a lot of the normal brain functions that had been destroyed by neurodegenerative diseases, essentially making old age a lot more pleasant and rewarding for them."

"But still you can't deny, Franklin …."

"Wait, let me finish my thought. You're particularly concerned about what's being done to the brains of children, especially before they become aware of selfhood. I'm guessing that you're troubled about the lack of informed consent in such cases. I agree, that's a possible problem. But try to look at the matter from the perspective of those children who suffer severe, debilitating deficits in brain function. Take the curse of autism. Until quite recently more than ninety percent of autistic children never grew up to lead any kind of normal life at all, and even the rest—the high-functioning autistics—remained damaged in many ways. Child rearing has been a nightmare for the parents of these children.

"Autism is part of a genetically driven family of diseases; as few as a dozen powerful genes are implicated, and when they don't work as they should, the consequences for both the children and their families are truly devastating. But the genetic errors responsible for these diseases occur very early in the neurological development of the child, long before the sense of self emerges. Indeed, these errors block the normal sense of self from *ever* developing! So shouldn't those who have studied these conditions strive to repair the damage, if they can, at the embryonic stage of fetal development?"

"I'm glad you used that example, because I've long wanted to talk to you about autism for other reasons. Themis and Moira were born with Asperger's Syndrome, weren't they? They're what are called high-functioning autistics, aren't they? That's why they were taken away from our compound in Tembagapura before they were two years old, correct?"

He paused before replying and as he did so I ordered us some wine from the flight attendant.

"Yes, the two of them were diagnosed as having Asperger's—which very much surprised me, I must admit, because that disorder usually occurs almost exclusively in males. The clinical symptoms became apparent late in their first year. I had them removed to the satellite facility we maintained in Timika, and I brought in specialists by the carload to treat them. I spared no expense; you must believe me. The treatment regimes had become very sophisticated by that time, and significant improvement was achievable if intensive treatment was begun very early and kept up indefinitely. Pets have been shown to be very helpful in the treatment regimes, and that's why, when they reached age eight and were returned to your compound permanently, you observed them bringing their dogs with them. By then they had become much, much better. But as you're aware, I think, some of the emotional deficits they still suffer cannot be repaired."

"As I understand it, two out of twelve is a very high ratio for this disease. As the *Memorandum* explains, you engineered our prefrontal cortex; as I recall, there's even a mention of the risk of autism in that document. So isn't it safe to assume that what you did to us caused this to happen to Moira and Themis, who were just the unlucky ones?"

He didn't respond for what seemed like an eternity. "Yes. I accept that charge—not as a certainty, but as a strong possibility. The genes that are implicated in autism are part of the large ensemble of genes responsible for the neurological wiring of both the various components of the prefrontal cortex and the neurons connecting them to other regions of the brain. Your mother and I knew we were taking certain risks with the protocol we designed. We worked day and night for years, trying to ensure that we had covered off the worst of the unintended outcomes that might occur. But yes, we realized that we couldn't guarantee we had eliminated them entirely. In the end we thought that the remaining risks were worth taking."

I looked directly into his eyes now. "Exactly as I thought. You took calculated risks with our minds. How could you possibly think you had a right to do such a thing? We were destined to become fully conscious beings, Franklin, although—I suspect—not to figure out that we had been engineered as part of an experiment. Did I guess right? We sisters weren't supposed to see the *Memorandum*, were we? I'm surmising that the program was laid out so as to work best if the 'subjects' weren't apprised of its intent. We were supposed to be just like your run-of-the-mill lab rats, blissfully unaware of the larger purposes we were serving. Except that things fell apart three years ago, didn't they? And because I told you that we were going to make a run for it on our own, you thought you had to leave a copy of the *Memorandum* for me, since I now had to figure things out for myself."

"I confess that your mother and I weren't intending to disclose the purpose of our program to the children whose genes we engineered. We assumed that to do so would be counter-productive in that it would cause them to focus on the gene manipulations rather than on accomplishing the program's goals. It's a bit like the situation we discussed long ago, when you asked me why I delayed so long in telling all of you that you are full sisters. I wanted you to concentrate on your studies, not on competing with each other for my attention and emotional support.

"Perhaps I shouldn't have left the copy of the *Memorandum* for you after all. Clearly you are bitter and angry toward me on this account."

"I'm sorry, Franklin, and I apologize for my tone. I *have* been both bitter and angry in the past, but I'm trying to get beyond those feelings and to look ahead. Try to forget how I spoke just now."

"Please, step back for a moment and just look at yourself, Hera, as I see you, and as I'm sure others must: You're a creative, resourceful, talented—and very courageous— woman. So are all of your sisters. Even Moira and Themis developed amazing skills and began to function pretty well in normal human company by the time they were teenagers. How can you overlook all this, and also the other things you read in the *Memorandum*? You referred—rather sarcastically, it was obvious—to the group of sisters as 'lab rats' and to the protocol your mother and I developed as an 'experiment.' Yes, we designed you, to be special, very special; to be able to go out into the world and help save human society from its downward spiral into chaos and the collapse of scientific civi- lization. Is that so unworthy a goal in your eyes? Am I supposed to regard myself and your mother as some kind of criminals for having had this dream?"

Now it was my turn to pause. Finally I replied, "Not crim- inals, but perhaps just a bit naïve. What we refer to as our mind originates in our brain-based capacities for thinking and feeling—and, above all, for *knowing* that each one of us, as a distinctive individual, is thinking and feeling. During every waking moment—and differently in our dream-sleep—we're able to brood upon our own self-awareness, that is, on our consciousness of the unstoppable flow of time and experiences. I do this constantly. That's what having a mind means to me. It's being conscious of the feeling of thinking and feeling. This is personal—and very, very private. Or, to use another word I love, it's ineffable. I'm not convinced that anyone should attempt to engineer this feeling or to make it part of some program of social transformation."

"Of course we all have a subjective feeling of self, Hera. But really, when you look around at your fellow humans, what do you see? Except for a fairly small percentage of outliers, we're pretty much all the same and behave in similar ways. Our minds are an integral part of this sameness—what we call normalcy. And these minds of ours are never static, either. At least in what we call modern civilization, most people are committed to making things better, a little bit at a time, including the ways in which we behave.

"Think about—I don't know, take any example—the way most of us believe we should treat the criminals in our midst, or domestic animals for that matter. Today, what most of us regard as appropriate behavior in this context is utterly different from what our ancestors thought a mere hundred or two hundred years ago. I'm referring to what we *feel* intuitively in our minds about such things. The way we feel inside us changes over time and is what prompts us to alter the way we behave."

"Fine, I grant you the point, but those changes in feeling weren't engineered by anyone. They came about through a social process of people interacting and talking, preparing studies and offering reasons, sometimes battling with each other in political or courtroom debates."

"What you've just described is actually a passive form of social engineering; in changing our minds, the way we feel about important matters, we necessarily change how our brains work. Consider for a moment the massive rewiring in the brain's prefrontal cortex during adolescence, something that became widely recognized only about thirty years ago. I'm referring to what we neuroscientists describe as the mind's faculty of judgment, the part of the brain we use to make decisions. People were astonished to learn that between the ages of twelve to eighteen or so, there is, first, a huge spurt of new wiring, and second, a selective culling of neurons and axons—specifically, of the ones that aren't being used.

"The point is, although this incredible, late phase of development is initiated by our genes, the process is completed successfully only if the person's social environment is supportive. Which means, only if there is abundant positive feedback for intelligent decision-making—and the reverse as well, of course. In other words, those aspects of the brain that we depend upon for good judgment need exercise, just as our muscles do."

"All right, I do see your point. What's called socialization in childhood development is a kind of engineering of the brain, and it's possible because the human brain is unique in nature, since it continues to reconfigure itself so long after birth. Human societies have always tried to shape and channel behavior into a kind of instinctive decision-making, so that individuals automatically follow established norms. As modern society evolved, this traditional channeling was replaced by extended schooling. In effect, this is a disciplining of the brain according to explicit rather than implicit norms. And your neurosciences tell us that the brain, configured by its genes, is not just receiving and storing instructions from outside. Its genes are collaborating with the effort and actively supporting it; in fact, in the absence of that collaboration, the social training wouldn't work."

"Precisely! So you see, from this perspective both parents and the societies they live in have been working hard to mould their children's minds from time immemorial. Your mother and I simply were taking this old effort one step further—applying what was learned about brain functions in the explosion of knowledge in our field that began fifty years ago. It's true that the two of us planned careful interventions in gene function, beginning at the embryonic stage, but as you know, I didn't stop there. I created a rich environment for learning—what you once called your 'tropical hothouse' in Tembagapura. The key to brain development is the ongoing interactions among gene functions and social environment, not gene manipulation by itself."

"I accept all this, Franklin. But what you fail to understand is how it *feels* to me to be spoken of—by you, my father—as a factor in an experiment. I hear you; I take in your words of explanation; I also recall my reading and Internet searches during our years in Alberta, and the discussions we sisters had there after I encouraged all of them to read the *Memorandum*. What I'm trying to tell you now is that your thoughts and your words—so dispassionate, calm, clear, well articulated—sound somehow strange to me. It's as if I'm listening to them over a poor-quality telephone line, distorted, broken-up, interrupted by static.

"How can I explain this to you? It's as if my sisters and I are standing close to you, but separated by a divide. That's it; think of what we've been engaged in here as a conversation between two people across a backyard fence. They're good neighbors and good friends, and the fence itself doesn't seem to mean anything to one of them—I'm referring to you—apart from demarcating the property line. But to me it marks a chasm across which I cannot stretch. And do you know why? Because unlike the friendly neighbors, who could conceivably exchange positions on the fence line without changing their relationship to each other, you and I cannot do this. You designed me; I cannot do the same. That fact polarizes our relation to each other; no matter how often we change positions, it stays the same."

"I agree, Hera; you and I cannot switch roles. That is certain. But again, in another sense, our relationship is just a small part of a much larger historical process. Remember when I observed a few minutes ago how people's behavior toward criminals and animals had changed drastically over the centuries? We're striving for the betterment of humanity, slowly but surely, first by hit-and-miss methods and now with greater precision, thanks to the science of genetics.

"History isn't reversible, however, and I don't think very many people would want to go back to earlier times even if they could—except for some of the religious fundamentalists I've read about. So, my answer to your analogy with the fence is, you're right, we can't trade positions—nor can any generation trade places with its forebears. Sometime in the future your generation will go on to make additional changes, hopefully for the better. Then your own children and their own further descendants will stand in the same relation to you as you do with regard to me! It's not a real fence that separates you and me, only a symbolic one. After another few generations come and go, it will fade from memory."

Once again I paused, not knowing how to reply immediately, turning over his words in my mind. "I confess, you're a first-rate interlocutor, Franklin! You make me think hard, and that's good. Let me put my response this way: What if I were to tell you that I've come to feel disconnected from the program you described in the *Memorandum?* That recalling it to mind leaves me cold and indifferent? What if I were to tell you that ever since childhood I've been becoming more and more conscious of feeling estranged from all of the most pressing concerns in the world around me? So now I ask you: Should I regard this aspect of my mind as a *therapeutic* problem? If I did so, would you consider it to be curable?"

He couldn't disguise the look of alarm on his face. "I would regard such a thing as nothing short of catastrophic, Hera. I've just turned over control of the Sujana Foundation to you, so that you could carry on the life's work that united your mother and me. I still believe what we did was right. And I want to resume my own role in this project, now that we'll soon all be back together. Are you saying you won't allow me to draw upon the foundation's resources any longer to advance my cause?"

"No, I'm not saying that." I had trapped myself. I had gotten carried away with the rhetoric of my own argument and didn't notice where it was leading me. I do feel this estrangement from the world's obsessions, deeply, at the core, but I'm also happy with what I find of myself inside me; I am *satisfied* with what I am and have become! Under no circumstances would I want to be 'changed' through treatment! *That* was what I was trying to get at a moment ago.

"Okay, Franklin, I can see that what I said is misleading. I wanted to make another point entirely and got sidetracked. About the fence, which is purely symbolic for you: It's much different for me, and that's what I was really trying to say. I've studied your *Memorandum* carefully, I've asked myself countless times how I feel about it, and I've often discussed it with my sisters. This is what's happened to me: I feel as if I've taken control over whatever there is in me that makes me different—the difference that you engineered into me. Whatever it is—and you would realize, of course, what I'm saying, why I cannot pin it down precisely—I feel that I now have assimilated it into my being and made it my own. In a way, I suppose what I'm postulating is that I have wrested away from you what you did, and what you intended, and have stamped it with my own identity."

He hesitated and then smiled. "I think I really do understand what you're getting at. I admit I never thought about what might happen in those terms, but now that I do, I see that what you say makes sense. After all, the gene manipulations I focused on certainly do have a role in engendering the sense of self in all of us, and, as such, they also play a defining role in the larger collective sense of human identity that must be closely related to it—what we call the feeling of empathy. What you're saying, in effect, is that in forging your sense of self, you were forced, in a manner of speaking, to integrate the changes I engineered with the normal human structures that had evolved previously in the human brain.

"Of course! Now it seems clear to me: What I did at the level of gene expression *in your brain*, you then had to integrate on a personal, subjective level *in your mind!* I knew this, actually, in an abstract sense, but until now, until speaking of these things with you, I don't think I ever grasped it concretely, as it were."

"That's it! Working it out with you has clarified things for me as well. I had to think hard in order to arrive at this point—I remember being terribly confused, being whipsawed back and forth inside my mind many times during my earlier years. By the time I was thirteen or fourteen, I had found the mental strength inside me to force together the bits and pieces of my self into something whole. Now I realize what I was doing then: I was appropriating your work for myself. It isn't yours anymore, Franklin. And the process isn't over yet. I have a vague yet quite firm sense that I'm being led down a path made for me—and my sisters—alone. I don't know where it's leading; there is an intimation of twists and turns ahead that prevent me from seeing the terminus. Only one thing is clear: I must follow it ...." I paused and looked out the window before turning back to him with a smile. "... But not just now. We're about to land in Miami!"

§   §   §

(05 October) Tonight there was a joyous reunion at the family's compound, set along a lovely stretch of secluded beachfront on Providenciales Island and encircled on land by a secure perimeter fence. I reintroduced Franklin to his now grown-up daughters, who tend to congregate in three subgroups, defined both by their differing intellectual interests and the practical needs of our collective.

"I am part of the group of four who specialize in business transactions, financial analysis, and portfolio management for the investments in our hands. Included here is our chief financial officer, Tina, as well as Tammy and Hex.

"The four interested in the sciences, especially biochemistry and molecular biology, are Gaia, Pan, Percy and Rhea, all of whom are keenly looking forward to being trained by their famous father." Franklin fawned over them, overjoyed at the prospect of superintending their further education. I've never seen him look so happy—after his many years of personal agony—and watching this scene filled me with joy.

"Ari, Moira and Themis are the sisters who have turned out to be the best mathematicians and statisticians, and they have also branched out into applied fields such as computer programming, encryption, and electronic security." Io had already had a chat with her father, where she told him that she had refused to attach herself to any faction, preferring to dabble in whatever happened to interest her at the moment. Moira and Pandora make up Io's small band of followers, whose rejection of my leadership position is now muted but still alive. "And of course there's our very precious Marco, now into his third year and growing fast.

"At the moment, our collective passion is the construction and stocking of our primate sanctuary. Our acquisitions program started while we were still living in Alberta, although we won't take the first deliveries until next month.

We've built temporary quarters for seventy animals within the family compound, and are in the process of hiring trained staff away from some of the world's leading zoos. Now that the foundation's huge resources are to be at our disposal, construction work on the first permanent sanctuary, located on West Caicos Island, can be speeded up. Our plan is to concentrate on the various species of great apes, all of whom are by now either extinct or threatened with imminent extinction in the wild—both lowland and mountain gorillas, chimpanzees, bonobos, and orangutans.

"When anyone asks us to explain this obsession, most of us simply say that we sense a mysterious yet overwhelming bond of kinship with them. We were delighted when we found out that the Malay word for the orangutan, whose scientific name is *Pongo pygmaeus*, translates as 'person of the forest.' We like to use the German term for this whole set of species, which is *Menschenaffen*, literally, 'human apes.' We've started to acquire our stock from a number of sources, including surplus zoo animals and those released from confinement in laboratory research facilities. But most of our purchases are arranged through agents operating in various parts of the world, who are either rescuing the apes from captivity in private homes, or extracting the last remnants of wild populations from the African and Asian jungles, just ahead of the poachers and purveyors of bush meat. We don't ask about the methods used by these agents, and the premium prices we offer assure us of a steady supply."

13 NOVEMBER 2032

I convened the first meeting of the newly constituted Sujana Foundation. As a family-owned foundation the board is drawn exclusively from our ranks, and is now composed of myself, Franklin, Ari, Gaia, Io, Pan and Tina. We struck two main committees, one responsible for asset management, and the other to superintend the construction and furnishing of a state-of-the-art suite of molecular biology laboratories within the compound.

Franklin told the other board members for the first time—only I knew earlier—about the stock of frozen embryos from the Group of 300 that had been stored for close to ten years in a building on Grand Turk Island. When our own labs are finished, the cryopreservation units will be transferred to our compound in Provo. I remained silent during this time and deliberately allowed Franklin to control the discussions at the meeting. I want the scientists among the sisters to have advanced training from him, and I want the most modern facilities available to be housed within the compound here. Everyone was delighted that we will soon be expanding the scope of our primate sanctuary, now that the foundation's resources could be used for this purpose.

All of these things will take time to bring to fruition, at least five years or more. There's plenty of time yet before I'll have to confront Franklin over other issues not now on the table. Whatever might come between him and me down the road, it's necessary—in order for my own longer-term objectives, now taking shape in my mind, to be realized—for father both to re-establish himself as a working scientist and to give the four scientist sisters the best training possible in biological sciences. Ever since we got to Provo I've begun encouraging him to re-enter the world scientific community, which in any case was eagerly awaiting his reappearance, so that he could once again participate in professional discussions in his field.

My only substantial intervention at that Board meeting was to suggest that we create one or two new business entities. The regular scans and analyses of world events, which are provided by a commercial service to which we subscribe, contain repeated references to the dangers posed by bioterrorism. Thus, at Gaia's urging, I proposed that we create a corporation to be called PathoGene, in order to specialize in this area. Franklin and I had discussed this in advance and he's interested and willing to help establish it. The new company will seek to develop portable machines for rapid DNA sequencing and gene-typing of new or unfamiliar pathogens, as well as techniques for the construction of defenses against them—drugs such as new antibiotics for the bacteria, and vaccines for the viruses. Its scientists will try to develop predictive models for the pathogens most likely to be engineered next for nefarious purposes, thus possibly anticipating them and having antidotes already in place.

Ari, Moira and Themis, our three mathematicians who have displayed a special cleverness in electronic security and data encryption, which by now is a rapidly escalating global concern, want to set up another small company, Troglodyte Partners—named after the scientific term for the common chimpanzee, *Pan troglodytes*—to provide consulting services in these fields. We approved this plan.

25 DECEMBER 2032

By no means is it all work and no play for us! To their other athletic interests, the sisters have now added diving and snorkelling among the coral reefs and shallow coastal waters. And at last many of them—more than half our number—broke free of our rather overly regimented lifestyle by becoming regular fixtures in the evenings among the tourists at the entertainment spots around town. True, I rarely join them, unless they virtually kidnap me. I cannot help myself; I stand a bit apart and watch over their comings and goings with a worried eye. I must let them be, and am well aware I couldn't stop them even if I wished to; if I did try to superintend them too closely, it would only create anger and resentment between them and me.

So I've done the next best thing—engage a private security firm that caters to the needs of the very rich and arranged for them to mount a continuous surveillance operation on all of us. I demanded that their work be done in such a way as to be utterly unobtrusive so that those being watched rarely, if ever, are able to spot the comings and goings of the firm's personnel. My instructions to the operatives were explicit: Do not interfere except where a clear and present danger has arisen, and then, if possible, do so in the guise of concerned citizens who just happened to be nearby.

And I've just found my own recreational preoccupation. One of the first residents in the temporary primate quarters at the compound was Lucy, a bonobo (*Pan paniscus,* the species formerly called pygmy chimpanzee), who had been rescued from a contract laboratory services company in Zimbabwe. Unfortunately, there are a number of these small companies in operation around the world, operating on behalf of unscrupulous larger firms wanting to have types of research performed on primates that would not be allowed in their home countries. For the first few months after she arrived Lucy screamed in terror and hugged the rear wall of her enclosure whenever a human approached. Only with the greatest of patience and tenderness did her keepers finally induce her to respond to their kindnesses, as she gradually allowed them closer proximity and finally physical contact.

Every evening I take Marco to see Lucy. We sit next to her enclosure and just talk to her, sometimes also listening together to classical music on our portable player. I'm reading a lot about bonobos and they fascinate me. They are the only apes who easily walk upright. Their sexual behaviors involve all types of pairings, including male-male, male-female, and female-female. In addition, bonobos express a preference for face-to-face positioning in copulation, and their sex acts can be initiated by either party. Adult females frequently engage in what is called 'genito-genital rubbing,' where two females, positioned one atop the other, mimic the thrusting motion of copulation and mutually stimulate their genitalia. These behaviors are not observed in either gorillas or common chimpanzees.

I suppose that at first the bond between Lucy and me was formed by my keen awareness that we had both been terrorized by stronger humans. What had started as a feeling of pity for the depth of Lucy's fear gradually turned into a powerful feeling of comfort and tranquillity for me whenever we spend time together. When I think she's ready, I'm planning to take Lucy from the sanctuary for short stays in my private residence and garden.

18 JANUARY 2033

Franklin has now publicized his whereabouts to his peers in the global scientific community, but he's resisting every entreaty to take up a university post, saying that he is content to be a private scholar. He's gradually catching up to his colleagues in neurogenetics after his absence from research, and beginning to initiate collaborations with other scientists using Internet communications. But his main priority is turning the group of four sisters into highly competent scientists.

Now that he has re-emerged from his self-imposed exile and become a public figure once again, there's an urgent item of business for me to attend to. I realized that I had to settle with the rest of Klamm's former clients in order to protect him, because he had signed the contracts. What I intend to do is this: Over a number of years, using agents employed by trusted intermediaries, I'll track them down and repay their deposits, with interest, from the substantial coffers we sisters have been accumulating. The story I'll tell them is that Klamm had perpetrated a hoax on all of them, forging my father's signature on the contracts. I won't care overmuch whether or not they believe me.

FEBRUARY 2034

I've now traced most of Klamm's clients—about a third of them have died or disappeared in the meantime—and I've obtained copies of the contracts. I'm trying hard to control my anger at Franklin for having put us into such jeopardy, but it's not easy, I confess. I barely run into him at all these days; he's so busy with the group of sisters in their labs. I'm concentrating on managing the foundation and working with Percy on the primate sanctuary expansion.

HERA'S JOURNAL (UNDATED FRAGMENT)

My sisters and I had been promised a holiday expedition to celebrate one of our birthdays, right after our annual medical check-up was finished. We are twelve high-spirited young girls and we always test the mettle of the best clinic staff when we arrive together. No amount of professional seriousness on the doctors' part could subdue our excitement either! Nor did the cool white light striking their bleached uniforms, making their wearers almost invisible against the colorlessness of the clinic's walls, floor and ceiling, have the slightest calming effect on our excited chatter.

If it had occurred to me that the staff complement seemed unusually large that day, I didn't recall remarking upon this fact to the others. For when each of us was accompanied at the same time into an examination room by a doctor, we all knew that the routines would pass more quickly and we could soon be on our way. Besides, we girls were well used to getting special treatment at all times.

I didn't recognize the man who closed the door behind me, but this, too, was unremarkable because our father was always having us looked over by an endless stream of specialists. I had already undressed and was sitting on the examination table when I realized that he hadn't yet spoken to me, so I turned to look at him as he approached.

Just as the doctor reached for me, the first terrifying screams pierced the walls of the nearby rooms. Instinctively I had turned toward the wall nearest me and in the same instant he pushed me down onto the table with one quick sweep of a powerful arm; my head snapped back to face his as he mounted me. I watched as the whole skin covering his skull dissolved at once, revealing the deep blackness and angular contours of an ape-like visage. The screams from the other rooms rose and fell in rhythmic chants. In a single thrust he penetrated me and blood poured onto the clean white floor.

That's the moment when I sat bolt upright in my bed, awake, bathed in sweat, my heart pounding. I recognized immediately the nightmare that had visited me occasionally for a number of years. I knew, too, that I must have cried out in terror in my sleep because the door to the garden adjoining the bedroom now slid back on its tracks, and Lucy entered along with the perfumed Caribbean night air. Her bare feet glided noiselessly across the polished wooden floor and she reached the futon in a few quick steps, sliding onto it next to me and gripping me with astonishing strength. I lay back again, shaking, and said to her, "Lucy, I'm so sorry, I must have frightened you with my cries again; you never seem to get used to them." The low soft sounds from her throat comforted me and I was able to fall asleep again.

When I awoke that morning she was gone. I realized I had been dreaming again, toward dawn, and as the memory came flooding back to me, I lay motionless in my bed, astonished. In this dream Lucy was still beside me, gently stroking me, her hand moving across my body, first shoulders, chest, and stomach, then sliding down to my pudenda, rubbing slowly at first then more quickly as I began to moan, until I came.

JANUARY 2036

One day about a week ago Franklin informed me that his troop of biology assistants was advancing well in their training.

"There's been a huge amount of scientific research done in neurogenetics in the twenty-five years since Ina and I first began thinking about our project, Hera."

I was sitting with him in the outdoor pavilion adjacent to the laboratories and offices of the foundation. It was a perfect Caribbean day, with cool ocean breezes nicely counteracting the sun's heat radiating from crystal-clear skies.

"But the most interesting thing is, it seems your mother and I had the basics right," he continued. "By the time—in 2013—I started the modifications on the embryos from which you girls came, scientists had located and mapped the main DNA sequences that control the development of the general functions for the neocortex and prefrontal cortex in the human brain.

"What was still lacking at that time," he went on, his enthusiasm mounting, "was a more complete set of detailed chromosomal markers that would allow us to zero in very precisely on the DNA sequences of particular interest for quite specific brain functions and characteristics. Also the markers for various disorders, such as schizophrenia, of course. During the decade that elapsed between the time your mother died and early 2025, when I was able to finish collecting and preparing the embryos donated by the Group of 300, those further steps had been accomplished. So in what I'm now referring to as our Second Generation, there will be some improvements on my first effort—not that you girls are lacking very much, to be sure! Most importantly, there is a good chance we'll be able to reduce further the risk that serious neurological disorders will occur in our new group of children. I'm thinking of conditions such as depression, or panic attacks and anxiety, and more serious ones, such as bipolar disorder or paranoid schizophrenia. Obviously this is a very delicate matter for us, now that we're going to produce a much larger group of children.

"But I've been worrying recently about the passage of time—with respect to the quality of the embryos that have been frozen at super-cold temperatures for almost twelve years already. This is my dilemma: I want to enlist the biology sisters as my full collaborators in the Second Generation project, so that they develop the competence to carry on with our mission after I'm gone. Although they are very fast learners, as you might expect, they're not quite at the required level of training and experience yet, especially in laboratory techniques. I estimate another two years of hard work will be required.

"So together with them I've formulated a new strategy. We want to discard the embryos we have in frozen storage and start over again—recruiting a new group of suitable donors and preparing their embryos from scratch. The main reason is, of course, the age of our inventory; the longer the embryos remain frozen, the more deterioration we could expect. But there are additional reasons as well. The most important is that in beginning anew, the sisters can be directly involved in all the many stages of this process— including the gene manipulation stage—an experience that will be invaluable for them. You'll not be surprised to learn that they're thrilled by this prospect. Finally, when we get to the gene manipulation stage, we can take advantage of the very latest applied research results in this field.

"We want to bring to the foundation board a request authorizing us to initiate the donor search process and all the subsequent steps—egg and sperm collection, IVF, and so on. This time we're leaning toward proposing a Group of 500 because we have both adequate financial resources and a larger complement of trained personnel at our disposal. We think it's vital that the non-scientist directors of the foundation should understand some of the basic issues involved, so I've asked Gaia to draft a special memorandum for them."

MEMORANDUM FROM GAIA SUJANA-STONE TO THE BOARD OF DIRECTORS, SUJANA FOUNDATION RE: THE SECOND GENERATION

The member couples of the new *Group of 500* will be chosen on the basis of an exhaustive screening of family histories; thus they will represent a very healthy cohort from a genetic standpoint. The target age is in the range of 25-30. The females in the group will be administered follicle-stimulating hormones, as well as other fertility drugs affecting oocyte maturation, in order to induce their ovaries to produce supernumerary follicles containing eggs—a process called 'super-ovulation.' They will undergo two cycles of this procedure and, based on the record of current experience, we can expect an average of close to 30 eggs per woman to be obtained—for a total of 15,000. The males will contribute a series of semen samples over a six-month period that will be examined for sperm viability.

Sperm will be sex-sorted (X- or Y-carrying), eggs will be mixed with sperm *in vitro,* and the result will be examined after twelve hours for signs of successful fertilization. On day 2, embryos will be at the 4-cell stage; each individual cell is called a blastomere. One blastomere will be separated out and put through preimplantation diagnostic screening for evidence of known inherited diseases and to determine sex. Germline therapy will also be done at this time; this is the set of modifications that will be fully inheritable in the future offspring of this generation. Embryonic development will be halted at the 8-cell stage and the embryos will be prepared for extended freezing using cryoprotectant chemicals. Once we have completed all of these steps, we can turn our attention to the recruitment and screening of the large cohort of surrogate mothers we will require.

Significant losses occur at every important step in this process. The IVF procedure itself has roughly an 80% success rate. Then at the first three stages of cleavage, beginning when the single cell starts dividing, there are additional losses in the range of 70-80%. Therefore, if one starts with, say, 100 eggs, then by the time the 8-cell stage is reached, one can expect to have 30 viable embryos. Further losses will occur during the freeze/thaw cycle, although these technologies have improved steadily over the years. Still, one cannot count on ending up with more than about 20 out of the original 100 when one is at the point of being ready for implantation in the wombs of either natural or surrogate mothers.

In the first decades after surgical implantation of embryos into the womb was carried out, success rates were rather low, around 25%; since then, dramatic improvements have been achieved in this regard. Sometimes the problem is with the cytoplasm, the area inside the cell excluding the nucleus, and the solution is to replace the cytoplasm using the egg of a second donor, which improves the chance of success while retaining the desired genetic material in the original cell nucleus. If you find all of this rather alarming, and are wondering whether we are just incompetent, relax! Most people are completely unaware of how many missteps occur in natural pregnancies and how few final successes there are—represented by the delivery of a healthy fetus—compared with the initial number of male/female couplings in cases where the partners are desiring to have a baby.

As indicated in the prior document (*Memorandum of 30 June 2021*), the basic strategy behind Franklin's scientific protocol for germline genetic engineering is to increase the density of the neuronal 'wiring' in the brain, focusing particularly on the prefrontal cortex (PFC). This neuronal density has two aspects, namely, the total number of neurons as well as the average number of connections among them. Since the PFC has important linkages with other regions, all the inter-regional connections should be enhanced as well.

Expression of the genes controlling these aspects of brain development is influenced by two classes of steroid compounds—the steroid hormones from the gonads and adrenal glands, as well as the neurosteroids produced directly in the brain. Steroid hormones include aldosterone, progesterone, estradiol, cortisol, and testosterone. Studies have shown that, in addition to all other effects, steroid hormones do have a significant impact on cognitive function.

The neurosteroids are one of four classes of neurotransmitters and neuromodulators, that is, chemicals that make communications possible within the brain. Neurotransmitters are the mechanism for the so-called 'signal transduction' processes among neurons—the way signals flow across the brain to its various centers, such as those for memory. The important neurosteroids are pregnenolone (which is also a precursor to all the steroid hormones) and DHEA, dehydroepiandrosterone, which is a precursor to testosterone. In the fetus, neurosteroids influence neuronal outgrowth and synapse formation. In adults, the very strong impact of neurosteroids on the quality of signal transduction processes means that they can affect learning and memory as well as emotional response.

One important fact should be kept in mind about these two classes of substances. Beginning in the early part of this century, both steroid hormones and neurosteroids were synthesized in the laboratory and turned into pharmaceutical products. For a long time now, both types of compounds have been administered therapeutically to treat a variety of conditions, such as control of epilepsy and convulsions as well as sleep disorders.

Our germline modifications primarily seek to increase the expression of those genes that code for neural development supporting the higher cognitive functions in the brain. For the most part, this is done by altering the rate at which the gene is transcribed or becomes active. In turn, the rate of transcription is affected by enhancers, also known as enhancer-binding proteins, that latch onto what are called promoter sites, which are the switches that turn genes on and off. This is a long-winded way of saying that we can use certain proteins to ask the genes we're interested in to do more work than they normally would in building neural networks in the brain.

Remember also the major theme emphasized in the 2021 *Memorandum*: Brain development goes on for almost twenty years after birth. After birth, however, environmental factors combine with genetic ones to determine the final outcome. In short, skill acquisition, memory, and reasoning abilities depend on the intensity of the continuous learning environment, as well as on the ongoing responses of the brain to that environment. This is why our primary emphasis is on a continuous and carefully structured program of learning.

Our scientific protocol calls for very careful monitoring and analysis—at various ages during postnatal development—of the levels of steroid hormones, neurosteroids, and other neurotransmitters in the brain. There is a possibility we could use corrective therapies if we find that the levels of particular substances are either excessive or deficient. But we are very careful in this part of the protocol due to the possibility of causing or contributing to psychic disorders.

In summary, our protocol includes the following modifications and procedures: germline enhancement of gene expression for neuronal tissue; an intensive, structured learning environment for fifteen years after birth; and regular monitoring of specific chemical compounds at intervals during the post-natal period.

One final note. As is emphasized in the 2021 *Memorandum*, the intention of this protocol is not to produce individuals who are all of a single type, nor to create people with specific sets of abilities, say, for mathematics. Rather, the core intention is to increase the *general capacity* of the brain's own higher cognitive functions. We expect that, in a large set of individuals such as the Second Generation will be, as a whole they will display higher-than-normal abilities across the entire spectrum of human intellectual disciplines.

That day in late January I had come straight from one of my walks with Lucy to the foundation's offices to meet Franklin. Every morning during Lucy's visits to my compound, the ape and I meander hand-in-hand among the lush gardens that extend outwards in all directions from my ground-floor rooms. Lucy mimics me when I stoop to smell the flowers. I refer to these walks as my therapy. For days now I've felt upset in a way I just can't pinpoint. To work out my frustration, I spent much of the previous night writing in my journal.

§   §   §

I'm quite sure it's the upcoming meeting with Franklin

that's been bothering me. I've been postponing it for weeks and that's not fair to him. Avoiding it hasn't done me much good either! So I'll spend all night, if necessary, writing out whatever comes to mind. I have to; I've promised to see him tomorrow.

Where to start? Perhaps my turmoil began with the item I read in a scientific journal about experiments with chimpanzees conducted some time ago in North America. These were trials that, at least on the surface, seem to be quite harmless, such as feeding chimps fish-based diets from infancy. This was being done to test the hypothesis that in the period between the emergence of *Homo habilis* almost three million years ago and its successor, *Homo erectus*, two million years later, it was access to African coastal waters and the abundant fish protein found there that jump-started the enormous changes in the hominin brain's size and complexity.

But I've also read that others are trying the more direct route of manipulating the genomes of monkeys and chimps to see if it is possible to stimulate additional neuronal growth in the neocortex and frontal cortex. Why, for God's sake? What are they looking for, apart from the fame and fortune that might flow from the notoriety of their success? I've followed this literature for years. A long series of observational studies of chimp behavior during the late twentieth century had demonstrated that these animals almost certainly do not possess higher cognitive functions, including the capacity for language, nor can those powers be induced to appear through extensive training in the laboratory.

Despite some limited capacity to recognize themselves (or at least some self) in mirrors and to mimic the behavior of other chimps seen on videotapes, these studies tell us that chimps don't have a sense of personal self, as humans do. As far as we can tell, they don't find in themselves "the 'I' that accompanies all of our representations," as the philosopher

Kant put it when describing the process of thinking.

So what are these scientists up to now? Do they actually think they might *manufacture* the consciousness of self in the chimpanzee? And what if they succeed? What then? Would they next want to insert their clever new stretches of DNA nucleotide sequences into the germline, so that upon mating, such chimps would pass on their new traits to their offspring? Have they actually thought about what it would mean to *succeed* in this endeavor?

Could they really be so—what's the word I want—naïve, or callous, or irresponsible, or smug, or just simply so supremely indifferent to what might ultimately flow from their search for knowledge? Whenever I read about archaeological discoveries showing the first traces of human self-awareness—not the tool-making relics, but rather the more artistic ones—I always recall the Aztec facial masks that turn up frequently among that culture's artifacts. Their common motif appears to be a scream of horror. (Is this the same horror that brings Conrad's *Heart of Darkness* to its close? Possibly.) For me this expression on the masks illustrates the origins of self-consciousness: The first awakening of an animal spirit to the reality of a wider world *inside* itself, "void and without form." That's the language in that marvelous sentence from the opening of the Book of Genesis in the King James translation.

Ever since I spent those days in the Biblical scholarship classes at the missionary college in Alberta, I've had a love for the Bible's poetic modes of discourse. I wondered often what the poet of Genesis really had in mind in his reference to the formless void. It couldn't have been the surrounding world of nature, which in his time obviously consisted of well-defined landscapes and endlessly varied plant and animal species. No, it's a metaphor that refers to something else entirely—what might be called an existential void. What I mean is this: For the 'first' man and woman who became self-aware—metaphorically, Adam and Eve—there was this sudden realization of a sense of separateness or psychological distance between themselves and the rest of their environment.

This also gives us a clue as to what the prior state of innocence is—the innocence all other animals have, by the way (as we surmise, at least): An immediacy of identification with the surrounding environment without the interference of the sense of self. This is easier to imagine with ocean-dwelling animals rather than land-based ones: They are literally immersed in their environment.

This sudden sense of having an inner self wasn't necessarily scary, but the next thought certainly was! For when they called out "What *am* 'I'? *Where* am I in the vastness I see above me in the night sky?" there was no answering reply. These ancestors of ours encountered no other speaking creatures who might explain why the strange interior voice of thinking had arisen suddenly inside their bodies. When did this first happen? Perhaps 100,000 or maybe only 50,000 years ago? We can all try this experiment for ourselves—just run a little interior monologue silently in your mind.

Now imagine what it must have been like when this happened for the first time! Until then we were all just darting around this way and that, scrounging for food or grooming each other in the tribe, the young engaged in raucous play, the adults chattering away, making the kinds of sounds we hear chimps make today, responding to the internal drives of which we were utterly unaware. Then suddenly, there it was! Another type of voice, silent, somewhere inside, its contents laid down in memory and recalled again. And one fine day, thanks to an accidental mutation in our *FOXP2* gene—something that happened to humans but not to other species of apes—we could form more precise sounds with our lips and tongues and begin to describe to others in the tribe what these inner voices were saying.

Well, this is probably a pretty crude version of the true story, to be sure, but it had to have happened, somehow, sometime, somewhere, for the first time. Whenever it was, who can doubt that it frightened these creatures to the very core of their being? They needed an explanation, so they embarked forthwith upon the construction of their deities: Every human culture, without exception, has peopled itself with gods and demons.

And what did these invisible beings do for them? They spoke back and answered their questions, they mapped out for them the hidden order and meaning of the cosmos—which they could imagine in their minds but not actually point to anywhere. And then the people were comforted. Until, that is, they stumbled upon other tribes and their false gods, the foul ranks of shameless unbelievers, and they could find no rest again until they had annihilated them or been annihilated in turn.

What a weird roundabout my mind has been taking these past few days! I've been hiding from myself, haven't I? I know what's occasioned this little journey, so why not own up to the fact? This all started when Franklin told me last week—enthusiasm brimming from every pore!—that we needed to discuss a specific timetable for the engineering of the Second Generation. That's what started all of my troubled reflections about the chimpanzee experiments and the first humans.

Face it, Hera, it's past time for you to own up: You're ambivalent about the foundation's new project and you've been so for a long time. Now decision time is at hand, and I realize I've been avoiding the subject, thinking about everything under the sun except the one question to which I must give an answer, because as the president of the Sujana Foundation—a post I freely accepted—my assent (or dissent) is required. He's determined to do it again, to do what he once did to my sisters and me, only this time using five hundred or maybe even a thousand embryos!

One part of me wants to say, "No! No, Franklin, never again! Don't you realize the enormous price my sisters and I have paid for being the living embodiments of your project? And I'm not just referring to what went wrong with your dream, yours and my mother's, when Klamm's new plan intervened. I'm not even concentrating on our all-too-narrow escape from a fate worse than death at the hands of Klamm's clients! No, it's more than that. It's simply the reality of waking up every day and realizing that one is a *constructed* entity! You did something to my sisters and me to make us different, first in our embryonic state at the inception of cell division, and later in the series of post-natal treatments dictated by your scientific protocol."

How could anyone arrogate to herself the right to do such a thing to another human person? Or to one of the higher primates, for that matter? The majority of people today, many trained scientists among them—including those living in modern, science-dependent economies—number themselves amongst the ranks of believers in one of the world's monotheistic religions, where God rules absolutely. I'm not a scientist, unlike some of my sisters; sometimes I think I became a theologian in Alberta. Every religion begins with a creation myth that claims creation is God's exclusive franchise. This much is—or should be—perfectly clear to every believer.

So what did those scientists, and the devout citizens who await with bated breath for the next magical therapeutic innovation for their decaying bodies, think they were doing in launching their engineering projects inside the human genome? Especially where germline modifications would allow new traits to enter the gene pool of the whole human species. Isn't the very idea of improving on God's design a simple case of the rankest blasphemy? Doesn't that type of enterprise merit one a ticket straight to Hell?

Curiously enough, there's precious little commentary on this point, especially among the ranks of working scientists who are also religious believers. I know; I've looked for it. And the oddest thing of all is that this blasphemous enterprise has been undertaken so casually, with almost no serious prior debate in legislatures or church assemblies. Being orderly folks, citizens and scientists alike appear to divide their mental compartments very tidily, one for biology, another for faith. They avoid dealing with troubling thoughts by never allowing them to arise in the first place.

Unlike the human brain itself, these artificially divided compartments for science and faith don't appear to be cross-wired. If they had been, the manifest contradictions between the two zones would be painfully obvious. And when one considers the frantic search for the so-called immortality gene, the silence in those mental spaces is positively deafening. *Surely to God*—so to speak—that's not only blasphemous, but counter-revolutionary! As Io is fond of saying, "Who in the Bible is described as the revolutionary usurper, intent on overthrowing the current ruler in the Kingdom of Heaven? None other than Satan." The leader of the Band of Fallen Angels seems to be a busy man these days.

Oh yes, Io; what a wicked sense of humor she has. I don't know why, but she and I just can't seem to relate to each other easily anymore. Except when we're having a party with a group of the sisters and their new friends here, getting a little wired on booze and dope. Then she takes over, letting her imagination run riot, and the rest of us just sit back and enjoy the show. At one of these gatherings a few months ago, I tried to raise a serious subject for conversation about my puzzlement over the facile acceptance of genetic re-engineering by so many people who nevertheless continue to think of themselves as true believers in one of the monotheistic faiths—Muslim, Christian, or otherwise. Io took over and delivered one of her soliloquies, leaping from her chair and pacing the deck of her veranda, where we all sat. I love her performances and often record and annotate them in my journal immediately thereafter.

"Why are they so sure that their God will even *recognize* them as products of His handiwork when they show up at the Gates of Heaven, for goodness' sake? Imagine the scene at the Pearly Gates when one of these beautifully modified artifacts of human ingenuity turns up and announces: 'Here I am, a true believer and faithful Christian, who has repented all my grievous sins before death and received absolution from my priest, your servant. I'm ready to be admitted to the Kingdom of Heaven and to join the Heavenly Host.'

"Standing before the petitioner is a bone-weary Saint Peter gazing at the endless series of souls stretching out before him into the distance, all of them a bit too cheerful at merely being in the queue, each as convinced as the next that her admittance is a foregone conclusion. We can imagine Peter's private musings: 'Good God, look at the lineup. Why does He always reject my petitions for additional staff support, sending them back with the same handwritten note, telling me to check the Book of Revelation? Doesn't He think I know it by heart?

> *And I looked, and, lo, a Lamb stood on the mount Sion, and with him an hundred forty and four thousand, having his Father's name written in their foreheads.*

"'Only 144,000 should be admitted, He says. And I tried to make it easy for you, He says. All you have to do is to check for my Name that is etched on their faces, He says. Well, easier said than done. There are billions out there whose whole dossiers have to be scrutinized because they all know the line about putting His name on their foreheads before they reach my desk. And, of course, to a soul they all claim membership in good standing in one of the twelve tribes of Israel.'

"Now watch Saint Peter, who, as you would expect, is up-to-date on all the sinners' tricks, as befits the Divine Gate-keeper, carefully scrutinizing this candidate's credentials, entering her particulars into his computer file, then request-ing her to take a number, and a seat, while he sends a DNA sample from her soul upstairs to the Holy Laboratory. Some-time later Saint Peter recalls her to the admitting desk after the lab results have come back. 'I regret to say that your candidacy has been rejected. Please turn in your immortal soul at the transit station in the next room.' The petitioner hears his words but cannot process them. She watches with horror as he deletes her entry on his computer screen. He calls out, 'Next, please.' She stands before him, unmoving, and screams: 'There must be some mistake! Please, redo the tests! The priest gave me absolution for my sins before I died.'

"He looks at her with the kind of patience only a saint can muster and thinks to himself, 'This must be at least the four-hundredth such case already today, and it's not even lunchtime. No wonder I'm getting further and further behind—look at the length of the queue! This used to be such a simple job. Does God know what's happening here? Does He even care?' Now Saint Peter glances at the soul standing before him and says, 'I'll try to keep it simple for you. According to the DNA analysis, you aren't made in God's image, so you can't enter the Kingdom of Heaven. As you should know, only beings formed "in His image" qualify.

"'Actually, you shouldn't even have gotten this far, but there's a glitch in the Holy Computer system, and I can't seem to persuade God that He's got to fix it. You shouldn't have been assigned a soul in the first place, that's what I keep telling Him. You should have been classified with the dogs and cats and cattle and horses, and all the other domesticated animals. Now please, move along; can't you see the length of the line behind you? How am I ever going to catch up at this rate?'

"As the conveyer belt starts to whisk her away toward the door leading to the transit station, she yells, 'I want to appeal! I insist on seeing a lawyer!' He smiles now and makes no reply as the door opens and she's dumped into the next room, which is packed to overflowing, standing-room only, where the machine dispensing numbers has run out of paper, where the sounds of wailing and the gnashing of teeth—speaking metaphorically, of course—raise a cacophonous din, where she can barely catch a glimpse of the bad-tempered Prince of Darkness, sitting crossly at his post. End of story."

She may have been having fun, but Io is onto something serious here. We sisters are, in fact, the products of an act of creation; we know in our hearts and minds that we *are* different from most other people, even if we don't understand all the ramifications of this fact. And it's also undeniable that we're living, breathing exemplars of the mammalian family *Hominidae* on earth. Whatever we are, as created beings, we're authentic in our own way—in and for ourselves, as a philosopher would say. And we don't—couldn't!—want to be otherwise than we are. For such a wish would constitute an insoluble paradox. To wish to be another kind of being would be to wish to *not be*.

And here's the rub. Since we sisters know ourselves to be different, and have accepted this fact—as we must, for what other choice do we have, really?—shouldn't we want to have more beings like ourselves here on earth? Isn't the small number of our little band one of the primary reasons why I've always, since early childhood, felt the presence of a menacing and all-pervasive fear? Wouldn't I feel safer, more secure, if there were more people like my sisters and me?

The engineering of the Second Generation will yield precisely such a result! Thus I *have* resolved the ambivalences that wrack me, haven't I? I just don't want to admit to myself that deep down inside, I've never doubted that a Second Generation should be created.

I've often wondered if I should ask father for a copy of his original scientific protocol—I've seen only the general description prepared for the two groups of donors—containing the details of the modifications that created us. But do I really want to know—or would I actually understand things better—if I learned which specific sequences in my DNA had been reconfigured? Would knowing this somehow set me free, or only make things worse? Isn't it enough to be aware that *something* had been done to make my sisters and me unlike other people? Sometimes I think, 'What would we have been like otherwise?' Then I immediately stop this train of thought because there is no 'otherwise.' There cannot be. The twelve of us are—actually exist—in the only form possible. If, after our mother's death, father had decided not to proceed with the project the two of them had conceived together, my sisters and I would not now exist.

To me this is the oddest feature of all within the ensemble of that weird and unsettling business we call consciousness of self. Our thinking brain uses universals as its default mechanism: It thinks in language and in number, and both of these symbolic devices have their foundation in generalizable or universal systems. Language makes communication possible because it is shared. Number is literally everywhere—and nowhere.

Yet all these universals are firmly embedded in a very singular 'I.' We come to know ourselves intimately—at least, those of us who do a lot of self-reflection, in whom the interior monologue never seems to switch off. True, we can deceive ourselves as well, so that this always-running tape of self-awareness doesn't necessarily display the one true and objective picture of reality. Probably there is no such thing as one reality. Moreover, it seems impossible to imagine oneself—*really*—as another person. Yes, fiction writers do it, and their characters can appear to be quite authentic to their readers and audiences. But does this mean that we know who they actually are? Isn't it possible that fictional characters deceive themselves, and us, just as much as we real people seem to do?

In the end it all comes back to the singularity of the thinking machine inside our heads. Each person can be only who she or he is and has become over time—apart from those who suffer from certain hallucinatory disorders. And the point is we do see those cases as instances that something is not right. This worries me constantly: I dread the day, should it ever come, when one or more of us might start to show unmistakable signs of a serious late-developing psychological disorder, a disease such as schizophrenia, or especially—God forbid!—paranoid schizophrenia.

Perhaps that's enough for now!

§ § §

These chaotic notions were still ricocheting in my mind the following morning as I headed for the offices to meet Franklin. My final thought was, 'Oh no, will they try to pin this butterfly to the wall as well? Will some experimenters try to get inside our heads to find out if there is just one tape running there, the one true tape, and lay it out for all to see?' I remembered reading that, almost fifty years ago now, someone had the bright idea of scanning the contents of the mind, stored in the network of the brain's neural memory structures, into a computer's digital storage device. 'Uploading' was the popular term coined for the idea.

Has this already been tried in the meantime? What

exactly did they expect to find when the computer drive was accessed after the scan? And, more importantly, did they expect—did they actually hypothesize for the experimental design—that the digitized mind now residing on the hard disk would signal back to them in newly formed sentences? That this 'thing' would be *alive* in there somewhere? Again, I recalled how Joseph Conrad's story ends: "The horror. The horror."

§ § §

"Hello, Franklin," I exclaimed as pleasantly as I could when I arrived, determined to banish my black thoughts for now. "How are you today? I'm afraid you're working too hard again."

"I'm fine, Hera. As I mentioned a few days ago, our little science group, your sisters and I, have undertaken an exhaustive study of the recent scientific literature, including detailed reports and evaluations on the relevant therapeutic applications published in the last decade. We've also corresponded extensively with our peers who are doing similar work around the world, and examined all the commercial therapies currently available. We wanted to re-confirm that the rationale behind the manipulations I carried out on the Group of 300 embryos in 2024-5 was still valid.

"What I sought to do then was to make only the minimally necessary intervention in the individual's genome, in the course of getting the exact traits I desired. As well, I wanted to reduce to the lowest possible level the probability of accidentally producing either other unwanted changes that are apparently benign, or—much worse, of course— unintended effects that could result in harmful neurological disorders. I'm pleased to report that these latest investigations of ours have provided the basic confirmation I was seeking. However, there is some crucial new information that we will be taking into account when we begin work on the new embryos donated by the Group of 500."

"Thank you for telling me that. I'm genuinely gratified that you and my sisters have taken so much care in preparing the groundwork for the next project. I know how hard you've worked over the last few years to improve the scientific protocol for the genetic modification of the Second Generation. I want to make it clear right away that I have no reservations whatsoever about proceeding. Quite the contrary: I have always been convinced that, whatever ethical or political qualms might arise about what we're doing, the creation of the Second Generation must be undertaken."

"I expected as much from you. Our calculations suggest that our surrogate mothers will be able to deliver one thousand healthy babies."

"Good," I answered with as much enthusiasm as I could muster. "Of course, what we'll be doing here on our little group of islands is not the only project along these lines that's coming to fruition around the world, is it? I don't follow all of the developments in neurogenetics research as you do, but I see enough, just in the media reports, to get an idea of what others are trying to do—and succeeding in doing, for all we know. Because like ours, many of the other projects are being carried on in secret, aren't they? What's your own assessment of the other experiments that we can assume are taking place?"

"You're right. A lot of what's apparently happening is not fully or even partially reported in the standard literature. All we have to go on in these cases are second- or third-hand accounts, which may be apocryphal. However, I must admit there are fairly reliable signs indicating some disturbing types of modifications, although no one has yet documented them with sufficient care. Most likely this is because the 'products' are being hidden away during their early years and maturation, both to evaluate the results and to avoid unwanted publicity. So it's entirely possible that in the future we'll suddenly be confronted with some very unpleasant surprises in the engineering of psychological traits. But no one can even estimate the chances of this occurring, or of how disturbing the results might be."

"Doesn't all this bother you, Franklin, even just a little bit? The same type of knowledge that you and your peers began formulating and publishing forty years ago, as well as all the advances since then, can be used for many different purposes. In fact, it can be used for purposes diametrically opposed to your own."

"Yes, without a doubt. But as you know this is true of all knowledge, including modern science. The inventor of the world's first sword-like instrument probably intended his innovation to be a more efficient means of harvesting crops or hunting animal prey. But think of how many horrible battle deaths also resulted from the unintended adaptation of his invention for purposes of war! There's no solution to this dilemma, Hera, otherwise it would have been devised long ago. We must push forward our present form of knowledge to its limits and then go further beyond still. There will always be a frontier of knowledge, and I believe we humans are programmed to conquer it.

"Every single innovation has the character of that original doubled-edged sword: Although intended for good, it will be applied to evil ends as well. Those of us who think of ourselves as being on the side of the good simply must resolve to win the race, every time, and keep doing so, for the competition will never end as long as *Homo sapiens* flourishes on earth."

I laughed. "That sounded like a speech to a science-awareness-day crowd, Franklin. I know you used to give those speeches, so I'm not surprised to hear it from you in person. But do you *never, ever* doubt that the last set of races will, in fact, be won by the forces of the good, as you term them?

What if events turn out otherwise in the end? Think ahead to the time when all of us will have helped to create instruments of power and manipulation so breathtakingly clever that *Homo sapiens* can do pretty much as it pleases on its home planet and even elsewhere within our solar system. Then add the last little twist to the story: The evildoers gain the upper hand just as these mighty powers are realized. What then?"

"I simply can't allow myself to imagine such a scenario," he answered immediately. "If I were to admit such a prospect, then what would I and others like me do? Would we lay down our tools like striking workers? Would we announce to the astonished public, 'We're terribly sorry, folks, but there will be no more science and technology research done, and no further innovations, until we're sure that the evildoers won't triumph in the far-distant future!'"

I inquired meekly, affecting innocence, "Have you and your peers ever considered such a strategy, by the way?"

Now it was his turn to laugh. "No, and the first one who suggested it would be promptly ostracized and put out to pasture, or shot—in some places anyway. Maybe it's just a problem of herd mentality, I grant you. The first ones to head off in a new direction fall victim to the waiting wolves. I don't know. But look, realistically, science and technology is such a vast international enterprise now, with facilities busily working away everywhere on the globe, funded by tens of billions of dollars annually. Purely as a practical matter, at this point, no one—or no group—could do what you suggest, even if they wanted to."

"Yes, I concede the practical problem. I suppose I was thinking more of the speculative side. Whether you had ever entertained the thought itself."

"What good would that do me, or anyone else? I, for one, have a chance to do something that, I believe deeply and unequivocally, is for the good of humankind. It may even be so beneficial that it can turn humanity in a new direction, where the forces of good gain the upper hand once and for all, and banish evil to the sidelines. You would have to concede that there is *some* probability, even if it is very small, that I, or others similarly motivated, will succeed. And that thought is enough to inspire me to carry on."

I paused before answering. "It's funny. I hear so much of that language—'good versus evil'—in our time. Doesn't it strike you as odd, hearing those words so often in this super-scientific age? Earlier today, on my way over here to meet you, I was thinking about the way people keep different dimensions of existence in separate compartments in their minds. In particular, how modern science and ancient faith seem to co-exist happily in today's world, despite the obvious fact that the two of them are based on radically opposed conceptions of reality—one materialist, the other creationist.

"Taken together, science, technology and innovation is a very rational enterprise that builds on the accumulated human understanding of how nature works. From this enterprise humans get new powers to control natural processes and produce benefits for themselves. But the idea that good will triumph over evil in the end isn't a scientific proposition; it's an act of faith."

He started to interrupt me, but I wouldn't allow it and instead rushed on. "Wait, let me finish my train of thought. When I refer to faith, I mean faith in God's plan for His Creation. Belief in the ultimate victory of good over evil is this kind of faith, and it has nothing to do with a purely scientific worldview. This is what troubles me so much about the continuous enlarging of human powers, especially when we get to engineer the genomes of all living things.

"Thanks to modern science in particular, these powers have become a reality in the world that humans have created. But as I said a moment ago, the idea that there will be a preponderance of good over evil in the uses to which these powers are put isn't a scientific proposition at all; it's an article of religious belief, a hope based on a doctrine of faith in an unseen God. What if this hope is betrayed in the end? What if it turns out that humans didn't quite understand God's plan for them after all?"

He waved his hand at me dismissively. "That's precisely why I never trouble myself with religion or superstition, Hera. It just confuses things, when it makes any sense at all, which isn't often. When I speak of bad outcomes, I'm referring to events that just happen, usually accidentally, and must be made right again. We just have to find out how to fix whatever's gone wrong, and our technologies tell us how to do this. What's the point in referring to evil intentions or some such nonsense?"

"Well, I'm not the only one using these terms. Our politicians started talking this way a few decades ago, when the awareness first dawned on them that there were many people who didn't accept the right of those with the strongest technologies to run the whole world. When those people fought back, with whatever weapons they could lay their hands on, they were referred to as evildoers, weren't they? You may not have noticed, but this language is still today very common among politicians.

"Remember, Franklin, we sisters lived for some time in Canada among religious believers, and we even included Bible study as part of the deal we made with them to take us in. You may not know this, but the one among us who seemed to become quite obsessed with religious expression is my dear sister Io. She became fascinated with the language of the Bible a few years ago. I find it interesting because she has an exceptionally keen mind, as you know. That's why I referred to this notion of the final triumph of the evildoers, who have been provided with their most potent weapons by those who were striving to do only good. Io has a very perverse rendition of the final outcome, as related in the Book of Revelation. You might be amused to hear it. Let me see if I can recall how it goes."

He grumbled, "Must we really dwell on this? Aren't we meeting today because we have far more important matters to discuss?"

I simply ignored his protest. "Please, bear with me just a minute; this won't take long. Oh yes, I remember now. Io's heresy—I'm sure she would have been burned at the stake for saying this in an earlier century—is that the Bible's rendition itself makes it clear that the bad guys win in the end. Satan gets to do God's dirty work for Him, and then, after the final battle on earth, God hauls His tiny band of perfect believers up to Heaven with Him, where, we're told, their occupation for all of eternity thereafter is to sing His praises. What an egomaniac, Io says. How boring and unlucky to be among the ranks of the saved."

I sensed that he was getting restless and annoyed, but I persisted. "Meanwhile, Satan and his band of demons have the bad people all to themselves. And remember, there are far more of them in Satan's camp than in God's. So the Devil wins on numbers alone. Think about the outcome carefully. After God departs for Heaven, why should we expect Satan to carry on punishing the sinners with hideous torments—the kind portrayed so lovingly in medieval paintings? After all, sin is disobedience to God's will, succumbing to the devil's temptations. So why on earth should Satan punish them for doing his bidding? After all, they're his kind of people, right? Besides, Satan doesn't answer to God; he never has—the Bible makes this clear. He's his own master. And now he owns the earth, or what's left of it, after all the destruction that's been rained down on it, as if the poor planet itself were somehow blameworthy.

"Those who failed admission to Heaven did so because they followed Satan's temptations and had fun. Why should their suffering be prolonged now that God has ascended to some far-off place with his little cohort of sycophantic praise givers? What those puffed-up loyalists didn't realize is, with God now gone, Satan intends to turn Hell on Earth into one grand, never-ending party. Loud music, drugs, alcohol, nonstop sex—you name it, they'll be doing it. And they won't have God's so-called servants, the fun-hating clergymen, around anymore to pester them and try to make them feel guilty about doing what their natures incline them to do. So, I ask you, why should we have any sympathy for the devil?"

As Franklin sat stone-faced in front of me, my recollections of Io's performance made me quite merry. "We were all hanging around one night at Io's place, drinking some good wine, and Io just got carried away with this theme; it was hilarious. Everybody else was trying to outdo each other in coming up with ideas—the more outrageous, the better. Io started the contest off by naming Satan the 'Resident DJ at the Hellfire & Damnation Café.' Its motto is 'Sin Around the Clock.' Then we all started contributing slogans that would advertise Satan's café to patrons on the Underworld Internet. Let me see if I can remember some of the better ones:

> *We have every drug ever banned by Christian authorities.*
> *All free!*
> *The bad have fun. The very bad have more fun. The evil*
> *are fun.*
> *We'll get you so high you'll be looking down on the angels*
> *in heaven.*
> *No do-gooders allowed. We threw out God Himself last*
> *night.*
> *Back by popular demand this week only! The Marquis de Sade*
> *in person!*

"All of a sudden Io got very serious and said, 'The bad guys win. Every time. End of story.' Then she left."

Franklin was extremely curt and ill-tempered when he finally spoke. "It's a lot of silly nonsense based on a very silly book, Hera. What's the point, if there is one?"

"I'm sorry you don't find it funny. We all did that night, but maybe it was the wine! Anyway, Io does have a serious point to make. She said something along these lines: Remember that God's great idea, the pinnacle of His creation, was to mould one special creature—the only one in all the infinite number of beings that He made then or thereafter—who would be formed in His own image or likeness. Then the serpent comes along, intent on spoiling everything, chatting up poor innocent Eve:

> The woman said unto the serpent, We may eat of the fruit
> of the trees of the garden;
> But of the fruit of the tree which is in the midst of the
> garden, God hath said,
> Ye shall not eat of it, neither shall ye touch it, lest ye die.
> And the serpent said unto the woman, Ye shall not surely
> die:
> For God doth know that in the day ye eat thereof, then your
> eyes shall be opened,
> And ye shall be as gods, knowing good and evil.

"Well, we were supposed to resist this ridiculous little blandishment, weren't we? Even though the Bible describes the serpent as subtle or cunning, what was so subtle about this pathetic little trick?"

I carried on, racing against his rising exasperation with me. "I'm still relaying Io's rendition. Eve should have refused the fruit when offered it by that 'old serpent,' who of course was Satan in disguise. What did she and Adam need the knowledge of good and evil for? Of what use would it be to them? In any event, neither of them was smart enough to just send the serpent packing, which makes you think that they weren't very bright. But in accepting the knowledge that supposedly makes us 'like God,' we crossed a line in the sand and there's no going back. What is this knowledge? It's our science, of course. What else is there in our possession that seems to make us 'like God'—the God who is the Creator of All Things?

"Read the *Memorandum to the Group of 300,* Io says. Now the modern scientist comes along and announces to God, 'I bet I can trump your deeds. I can find out exactly where the seat of this moral center is, the one you implanted so that humans could tell the difference between good and evil, as no other animal can. And I'm so smart, once I find it, I could re-program it a bit, or even just delete it if I wanted to, like a software file that's no longer needed. Then I'll have a version of your precious *Homo sapiens* that won't know good from evil even if it tries. I'm pretty sure you won't want this version back on the Day of Judgment. But I can find a few uses for it down here in the meantime.'

"What I think she's getting at is this. It's not the application of knowledge to evil purposes, but just having the knowledge of how to create life itself that puts us across the line in a religious sense. Do you see what she means?"

His response was to stuff his papers into his briefcase and start to walk away; when he was a few paces away he turned and said angrily, "I'm sorry, Hera; you've lost me. I've waited patiently for weeks to have a serious conversation with you, and my thanks is to have you waste my time with a farcical religious exposition. I don't understand what you're getting at, or why you think that this crazy stuff is relevant to the issues about genetic engineering. Somewhere along the line you and Io apparently have become theologians. I'm just a working scientist doing what he thinks must be done if humanity is to escape its headlong rush into universal chaos. Can we leave the Bible out of this from now on? I realize that many people—including natural scientists—describe themselves as believers in God in some sense, but there are also plenty who don't. Nor do non-believers think you need a religion in order to have morality and a distinction between right and wrong. I'm with the non-believers, so all this biblical nonsense is irrelevant to me."

He turned to walk away. Clearly he was very annoyed and I realized I had pushed him too far. "All right, Franklin, I do apologize. Please sit here with me just awhile longer. I freely admit that my comments on these subjects are rather inchoate, which bothers me as well as you, since I take pride in thinking clearly. So let's turn to the subject you wanted to talk about, the plans for the Second Generation. One of the outstanding matters is gender."

"Good, I'd much rather talk about real issues," he answered at once, returning to his chair. "And the one you mentioned is very real to me. Ina and I had no wish to create a separate little subgroup of the human race that would treat its special genetic enhancements as its own private property, so to speak. In fact, exactly the opposite. We were both very disturbed by the trends we had observed already by 2012, just before she died, because the rich and privileged strata were already starting to talk about restricted mating among their offspring, after genetic enhancements had been carried out on them. They were thinking about conserving certain types of enhancements—affecting both physical appearance and mental qualities—within their own circles, and not allowing them to be available to the masses."

I interjected. "We know that some of these ventures have been carried out during the last few decades."

"Yes, they have, and I remain completely opposed to such a thing. We don't want to create a private tribe by having our own males and females interbreed with each other. The whole purpose of the original project was to spread our genetic enhancements as quickly as possible through the human population as a whole. Having only females in our group is the best way to do this. The types of modifications made in my protocol cannot yield their intended results only at birth. The correct kind of childhood and teenage learning environment is just as important. Our best chances of success involve training our mothers-to-be to raise their children properly. If, on the other hand, we were to choose to engineer only males, the probability they would adhere to the protocol's elaborate child-raising requirements once they were marrying and having children of their own is slim indeed.

"And, by the way, part of this training will be to impress upon these girls the importance of following the protocol for up to twenty years after the birth of their children. I interpret some of my failure with you sisters as a direct result of the abrupt termination of my program when you suddenly became separated from me. The higher-level attributes in the prefrontal cortex, which I hypothesized could be the basis of the humanitarian mission you would carry out, become fully formed only at a very late stage in a young person's development. That stage was truncated in your case."

I had no intention of revisiting these sensitive topics right now, so I simply said, "The main point is that you want to select only female embryos for the Second Generation. Your reasoning is that females are much more likely to take your protocol seriously when raising their children. So, on balance, your objectives are much more likely to be realized by making this choice."

"Yes, and I want to be sure you understand the other implications of this approach, since you haven't been trained in biology. The process of natural selection would dictate some loss of our germline modifications when the children to be known as our Second Generation themselves mature and reproduce. This results from the fact that many of the modifications dictated by the protocol are made on the X chromosome, the so-called female chromosome. And we do so because out of all 23 that humans carry, this particular chromosome happens to have a large number of genetic sequences responsible for brain development. When the second generation has children, one would expect half of the daughters in that cohort to be carriers for our dominant gene modifications; the other half will not. This is because in them, one X from the mother—our modified individual, represented as X*—is mixed with another X from the father—unmodified. Since we carry only one copy of our sex chromosomes in our gametes, or sex cells, what we are talking about is essentially a random process in which the X and X* are distributed in the next generation.

"I've been assuming in these illustrations that natural selection continues to operate, Hera. However, recent technological advances in rapid genetic screening of entire genome sequences, using microchip arrays, give rise to another possibility entirely. In the future, parents could, if they wish, screen candidate embryos after IVF and select for re-implantation only those that are carrying the desired modifications. In order to do this type of screening, one has to know where to look in the genome for the modified sequences; so, with respect to the modifications we will be making, I intend to publish my protocol after the children from the Group of 500 are born so that others can use it. Of course, while this screening is being done, a check for inherited diseases can also be made. Any embryos not showing the modified genes would be discarded. I fully expect that a high percentage of parents will opt for these procedures.

"Therefore, after a number of generations have passed, we can expect the X-linked modifications we engineered to become well established in the human gene pool. The bottom line is, after we introduce these changes they will slowly spread throughout the population and become widely distributed in the human genome, and there will be no turning back."

"OK, I think I'm clear on what you just explained. If I remember what you said at the beginning of our conversation, you've completed the scientific review of the gene modifications you carried out in 2024 on the embryos before freezing them; you concluded that the protocol you used then is still valid, although you do intend some further modifications. So now the first tasks that await us is recruiting and screening the new donor couples, collecting eggs and sperm from them, and fertilizing and preparing the embryos."

"That's right, and we'll have to get started on that job right away. Of course, I'll also be writing to the members of the Group of 300, explaining why we had to discard their embryos due to the unexpected delays we encountered. I'm sure they'll understand. They will know that they themselves have passed the optimal age for producing healthy offspring. They were a highly motivated bunch. I won't be surprised if some of them offer to help us in recruiting the new donor group."

"And later on, when you are choosing the surrogate mothers, do you intend to involve the couples among the Group of 500 who donated the eggs and sperm? Also, of course, involving them when these children are being raised? That was part of your original plan for the Group of 300, wasn't it?"

"Yes it was, but I'm not sure that we should make that offer to the couples during the recruiting process this time around. The world has gotten much more unstable during the intervening years, it seems. We may need to proceed in extreme secrecy and protect our mothers and children behind high-security enclosures. So I'm considering writing up the legal agreements with the donors in such a way that our foundation will have the option to proceed without any involvement of the natural parents in either childbirth or child rearing, if that appears to be the best course to follow when we get to the implantation step."

FEBRUARY 2037

Gaia presented the necessary motions to a recent Board of Directors meeting. "Anticipating your approval, we've had preliminary meetings with some prospective donors during the last few months—including reviewing with them a slightly revised version of the 2021 *Memorandum*. As a result, we're convinced we'll have no trouble in eliciting enthusiastic cooperation from the type of couples we are targeting. Everyone is alarmed by the trends in world events. They can only guess at whether we'll succeed in our objectives or not, but they're eager and willing to help us try. We'll have no trouble at all in filling our quota."

I called for a vote and the board gave its unanimous approval. "What's your expected timeline?" I asked.

Gaia answered, "A minimum of three years. We four scientist-sisters will be continuing our training while the donor recruitment and screening process is taking place. We've allocated two years to that phase. The third year will be devoted to preparing something on the order of 15,000 embryos. We have already begun the hiring and training of a large batch of skilled lab technicians to assist us with this task."

I adjourned the meeting. Franklin had allowed Gaia to carry the entire conversation, saying not a word. He's not looking at all well to me.

Just returned from the hospital visiting grandfather, who has suffered quite a serious heart attack. *(Sub-Compiler's Note: Enter Marco!)*

He's had some unmistakable warning signs throughout the past year, such as repeated bouts of illness that kept him away from his laboratory for extended periods. His doctors counseled him to ease up a bit in his work, but he refused, telling them that his project was falling behind schedule again. He's expected to recover, although the doctors have now ordered him to stay away from his lab for at least another year. I had a long talk with mother a few days ago, and it was a bit unsettling. She's become quite careful when talking about her father and the upcoming procedures to create the Second Generation.

Just before his heart attack, Franklin was very critical of her for 'dragging her feet,' as he put it, about forming a management team at the foundation to direct the recruiting of the small army of surrogate mothers who will carry the children, and for getting the facility ready in which they will be housed. He had started to express these criticisms of mother to many of the sisters, especially to Io, who has been spending a lot of time with him lately. She's rarely left his bedside since he was hospitalized three weeks ago.

Mother asked me to start keeping a running journal of events and observations for her, since she's become far too busy recently to do this for herself.

To be fair to Hera, I think Franklin has underestimated the sheer scale of the new project, in terms of logistics. The permanent population on the Turks and Caicos Islands is far too small to form the sole recruiting pool for the surrogate mothers, since obviously we will demand documented proof of consistent good health over a long period prior to acceptance. The foundation will have to search more widely among the other nations in the Caribbean in order to come up with the list of two thousand candidates who could pass the first health screening. Then there will be various rounds of personal interviews and exhaustive medical exams, blood tests, and X-rays by doctors working on contract to the foundation before the final list of approved persons is drawn up.

As far as I'm concerned, one of the reasons why things have slowed down is that Hera has become increasingly upset with her father's criticisms of her. Their relationship seemed to turn sour sometime in the last year, for reasons that are not entirely clear to my aunts or me. But it was getting pretty serious in the few months leading up to his heart attack. I overheard them one day in the pavilion—they were arguing in loud voices—and Franklin said to her then that he was thinking of requesting a board meeting of the foundation so that what he called her 'failings in leadership' could be discussed by the directors. Apparently he got sick before this could take place.

She told me a few months ago that the increasing frequency of the fights with her father, and his tendency to become more verbally abusive to her over time, was wearing her down. Mother hasn't looked well to me, at least not like she usually has in the past. She says if it wasn't for me and Lucy and her dog, Magnus, and what we mean to her, she wouldn't know what to do. I told her I wanted to help in any way that I could.

Last week Hera told me that she had had to add a new

project to her already heavy workload; she'll get a little help from Tammy on it, apparently, but it seems that the whole tribe is working flat out on their various assignments—except for Io, of course, who seems to follow only her personal agenda. Anyway, this new project involves a group that wants to set up a long-term working relationship with both the Sujana Foundation and our company, PathoGene. Their organization, which is based in the United States and contacted us first about three months ago, has a strange name: The Vandenberg Colony. I'm not entirely sure yet just who is involved and what exactly their purposes are. Hera has obtained some information from them, although she had to pledge to uphold the strictest level of confidentiality about it.

Its president is General Philip Ziegler, who's apparently a two-star general in the United States Air Force, although he's still in his thirties. The Colony apparently is a kind of secret society—only those who are members know it exists. General Ziegler sent a document to Hera that outlines in general terms the membership and objectives. Mother said I could copy some passages from it as long as I kept my journal locked away in the foundation's safe, where she keeps her own journals and business documents.

MEMORANDUM RE: THE VANDENBERG COLONY

The Vandenberg Colony is an association of like-minded individuals whose names are known only to the board of directors. No written record of membership exists in any location that is not fully protected with the highest levels of military security. We have come together for purposes of protecting our mutual interests in a time of increasing social and political chaos throughout the world. We are convinced that we can no longer count on established governments, not even the Government of the United States, to safeguard those interests.

The Vandenberg Colony takes its name from the Vandenberg Air Force Base (AFB) in central California, home of the launching sites for all rockets headed into space. The Colony has entered into a confidential contract with the United States Air Force, under which the base perimeter will be expanded gradually, with funds provided by the Colony, as contiguous property is acquired either on the open market or by exercising powers of eminent domain.

This arrangement was made pursuant to a federal law, enacted by Congress in 2035, that permits the US armed forces and national security agencies to enter into agreements with private parties, and to provide services to them under those agreements. As you know, the reasons for this law arose largely because the costs of maintaining both the military and security agencies have escalated rapidly in recent decades, due to the proliferation of anti-American terrorist activities around the world. These costs became so high they could no longer be funded exclusively from public tax monies, and so additional sources of revenue became necessary.

Once they take up residence near Vandenberg AFB, the members of the Colony will receive full security services for their persons and property from US government agencies and the military. Since the Colony is a privately incorporated entity, members (including their families) may be citizens of any country in the world. Membership payments are on an annual per capita basis, according to a fee structure approved by the board of directors, and each Member may designate up to 50 individuals to be covered under the terms of the Colony's charter. By special act of Congress, all individuals included in the Colony's membership are issued permanent residency permits, and are treated as if they were officials in their home countries' diplomatic service.

Each Member's initial capital contribution provides for the lease in perpetuity of a five-acre plot of land within the Colony's security perimeter, all of which is now legally a part of Vandenberg Air Force Base. Thus all of the Colony's territory is covered by the access restrictions common to a high-security military installation, and, of course, is off-limits to unauthorized persons at all times. Each Member is required to construct a private compound on his plot within three years of acquiring it. The approved architectural designs all have full computer-controlled security systems. The perimeter, as well as interior roads and streets, are patrolled continuously by armed military forces, and full electronic and satellite surveillance is supplied as well.

Participation in the Colony is presently restricted to a maximum of 500 members, and therefore to a maximum of 25,000 registered individuals. Current members are drawn from every region of the world, and the membership complement is now full and closed. The Colony has opened a waiting list for future membership on a first-come basis, and at this time there are almost 200 applicants on the list.

I must admit I quite like the aura of mystery surrounding the Colony and its membership! Hera told me she understands that the initiation fee and initial capital contribution is something like 100 million euros per Member, and average annual fees total about €5 million. There's an additional voluntary subscription for those wishing to take part in an unnamed special project, priced at an astonishing 300 million euros! Participation in this project is limited to forty members and apparently the list is already full and closed. According to Hera, most of the very richest families everywhere on earth are among the current members, and those on the waiting list are applying every type of pressure they can think of, including offers of premium fees and simple bribes, to be accepted as soon as possible.

OCTOBER 2039

Hera revealed to me today a vague description of this special project, and it's amazing! Each subscriber is entitled to put one name on a roster, female or male, who will join a privately funded expedition to Mars sometime within the next twenty or thirty years! Not only that: This expedition, totaling about fifty people in all, will set up the infrastructure for a *permanent* Mars Colony. Others will go there later to occupy it if the expedition is successful. Apparently this plan has been in the works for a long time. I'm dying to find out more.

At our last meeting I asked Hera, "Why did The Vandenberg Colony contact you, of all people? Why are they interested in us? Or have we become a member?"

"No, it's simpler than that. General Ziegler called me one day out of the blue and asked me to meet him at a US security installation located in the Bahamas. You don't say no to a two-star USAF general! They're interested in PathoGene's technologies and, more generally, in our expertise in neurogenetics and molecular biology. Your grandfather's work is extremely well known around the world, and despite his three-year 'sabbatical,' as he refers to his stay at the clinic outside Cambridge, once he resumed his research he quickly regained his standing among his peers as the leading scientist in his field.

"There are two reasons for the General's keen interest in what we're doing. The first stems from the increasing virulence of the bioterrorist threat around the world. As you know, for a while now some terrorist groups have been targeting rich families directly, and extracting protection money from them, instead of concentrating their attacks only on governments and multinational corporations. Their engineered pathogens are getting ever more deadly and difficult to counteract, partly because the equipment and techniques used for molecular biology, especially for tinkering around with rudimentary organisms like bacteria and viruses, get simpler every day.

"Already a few decades ago, applied microbiology had become virtually a 'backyard garage' type of operation. There are plenty of recruits in the terrorist organizations who have obtained enough scientific training to become rogue gene jockeys. After all, in the advanced economies, all high school students today play around with unicellular organisms in their biology labs, using gene guns and probes to insert and remove DNA fragments. It's regarded as fun."

I listened carefully and took some notes as Hera went on. "They're very interested in PathoGene's expertise, especially our patented technologies for rapid DNA sequencing of new pathogens and accelerated development of countermeasures. But it's the second reason that explains why General Ziegler had to brief me on the Colony itself, as well as on its project involving the expedition to Mars.

"As you know, a lot of preliminary exploration has been undertaken on Mars using computer-controlled robots. NASA has mapped extensive portions of the surface and sent probes deep below, looking for water deposits and analyzing the planet's near-surface mineral and metal composition. Apparently they've found vast underground aquifers, promising not only an abundant supply of pure water, but also a basis for producing hydrogen to fuel their shuttle rockets. They also found sufficient metal and mineralogical deposits made up of familiar elements, so that with portable high-energy chambers they can fashion construction materials on-site.

"But what they fear most of all is encountering previously undetected infectious microbes, unlike anything yet known on earth, that would wipe out the entire colony almost instantly because the settlers wouldn't have any immunities to them. This is the second reason for their keen interest in

PathoGene's technologies. I've already signed a contract between the Colony and PathoGene under which we'll start developing a prototype for a portable, self-contained Microbial DNA Sequencer, and associated devices, for transport to Mars. Since Franklin isn't expected to be back in his lab for a year or more, two of our biologists—Rhea and Pandora—are now working on this task at PathoGene, which has increased the firm's productivity enormously."

"First, of course, they must have checked us out with undercover agents, right?"

"Indeed they did, Marco! For awhile our islands were overrun with US spooks doing background security profiles on all of us. We passed with flying colors, although some of them did wonder whether we were training our apes to be undercover agents with listening devices implanted under their skins! Anyway, they're so good at their jobs that, as far as I know, no one else suspected what was happening.

"No, that last statement is not quite accurate: The girls over at Troglodyte Partners picked up some of the electronic scans, but the equipment that the spooks were using is so advanced, they couldn't break the encryption. By the way, part of the contract I signed provides for technology transfer the other way. Troglodyte Partners will gain access to some of their very nice snooping toys under license.

"This has all transpired within the last few years. I regard this as one of our highest priorities because I think that, sometime down the road aways, we might need the Colony as much as it now perceives it needs us. We may not remain immune forever to the political chaos sweeping the world. And if our genetic engineering capabilities ever become more widely known, even to a relatively small circle of players, we may be either targeted for sabotage or recruited—being made an offer we couldn't refuse, as they say—into somebody's terrorist campaign. In that case we'll need Ziegler's protection.

"Like the Colony, apparently, I've also become more concerned recently that the gradual sea-level rise around the world will exacerbate the existing political and social tensions. It's not so much the amount of the sea-level rise to date, but the uncertainty about whether it will continue to happen at the same rate or—and this is what scares people—suddenly get much, much worse. People's nerves are already on edge, mostly because of terrorism, so any added uncertainty about another entirely different set of bad news really gets to them. Therefore, the effect is magnified out of all proportion to the danger, at least to the danger we now can see with our eyes. We have an elaborate operation here. We have to think ahead as well, try to anticipate events, and do some scenario planning. When you're a little older I want you to help me with this file."

"Oh yes, please, I'd love to be involved with this. It would give me a nice break from my studies once in a while. Could I start now?"

She gave me the nicest smile. To be fair, she indulges me a bit. I knew she wouldn't be able to say no.

"Okay, Mr. Marco. Although you just turned nine two months ago, I will concede that you are mature beyond your years. You do remind me a bit of myself when I was your age. So I'll give you access to the file and you can pass on your considered opinions to me whenever you like."

She handed me a couple of manila folders. "You should know that I've already broached the subject of our own security concerns with General Ziegler. You'll find in the files a first draft of a *Memorandum of Understanding* between the Colony and our foundation. Obviously, Ziegler is a man who thinks ahead. When I raised the subject with him, he grinned rather coyly and said that he had already placed our entire operations and facilities under a first-level watch. We're now routinely included in his analysis of daily satellite scans of the areas surrounding vital facilities. We're also included, in a preliminary way, in his contingency plans for emergency evacuation and relocation.

"Clearly he and his associates think very highly of our expertise and its value to them. The MOU between the Vandenberg Colony and PathoGene is designed to document our awareness of our mutual interests and to formalize a method for cooperating in the future. It will indicate in broad outline what kinds of steps will be taken, by both parties acting together, if certain specific chains of events should unfold. He and I have already agreed in principle that, under a number of worst-case scenarios, the Colony will assume responsibility for relocating all of us to a secure place to be specified later. This means our entire operation—including, of course, every one of the primates in our care!

"That should do for the time being, young man," she said, laughing. "Now off you go! I believe it's time for your riding lesson. I hear you're becoming quite the expert horseman."

§   §   §

I've now had a chance to read the entire set of documents about The Vandenberg Colony that General Ziegler gave Hera at their meeting in the Bahamas. I was particularly interested in the Appendix to the colony's charter, which provides a brief account of the background events leading up to its formation. Some of the information in it presumably came from top-secret briefings by the US national security agencies, since I've never seen this material published anywhere.

The Vandenberg Colony Charter
Appendix: History and Background

This Appendix, prepared in December 2038, provides members with the perspective of the board's security and intelligence advisory committee, which includes senior officials from the US agencies responsible for threat surveillance and risk assessment around the world. The steps that led to the incorporation of The Vandenberg Colony can be traced directly to events that took place on 11 September 2031, which marked the 30th anniversary of the infamous attack on New York's World Trade Center. Although similar attacks had occurred at regular ten-year intervals beginning in 2011, these latest were by far the worst. The coordinated terrorist assaults unleashed seven years ago provided final proof, if any were needed, that national governments were no longer able to offer acceptable levels of security to their citizens against such operations. The official casualty and property damage figures are often cited: 20,000 deaths and 100,000 serious injuries across Europe and North America combined, with property losses estimated at 800 billion euros.

Reliable confidential documents reveal that the actual casualty figures could be 50% higher in both categories. However, even the official numbers frightened our populations and demoralized our governments to the point where neither seems able to think or act appropriately. Appeasement has been the order of the day ever since, but we all know where that route leads in the end. The families of the wealthy around the world have concluded that they cannot rely upon conventional forces marshaled by governments to protect them. We have charted an entirely different course, using a form of public–private partnership to achieve our goals. And we have moved in this new direction for the simple reason that we foresee further and worse trouble ahead.

Governments in Russia, India, China, Central and Southeast Asia, and most of Central and South America have been slowly crumbling under the stress of endemic social, economic and environmental chaos. All of this leaves a fast-shrinking network of oases of relative political stability: Mexico and the Caribbean; the European Union (although its eastern and southeastern borders are highly unstable); Japan and South Korea; Australia and New Zealand. The security of the United States itself has, of course, been strengthened greatly by the recent peaceful absorption of both Canada and Québec, assuring access to their oil sands deposits and vast freshwater resources, and also extending our command over the oceans in the Northern Hemisphere right up to the Arctic Circle.

Finally, we add the corrosive uncertainty that attaches to possible future climate events. To date climate change impacts—such as extreme weather events, average temperature increases, and sea-level rise—have remained within the higher part of the range of estimates, as first laid out in scenarios prepared by the Intergovernmental Panel on Climate Change (IPCC) in its *Third Assessment Report* issued in 2001. But the most recent figures, from the Tenth Assessment Report (2038), showing that global greenhouse gas emissions are still on a strong growth curve, have prompted experts to insist that the accumulated future impacts will be much more severe than previously estimated. In addition, the very visible scenes of collective hysteria associated with relatively small sea-level rises in low-lying populated areas have gotten everyone on edge.

Most people are unaware of how large is the percentage of the total human population now living along coastlines whose habitats are at some risk from sea-level rise. Taken in isolation, neither the recent climate-related events nor the uncertainties about the future would have been sufficient in themselves to induce widespread panic. But they are not occurring in isolation; rather, they have just become one frame in a larger picture of looming chaos.

The two most probable future scenarios may be sketched as follows. In the first scenario, the combination of terrorism and social chaos on the one hand, and rising sea levels on the other, sets the restless populations to Europe's east and southeast into motion, and the last friendly portion of the great Eurasian land mass is eventually overrun in an orgy of destruction. The zone of stability shrinks to North America and a few still-powerful island-states, but the governments and peoples there devour their own strength in a frenzy of self-loathing—until the others start to fall like dominoes, one by one, and only North America is left. You can guess how that scenario finally ends.

However, the second scenario is the one that we intend to see through to success. By careful advance planning, a series of secure colonies will be established in favorable and well-defended locations around the world. Members' wealth will be converted into the portable commodities most desired in a chaotic world—gold, diamonds, weapons, energy, pharmaceuticals, and so on. They will be linked in a defensive alliance through satellite communications, control of the skies, and access to the most advanced weaponry ever developed, including biological warfare agents. They will have large client populations on their perimeters who will supply them with necessities in return for protection against marauding bands of vandals. They will possess sufficient firepower to wipe any who threaten them off the face of the earth.

I realized just how important we must be when I thought about the alliance we are building with The Vandenberg Colony. We're no little band of twelve sisters and a baby anymore! If I think ahead just a few years, we'll have one thousand pregnant women in residence in their own building. We already have an extensive array of laboratories and business offices, and as a group we have been accumulating personal possessions at an alarming rate! Perhaps this latter element reflects the fact that my aunts fled their birthplace with not even their own clothes on their backs and with nothing but a few personal mementos in their pockets.

And we have our primates, now numbering more than 250, who are starting to produce many offspring. The keepers say this is not surprising, since we have provided them with large, secure enclosures, each devoted to one species and all covered in trees and vegetation, where they can roam around to their hearts' content. Only the keepers interact with them, and nobody except our staff is allowed to mingle with them—except for Lucy, who has bonded with Hera; the rest of us, however, are permitted to ascend the viewing platforms built at the edges of their enclosures.

§　§　§

I love spending time in Hera's private house, where I have my own set of rooms. Roberto, who prepares our meals and organizes our schedules, also lives there. Hera had it designed in Japanese style, as a suite of connected chambers arranged in a small square around a central courtyard, with large gardens beyond its outer walls on every side, so that we are enclosed in a sea of plants and flowers native to the Caribbean. Her inner courtyard is an amazingly peaceful place, filled with ancient trees, plants and rocks imported from Japan, with water flowing and bubbling continuously everywhere. When I sit there the entire world seems to be shut out, and it's a wonderful place for meditation and working on my assignments.

In her outer gardens Hera favors the native dry-loving succulents, the cacti and agaves, as well as the Islands' wonderful flowering shrubs and vines, arranged by species in plantings under the cover of larger trees. Nearest her bedroom in the outer gardens she keeps the native orchid,

Enclyclia altissima—the tallest member of the orchid family, as indicated by its name, reaching up to two meters in height—and a few varieties of frangipani (*P. rubra*), whose intense fragrances float inwards whenever a door is opened. The house and outer gardens are enclosed by a perimeter wall that gives us a wonderful sense of privacy and peace.

Hera's own rooms are also in Japanese style, built all on the same level except for a few steps up or down here and there. The floors are of highly polished hardwoods—recycled, she said, 'since there's nothing much left in the tropical rainforests'—and all her walls are draped in off-white linen wallcovering. One enters some rooms through *shoji* doors. Interior entryways between other rooms have *fusama* doorways, all made of the most beautiful cypress wood. The inner walls and the flooring are of modular construction, set on aluminum frames, so they can be disassembled and moved easily—a sign of her sense of impermanence, I guess.

All of Hera's rooms are sparsely furnished, but every piece there—mostly lacquered or varnished furniture—is beautiful. Many Japanese wood-block prints cover the walls, and there's an old bonsai tree in each room. Antique bowls and platters of celadon porcelain and very old *cloissoné* pieces from China are displayed in cabinets. Hera sleeps on a futon close to the floor, but indulges herself shamelessly, as she puts it, with her silk bedding. In one room is her piano, where she plays for Lucy for an hour a day whenever they're together.

I'm in shock every time I go to visit Io, however. Especially if I have just come from Hera's place. Io's compound contrasts with Hera's in every way you could imagine. She loves African art as much as Hera loves the Japanese style. There are wooden masks and figurines everywhere. Io admires especially the Dogon statuary—her collection includes both the female and the hermaphrodite types—and the masks carved by the Fang and Bambara tribes.

Her furniture is made of quite rough woods, sometimes unfinished and drab, but what makes up for this is that everything in her rooms, and most of the walls as well, are draped in cloths of riotous colors, with African, Aztec, Mayan and Navajo designs. Thin rugs of the same designs cover the floors and are sometimes piled three or four deep. Outside she has large rock gardens planted with herbs amidst stands of Caribbean pine. Only the tiny flowers produced by herbs appeal to her; larger flowers, she insists, are 'too sensual and provocative for the daylight hours.'

Her bedroom is what she calls her lair. She has an enormous four-poster bed covered with a silk canopy, with bedding of the finest black silk. Her precious cats, a Balinese and an Egyptian Mau, are usually found there. There are soft multi-colored lights, computer-controlled, set in the ceiling and walls, and a big sound system that can be heard in some of the adjoining buildings. She tells me that when I'm older she'll show me her fine collection of dildos and other pleasure implements. I heard Hera telling Ariadne once that Io holds wild parties in the houses outside the compound and invites people from town to them.

§　§　§

I want to set down a few words about Magnus, Hera's big and beautiful male Great Dane, who is now a little more than two years old. Hera says that he's my dog as well as hers, and I do spend a lot of time with him, especially since Hera has become so busy with work. And she also needs to spend some time with Lucy when the chimp is visiting.

I take Magnus for long walks at least once a day, sometimes more, along the beach and through the grove inside our compound. The Turks and Caicos Islands are very dry much of the year; often the only significant rains are in October. There is some tropical deciduous forest left here and there on the islands. The forest grove in our compound is an older one, having some lovely stands of Caribbean pine and mahogany covering the dense shrub undergrowth. Magnus loves to play hide-and-seek with me in our private forest.

Hera got Magnus after her relations with her father started to turn sour. He's a large man and can appear intimidating when he's angry, although he's not physically violent, as far as I know. But as their conversations gradually turned into repeated arguments, he often raised his voice at her and has sometimes been verbally abusive. She knew that it would be impossible to change him, and she couldn't stop talking to him because the foundation's main project is approaching a critical point.

So she decided to deal with her problem indirectly by getting a big male dog that would be very well trained to obey her commands—and thus could be taken everywhere she went. Magnus took to his training routines like a duck to water: He loved the interactions and excelled at his duties. Hera said once that he was smarter than many people she has met. He could be left off-leash, and she could be confident that he would respond at once to whatever command she gave.

One day she remarked to me, "You know, Marco, I used to have trouble explaining to Franklin what it was like to have a mind that could 'see ahead,' in a way. What I mean is that my mind is hyper-attuned to pattern and order, and I can grasp the outlines or trends of developing events much more quickly than most people can. Now I just explain it by referring to Magnus! We've spent so much time together in the last few months that he's started to show an uncanny ability to anticipate what activity is about to take place for the two of us.

"I think he does this by being able to pick up very subtle signals from me, signals that I'm unaware I'm even sending, such as body language, tone of voice; he also pays attention to my sequence of activities during the day, the passage of time, and maybe other things. So once or twice during the day he'll just get himself up and move to the right place, as if to announce that he knows what should be happening at that point and that he's ready. It's delightful."

She laughs when she refers to Magnus as her 'alpha dog.' It seems he's just made that way; he regards himself as being at the top of the heap and expects other dogs to accept this fact. He's apparently prepared to test this hypothesis with every other dog he encounters. That's why Hera has trained him so well, so she can control his proclivity to 'sort things out.' She says that dominance hierarchies in dogs is their way of creating a well-ordered world. "Just like me," she says of Magnus, "always looking for the pattern that conveys meaning."

I've seen Hera accompanied by Magnus on her way to meetings with Franklin. Magnus is generally very friendly, at least with people he's been formally introduced to, and loves getting attention from one and all. But he is Hera's dog and he knows it. When she sits he lies down right beside her. Even when he dozes off you just know that he's alert and on duty, and I've seen the result.

Once Hera and Franklin were having a reasonably pleasant talk that escalated quickly into an argument, and he raised his voice, quite suddenly. Instantly Magnus—who had been fully stretched out, dozing—was on his feet, every muscle tensed, eyes blazing. Franklin visibly recoiled in his seat, expecting the dog to lunge at him. Since Magnus is so well trained, however, he immediately looked to Hera for a command. She made eye contact with him and said, "Magnus: Stay! Good boy." And he relaxed again after accepting the praise. In future there were fewer occasions during which Franklin let himself get out of control.

It's altogether different with strangers. Magnus never lets

his guard down in their presence, never dozes or allows his gaze to wander. Hera says that the other thing about Magnus that reminds her of herself is his keen intuition about situations that might represent risk. She and I were walking him one evening, on a leash, outside the compound on a training exercise when a stranger approached. We didn't think the man posed a danger, but Magnus sensed otherwise. Magnus stopped and just stood in place with every muscle tensed.

He had been reading the stranger's body language and apparently didn't like what he was seeing. His gaze locked onto the man. He let out a very low, almost inaudible growl that Hera and I, standing right next to him, could barely hear. She knew from previous experience that he had not acted this way in other, very similar situations. There were times when strangers passed them by on the street and he barely took notice. But this time was different. The man stopped in his tracks and froze. Hera said, "Magnus: Heel! Walk on! Good boy." And we passed by the petrified figure without incident.

NOVEMBER 2042

(Marco's Journal) All but a few of the sisters managed to make it to the airport to welcome their father back from his long stay abroad for medical treatment. Four months after he suffered his heart attack it was clear that he wasn't going to recover without major surgery, so we sent him off to a world-class cardiac facility in Edmonton, accompanied by Io. His quadruple-bypass operation seemed to go well at first, but serious complications intervened, including a series of strokes. For the past two years he's been cared for in a fine private clinic in Calgary—the same one in which I was born!

Io has been with him—or at least in the vicinity—almost the entire time, except for making short trips back to Provo. She took him on frequent outings through the Rockies and, so far as we know, obeyed the doctors' strict instructions that he was to receive no news whatsoever on any matters of science or foundation business. As for what else she was doing, none of us has the slightest clue. Pandora made quite a few quick trips to Calgary during this period; apparently she and Io spent a lot of time together in Vancouver, but that is the sum total of the information we were vouchsafed.

When we got our first look at him in the airport's VIP lounge, he appeared to be fully restored to health. This impression was reinforced by his instantaneous outburst upon hearing the reply to the question he posed right after our exchange of brief hellos. "Do we have a Second Generation?" he demanded.

Everyone looked at Gaia. She has never been intimidated by him, however, and she replied coolly, "Not yet. But soon, I expect. And that's the sum total of the answer you'll be getting right now. Let's go home."

Gaia had led the team of talented sisters and technicians who labored for six months in the latter half of 2040, fertilizing 10,000 of the donated eggs and then shepherding the zygotes onward to the 8-cell stage; the approximately 3,000 viable embryos that resulted are now resting peacefully in their cryopreservation chambers. By a fortuitous coincidence, this Herculean task was completed just in time for Hera to be able to reassign Gaia and Percy to PathoGene, where they joined Pandora and Rhea on the urgent tasks contained in the contract with the Vandenberg Colony. Their keen and restless minds welcome any new challenge and none of them needed any cajoling from Hera to take up this new assignment. Clearly they were ready to be released from their father's tutelage and strike out on their own. Since at this point I pretty much manage this file single-handedly on Hera's behalf, I'm familiar with their successes and with the praise emanating from our satisfied client.

MAY 2043

(Hera's Journal) "How very nice to see you back at work again in your lab, Franklin! The long period away from it on doctor's orders must have been trying for you."

"You don't know the half of it, Hera. I've just turned seventy years old. I can't expect to have all that much time left, especially not time when my mind is still sharp and I feel motivated to work. And, of course, the rest of my team was reassigned to another project while I was away, so no further progress was made on mine. By the way, have you finished the recruiting and screening procedures for the surrogate mothers?"

"No, I'm sorry, we're still not done. Frankly, it's been much more complicated than I ever imagined it would be, even with Rhea's help—she's the one actually monitoring the medical screening. We ended up rejecting more than half the candidates on the second round, and the process itself was incredibly time-consuming."

"I'm extremely disappointed to hear this news. Are you telling me that we won't be able to assemble the women and do the implantations for—what?—another year or more?"

"I'm afraid so. Look, I've got to run for another appointment. And I do want to talk to you at greater length about some aspects of our project that are still bothering me. Would you like to come to my place this evening, along with Gaia and one or two others? Would you mind if Marco joined us? He's become my indispensable executive assistant over the last few years. We've got so many things on the go that I can't handle them all myself anymore."

"Invite whomever you please—it's your house. And Marco's a fine young man. We had long conversations about everything under the sun while I was hospitalized here a few years ago."

So he and Marco and Gaia came to dinner at my house that evening, as did Tina and Ari, with whom I've been trying out some ideas. Marco accepted on condition that he could just listen. Roberto prepared an extravagant meal for us, to high praise from the fortunate diners. Later, after taking a walk through my gardens, we settled down in the courtyard and I opened the conversation. I had been dreading this moment but couldn't postpone it a moment longer.

"While collaborating with Rhea on the recruitment of surrogate mothers I reread your *Memorandum to the Group of 300* several times, Franklin. I focused specifically on your reasons for believing that engineering their embryos was not only desirable but also necessary. The reason given was that others in the world could be presumed to be experimenting with regressive forms of behavioral genetics and engineering. Therefore, someone like you had to mount a counteroffensive and try to design better types of people. Is this a fair account?"

"Yes, as far as it goes. Remember, though, your mother and I had good grounds to believe then that we were quite aways ahead of anybody else, at least with respect to understanding the genetic basis of neurological functions. As far as I can tell, we were right. Thus we weren't necessarily reacting to what others had accomplished, but what we feared they might try. What she and I really were striving to do was pre-empt the field and set a standard for others to aspire to—a standard driven by a vision of goodness and humanitarian ideals, of course. And in this sense, we also thought that what we sought to do was a good thing in itself, even if it had no additional practical objective."

"Still, the tenor of your *Memorandum* suggests that you were thinking of your creations as being instruments of a higher purpose, who would help save the civilized world and the scientific enterprise from descent into chaos, if I remember some of the language correctly."

"Fine, if you wish, you could say that in one sense we were launching a pre-emptive strike on our opponents by developing such instruments before they were in a position to do so. If you can beat them to it, and continue to stay out in front of them, you're in a perfect position to say, 'I'm way ahead of you in this game, and if you dare to threaten me, your people will suffer the consequences of our superiority.'"

Ari responded. "Somehow that sounds very familiar to me. Yes, I remember now; it's the balance of terror argument underpinning the Cold War ideology of both sides— the Soviet Union and the United States—for almost the entire second half of the twentieth century, isn't it?"

"Perhaps it is, and by the way, it worked, if I'm not mistaken. Humanity was spared a nuclear holocaust between two massive superpowers. We're in a new phase at this time, but the battle itself is really no different. The enemies are amorphous now, highly distributed, more devious, sometimes hiding as sleepers among us for years or decades. But they're all the same underneath. They all have some cause they want to advance. As long as we can speak to them from a position of strength, having more advanced weaponry than they do, we can guarantee that their people will suffer far worse than ours will if they decide to pick a fight with us."

Ari broke in again. "But don't you see that this is a completely different type of human conflict? There isn't any coherent clash of ideologies anymore. It's not like it was early in the twentieth century, with two social ideologies battling it out for supremacy in the West, each of which—capitalism and socialism—could marshal great systems of ideas in its defense.

"No, not anymore. What lurks behind the current crusade is the vision of Armageddon, the Apocalypse, the End of Days, Franklin. For the religious fundamentalists, whether they are Islamic or Christian, modern civilization itself appears to be the main enemy. It's always helpful to have a visible target when you're fighting demons, which tend to be rather elusive! The fundamentalists regard our society as thoroughly decadent, too attached to the betterment of life on earth. They say, 'The difference between us is that we love death as you love life.' The cry is not, as it once was, 'down with man's inhumanity to man.' Rather, it's 'slay the unbelievers whose very existence is an affront to God.'"

I picked up the thread of conversation. "Exactly, Ari, and that's because now the perceived problem isn't injustice but blasphemy. And this change is no trivial matter. From the religious standpoint, injustice on earth is to be endured, not overthrown, because it's unimportant in the end: What matters is the salvation of your soul. Blasphemy is something else entirely. As a believer you are duty-bound to extirpate it, *here and now on earth*, even if you should perish in the attempt, not so much because it may offend you, but because it's intolerable in the sight of your God. Indeed, if you should perish in the attempt, so much the better. That merits you a ticket straight to Heaven.

"To them the modern world is Sodom and Gomorrah writ large. The point about those cities is not to capture them. The point is to destroy them utterly, to rain down fire and brimstone upon them until nothing remains."

I stopped suddenly in mid-thought and looked at him. "Oh dear, I've gone and done it again, haven't I? I got carried away with my own thoughts. Please forgive me. You said I could be tiresome, and you were right!"

But Franklin smiled. "Hera, it's not that I don't enjoy listening to you, provided I'm in the right mood, of course. Even when you go off on one of your rants, which, for reasons I cannot fathom, always seems to dredge up the religious twaddle I despise so. The problem I have is I never know where your arguments are supposed to lead. What's the point? Where are you going with all this?"

"OK, you asked for it. Here goes." I paused momentarily and shifted in my seat for maximum impact. "I actually dreamt this not too long ago. All of humankind are passengers on a very long train. They have always been in the habit of waging no-holds-barred combat with each other, and no compartment is spared. For five thousand years now, and still counting, the train speeds down the tracks following signs marked 'Next Stop: Civilization' as blood and gore pour unstoppably from the doors and windows. And up front in the locomotive, lending the engineer a helping hand, stand the technicians who forge weaponry for the feuding passengers in the engine's white-hot furnace.

"As time goes by these technicians get better and better at their craft. With their help the passengers raise their killing proficiency by the hour. The cries of triumph are deafening. Finally the train slows down and pulls into the next station. But now the entire train is utterly, eerily silent. It's the silence of the graveyard. They're all dead, all of the riders in the compartments, all dead. Only the engineer who was driving the train remains.

"The engineer remarks, 'They can't say they weren't warned. They should have paid more attention to their precious Word of God, then they would have known what to expect. It's all there, set out in plain language in their sacred Bible, in the Book of Zephaniah, so that even the dumber ones might be able to get the point:

> *Neither their silver nor their gold*
> *will be able to save them*
> *on the day of the Lord's wrath;*
> *in the fire of his passion*
> *the whole earth shall be consumed;*
> *for a full, terrible end*
> *he will make of all the*
> *inhabitants of the earth.*

"Then he grins and removes his mask. It's Satan."

He fairly roared with laughter. "Oh please, Hera, spare me, not again! Not Jehovah, Allah, Jesus, Satan, or any of them. What did I do to deserve this? Am I being punished for the act of naming you all after Greek goddesses? If so, forgive me. Maybe you should all change your names. Would that put a stop to these useless references to religion?"

"Hera, don't you remember?" Ari asked. "I told you about an actual event like that—minus the part about Satan, of course. Your mind must have incorporated it into your dream! These events took place along the new border created to separate India and Pakistan in 1948, when hundreds of thousands of Hindus and Muslims began fleeing for their lives in both directions. Some were attempting to travel by trains that were stopped by mobs on each side before they could reach the border. The trains moving south from Pakistan into India were full of Hindus, and those going the other way had Muslims, men, women, and children. On certain trains all the inhabitants were slaughtered by their foes before they could cross the border. Then the trains were sent on to their destinations. When the cars arrived and those who had been awaiting them opened the doors to the compartments, they found nothing except dead bodies."

"Yes, now I remember," I added quickly, "but I think it was my reference to Satan that chiefly upset Franklin!" Looking at him I said, "I don't mean to provoke you—honestly. I'm just playing with metaphors. The point I wish to make is simple. Let me re-label one of the players in my dream and call the technicians 'scientists.' In your eyes your duty lies in carrying the death-struggle right into the locomotive itself. The good ones, among whom you count yourself, will try to fling the evil ones out of the speeding train, and vice versa. When their ranks are thinned Satan will pitch in on their side, so you'll try to toss him out, too. Then you'd start throwing so many wonderful goodies back to the warring passengers—no more weapons, but useful things, like medicines—that they'd stop killing each other and start enjoying life, all of them.

"Yet as I said to you once before, please tell me why you're so very sure that your side will be in the victor's seat when the train pulls into that station. Tell me again why you won't even consider your other option. Pull the brakes on the train, without warning, so that all the bad ones are suddenly thrown off-balance. Before they can regain their footing, disable the engine and jump off. Say to the passengers, 'This train has gone as far as it's going to go until you have learned to stop killing each other and can live together peaceably.'"

"Please don't give me that line again, Hera; I've listened to it for years and I find it no more persuasive now than it was the first time. It's obvious why it can't happen as you propose. Science and technology are just too big now. No group would stand a chance of succeeding. So I'm afraid that your first scenario, which you attribute to me, is the only one that stands a chance: 'Fight the evildoers to the death and hope to be the last man standing when the battle's over.'

"I may have misspoken the last time we talked about this. Perhaps I left the impression that your idea was unrealizable only because of an insuperable practical obstacle. If so, I didn't make myself clear. I don't agree with it as a matter of principle. It can never be right to try to stop the march of knowledge. We have no choice. We must know all that we can know. That is in our nature. It must be in our nature because why else would we find ourselves in possession of this marvelous instrument—our brain—by means of which we know so many things?"

"But Franklin, from the standpoint of modern science aren't we just another evolutionary accident, like all other creatures who ever were or will be?" Ariadne asked. "Imagine a few twists or turns along the way, which could easily have occurred, and we wouldn't even be here at all. The big asteroid that crashed into the sea 65 million years ago off what is now Mexico, which probably wiped out the dinosaurs, is a good case in point. What if we spotted it heading our way today and it was due to arrive in three weeks time? And what if it were ten times as big as that earlier one? Hollywood may fantasize about rocketing some macho males up into space to intercept it, but in real life that won't happen. It would be all over. Our being here isn't part of any grand design. What you just said sounds a lot like creationism to me."

"All right, forget I ever put it that way," he conceded. "The point is, we're made this way. We just happen to have evolved so as to want to know. Is that any better?"

"A bit," I remarked. "But I think I see where you're heading. We've been there before. You intend to separate the instrument from its uses. Science is, for the modern mind at least, the most cunning instrument ever devised by man to take the measure of nature. Every prior attempt looks not only poorer by comparison but downright pathetic. Still it does have something important in common with those earlier failures—namely, that it is, after all, only the *instrument* whereby we seek to unveil nature's secrets.

"And any attempt to blame the instrument for the uses to which it's put is absurd. As a method of discovery, science is an artifact of consummate beauty: subtle, precise, elegant, breathtaking in its scope, self-correcting, sceptical, humane, universally accessible, and rigorous. Many of the uses to which it is put violate the very premises on which it is erected. But whose fault is that? Only in magical thinking do you curse or praise the instrument."

"I couldn't have expressed it better myself, Hera. You always were an excellent pupil."

"Now I will come to my point, Franklin. What you believe, if I can put it in slightly altered terms, is that the instrument is 'innocent.' And by definition no blame attaches to something that is innocent. Am I right?"

"Exactly so," he said.

My rejoinder was swift. "What if I said to you that this is precisely the mistake that could prove fatal to us all?"

"Then I would disagree, wholeheartedly. Why would you say that?"

"You're going to be upset with me again when I give you my answer. But you invited me to explain, so you'll have to bear with me. Let me start by asking you this: Why didn't Adam and Eve refuse Satan's gift of the apple? Why were they so keen to surrender *their* innocence? What exactly was the benefit they were seeking?"

He roared with laughter again, and his subsequent remarks were entirely good-humored, not sarcastic as I had expected. I think it's in part because Roberto had chosen excellent wines to accompany the meal he had prepared for us, and Franklin was thoroughly enjoying himself for a change. He pretended to call for aid to the dozing Marco stretched out on a nearby bench.

"Marco, help me, I beg you! Your mother is incorrigible! Every time we talk about science, she turns the discussion a hundred-and-eighty degrees around to religion." He turned back to face me. "Hera, I won't let you get away with this—for your own good. You said you wanted to talk to me in order to help you clarify your own thoughts. How on earth am I supposed to help if you keep twisting your arguments into knots?"

"Please bear with me," I said, laughing with him. "It's the only way I know how to deal with these questions. You see, people like you always want to talk about science's social role from within the standpoint of science. You look at its own internal operating values—openness, tolerance, self-doubt, scepticism, democracy, rationality—and you say, 'All of society should work like this. Things would be so much better if this were the case.' So then you announce to your fellow humans, 'Here, take these values and apply them to the rest of your affairs; you'll be so much happier than you are now.' But you haven't a clue, Franklin, you and your peers, about what most people actually want."

"She's right!" Tina exclaimed. "The simple truth is, most people don't want those values to govern their lives. In fact, they want pretty much the direct opposite! They want belief, not scepticism; social group cohesion, not openness; certainty, not doubt; conformity, not tolerance; male domination, not democracy; and rather than rationality, they want faith. According to public opinion surveys done fifty years ago in the United States, which was even then the most science-hyped of all nations, the overwhelming majority of American citizens affirmed their strong belief in three things—a personal god, the afterlife, and UFOs. And they haven't changed any since then."

"Again, my dear daughters, with all due respect, I've missed the point. You must forgive me. As a humble laboratory scientist I have difficulties trying to follow popular thinking."

"That's a great pity," Tina replied. "For these people are your real clients, the ever-so-grateful beneficiaries of the technological bounty that tumbles out of your laboratories. They pay your salaries, at least for the university-based ones among you. They expect something in return: Science is expensive these days. But I think what Hera's getting at is that somewhere down the road, when it's far too late to turn around and go back, they may very well realize that they ended up with much more than they bargained for from modern science. Much more."

"And just what would that be?" he shot back.

"May I return to the serpent's temptation? Please?" I begged. "Before they bit into the forbidden apple, one would have thought that Adam and Eve had everything they could possibly want—comfortably bedded down in the Garden of Eden, no jobs to head off to in the morning, just plucking fruit off trees, no pain and suffering, guilt-free sex. Remember that already at that time—*before* the Fall—God had granted Adam 'dominion over the fish of the sea, and over the birds of the air, and over the cattle, and over all the wild animals of the earth, and over every creeping thing that creeps upon the earth.'

"That's a quotation from the Book of Genesis, of course. This was in Eden, before the Fall, so we may properly call this 'innocent dominion.' Adam didn't earn his power over nature 'by the sweat of his brow,' as the Bible says elsewhere, nor discover it through laborious experimentation at the scientists' workbench. No, it was granted to him by God, freely and without charge. Living was easy."

"And your point is?" Despite his good humor that night, Franklin always found himself losing patience when any discussion got stuck on religion.

"I'm coming to that, believe it or not!" I, too, was determined to remain in a buoyant mood. "The point is that after the Fall, *everything changed.* There was and still is no more innocence and thus there is no innocent dominion. Humans have to work their way back to God through temptation, pain, and death, all the while keeping their ragged souls pure enough to qualify for readmission to His presence. And the worst penalty for the Fall is imposed upon women, isn't it: The pain of childbirth. Anyway, being good is quite an impossible task for most of humanity, but they have to try at least.

"And try they do. But now dominion had to be earned, and for a very long time, the outcome hung in the balance. Humans didn't rule the earth, quite the contrary; at times—think of the Black Death—they just managed to hang on by their fingertips. Not until fairly recently could it be truthfully said that humans had, once and for all, regained the upper hand over nature and all the other living things of the earth. The new powers from modern science and technology were what tipped the balance in their favor at long last. But I think it would be fair to say that for anyone who takes the biblical parable of creation seriously, one thing was not permitted: To change the rules of the game."

"What game, Hera? What rules?" he demanded gruffly.

I paused momentarily before replying. "To alter both our own nature and the natures of all God-created species over which we had re-established our right of dominion."

"You mean engineering their DNA?"

"Exactly. This could never be seen as a legitimate response to the challenge posed by God to humankind after the Fall: 'By your disobedience you have cast yourselves out of My presence. You must find your way back to Me.'"

He interrupted. "Well, if I might interject just a little scientific terminology into this theological discourse, Hera, humans have been engineering the DNA of some plants and animals—not many species, to be sure, but very important species to us—for a very long time. In fact, we've been doing this ever since most of us stopped roaming around the forests and settled down with our food crops and domesticated cattle. Not only that, we've been doing the same kind of engineering on our own genes, by building permanent settlements and thereby selecting those types of individuals and traits best suited for this new way of life. Was this all a hideous violation of 'the rules of the game,' to use your expression?"

"No, actually, it wasn't," I answered, "because humans didn't intend to violate God's order when they started cross-breeding different variants of the same species. At the time when this began, and right down until the last hundred years or so, people didn't even know that each species had a genome that defines its traits—within normal limits of variation, of course. So they weren't setting out to create new species. They may have bred their cattle or corn-plants selectively, to accentuate certain traits, but they expected to get creatures out the other end that would still be recognizable to them as cows and corn."

"And yet, the fact of the matter is, that they *were* engaged in engineering these genomes, even if they didn't know they were doing so at the time."

"Now you're the one who's speaking in metaphors, Franklin. You're like the rest who say, 'We've been doing genetic engineering for millennia. What's the big deal about doing some more now, especially since we finally have some idea of *what* it is we're actually doing for a change!' I'm sorry, but this is just sloppy reasoning. First of all, it does

matter what the underlying intention is, or was. Our ancestors were just trying to survive, and they used their social
skills and reasoning to change the environmental conditions
that, in turn, unbeknownst to them, affected their reproductive success. They had not the slightest idea of what the
evolutionary rules of the game were—most of them, in fact,
attributed their success to God's benevolence."

"Our intention is the same, Hera—to survive and prosper. At last we've discovered the 'genetic rules of the game,'
and can now take advantage of that knowledge. But the
game itself hasn't changed a bit."

"Oh yes it has! Because until now, no single species ever
controlled what you call the genetic rules of the game. No
single species could decide, on a whim, to re-engineer some
or all of the others. Or just to create brand-new entities from
scratch. As you know, some decades ago already, scientists
constructed what's called the minimally necessary genome."

Franklin jumped in right away; we were now on his very
own turf. "Of course. This is the set of 200 or 300 genes that
can in principle confer environmental viability on an organism. In other words, an organism with this set of genes has
the ability to take up energy and nutrients from its environment, as well as to reproduce true to type, that is, to propagate its kind."

"Precisely," I replied. "This minimum genome is a kind of
biological platform onto which an infinite variety of particular traits can be uploaded. One could imagine the God of
Genesis building such a platform and then churning out
one type of species after another, on an assembly-line basis.
One would emerge as an aquatic or air-breathing land
organism, it would feed on this or that type of nutrient,
would have a specific degree of motility, be a certain maximum size, and so on. All this is now at our discretion. We can
create—or destroy—whatever we like for whatever purpose
we fancy.

"We stand in God's place and are reformatting His hand-iwork—including ourselves, of course, as you well know, having done it in your laboratory. No other species can do this. This is the new game and these are the new rules of which I speak. We crossed the line when we decided we had the right as a species to do this."

"What line?" he said abruptly, now clearly annoyed.

Again I paused. "The moral line. We lost the right of dominion when we did this."

"What could you possibly mean, Hera? Your own exposition shows that, far from losing it, just the opposite happened: We humans reinforced our dominion in precisely this way. I agree with you. With our current and expected future techniques in molecular biology, we will be the masters of creation. We will soon control the fate of all existing things and can do with them whatever we want. And, as you just said, we can even add entirely new species at our whim, things that have never before existed on earth and may never have come into existence were it not for our clever technologies. But we earned this position through our genetic endowment and our intelligence. All that remains is to manage the results."

"I'm trying hard to be precise," I responded, keeping my voice as calm and even as possible. "I didn't say we lost our *actual* dominion over other species. Indeed, that would be a self-contradictory claim, as you just explained. No, I said that we lost the *right* of dominion, or more precisely, the *exclusive right*."

"What additional benefit does this exclusive right, as you call it, confer on us? What difference does it make if we lose it, whatever it is?"

"Just this. It's a virtual certainty that in engineering the human genome according to our own will and purposes, we'll make mistakes. We'll get results we didn't intend. Both in the cases of the human genome and in others we work on."

Again he felt himself to be on his professional home ground. "That's already happened, many times, and it's well discussed in the scientific literature. Ask your biologist sisters; they know all about these things. Reported cases go back to the beginning of this century. The first instance of a serious mistake was the inadvertent creation of a super-lethal mousepox virus by Australian researchers. They were not, of course, trying to produce such a result, especially since the mousepox virus bears some relation to smallpox, one of the weapons most feared by humans in nature's arsenal. But it happened, and, more to the point, they couldn't understand how it might have happened. Anyway, there have been other cases since then, and we've learned something useful from each of them."

Suddenly he stopped and stood up, and his action seemed to symbolize the awakening in his mind of a different thought entirely. "Wait a minute, now. I've just had a funny feeling about where all this discussion is leading. Maybe I'm getting a bit slower of mind in my old age, because I should have twigged to it sooner. Do you have this sense too, Gaia? You haven't said anything so far tonight, but I presume you've been listening."

Both he and Gaia looked directly at me; she raised her eyebrows as if to say, "It's your conversation." He was angry now. "You don't want to proceed with the Second Generation project, do you, Hera? That's where this high-minded talk has been headed all along. Why don't you just admit it, instead of leading us on a merry chase through this maze of ideas? You don't want to go ahead, do you? Please answer me."

I was silent for a moment, and without my willing it, my eyes avoided his gaze. "You may be correct, and I apologize if you think I've been avoiding the real subject. I guess that's been part of my problem. For me it's obvious that what you call my 'maze of ideas' is quite relevant to what we're planning to do. Yes, I do have serious doubts about the wisdom of creating a thousand new babies according to a design. Hear me out, please, I'm not saying that I'm against doing so, just that I'm of two minds, and I haven't yet been able to resolve the matter for myself. These doubts have been forming in my mind over the past several years, but it never seemed appropriate to me to raise them during your battle with your health. Then we all got so busy with daily routines, time passed and the right opportunity for discussion never arose. So here we are."

"I have a clear sense of what is on your mind," Gaia finally said. "Of course, as you well know, I've been heavily involved in the neurosciences research and the gene-modification protocol for the Second Generation. But I don't mind having this conversation, Hera. These are serious issues you raise. I haven't participated, but I'm following your discussion with Franklin very closely. I'd like you to continue, until you feel you've brought up every issue that's important to you." She turned to face Franklin. "I want to hear the rest of it."

Did he look disappointed? Or just resigned? I couldn't tell. He cast an angry glance in my direction, sat down again, and said, "Fine. Carry on, then."

I launched right back into the discussion. "I want to do a thought experiment with you, Franklin. Sometimes this is the only way we can lift our eyes above the trajectory of routine discovery, which occurs one experiment at a time, and try to look far down the road in the direction we're heading. There is some discrete probability—naturally, I can't attach a number to it, but grant me just the theoretical chance—that, in tinkering with our own genome, we'll end up creating a being that is different from *Homo sapiens* as it has evolved naturally to date."

His voice expressed the anger that showed in his face. "Why talk about purely theoretical possibilities? You and your sisters *are* such beings, as I believe, and as I think you believe. You are different in some very important respects from what would have been the case, say, if your mother and I had had natural children rather than expertly engineered ones. In other words, instead of only a fully random genetic shuffle from two parents, you also have a certain amount of directed genetic forcing. That's all. But you're still humans, aren't you?"

I was determined to follow the thread of my own argument rather than reply to his question. "I'm speculating about the possibility of much more significant forcings, as you call them, by which I take you to be referring to deliberate acts of genetic manipulation. Actually, such forcings could be either intended or inadvertent; it doesn't matter in this context. I'm asking whether you can conceive of even the possibility of someone engineering a set of beings—let's call them 'new people'—who would think so differently from the rest—'old people'—that they would decide to remain apart from the older models? In other words, these new people would make a compact with each other not to interbreed with old people, but to breed true to type among themselves.

"This wouldn't be a case of hybrid sterility, as happens when a horse is crossed with a donkey and the offspring—mules—are sterile. So I'm not presupposing that the new people are unable biologically to breed successfully with old people, but rather just the existence of a conscious decision on their part along these lines. As a working molecular biologist, can you concede that just such a thing *could* happen one day?"

"We're being speculative, you said? All right then, logically, no one can rule out this possibility. As I recall, you and I discussed this once before. There are rumors that such experiments have begun already, and there's even a name for them: 'gated genetic communities.' There's no hard evidence yet, but it's not surprising that, if they do exist, no one who's involved wants to advertise that fact to the rest of the world. But remember, biologists know that there are real disadvantages to restricted gene pools, so maybe those folks will find out it wasn't such a smart idea after all."

"OK, we agree at least that the possibility is there. Now indulge me just one step further. Let me work out my thoughts, for my own benefit. I'm not so foolish as to believe that I'll persuade you to adopt them. Suppose that the new people not only decide to become a separate subspecies of *Homo*, but they discover they have special powers that enable them to subject the old people to their will. In fact, they proceed to turn all the old people into the equivalent of our domesticated animals. The new people have their own legal system, of course, and the rights and privileges they enjoy under it do not extend to old people.

"In fact, under their laws new people have the legal right to discipline old people in whatever manner they choose, or even to kill them without compunction or fear of any consequences. They keep old people around as domestic servants and to provide entertainment, like our household pets. Of course, the new people control all further attempts at breeding by the old people. Over time they find that the more intelligent among the old people are too much bother, always making unreasonable demands on them, so they select them out, and gradually reduce the average IQ of old people to a point where they are docile and more easily managed."

He simply couldn't contain his exasperation with me any longer. "Oh Hera, this is ridiculous! How can I deny your claim that the theoretical possibility exists for such a future? But stop dishing out worst-case scenarios; they're just not helpful! If it appears that such things may be in the works, the rest of us will join together and find a way to stop them. You can imagine dozens of similar scenarios if you wish.

Most of them will never come to pass. All you will succeed in doing is to scare yourself straight into a catatonic state."

"All right, I admit it; all of this does frighten me. Compared to you, I just don't have as much confidence that the power of creation can be so easily managed by the societies we see around us. For God's sake, Franklin, look about you! There are people trying to make horrible weapons out of pathogens and radioactive materials, whose model of a good society comes straight out of the fourteenth century! Aren't you just a little bit afraid of what such people will do when they gain the power to modify and create living species?"

"Hera, I will grant you this much: We live in very perilous times. Maybe it would be better if we humans had sorted out the conflicts among religious faiths before these powerful modern technologies had been forged. But for whatever reason, we didn't, and now it's too late, because no one can reverse historical time. We can't turn the clock back. We can only press forward."

I didn't reply at once. I was angry mostly with myself for not being able to put my own argument into a clearer and more convincing form. "Actually, I believe that there are many in our midst who do indeed want to reverse historical time. This is one of the issues that bothers me most of all. Their fight seems to be with the whole of the modern world."

"At times during our conversations it did occur to me that your problem is not with science, but with organized religions. You and I always seem to start talking about science and end up with theology. Doesn't that strike you as odd?"

"The two interpenetrate in the story of creation. I know that to you science is one thing and religion is something else entirely. However, I see the matter quite differently. Once people got an inkling of what possibilities lay dormant in the knowledge about genomics, their ordinary dreams about a comfortable and rewarding life instantly deserted them. Immediately their fantasies turned to greatly extended life spans, even to visions of immortality, and to tinkering with every aspect of their bodies and minds, searching for perfection—or just experimenting, to see what would happen. Generally speaking, they wish to do with their mortal forms *whatever* they happen to want to do at any moment in time. And it would all be just innocent fun.

"This is exactly why we need to remember what the great religions teach about creation: *There is no innocence anymore.* As I mentioned a while ago, the story in the Book of Genesis tells us that before the Fall humans shared their moral innocence with all other animals, and of course, that was God's own original design. It says that God's acts of creation during the world's first six days—including the creation of humans—occurred entirely within the state of innocence, before the Fall, before the ingression of evil. But humans cannot gain access to that primordial state of innocence after the expulsion from the Garden—remember, God sets a fiery sword at the gates of Eden to bar them from ever re-entering."

He sighed, clearly exasperated. "Here we go again. Look, the story you relate is just that; a little fable invented a long time ago by some primitive desert tribes. It has absolutely no relevance for our modern scientific age, and I simply cannot fathom why you insist on repeatedly bringing it up in these conversations of ours." He slumped in his chair, morose and bad-tempered, clearly wishing now that this dialogue would end. But I was equally determined to press on.

"That's where you're quite wrong! What happened was that modern science picked up and recycled the moral of that little fable, as you call it. Wait a minute, please, let me fetch something from my study, it'll only take me a moment." I ran from the courtyard gardens where we were sitting through the doorway into my study and returned within seconds with a small, framed document. The eyes of everyone present—except for the dozing Marco—were upon me as I resumed my place.

"I keep this on the wall in my study. It's a quotation from a remarkable seventeenth-century philosopher, Francis Bacon. Listen to what he wrote, more than four hundred years ago, in 1607 to be exact, in a small work entitled *Thoughts and Conclusions on the Interpretation of Nature*. His ideas are so beautifully expressed:

> *And indeed it is this glory of discovery that is the true ornament of mankind. In contrast with civil business it never harmed any man, never burdened a conscience with remorse. Its blessing and reward is without ruin, wrong, or wretchedness to any. For light is in itself pure and innocent; it may be wrongly used, but cannot in its nature be defiled.*

"Isn't that wonderful? I love the way he puts it. Bacon's phrase 'civil business' refers to politics, of course, and 'the glory of discovery,' which he juxtaposes to it, is a reference to science. He was trying to persuade us that knowledge of the way nature works is always 'innocent'—his own word, not mine. But he was terribly mistaken, I fear!

"Knowing isn't innocent at all. Perhaps it's driven first by wonder, the natural impulse of a pattern-seeking brain to comprehend the regularities in its environment. Yet quite obviously it's impelled in equal measure by the straightforward motivation we all share—the drive for self-preservation—and, as well, by the interests of greed, power, ambition, influence, pride of place; what used to be called the striving for honor and preferment.

"Above all, Franklin, knowing about *our* nature couldn't possibly be regarded as innocent because this is the most fateful and earth-shaking kind of knowledge our brains can possess! To discover what we're made of, so to speak: What could be more momentous than that? Some will argue that examination shows we are morally corrupt in our very nature, doomed by original sin to everlasting torment unless we repent and are forgiven by an all-powerful and insubstantial deity. Others will maintain that we are pure products of evolution, which is a random walk through time by the DNA molecule, a journey having no special purpose or meaning. Both are marvelous stories, to be sure. Yet, to imagine that we are or could be blithely indifferent to the *consequences* of choosing to believe one or the other of these competing stories is just rank naïveté.

"It's simply ridiculous to think that, having decided to accept the second of them, we could then regard knowing how to re-engineer all natural life on earth as an 'innocent' enterprise, as if it were a kind of child's game. On the contrary, this is a deadly serious business, and moreover, one that we're not equipped to oversee. No matter how clever we become, we are not gods, we did not create ourselves or the world of nature, we do not understand the purpose or meaning of life. To imagine that our knowing about nature is innocent is to suggest that we are back in the Garden of Eden, toiling happily alongside God as He was busy creating life.

"Remember, there are no guideposts inside the gates of Eden to distinguish between what we should and shouldn't do. Everything is possible—and precisely for that reason, it's too dangerous a place for us to be! We'll surely lose our way by experimenting freely with the creation of life, and that's what worries me so much. We aren't equipped for this kind of expedition. It's being undertaken helter-skelter, in laboratories all over the world, in the context of economic interests, social and political institutions, and ethics guidelines that have virtually nothing in common with each other. The *only* universal is the methodology of science itself; every

other aspect of this busy enterprise is dependent on particular circumstances. We must bring it to a stop, at least
temporarily, before it's too late, before we realize we can no
longer find our way back to the world where, however imper-
fectly, we work out our sense of what's right and what's
wrong."

He got up abruptly from where he was sitting. "I just can't
take one more minute of this babbling! I'm exhausted from
trying to follow your reasoning. You've worn me out. My
head is spinning. I fear I'll be unable to do any useful work
tomorrow, and there's much to do."

"No, please, don't go just yet, I'm almost finished, but I
need you to hear the rest of what I have to say, and I need to
hear your reaction to it, no matter how hostile. I'm sorry, but
I must insist: I've been wrestling with these ideas for at least
five years now, and I feel that—*finally*—I've understood
what's been bothering me all this time. It was Francis
Bacon's use of innocence, when referring to science's investigation of nature, that catalyzed my thoughts and allowed
me to see the deep, underlying affinity between the two
creation stories—one religious, the other scientific.

"You have always remarked to me during these conversations between us, 'Hera, why do we set out in the beautifully
logical domain of science and immediately thereafter find
ourselves in the bizarre realm of theology?' Well, here's my
answer. Look closely at how Bacon phrases his point: He
talks about the process of knowing, in the abstract, rather
than about the scientist who is engaged in that process. In
effect, when referring to the process of knowing about
nature as innocent, what Bacon put on the table is the idea
that the scientist has no responsibility for what he or she
finds in that investigation. He suggests that although someone else may wrongly use the resultant knowledge, the
knowledge itself is 'pure.'

"What exactly does that say to us? Precisely this: *The*

discoverer has no responsibility for what others may do with the find-ings! 'Here it is, this marvelous new knowledge with so many beneficial applications; my findings have been peer-reviewed, published, and replicated, and now someone else has to take charge of things from this point. If anything bad should happen as a result, that's not my problem. Go set up a government commission or something if you think the consequences must be dealt with. Don't bother me with your problem, however; I've got other research to get on with and new therapeutic applications to commercialize.'

"Wrong! Wrong! And especially wrong when we're deal-ing with knowledge that penetrates to the core of our being, to our very heart and soul—the knowledge of the creation of life. Now do you see the connection between science and religion? In the religious version, at the end of days God just walks away from the remnant of his most precious creation. He looks at them with scorn, as they writhe in agony under the demons' tortures, and pronounces, 'Well, you had your chance, you screwed up, and now I'm leaving you to the everlasting tender mercies of these fine fellows.' *He created those tormented humans, the ones He was abandoning, for God's sake!* They were made to His *design!* It was the bloody design that was faulty! And He just washes his hands of the whole business and takes off to Heaven."

"Stop, Hera, I'm leaving. No more of this silliness, please."

"Franklin, just wait, two more minutes is all I need. You're not listening to me! Mary Shelley tried to make us under-stand this same message more than two hundred years ago. She wrote another creation story. The level of sheer despair in her story—the despair felt by the mutilated, nameless, quasi-human being of Dr. Victor Frankenstein's creation—is heart wrenching. After initially agreeing to acknowledge the reality of his creature's agony, and to assuage it by preparing a mate for him, Frankenstein cruelly reneged on his prom-ise. He walked away. 'Not my problem.'

"Well, damn him, it *was* his problem! Or he should have seen that it was. And it's yours, too, Franklin, yours and that of your peers who are similarly engaged in creating and engineering life. It's the problem of those of your colleagues who have been fooling around with chimeras, and constructing new kinds of living entities by infusing some creatures with stem cells from other species, including humans. Just pour a few million human stem cells into the brains of a monkey or an ape, and see what happens! Or put some of them into a rat embryo and see if you get human germ cells, eggs or sperm. When you're finished, no problem; just terminate them and start another experiment. Of course, we'd never do the opposite experiment on humans—that would be highly unethical—but we can do whatever we please with all other species. Religion told them that, by the way."

He let out another long sigh. "Your two minutes are up, Hera. But if you really want to know, my response would be exactly the same as the one you related, referring to your imaginary discoverer: If someone else does bad things using the knowledge I created and published, that's not my problem. It's not in my power to control what others do and I don't feel responsible in the slightest degree. And I won't be detained here against my will any longer. As usual, you rant on and on and never get to the point."

"You want the point? Here it is, then. I'll put it to you in the form of a question. Let's assume you found yourself in possession of the means to stop everything in its tracks—all new scientific discovery and its applications, everywhere. Would you be willing to do so, and explain to your colleagues, 'Let's just think things over for a while before we push on again, until we can sort out this issue of what responsibilities we investigators have for the discoveries we make, and how we might best discharge those responsibilities.' Would you do it?"

His accumulated agitation and annoyance showed through in his tone of voice. "No! A thousand times, No! I hate hypothetical questions, but I'll answer this one, and the answer is No. Shutting down further science-based discovery and innovation is no solution to whatever crises confront us. We must advance. That's all there is to it. I'm very tired and I've got to go to bed. The problem we members of this family have in front of us right now is not how to save the world from scientific discoveries, but making a decision about our own very important innovation. We have a formal process—fortunately—for authorizing the Second Generation project to proceed. The board of directors of the foundation makes that decision. We'll call a board meeting soon and see how the vote goes."

The tension in my beautiful courtyard was palpable and I sensed that everyone had had quite enough for one evening. My guests got up and made ready to leave, and Gaia came up to embrace me. "I'm sorry about the ill-feeling toward the end of the evening. Let's you and I get together soon and continue this conversation." Tina, too, gave me a hug and remarked: "Look, young Marco has fallen fast asleep on the bench. No wonder. He must have been bored to tears." Ari laughed and said, "I think he was exhausted. He's such a busy young man." The three sisters said good night to me and walked off together.

Franklin was halfway out the door when he turned and said suddenly to me, "Hera, can I have a short private chat with you before I go?"

"Of course." The civil tone he employed was a welcome relief from the rancorous debate we had concluded a few moments ago. Actually, I hate bickering with him, and I always have, even at those times when the need for a brutally frank exchange between us was—in my opinion—dictated by circumstances. After all, we've faced life-and-death challenges in our time! I hate to see him become so upset with me, especially now, after he's gone through such severe illnesses. So I was delighted to hear his change of tone and was resolved to respond in the same manner.

"This has been our first opportunity to resume our long talks since I became ill. You girls will celebrate your twenty-ninth birthday in a few months' time. Your biological clocks are ticking, as the saying goes. Are there any plans in the works right now for marriages and families?"

"I fear not. Nothing's changed since we last spoke of this. My sisters rarely raise such issues with me anymore. I suppose they feel that they're old enough to judge their own feelings and make their own decisions—as they do." I had a sinking feeling in the pit of my stomach. Of all the topics he could have chosen for us to chew over, this was by far my least favorite.

"I was afraid of that. Those decisions include—for at least two of them, Tammy and Hex—having a child and raising it here, inside the foundation's compound."

"Yes, and you undoubtedly also know that the two mothers decided to have a child on a purely personal basis—there's no special program for their education or anything else. The children have been enrolled in the daycare center we operate here in our compound for the youngsters of our staff personnel. Tammy and Hex want their girls to have normal lives."

"And the fathers?" he asked, with considerable irritation in his voice.

"As far as I know, neither has a continuing relationship with the father, whoever he was. I suppose they're men they met and got to know among the tourist crowds here. I discussed this with each of them, of course, because we would have had to make special arrangements if either of the fathers was going to live among us. But they chose not to request this. My guess is that their decision has something to do with how closely we sisters bonded during our first eight years in Tembagapura, before you came to stay; then when we fled alone and in terror to Alberta, and during the time there while the threat to our lives persisted, until Klamm was killed. Also, they all know that we're different from other people, and that we may be threatened again, somehow, and so they want to preserve that close bond among us in case we have to rely on it again for our safety. That's how I read the situation, in any case.

"This may have something to do with what you did to us! Over the years I've conversed a lot with my sisters about such things. Although the rest of us are not like Moira and Themis, who are unable to relate normally to other people because of their genetic dysfunction, we do seem to be a bit wary of close contact with others and to have difficulty in forming long-lasting emotional bonds, such as marriage partners do. So maybe you should accept part of the responsibility."

"So, now it's my fault," he said, unable to disguise the sudden bitterness in his voice, "Well, the bottom line is, there'll be no normal families from the lot of you."

I tried my best to maintain the same civil tone in which he had opened this conversation, but I had a feeling it was not going to last. "I know how disappointed you must be. But I'm powerless in these matters, as I told you earlier."

Suddenly and without warning, that bitterness in his voice turned to vitriol, although he still kept his voice level. "You don't know the half of it, Hera! Disappointed is hardly the right word to describe what I feel. Outraged would be better. What a betrayal of your mother's memory! And you're entitled to know that I do hold you chiefly responsible for what has transpired. From a very early age you were always their role model, weren't you, except for Io and one or two others. They looked up to you, they consulted you, they brought you their problems. And yes, you responded, you accepted that role, freely and willingly. So they followed you. And look where you've led them. Even the ones who have children show no interest at all in carrying out the special educational program I designed. I'm left with a gaggle of self-indulgent spinsters whose genes, so carefully nurtured, will vanish up the crematorium chimney."

"Perhaps you'd better go. There's no point in pursuing this line."

"Yes, I'm going. I'd much rather talk to Io about these things nowadays anyway. I've grown quite fond of her since my illness felled me. She took such good care of me in Canada, and almost every day we had the most wonderful long talks, about all kinds of subjects. She has such an interesting mind!"

"I'm fully aware of what a fertile imagination she has," I replied cautiously. In retrospect I should have left well-enough alone and just bid him good night there and then, but somehow I couldn't stop myself. "And now, as I've heard, she's been hanging around your lab every day. It's curious, don't you think? She never took a serious interest in biology before, although with her quick mind she picks up a pretty good smattering of whatever catches her fancy. I've wondered what she was up to."

For the first time that evening he lost control and began shouting at me. At once Magnus, who had been dozing, lying on his side, rolled into an upright position on the ground, alert and watchful.

"She's not 'up to' anything, Hera! She enjoys spending time with me. Is that a crime in your eyes?"

"Take it easy, Franklin. This kind of stress isn't good for you."

"Don't patronize me!" Glancing at Magnus, he lowered his voice again. "You may be interested to know that one of the things Io and I have talked about most often since I returned to Provo is exactly the subject I raised with you a moment ago. Io tells me that she's realized it was wrong of her to be so influenced by you in matters of marriage and family, and that she's trying to get her life in order so that this will come together for her. She also says she's working hard on the other sisters to follow her example, and judges that she has some real prospects for success. There's still enough time for this to happen. Naturally, I'm delighted, and I told her so."

I just couldn't suppress a chuckle. "So she told you all that, did she? She hasn't also, by any chance, invited you to any of her orgies across the road, has she?"

He lost control and yelled at the top of his voice. "I don't know anything about orgies! I do know that she seems to be acting a hell of a lot more normally these days than you are! My God, Hera, the only close personal relationship you're known to have is with a goddamned chimpanzee!"

As he blurted out these words, Magnus sprang to his feet and Marco, startled, awoke. I walked over to them. "Magnus: Sit! Good boy. Marco, get his leash and take him for a walk. Now, please." I accompanied Magnus to the gate, stroking his back. "It's OK. Go for a walk with Marco." I watched them walk away fifty paces or so, my fury escalating with each passing second, then I wheeled to face Franklin in full rage, shouting back at him.

"Don't you *ever* say such a thing to me again! Who do you think you are, a harem-keeper? Are my sisters and I supposed to be your obedient slaves? Snap your fingers and we do your bidding? When you speak to me like this I'm reminded of all the disgusting images that fill the news stories from so much of the world! You know, where the white-robed mullahs and preachers are screaming imprecations and death threats, their faces contorted in hate? Meanwhile, there in the background, the silent ranks of terrified women slink by, swathed head to foot in suffocating black robes so as not to be accused of beguiling these holy ones with a glimpse of their flesh! Ancient doctrine teaches that the mere sound of a woman's voice in public can arouse sexual frenzy in the male—and that should it do so, the fault lies with the woman. What a horrorshow! What contempt for the mothers of their children!"

He was shocked, never having seen me in such a state before. He tried to break in. "Hera, really, how can you believe …." But I refused to allow him to stop me.

"Don't interrupt me! You think you're so different from them, but are you? Really? You're a modern Englishman, you're quite sure, you're not like those mullahs." Now I paused, and without my willing it, my voice suddenly turned softer again. "Do you remember, when I was little, you had me listen to all of Mozart's operas? I fell in love with them, but especially with his *Abduction from the Seraglio*. Do you recall that? I was young and proud, and I imagined myself as Blonde, the captive Englishwoman in the Turkish castle, fearless and defiant, standing up to Osmin, evil master of the harem, even mocking the deep voice-tones by which Osmin tries to intimidate her, until he laments:

> *O Englishmen! Such fools you have been*
> *To give your women their freedom!*

"That was written about two-hundred-and-fifty years ago. How much has changed, really? For God's sake, Franklin, have you forgotten? You *designed* us to be brood mares! We were the vessels carrying your little packets of new genes that would remake the world."

Finally he managed to force his way back into the conversation. "Hera, you're forgetting that your mother was an equal partner in our plan. She …."

Instantly I interrupted him and raised my voice again. "I don't care *who* was involved! If she were here I would say the same to her: You have *no rights* over our destiny! None! Whatever you thought you were doing with the embryos out of which we developed is your business, but it was over the moment my sisters and I were born out of our surrogate mothers' wombs. We are free to make our own lives and we intend to do just that. You had better try to understand and accept this—or there will be nothing but trouble between us from now on!"

He tried once more to speak but I raised a hand and

stopped him. "No. Enough has been said. Just remember this: What my sisters and I do with our personal lives is our business and no one else's. You and I shall never speak of this again. Now get out of my house."

§   §   §

After he left that night I couldn't contain my tears. I went into my bedroom and shut the door behind me so that when he returned, Marco wouldn't see me weeping. I didn't care a whit what Franklin thought about my life: That's not what precipitated my reaction. Ironically, it was his indirect words of praise for me, his brief reference to my long years of caring for my sisters, that brought it on. But why now when that period was largely over, as I had told him, truthfully, this evening? My sisters take care of themselves. Their regular chats with me continue—except for Io, of course—but more often than not along the lines of friendly banter, which is relaxing, not stressful at all. No, it isn't the past. It's contemplating the future that's dragging me down.

For Franklin, the preparations for the Second Generation are all a matter of logistics—testing the viability of the frozen embryos; obtaining and furnishing a 1,000-bed facility; recruiting and screening the candidates for surrogate mothers; implanting the fertilized eggs. The final stages are fast approaching. Again, it isn't my involvement in these preparatory steps that's weighing on me right now. Rather, it's imagining what the future holds. Once I cared for my eleven sisters. Soon there could be a thousand babies to nurture and prepare for adulthood!

Who's going to oversee all of those headaches for the next two decades? Not my father, certainly, who, I'm willing to bet, doesn't have many good years left in him, given the pace at which he's driving himself and the seriousness of his heart attack. Not my sisters, I'll bet, who have their own private preoccupations. I'll wager that none of them will show the slightest inclination to become nursery attendants for a huge new tribe. No, overseeing the new flock will fall almost entirely on my own shoulders, as always. And as this thought has been slowly sinking into my consciousness, I'm beginning to admit to myself that I simply can't face the prospect.

In truth, it's everything all together—the impending, soon-to-be-irrevocable steps to create the Second Generation; the disturbing analysis of world trends in the Colony's documents; and the never-ending responsibilities associated with the presidency of the foundation. But I won't try to fool myself any longer into thinking there's no personal side to the bouts of depression that have been coming upon me with increasing regularity.

No, there's a large, purely personal quotient as well, including dealing with my father's increasingly vocal anger and disappointment, directed almost entirely at me; a nagging fear that Io will pose serious problems for me in future years; and, underneath the joys of my daily routines with Marco and Magnus and Lucy's visits, the self-appointed loneliness of a life without a partner. I have reached my Rubicon. I'll have to cross it, without knowing what's awaiting me on the distant shore.

There are two tasks that must be discharged at my office tomorrow. First, I must sign the now-completed *Memorandum of Understanding* between the Colony and the foundation that Marco has placed on my desk. He'll have to manage that file by himself for a while. Second, I must authorize the papers naming Athena as Acting President of the foundation. Then I'm going to lock the door and leave. I have no idea when or if I'll ever reopen it.

The words 'and darkness covered the face of the deep' pass unbidden through my thoughts these days. I'm at the end of my rope and the abyss has opened beneath my feet.

Soon I'm going to let go. It's going to be a hard fall. The climb back up and out will be much harder still.

January 2044

My flight landed in Denpasar, capital of Bali, at the height of the rainy season. I'm making my first-ever visit to my mother's home province, something I've wanted to do for a long time. Following my withdrawal from the everyday life of the family compound in Provo, I felt restless and uneasy, and after six months or so had passed my doctor suggested taking a long trip away.

I flew eastwards from the Caribbean first to London and then directly from Heathrow to Kuala Lumpur, continuing on to Bali via Jakarta. As I peered down over the Asian skies on the last leg of my journey, the notorious and by now omnipresent 'brown cloud,' the lethal mixture of dust, greenhouse gases, and other airborne pollutants that are now a permanent fixture of Asia's ruined skyscape, was visible everywhere.

There was no longer any need for me to stop in the city of Jakarta, because my mother's family had permanently relocated back to their property in Bali five years before. In the letters they sent to me in Provo they reported how they had grown increasingly fearful of the intensified social strife in the Indonesian capital, as more and more desperate peasants crowded into the larger cities from the outlying districts, victims of poverty and endemic religious conflict. The coastal fringes of Jakarta were already close to the prevailing sea levels when the gradual climate-induced rises had begun early in the twenty-first century. Those living along the coastlines kept raising their miserable huts on stilts, but these alterations offered them little protection from the storm-driven surges that arrived more frequently with each passing decade.

I had read somewhere that even a hundred years earlier this small amount of sea-level rise wouldn't have represented such a human catastrophe, for at that time Jakarta, like other coastal cities around the world, was a mere fraction of its current size in population and area. In most parts of Southeast Asia and elsewhere, however, for almost the last hundred years, huge populations had been draining out of the interiors to the coastal cities, fleeing some form or other of social or environmental disaster. As the dispossessed continued to pile into the swollen metropolises throughout the second quarter of the twenty-first century, they were now being greeted by the rising seas.

At Denpasar airport I was met by members of my family's security detail and driven to the interior, journeying from the coastal lowlands past stands of bamboo and palms, then encountering the terraced rice paddies and Bali's ubiquitous Hindu temples as the land began rising toward the mountains. The endless stretches of flowering shrubs, and especially the oleanders and sweet-smelling frangipani, brought sudden and comforting images to mind of my own gardens back in Provo.

Finally we reached the spectacular highlands of northwestern Bali, framed in the shadow of Mt. Agung, its volcanic peak soaring past three thousand meters in elevation, dormant since 1965 but due to erupt again before long. As my transport arrived in the steep alpine highlands, the plunging mountain streams, their banks blanketed in tree-ferns and wildflowers, became visible from the roadway. None of the chaos in the cities intruded here. Other than the screams of the monkeys in the surrounding forests of pine and cypress, nothing yet disturbed the pervasive refinement and grace of the Sujana family's immense landed estate.

Inside the grounds of this private territory I had the well-appointed guesthouse all to myself, and I spent every day on solitary hikes in the foothills, with the sleeping volcano visible at every turn. I sought rest on the steps of the tranquil temples that dotted the landscape, and in the shelter of the immense banyan trees during the afternoon downpours. I absorbed the silences of Balinese cemeteries in the shadow of the strange kepuh trees. The family members sensed my need for solitude and I saw them only in the evenings at dinnertime. Before departing from Bali I set out to cross the main island to visit the monkey forest at Ubud and then to walk among the wild bird populations in Bali Barat National Park.

I took my leave of this island after a stay of four months, not yet on the road to recovery but with replenished mettle. Back at Denpasar I chartered a small executive jet and, after borrowing three members of my family's private security detail, set a course for Papua Province. On that stressed-filled flight fifteen years earlier, I had been totally absorbed in our own drama and had cast no more than a few fleeting glances out the plane's window. So I instructed the pilot to fly atop the Sudirman Range, the western section of the Maoke Mountain Range that dominates Papua's central highlands. I wanted to admire the full splendor of the soaring 16,000-foot peak of Mount Jaya—the current name for what was once known as the Carstensz Pyramid—and to see our birthplace, nestled on its slopes, from this perspective. I was also looking for the Carstensz and Meren equatorial glaciers sitting on the mountaintops.

They were gone. Elevated temperatures had caused them to retreat at an accelerating rate in the second half of the twentieth century, and the first half of the succeeding one had finished them off. I asked the pilot to fly over the Lorentz National Park, a World Heritage site, its territory of 6.2 million acres making it the largest nature reserve in Southeast Asia, and finally the village of Tembagapura. It appeared deserted and its airstrip was littered with abandoned vehicles, so we landed at Timika.

My security detail and I were met by military officials and taken to the local army base. As a courtesy to my influential family, an armed escort and two helicopters were put at my disposal for the journey up the mountain to my first home. Disembarking in Tembagapura, we found a ghost town. The members of the indigenous peoples who had reclaimed the area after the foundation's support staff had fled, and who were engaged in sporadic combat with the Indonesian military, melted away into the surrounding jungle after sizing up the contingent's superior firepower. I wandered among the ruins of dynamited and looted structures while my escort stood guard.

I did not recover any sense of belongingness here. It was as if my childhood had been blown up along with the buildings themselves. As I glanced up at the mists swirling around the higher peaks, I regretted never having persuaded my father, while we all lived there, to mount an expedition further along the roadway leading up the mountain from Tembagapura, going 7,000 feet higher still, where, I had learned, a group of buildings housing colossal processing machines once stood. But this idea had been even then only an urge for an adventure to break the monotony of our daily routines. Even then I knew that all I would have found there was a set of rusting, fog-shrouded ruins, signalling mutely to the creatures in the encroaching montane rainforest that the industrial tentacles of the West had once coveted this site and then abandoned it, never to return. I told my escort I was ready to head back to Timika.

I had one errand to run there. When I arrived in Bali I had asked my family to use their connections to track down a man by the name of Bobby Haryanto. Bobby was a professional gardener who had supervised the local staff as they built and tended to the wonderful gardens in Tembagapura. Wandering among the abandoned and demolished structures during my visit there, I came upon the traces of those gardens, once full of native flowering plants, and now mostly overrun with weeds. Bobby had been found, still healthy but living alone and in poverty in Timika, having been without full-time work since the sisters' exodus from Tembagapura. So I headed to Timika to ask him to come back with me to Provo and take up a permanent position there, caring for my own gardens. My mother's family arranged for the quick processing of his Indonesian passport. An entry visa for his new home was no problem.

I had resolved some time ago that upon leaving Papua on this trip I would retrace the main stages of our original journey. My chartered plane returned to Denpasar where I boarded a series of commercial flights to Darwin, Sydney, Los Angeles, and Phoenix, and after a brief stay in Arizona, I continued on to Vancouver and Calgary. I expected the next stop on my tour to be joyful and I was not disappointed. After visiting briefly the offices of our law firm in Calgary, which we continue to retain for some of the foundation's international affairs, I booked a limo and driver from the security company that had watched over my sisters and me during our stay in Alberta. Remembering the lucrative proceeds from that contract, the firm refused to accept payment for this service.

At her sister's farm near the town of Black Diamond, where Marco had been raised, Mrs. Walter—now old but still lively and clear-minded—was waiting for me. With her were a few of the other people who had cared for the twelve Indonesian girls who had mysteriously shown up one day and vanished again, just as mysteriously, thirty months later. I was implored to tell them everything about our new lives, and all present pored over pictures of the sisters and the compound where we lived.

I was forced to describe in agonizing detail the nature of our daily routines. My hosts gushed over the photos of the handsome young Marco as I handed over the personal letter he had written to them. I showered them with the gifts that my sisters had loaded into my baggage. And there was so much excitement in the room that, when the matter of marriage and babies arose, I managed deftly to change the subject without offending anyone.

JUNE 2044

I'm back in Provo, after winding up my travels with a month-long self-indulgence on a tour of some of the finest hotels and restaurants across northern Italy. Almost six months has elapsed since my departure. My psychiatrist's hope was that the visits to Bali, Papua Province, and Alberta would once again ground me in my personal history, so that I could reconnect with the sources of my inner strength. In truth I do find that these journeys have sucked some of the sting out of the emotional pain induced by more recent events in Provo. I am not yet cured by any means, but I do feel that I touched bottom sometime during this trip. I have to touch bottom before I can hope to rebound again through the darkness to the light.

I was standing in my gardens earlier this evening, examining the new growth on my plants, exhausted from the intensity of my reunions with Marco and Magnus, when Athena found me.

(Marco's Journal, 15 June) I had warned Hera that Athena would come looking for her that very day, hours after her return, with a load of worries and problems about everything that had happened since her departure. If Hera had guessed this might happen, as she undoubtedly did—because she had left no forwarding address and refused to take her cell phone along on her trip—the look on her face indicated that the intrusion was no less unwelcome on this

account. I preferred to leave my own tales for later, but the truth of the matter is I, too, had had a positively miserable time of it during her absence.

It seemed that whenever he was not busy in his lab Franklin spent half of his time railing about what he called Hera's 'wilful obstinacy' and 'bizarre religiosity.' The other half was devoted to hassling Athena, trying to get her to do his bidding, and suggesting to all the other sisters that the Acting President clearly was incapable of running the foundation.

For her part Tina had adopted a simple coping strategy: She refused to make any but the most trivial decisions, such as processing payroll requisitions and ordering office supplies. For everything else she dutifully drafted an elaborate memorandum and stuck it in a file marked 'Attention— President.' Since Hera had drawn up the delegation of authority in careful legal language, there was nothing Franklin could do except fume and threaten to call a board of directors meeting—which he knew few of the other directors had any stomach for. None of them saw any reason why everything couldn't be put on hold until Hera got back and resumed her duties. And Io had simply dropped out of sight, although it's said that she shows up almost every evening at Franklin's apartment.

And I must confess Franklin was also putting a lot of pressure on me during the months that Hera was away. It's clear that he wants me to side with him, as he puts it. He says that, since Hera is—as far as he's concerned—no longer capable of running the foundation, he expects that the directors will soon ask him to step back into his former role, temporarily, until he can groom a new successor. He had told me he sometimes contemplates going outside to recruit a non-family member for the presidency. On the other hand, he mused aloud one day that maybe Io is ready to take over.

He urged me to move out of Hera's house and into my

own apartment, and recommended I consider going abroad, to England or to the United States, for a university education. I thanked him for this advice and told him I would think about it. But after a while, since I didn't appear to be following his suggestions, he started ignoring me.

I was standing in the courtyard gardens with Hera and Magnus when she told Tina that she had no intention of resuming her duties. Tina couldn't believe her ears.

"Hera, you must. I only agreed to do this while you were away."

Her reply was blunt and took Tina completely by surprise. "Indeed. And your way of dealing with your responsibilities was to write a memo and slip it into a folder for my attention?"

"But," she protested, "there was so much tension and anger created by Franklin! He was insisting I call the board meeting that is required before the final steps leading to embryo implantation can proceed. I didn't think this decision should be taken in your absence. I stalled for time by making a series of procedural excuses."

Hera replied coldly, "Tina, the minutes specify that the board meeting you're referring to should be called by the president, after consultation with a majority of directors, following a written request to that effect from the Scientific Director. Franklin put such a request to you four months ago, you said. Your duty was to follow those directives. You had plenty of preparation for assuming this role, which is why I asked you to accept it. And you agreed. I'm tired of always being expected to pick up the traces. And I'm not going to do it anymore. If you can't do your job, then resign so the directors can replace you with someone more capable."

Tina broke into tears, turned, ran through the garden, and kept going. Hera just remained standing there, stroking her dog's back, lost in thought.

I stood there, stunned and silent. I had never before witnessed Hera speaking to one of her sisters in such a harsh manner. She's not well, I thought to myself.

The next day Franklin gave me a note to deliver to her. "Dear Hera, I see that you're back. Athena has written to all of the directors, enclosing her letter of resignation as Acting President. This means, of course, that the position automatically reverts back to you. I wish to call your attention to my memorandum of February 1, requesting the convening of a directors' meeting to authorize the final stages of preparation for thawing and implanting the Second Generation embryos. Athena refused to do this, even though I showed her the earlier board resolution and explained to her repeatedly what her responsibilities were. I now make this request officially to you. Since there has already been an intolerable delay in this matter, I expect you to act expeditiously on it. Yours sincerely, Franklin."

Hera scanned it quickly and gave it back to me with the comment: "File it." She struck me as being both tired and depressed.

"Sit down, Marco. I'm not able to pay attention to much of anything involving business these days, as you've probably observed. But in all fairness I can't impose on you the entire burden of dealing with the Colony. Is anything happening?" She was petting Magnus as she spoke, and he appeared to be trying to lick the skin off her face.

I told her I had been extremely fortunate because there had been very little for me to take care of, apart from routine communications. Ziegler advised me a few months ago that he was most impressed with the products and research that PathoGene was delivering. However, there was one new development.

"Ziegler proposed a revised contract, with a significant expansion of the deliverables as well as a closer relationship with us. He wanted to send some of his people down here for advanced training in our facilities. He was very keen to get started so I had to make a decision. I said yes, and they're already here. I put the new contract in front of Tina and asked her to sign it, which she did."

Hera interjected, the bitterness in her voice all too obvious. "Another decision she didn't have to make for herself."

Her tone alarmed me. "I hope you don't think I did anything wrong. Are you upset with me?"

"No, Marco, I'm not upset with you, not one bit. On the contrary, I'm proud of you for taking this initiative. It doesn't even matter if I agree with your decision or not—although I do happen to agree with it. I had hoped you would do exactly as you did. Thank the stars you are here. Now, Magnus is telling us that it's time for his walk. Take him, please."

(Hera's Journal) My God, it's slipping away from me again. I don't even feel like going with Magnus for his walk. I haven't sent for Lucy. I haven't sat down at my piano. What's happening to me?

(Marco's Journal, 16 June 2044) Trouble! Franklin has insisted on having a meeting with Hera and has given her twenty-four hours to reply. He wants Io to be there, too. Apparently Hera never answered the first note from him that I delivered. She mentioned the new demand to me at dinner tonight.

"What are you going to do, mother?" I don't know why, I just felt like resuming my old form of address. "Are you going to see him? What do you think he wants? Is it serious?"

"It's certainly serious in his mind, Marco. It's about holding a board meeting and getting started with the Second Generation. But I haven't decided yet how to reply. I'm sorry, I think I'd rather be alone now. Do you mind?"

(Marco's Journal, 17 June) More trouble! Apparently mother didn't answer Franklin's second note either. Now he's sent another to say that he and Io will be at Hera's house at 5pm tonight. I don't know what she's going to do. Will she call security and refuse them entry?

Just before 5 o'clock this afternoon Hera came to my room and asked me to join the meeting. When Franklin and Io arrived she said simply, "Come in; let's sit in the courtyard."

Io embraced her. "I'm glad to see you back, sister. I hope to make part of that trip myself someday. Just to Bali, which I'm dying to see. I'm not really interested in going back to Alberta, and certainly not to Papua and Tembagapura."

He didn't waste any time getting to the point. "Hera, I think it's time for you to step down as President. I don't imply any criticism of you or your decisions in saying this. It's simply that no decisions of any kind are being made. Things can't go on like they are. Do you know how long your biologist sisters and I have been working together toward the goal of creating the Second Generation? Almost a decade. And I turned seventy-one a few months ago, so I just can't wait much longer."

"I am sorry, Franklin. I've been going through a difficult period; that's no secret, I'm sure. I thought I could entrust things to Athena until I felt better. I'm disappointed in her, I must admit. I started sharing responsibilities with her almost fifteen years ago. I thought she was ready. I was wrong. I know something must be done, but I can't seem to settle my mind on a solution."

Io spoke up. "Hera, dear, why do you take so much onto your own shoulders? Can't you start sharing the load with the rest of us? I realize there was a time, back in Tembagapura, when you alone seemed to sense the danger we were in. No one else—not father, not I, nor any of the other sisters—was able to see it. Only you. You saved our lives,

Hera. Every one of us will be grateful to you until the end of our days."

"Io's right, Hera," Franklin said. "I didn't see the real danger any more than your other sisters did. You not only saw it, you devised the plan to head it off. I told you when you suddenly appeared at my clinic in Cambridge how proud of you I was. Despite the arguments we've had since moving here, I've not changed that opinion, not a bit."

Io added, "No one should be surprised, least of all you, that all this stress and anxiety over the years has caught up with you. First it was Tembagapura, then you organized everything for us in Canada, and then you did it all over again on a far grander scale here in Provo. And that was just our living arrangements. Here it's been the asset management for the foundation, the primate sanctuary, and Patho-Gene. No one person should be expected to oversee all that. Not even you."

(Hera's Journal) I was listening to them with one ear while my mind wandered. It was all true, every word of it, and I can acknowledge this without immodesty. I did all that. I'm proud of it, too. But I *want* to stop. No! Actually, I don't want to stop. It's not a choice I've made. I just can't do it anymore, even though I try. Since I returned to Provo I get up every day, saying to myself, 'Today is the day I'll go back to the office and take over again.' But I never even get out the door of my house. If I can get out of bed, which doesn't happen every day, the best I can do is to make it to the courtyard or the gardens. I still haven't sent for Lucy, because I can't seem to make any decisions at all, no matter how minute their scale. I've started to accompany Magnus and Marco on their daily walks, thank God. But that's about all.

I half-heard Franklin speaking again through my reverie. "Do you agree that it's not wise for you even to try to carry on in your condition? Let someone else take over. We all know it'll only be temporary. All your sisters know that you'll be back before too long."

"Or don't try to prepare yourself to come back," Io added. "Do something else. Take off and travel again, for a year, or two years, or five. See the whole world. Maybe you'll meet your one true love in some exotic place, in darkest Africa, perhaps, or in the middle of Antarctica. Or stay here and take up horseback riding, or tennis, or gardening, or cooking. Or watch over the running of the primate sanctuary. That was your idea, and you love them. All of them, not just Lucy. They're wonderful companions. I wish I could have the kind of relationship you have with Lucy. You can do anything you want. Take the time to find out what it is."

I was still tracking their words while letting my mind run free. Then my mental circuits cycled back to the gathering around me, including the silent Marco, who sat there petting Magnus. My, but they're being awfully nice to me, I thought. What's come over them? The two of them are just like a tag team; the second takes up where the first leaves off. They want to push me out and take over the running of the foundation, but they want me to make it easy for them, too. Well, why not? I'm done with it. Let them have it. I don't care anymore.

"All right, Franklin. Do you have an alternative plan then? Have you and Io agreed on a proposal you'd like to put before the other directors?"

"Yes, we have. Let me back up a minute though. If we were still at the point we were in our planning, say, ten or even five years ago, and you had begun to experience this type of personal difficulty, it wouldn't have mattered so much; anybody could have stepped in, or we could just have brought in an experienced manager from outside to run things for a while. But we're not still at that point. We're ready to embark on one of the most exciting, ambitious, and—to tell the truth—possibly momentous human projects since the dawn of civilization. The future of humanity itself may turn on whether we succeed or fail. But we will surely fail without strong leadership. That's a certainty."

"I don't disagree with you at all," I remarked, my voice flat and entirely without emotion. "So what's your plan?"

"We think that I should step back in, just for a year or two, and that during this time I should groom Io to take over for a while after me. She's willing to do it, although I had to twist her arm a bit." He looked at Io, whose face displayed no reaction. "We believe that if you'll support this plan, all of the other sisters, and not just those who are directors, will be both happy and relieved."

So that was it. Io is ready to take over. Indeed, Franklin was going to 'groom her for the role.' Who would be grooming whom? My mind was now fully alert and racing because they would soon want their answer—in fact, clearly they weren't prepared to leave without one. Well, why not Io? She's both smart and cunning. Maybe she would make a great businesswoman and team leader.

Still, I wondered. Why does Io always make me so uneasy? I already knew the answer—at least the answer I had begun to formulate long ago while we were both still in Tembaga-pura. In truth, Io makes me uneasy because she is so utterly and shamelessly undisciplined in her mind, because she has absolutely no fear of whatever she finds there welling up from within. She has never accepted the idea that the judging part of the brain should rule over the others. "How undemocratic," she once said to me, on one of our daylong hikes in the hills above our ranch in Alberta. "There are more than enough dictators in the world outside. Why should we tolerate yet another one within?"

Io carried on in that long-ago conversation. "Sometimes I'd just like to reach inside my skull and strip off the layers, one by one, starting with the prefrontal cortex. Then I'd say to the old mammalian predator's brain I had exposed, which we still carry underneath all that hominid baggage, 'You're free now, go and do whatever you want.' But I would-n't stop there. I'd rip off more layers until finally I came upon that quick and fearless reptilian brain still lying there, deep down, half-asleep, oppressed by all that rubbish piled on top of it. And I'd say, 'At last, you're now free, too; go and do whatever you want.'" Then she had burst out laughing and walked away.

Suddenly I felt Franklin gently touching my arm. "Hera? Hera? Are you all right? I think you've been daydreaming. Maybe you didn't hear my question. Do you agree with our plan? Will you advise the sisters you support it?"

I stared blankly into space in the direction of my gardens. "No."

There was silence. Magnus sensed the tension in the air, stood up, yawned, and walked over to me. I stroked his head and he licked my face.

Franklin had had enough experience in these situations by now to know better than to raise his voice. So he just glanced at Io and she nodded, then he spoke softly to me. "There's no point in continuing this conversation, is there?"

"I suppose not," I replied.

He and Io stood up. "Then you leave us no choice," he said gravely. "We'll have you removed from your position."

"And how to you propose to do that?" I inquired, feeling inattentive or distracted, my own voice barely audible to myself, as if I were floating underwater.

"We've already explored this matter with a leading law firm, thinking it likely you would react exactly as you have done. Tomorrow we'll circulate a memorandum to the other directors—two of them have already agreed to support it, so it will have the four signatures necessary to trigger an official meeting of the full board. We'll put a draft resolution before the board asking you to resign immediately. Failing that, we'll ask the board to require you to step aside temporarily, to undergo an independent psychiatric evaluation and, if you refuse to agree, to dismiss you.

"A board can tolerate a certain number of wrong decisions at the hands of its CEO," he continued, appearing to be trying mightily to keep from raising his own voice. "What it can't tolerate is no decisions at all. We think we can persuade a majority of directors—we only need one more vote—to go along with this plan. If you do consent to the evaluation, we're pretty sure you won't come through it with flying colors. One way or the other you'll be out of office within three months at the latest."

Obviously Marco could contain himself no longer, for the first words he uttered that evening burst from him like a flood tide. "You can't do this to her!" he shouted. "Are you both crazy?! Don't you remember what we've all come through? If it weren't for Hera none of us would even be here!"

Franklin spun around to face Marco, and in his rage he forgot about Magnus. "Shut up, you little brat! Keep your nose out of this!"

His anger swept my mind clear in an instant and I managed to grab Magnus's collar a split-second before he would have lunged at Franklin. At the same time I barked a command: "Magnus: Stay! Good boy." With the greatest reluctance he obeyed, although his fierce gaze never strayed from Franklin's figure.

"Take him for a walk, Marco, please." He was about to protest but gave in when he met my eyes.

When they'd gone I said, "None of that will be necessary. You will have my resignation. I ask only that it take effect in mid-September, on the day of our thirtieth birthday. That's a little less than three months from today. So you'll get your wish after all, right on time."

He had gotten what he came for and could afford to proceed very gently now. "I knew you would see reason in the end, Hera. Believe me, you'll be much happier once you're away from all this. Don't forget what Io said: You can do whatever you want with your life. Start trying to figure out what it is."

I remained silent. Io just watched her father, saying nothing, as he went on. "But we do need some guarantee that this will happen just as you said. The foundation's affairs are at a critical point. Any further delay in putting new leadership in place will jeopardize the whole project."

"Send a staff member over tomorrow with the resignation letter," I answered. "I'll sign it and it can be witnessed. Will that do?"

"That will do just fine. And now perhaps Io and I should be going."

On the way out, Io gave me another warm embrace and kissed me, but said nothing.

I was sitting in the living room when Marco returned with Magnus and asked what had happened. So I told him. The anguish was apparent in his face.

"No, mother, you can't do that; you can't sign the letter! You know that this is just a plot cooked up by Io to take control of the foundation and its assets. I used to admire my grandfather, but in my opinion he doesn't think very clearly anymore. All he cares about is his project. He doesn't realize that Io will be waiting in the wings, ready to take over when he dies. And who knows what will happen then? Please don't do this."

I looked at him blankly, feeling as if I were struggling to contain the thoughts within me that, I knew, should remain unexpressed. I failed.

"Io's your mother, Marco. Not me. She wanted it this way. She refused to accept you when you were born, so I took you, and put my name on your birth certificate. But she's your mother."

Oh God, why did I say that? Why did I say that right now,

just when everything else was falling apart around me? No sooner had the words left my lips than I wanted them back. Too late.

Marco staggered, sat down. Tears welled up in his eyes. I moved to him but he brushed me away and refused to look in my direction.

We sat, distant, as an eternity passed between us. It seemed he was trying to put all the pieces together that I had just blown apart for him.

"So, you've been holding on to that information. Why did you wait so long to tell me? I had a right to know long before this. You let me go on for years calling you 'mother,' and you said nothing, letting me make a ridiculous fool of myself. How could you be so cruel?" He ran from the room.

I wanted to go after him but I couldn't. I couldn't summon the will, not even to cross the floor as far as the doorway. I simply turned out the lights and lay on the sofa. Only two things were clear in my mind. Tomorrow I would sign the letter. And then I would seek out Marco and try to explain myself. There is nothing else in my agenda book, and when those two items have been crossed out, I'll be finished at last and can put it away for good. No, there was a third item. I should send for Lucy, one last time.

AUGUST 2044, MARCO'S JOURNAL

All summer long a relentless hot sun has been beating down on the dry islands of the British West Indies. Much of the same had occurred last year. The forecasters had warned back then of a fierce hurricane season to follow in the fall, and they were not mistaken. Two years ago the foundation had accelerated its construction schedule for an elaborate network of secure tunnels and caves within the primate sanctuary where the terrified beasts could ride out the windstorms. The rate of shoreline erosion throughout the low islands of the Caribbean is mounting, although we have a decent margin of safety yet around all our properties.

§   §   §

(Io's Journal, 14 August) Only a month to go and it will finally happen! How long have I been waiting for this day to arrive, O Lord? The same length of time that I've been held under the thumb of my dear sister Hera—almost a quarter-century now. Yes, amazingly, she was little more than five when she started bossing the rest of us around. She wouldn't have gotten away with it if we'd had a normal set of parents, or even if the rest of the pack hadn't been so bloody subservient and afraid, kowtowing to her without a murmur—actually, worse than that, *asking* to be led around by the nose.

And now it's over. No more earnest suggestions from her as to how I might improve my attitude or change my deportment; no more helpful hints as to what to wear and how to behave with men; no more spying on me when I go out to have fun. Maybe it wouldn't have been so bad if she'd actually lived up to the big reputation she has—in her own mind!—for working so hard to protect us because we didn't have parents.

Or, once we finally learned we did have at least one parent, if Franklin had told her to stop lording it over the rest of us. She had him too nicely wound around her little finger. But in the end she didn't protect me, did she? Supposedly she was on top of everything, had it all figured out, but she wasn't quite clever enough to spot Klamm's plan in time, was she? I'm the one who discovered it—the hard way. So I'm the one who should be thanked for saving the sisters' skins. But do I get any credit? No, Hera takes it all.

'There'll be some changes made,' as the song goes, everybody can count on that. All I have to do is to humor Franklin for awhile. He's aging fast and getting a little slow upstairs at the same time, so it shouldn't be too long before he has to hand over the reins to me. Thank goodness he put in all those tedious years of training with those girls he calls the 'biologist sisters' before he started getting senile. According to him they've become a very clever bunch in the laboratory, the equal of many of the university scientists he used to hang around with.

But like lab rats everywhere, they don't seem to notice very much of what's going on in the world outside. Just give them some good equipment and tell them what kind of fiddling around you'd like them to do in the cell nucleus, and they're off and running. They race each other to see which one is the smartest and can finish the work first. Then they bring it to you and say, "Here it is, done." You say, "Thanks." They say, "So, what are you going to do with this stuff?" You say, "I'll get back to you on that. Here's your next set of hoops to jump through."

Oh yes, I just remembered that I must make an effort to improve my relations with Marco. Maybe I shouldn't have dumped him on Hera as soon as he dropped from my womb. She just used him as another way of getting the upper hand over me. "Look how dedicated and self-sacrificing Hera is," everybody kept saying, "taking care of Io's brat on top of all her other worries and responsibilities. Isn't she wonderful!" Sometimes I just can't stand how sanctimonious she can be! Or how the others fall for the 'selfless, brave, clever Hera' line every time.

I should have known I was making a big mistake in letting her raise Marco. She's turned him into another wimp and do-gooder, and no doubt she's filled his head with rubbish about me. But it's not too late; he's only fourteen, and besides, his male hormones are kicking up a storm right now, as I found out to my satisfaction. Too bad I couldn't let him know that I was the one who found that special companion for him this summer.

I must allow father to have his last little bit of fun breeding his precious Second Generation. He'll not be with us too much longer after he's finished that job next year. Then who knows? I've spent a lot of time at his lab in the past year trying to figure out what this new crop might be like. He figures they'll be better versions of us, and by better I mean more souped-up in terms of mental functions, and more able and willing to carry out his precious mission to save humanity. In other words, they may very well turn out to be a small army of insufferable do-gooders! This is decidedly not a happy prospect, if I'm the one who's going to be stuck with suckling them—metaphorically speaking, of course!— and shaping their clever little minds.

The great unwashed in the world out there, whom these precious babies are supposed to help, won't be the slightest bit interested in what they'll have to offer by the time the kids have grown up. The nations and peoples of the planet aren't waiting for someone to create paradise on earth for them. They're longing for that other paradise in the sky. They're waiting for deliverance from their sins and they're getting impatient for the big day to arrive. There are so many crimes to be avenged, so many accounts to be settled at last. They've been told over and over again by every cheap wandering preacher that the final battle between good and evil is due to start momentarily. "Well, where is it?" they bleat. "Bring in on. We're ready. Get it over with."

A new crop of a thousand do-gooders, more or less, will be useless for answering these prayers. What's needed instead are fierce warriors, mounted on fire-breathing steeds, who will be prodigious slayers of infidels and evildoers and who will know how to 'get it over with.' We need a thousand—no, millions—like Achilles, the scourge of Troy, who filled that besieged city with widows and orphans. But you don't find warriors like Achilles hanging about in the bazaars and slums, do you? No, you can't find them ready-made anywhere anymore. You have to manufacture them, once you've perfected your prototype.

Most likely this Second Generation will turn out to be just a pointless distraction. Maybe the whole lot of them could be trucked off to a nunnery to get them out of the way. I've heard that the churches are rather short of good staff these days. But who's going to feed that many useless mouths for a lifetime? No, if they start turning out as I fear they might, they'll just have to be recycled and composted. We can't be wasting the foundation's resources on completely impractical ventures, not when there's so much to do to get ready for the great battle.

I need a warrior prototype, and soon. I've already told Pandora to start thinking about this—confidentially, of course. There must be other biologists around who have some ideas that would be helpful to me. I've heard that there are a few who are on the run, moving from country to country, because they've upset the do-gooders. They sound like the kind of people I could use. Once I have control over the foundation's money I'll be able to buy them by the dozen.

I've started to design a breastplate to wear when I lead my warriors into the final battle. The veil lifts, the seals are broken, and the four horses thunder forward. I'm the second rider, astride the bright red horse, as foretold in the Book of Revelation:

> *When he opened the second seal,*
> *I heard the second living creature call out, "Come!";*
> *And out came another horse, bright red;*
> *Its rider was permitted to take peace from the earth,*
> *So that people would slaughter one another;*
> *And she was given a great sword.*

I like that word 'permitted'! My armor will strike terror in the hearts of the wicked and inspire my soldiers to the slaughter. My breastplate will reflect light from the raging fires of hell so brilliantly that even the heavenly host will tremble.

But first I must take control of the foundation and create my prototype warrior. There's no time to waste. Armageddon approaches. I can almost taste it. It's the salt air on the ocean breeze. The taste of blood. I'm ready for battle. In another month I'll have access to the treasury. My warriors will be expensive beasts, but well worth the price.

§   §   §

(*Marco's Journal, 15 August*) This has been a terribly hard summer for everyone. I moved out of Hera's house right after she told me that Io was my mother. I was going to take one of the vacant apartments in the compound, but Io said I should stay with her for awhile, and it did seem the right thing to do, given the circumstances. She's been very nice to me since then and we've been doing a lot of fun things together—horseback riding, snorkelling, water-skiing, swimming, and listening to her collection of rock music.

Io said last night, "You and I never had a chance to bond, Marco. It's such a shame. I'd like to try to make up for it now, even if just a little bit. It always hurt me to think about what Hera did back then, when you were born. You never knew about this, did you? Of course not; why would she tell you? While I was still in hospital, after I gave birth to you, she ordered the doctors to drug me and I didn't know what was happening. I was delirious. It went on for weeks, I think.

"By the time I was released she had already taken you away. Then she hid you on that farm outside Black Diamond and it took me ages to find you. But by then you had a wet-nurse, my milk had dried up, and you didn't know I was the one who had carried you in my womb. Then Hera took you for herself. She couldn't have her own baby so she took mine and pretended you were hers, even putting her name on your birth certificate."

Quite frankly, I don't necessarily believe any of this story, and I still go to see Hera as often as I can. She's been very good to me for a long time and I don't intend to forget that. Above all I wanted her to know that I would still take care of the business deals she had assigned to me.

"You don't have to worry about the Vandenberg Colony file," I told her. "I'm staying on top of it. We can discuss it on whatever schedule you prefer. I enjoy that work and I think I now have a really good feel for the relationship between the Colony and us."

"That's wonderful; I can't tell you how much I appreciate it. I have a sense that we'll need to rely on Ziegler a great deal in the future, so it's important we keep up our end of the bargain."

"I'd like to help in other ways, too, if I could. Are there other files I could take over? I know that it's been difficult for you to manage so many responsibilities. Maybe I can do more."

§ § §

(Hera's Journal) I looked at him with tears in my eyes. It had broken my heart when he left, but he had done what he had to do.

"I'm not sure, Marco. Things are up in the air right now, as you know. Still …" I appeared to hesitate, lost in deep thought, although in fact I already knew what I was going to say. "… why not? There are files that have to be managed no matter who's running the foundation, and you've proven yourself. I'd like you to start by keeping an eye on Patho-Gene for me. The work it does is top-secret. It would be very serious if there was a security breach.

"Tell you what. I'll give you a note to take to the sisters who run Troglodyte, saying that you are on this assignment. I want them to help you run a thorough security scan on PathoGene to see if anybody has been trying to pull off electronic break-ins—that sort of thing. They know they can bill the foundation for these services. I'll give you the keys to my office and advise you what company files to review so that you're aware of their approved projects. Find out if they're working on only what they're supposed to, and also if they're doing anything they shouldn't. Also, take their financial statements to Hex and ask her to go over them with a fine-tooth comb to make sure neither the bookkeepers nor the accountants are working any scams on us."

I knew that Marco would be thrilled. He loves exactly this kind of work—a bit of cloak-and-dagger under the guise of routine management. Also, he enjoys working with the Troglodyte girls, and finding out about their latest successes in hacking into other people's supposedly secure network communications while fending off others' attacks on them.

"Oh yes, I'd be pleased to do that. I'll get right to work on it tomorrow and prepare short summary reports for you."

"Thank you. Can I tell you also how grateful I am that you haven't forgotten Magnus? He would have been devastated if he couldn't look forward to his walks with you. I've been spending a lot more time with him lately, too, but he needs to see you as well. You know that, don't you? You won't get too busy, will you, with your new job on top of everything else you're doing?" I was being careful not to raise the slightest complaint about the time he was spending with Io.

"You know me well enough to understand that I couldn't and wouldn't neglect him. That won't change, even with my new job."

"Marco, as long as we're chatting about this and that, can I bring up another subject and talk to you about motherhood now?" Both of us had been avoiding this subject since he had moved out, but the unbroken silence between us on it was becoming simply intolerable for me. I didn't wait for his answer. "My dilemma about revealing to you that Io was your birth mother was no different from that faced by the parents of most adopted children: When is the right time to tell the child? You can surmise that the answer is that there's no infallibly right time, only an awful lot of wrong ones. In our case the right time never seemed to come. There were always so many other pressing items of business. That's not an excuse, only an attempt to make sure you know that I was thinking about it.

"I thought about telling you, often, but I never did it. The longer I procrastinated the harder it got. I'm so sorry. And you need to realize one other thing. I'm not privy to what Io has told you about how this all began, but I can make some pretty good guesses at the story she has invented for you. All I will say on that score is that I didn't ask to become your adoptive mother. I begged Io to keep you. She refused—and she made some awful threats, about what she would do if I didn't agree to take you, which I won't detail right now. I won't ask you to forgive me. I'm only asking you to believe that I'm telling you the truth."

He hesitated before replying. "I didn't move from your place because I thought you had done something terribly wrong, Hera—after I got over my initial upset, at any rate. It was a coincidence, really. It was time for me to make a change. Other people had said that, too. When you told me about my mother that night, without warning, it just made my decision easier. But I'd rather not take sides. My new experiences this summer have been good for me. I'm not concerned with who is telling me the truth and who isn't about things that happened a long time ago. But I will say that if I were forced to choose, I wouldn't hesitate to say that I think you always speak the truth when you tell me something."

I embraced him. "Thank you for that. You know, when I asked you to stop calling me 'mother' a couple of years ago, on the grounds that our new business associates might find it odd, I just invented that reason on the spot. It was true; Ziegler might well have questioned whom he was dealing with a bit more because I did reveal to him that you were helping me on this file. But it served a second purpose as well: I was trying to ease us both out of a situation that was growing more awkward by the minute, for me at least. It was a temporary solution. Only I never got to the permanent one. Until I just blurted it out that night."

"I think we can leave it at that. The wound is starting to heal because I really am enjoying everything I'm involved in right now."

"Will you come and visit me whenever you have time?"

He embraced me in return and said, "Of course."

Tonight I played the piano for hours. Lucy was sitting on

the floor nearby and Marco was sprawled in a chair, listening, until he fell asleep halfway through my little concert. I think he's rather exhausted from his new schedule. When Lucy is here I can't include Magnus because the poor thing is terrified of him, so he has to stay in Marco's old room.

For the last few weeks I've been practicing the works of one of my favorite composers, Erik Satie, and especially his pieces known as *Gnossiennes* and *Gymnopédies*. They bring me an incredible sense of peace and tranquility, which I desperately need. I've borrowed my interpretation from an old CD recording by Reinbert de Leeuw. His tempi are so incredibly slow in these pieces that you find yourself occasionally wondering if something's wrong with the disc player.

Sometimes he holds a single note for as long as two or three seconds, and inside those spaces one becomes suspended in time. The next note breaks the spell momentarily but then immediately recreates it, and these sequences can go on for several minutes. Satie's melodic structure produces the smoothest of transitions from one episode of suspended time to the next, making you feel as if you were a baby being rocked ever so gently in its mother's arms.

I think that music is the only one of the human arts that can control the onrushing flow of time. It seizes hold of the hands on the stopwatch—beating out the seconds with an unwavering regularity—and stops them, imposing its own meter. No longer are the units of time identical; they have been broken apart, resized, and laid down again in a new pattern.

But to realize what's being done by the composer, you have to allow your entire being to surrender to music's capture of time, to will yourself to be absorbed by it, to be taken up like a drop of water in blotting paper. If you don't make this choice, the composition will sound very boring, as if there's not enough happening, which is the reaction I get from some of my sisters when I play these pieces for them in de Leeuw's style. But for me, quite literally, it can bring the whirling globe to a dead stop. It's what I need in order to regain my balance.

Lucy also sits and listens patiently when I talk to her. I've been doing this a lot recently. The feelings of lassitude and inertia I've been battling this past year appear to lurk inside me, waiting patiently for a chance to escape, just like my migraines. I suspect they've always been there. The migraines emerged first when I was quite young. The headaches appear to be a kind of relief valve for the psychological pressures within my nature, especially my intensity of focus, my need for recognition from teachers or others judging my performance, and my overwhelming sense of responsibility.

For a long time my migraines were so regular, almost like clockwork, and each time they passed I felt such relief that I immediately plunged right back into my work again. I would wake up the next day, after a night of pain, feeling refreshed, just like the mornings that break clear and sunny after an overnight shower. Sometimes it seems like my headaches were designed to produce this whole cycle so that I could be re-energized for my tasks.

My very different bouts of lassitude are certainly a function of mild depression and anxiety. This disorder was bottled up inside me for much longer than the headaches. On the one hand, it seems to operate very much like my migraine cycle, in that it was released when I slowed down or stopped the pace of work-related activity. But on the other hand, it also escalated gradually in intensity. What I noticed first was a loss in my decision-making ability, whereas until then I had always loved the decisiveness that came so easily to me. Then ever so gradually that ability continued to deteriorate until I couldn't summon up the will to make decisions of any kind anymore. And unlike my migraines, this cycle doesn't have a kind of automatic restorative mode built into it. When it finally succeeds in firmly taking hold, it simply doesn't want to release its grip.

The depressive cycle is insidious. It asks you quietly to let go and step back, supposedly just briefly, for a little while, but when you take the bait, so to speak, instead of re-energizing you, it takes advantage of every pause to drive you downwards another notch. It's like gliding down a precipitous mountainside through one spiralling hairpin turn after another, all the way to the bottom. Then, having landed there, you look up and say to yourself, 'It's so far to climb back up again, I don't have the energy to even attempt it, so why not just stay here for awhile?' But a little while turns into a longer while, and so on. That's how it's been for me this past year.

Not everyone is the same, however. I know what I can do when I am in top functioning form, and I remember those times clearly. I could try to make the slow climb up the spiral I rode down, repeating every turn in reverse, and I would probably succeed, sooner or later. Perhaps for some that's the only thing to do if they're going to shake off these bonds. But not for me. There's just not enough time. And everything I've struggled for all my life is now hanging in the balance.

If you are daunted by the immense mist-shrouded peak that looms above and don't think you can get back up and over the mountain, you can try going underneath it, through the mind's deeper passages. But only if you are well equipped to do so. My brain was superbly engineered by my father, who constructed for me swift new highways through dense neuronal thickets unavailable to others. His wizardry opened up for me countless subterranean cortical shafts others fear to enter. I was outfitted like the best white-water rafters to ride the wild underground rivers of thought and still remain afloat. And in those gloomy caverns, I saw marked out before my eyes, lit up like a row of illuminated beacons along an airport runway, the one path that led unerringly past the false turnings to the opening on the far side. As I followed it, the darkness receded before me.

I will find a way to retain control over the Sujana Foundation and its Second Generation project. First of all, I must direct my energies toward resolving the dilemmas I feel about our undertaking, once and for all. It's not fair to keep the other sisters who are working on it indefinitely suspended in mid-air. I've put my strong concerns on the record in my conversations with Franklin and Gaia, and they still seem persuasive to me. In a nutshell, once people start going down that road using germline modifications, there's no turning back, the die is cast, the new genes are out in the environment. Then there's a good chance we'll all lose our way because we won't know anymore what it means to be human. After we've altered a sufficient number of the traits that were thought—up until now—to define who we are, who will be able say anymore what is human, what's non-human, and especially, what is inhuman?

On the other hand, our project consists in readying a large group of possibly exceptional people to take a prominent place on the world stage. For all his personal faults, Franklin is a great neurogeneticist, perhaps the greatest who has ever lived so far. In part that's why he's so frustrated and anxious now. He could have saved himself a lot of time and trouble by simply touching up and re-using the old scientific protocol—the one he developed for us sisters—on the Second Generation.

But he didn't. First, he reworked it extensively in the early 2020s, intending to apply it to the Group of 300 embryos. Then, together with his group of acolyte daughters, he spent another five years of hard work, trying to make his modifications more precise and fine-tuned for the Group of 500. They analyzed and synthesized a tremendous amount of new scientific research, primarily designed to lower the probabilities of accidentally causing neurological disorders as a result of his modifications. Then he patiently worked through a near-endless series of discrete chromosomal markers, trying to attune his protocol with the latest research insights.

Our Second Generation, therefore, will have a much better chance of becoming normal types of people who also just happen to be endowed with exceptional higher-cognitive functions. But even his original explanation of his project, written for the Group of 300, makes it crystal clear that the embryo manipulations are only the first in a long list of carefully planned interventions. The very nature of the project demands that it should go on for as long as the prefrontal cortex continues to develop, that is, from the developing fetus to age eighteen and beyond.

Maybe that explains some of the difficulties we sisters encountered, as he himself often suggested. The supportive learning environment my father created for us began to break down when we were about twelve. Certainly, well before that time, I sensed some of the tensions between Franklin and Klamm and was aware of my own fears about Klamm's intentions, and I'm sure that some of my other sisters did, too, at least partly. So perhaps our histories are not at all indicative of what the outcomes might have been if the original plan could have been fully implemented as planned.

Do I have the right and responsibility to deny the world the chance to see what these special beings might do? I can't make a final decision just yet, but I have promised myself I will do so very soon. Only one thing is for sure—if we do decide to proceed with the project, I have to stay in charge over the long-term. Even if he wanted to, my father cannot direct the post-natal phase of development for the Second Generation. He'll be too old at that point. So what then? Am I really prepared to leave that entire group to Io's tender mercies? That's absurd. I know that. It would be far, far better to repeat what I did earlier—this time, however, taking action earlier in the process. I would have to find a way to make sure the embryos were destroyed by pulling the plug on the cryopreservation units.

The alternative is unthinkable: How could I let a huge group of wonderful children arrive in the world, and then leave all of them at the whim of whatever interests just happened to be controlling the foundation's affairs at that point in time? Monstrous! The results might cause us—all of us who helped set up this experiment—to be looked upon with horror and revulsion for as long as civilization endured thereafter.

I cannot and will not allow this to happen. I will take back control of the foundation.

15 SEPTEMBER 2044

(Hera's Journal, 5am) The morning dawned clear and sunny. Today the sisters turn thirty and our birthday party is due to start promptly at 8pm. The foundation's board of directors meeting, at which my resignation letter is to be acted upon, is scheduled to begin at 3pm sharp.

§   §   §

(Io's Journal) I've been tallying the votes and lobbying the directors throughout the summer months. The total of seven voting directors means that four votes are needed for my side to prevail when the motion is made to accept Hera's letter of resignation. At this point I know that Franklin and I can count on Pandora to support us, but Ari and Gaia are sure to oppose the motion. If Hera shows up—having changed her mind—and votes against us, the count will be even at three-three. So, Tina—who to this day bitterly resents Hera's criticisms of her performance as acting president—holds the swing vote. What a lucky break: It's in the bag.

§   §   §

(Hera's Journal, 6am) Over the last week or so I've been assessing the likely outcome of the voting at the board meeting later today. If I try to withdraw my resignation, I'll lose by a

margin of 4-3. At that point it will be all over. But I've hit my stride again, just as I used to do in years past when crucial decisions approached. I find myself brimming with confidence and determination. Given what I've faced in my life up until now, why should sidestepping a small problem at a board of directors meeting pose an insuperable obstacle? I planned our escape from the jungle hideout in Tembagapura, the choice of a safe hiding place in Alberta, and the final showdown with Klamm. All of those operations showed a meticulous attention to detail, good strategies, and the anticipation of potential obstacles. Why should I vary a successful formula?

Only one element of my new scheme isn't under my full control. I've always held firmly to the view that whatever I did on behalf of the sisters' collective interests must be supported by a clear majority in the group as a whole. The choice of a subset of them to act as directors for the foundation is an artifact of legal convenience. My real, live constituency is the band of sisters—all twelve of us. So I should do my imaginary counting exercise with the larger group in mind.

Solidly against me are Io and Pan. I regret very much that I can no longer count on Tina, my close comrade-in-arms for fifteen years. If I could take back my harsh words of criticism of her I'd gladly do so in an instant. My excuse—a lame one—is that I was not at all well when I uttered them. Recently I sought to repair the breach with her, but I was rebuffed. Who could blame her, in view of how mean I was?

Moira has always been a complete mystery to me. Despite my best efforts to connect with her throughout my life, I've never managed to overcome her isolation and reserve. She's been in an especially ugly mood during the last six months, and no one knows why; she's also begun to hang around Io a good deal. I have to suppose that, for whatever reason, she's gone over to Io's camp for now.

If I were soliciting my sisters' support in 2030, after our successful escape from Papua, or anytime during the early years after our arrival here in Provo, I wouldn't even have bothered to tally the count. The memory of what lay behind us, and of my role in leading them out of the wilderness, would have been fresh in their minds at those times. But things are different now. A dozen years have passed since our arrival in the Caribbean, and that period had been peaceful, productive, secure, and even fun, as the sisters managed to overcome their earlier fears. Who among them—other than I—could call up into imagination anymore the horror of Klamm's plan and the narrowness of our success in slipping from his clutches?

Among the biology group, Pandora is Io's closest buddy, but Gaia has always been close to me and I can count on her full backing. I'm worried a bit about the other two—Percy and Rhea. Like Gaia and Pan, the two of them have spent the better part of their working hours for a decade in Franklin's company. How could they not have been influenced by his ways of thinking during their long apprenticeship? His influence might have been subtle, subconscious rather than explicit, but it would hardly have been entirely absent. When I lay out for the sisters the full story of the conflict over the foundation's leadership, will they follow him now rather than me? I simply don't know.

As for the rest, Ari, Hex and Tammy will be with me, but Themis is an unknown quantity. Like Moira, Themis has a good deal of trouble dealing with situations involving interpersonal conflict. And when—as I expect—she sees Moira allied publicly with Io, she may join them. If so, and if they stand united, I'm in trouble with my leadership in the whole band for the first time in my life. Under a worst-case scenario I could end up with only four solid supporters out of eleven. The sisters' caucus isn't a formal proceeding in any sense, but it won't matter. I will have lost the moral basis for leadership.

And I cannot endure the prospect of just sitting around here in the coming years, watching Io do what she pleases with the foundation's resources—and, more importantly, the collection of embryos. I'd better pack my bags, just in case.

But first I'm going to have breakfast with Marco. I wanted so badly to take him into my confidence about what I've planned for today, but I just couldn't take the risk. I have no way of determining if his relationship with Io has blossomed sufficiently for him to contemplate an act of betrayal. This morning all I can do is to ask him to wait until it's all over before deciding whether he can continue to trust and respect me. On the other hand, I consider the possibility he would actually betray me to be so unlikely that I will alert him to expect some highly unusual events to unfold this day.

(7:30am) After we finished our meals I swore him to secrecy and said, "Things will happen among us later today unlike anything you've witnessed in your life up to now. I'll be blunt: The events will certainly upset you, perhaps frighten you, maybe even cause you to abandon me and the entire compound. I hope and pray this won't be the case. For security reasons I can't tell you what's going to take place later. And I must start down the road I'm on without knowing if I'll succeed or not. For sure, by the end of this day, either I or some of the others will be forced to quit our compound here, permanently.

"I hope to be able to explain it to you later today, if all goes well. But if events go very badly for me, and I have to leave right away, I may not have an opportunity to talk to you again and explain to you why I chose this course of action. I love you, Marco, with my whole heart. You are my treasure. I have to go now. God be merciful to us."

Without giving him a chance to reply—what could he say, since I had given him no information?—I jumped up and hugged and kissed him before I left.

§   §   §

(Marco's Journal) I looked at her as she walked away. I have a pretty good idea about the kind of trouble that's brewing for the board meeting this afternoon. Obviously Hera has decided that I can't help her in this case, so I'll just have to wait and see. But I've already made up my mind what to do if she does take off later today: I'm going along, even if I have to hide in her luggage.

Thank goodness I decided to spend my free time during the summer doing much more than just working on my assigned tasks and cavorting in Io's company. I was determined to make up my own mind about what had happened between Hera and Io after I was born, which is why I had sought out all my aunts, one by one—all except Moira and Themis, that is, who flatly refused to talk about the subject. I wanted to make my own assessment of why things had turned out as they had in the years leading up to Io's pregnancy and beyond, when I was sent as a baby to the farm outside Black Diamond. The conclusions I've drawn might have been obvious, might have been arrived at without my conducting such an elaborate investigation, but they are firmer and clearer in my mind because of it.

I've concluded I can trust Hera as I always have done. No one is perfect, no matter how well engineered she is, and it seemed to me that she might have handled the matter of my awareness of the circumstances of my birth a lot better. Nevertheless, neither can I fault her all that much. And although I've enjoyed Io's company immensely these past three months, I'm not deaf and blind; I know that she was making a determined effort to be on her very best behavior with me. She had come looking for me and showered her attentions on me, in more ways than one. Knowing Io as I do, I have to assume that she had her own reasons for playing this game.

There's only one aspect of this summer's holiday experiences that I don't intend to share with Hera, namely my sexual escapades. It was good of Io to help me gain access to the safe houses outside the compound perimeter for my meetings with my girlfriend. Then Io pissed me off by peppering me with questions, wanting to know all the 'details,' as she put it. This annoyed me considerably and I started avoiding her. I've been much happier since I moved out of Io's guestroom and into my own apartment in the family compound.

§   §   §

(Hera's Journal, 9am) Dear Marco! How happy I am whenever I spend time with him! And he seems a lot happier, a lot more relaxed since he moved out of Io's digs. Of course, I knew the minute he moved out, but didn't know if it had been occasioned by any unpleasantness between the two of them. I was delighted for him, too, when the security people took note of his liaisons in the houses and brought the matter to my attention in their weekly reports. I am in truth his real mother, after all, and yes, I confess, I am terribly overprotective where Marco is concerned. Thus I felt that I must authorize a modest investigation, just to be on the safe side, to obtain a bit of a profile on his new partner. I also asked the agents, after interviewing her, to gain her consent for a thorough medical exam at our private clinic, and happily she agreed. They advised her in no uncertain terms not to mention their request to Marco.

I recall very well my feeling of vague unease thereafter. Something was bothering me, although I couldn't put a finger on what it was, so I sent the agents back for another interview. What a shock it was when the young woman revealed that some 'nice lady,' whose name she didn't know, had arranged her supposedly chance meeting with young

Marco at the beach! The lady—who, I deduced immediately, must be none other than Io—was, she said, paying her a handsome weekly stipend for the time she was spending with him.

This mystery patron had also ordered her not to use birth control, but to tell Marco specifically that she was on the pill. She was assured by the lady that if she became pregnant, her baby would be adopted and all expenses paid. My agents took her back to the clinic and she was given a contraceptive. The agents told the young woman on my instruction that she was free to continue to meet Marco. Of course, I was so pleased to learn through reading the interview transcripts that she was actually quite smitten by him. Finally they asked if there anything else they should know about her arrangements with the mystery lady. Probably it was their slightly menacing tone that persuaded her to make a clean breast of things—the lady had asked her to collect some of Marco's semen in a special container she had given her, and she had done so.

At that point the agents said they were finished with her, but they also warned her that if she ever revealed either to Marco or Io that they were watching, or that they had met with her, the local sharks would be enjoying a special meal at her expense. I haven't yet been able to figure out what, if anything, Io was up to—whether she was just playing games, or whether she had some nefarious purpose in mind—but I made a commitment to myself to delve into the matter again when I got the chance.

Following my breakfast with Marco I had summoned my driver and directed him to deliver me to one of the large tourist hotels in town. At the brief meeting there certain arrangements, previously discussed, were confirmed. Then back to the compound just before 11am. Yesterday I had sent a note to all the sisters except Io; the note said that I wanted to do some special planning for the wild thirtieth-birthday bash to be held that evening, and to please come to a meeting at 11am the next morning at my house. In the note I told them that I'd rented a private room in a luxury hotel for our celebration, and I encouraged each of them to invite friends and lovers, if any were in town, to come to the party.

Precisely at eleven I walked in and surveyed my living room. I'd hoped that all ten might be there, but Pan, Moira and Tina didn't show. After the greetings I quickly got down to business.

"I apologize for summoning you here on what you'll soon learn are false pretences, but by the time I've finished, I hope you'll understand why. You all know that there's a special meeting at the foundation offices later today. The directors among you know the reason for the meeting, but others may not, so I'll summarize what's been happening for everyone's benefit. Earlier this summer, under severe pressure from Franklin, I agreed to resign as president today and allow him to resume that post. However, I have since reconsidered and will ask to withdraw my resignation at the meeting. Immediately thereafter I expect Franklin to table a motion that will compel me to resign. I expect his motion to pass." There was an audible stirring in the room.

"Other motions, which I guess will also be approved, will authorize the appointment of Franklin as president and Io as senior vice-president. Io will probably succeed Franklin in the presidency not later than two years from this date. All this will be done in accordance with applicable by-laws and will have the force of law."

The sisters who had been in the dark about the foundation's business were abuzz. Some clamored to speak. I begged them to wait until I was finished with my background report.

"There will be plenty of time later, if subsequent events turn out as I hope, for full explanations of every detail for those of you who want them. But I cannot dwell on them now. Decisions must be taken today that will profoundly affect the futures of every one of us. The bottom line is all that's important at the moment. And the bottom line is this: I've decided that I'm not prepared to accept the outcomes of those motions before the foundation's board, even though they would be perfectly legal and proper in form.

"There is only one vitally important reason for my decision. I have come to believe that if the foundation's senior management is restructured along the lines I have indicated, and thereafter the board decides to proceed with the Second Generation project, the future welfare of all the members of that forthcoming generation may be in the most serious jeopardy. I say 'may be' because, of course, I have to assess the likelihood of certain future events taking place. My assessment is that it is highly probable that the health and well being of the Second Generation, and perhaps their lives as well, could be at risk from those who may be controlling the foundation at that time. I intend to ensure that this does not come to pass."

Some in attendance were now calling out questions, but I was determined to carry on for the moment without giving them the chance to take the floor just yet.

"As we are meeting here at this moment, certain actions are being taken within our compound that have been authorized—very reluctantly, I might add—by me in my capacity as president of the foundation. The actions are being carried out by a special contingent of highly trained and armed professional security personnel, based nearby in the Bahamas. They are here now.

"First, one group is heading to Franklin's apartment and—how shall I put this?—will be taking him into custody, as it were. He'll have all his personal effects removed to one of the safe houses across the street from our front gate, and this house will become his permanent residence from now on. For the time being he will be forbidden to enter this compound, including what used to be his laboratory. He will be free to move around on Provo, but not to leave Providenciales Island. There will be a private security watch on him twenty-four hours a day, and he will have to wear an electronic tracking bracelet whenever he leaves his house."

There were loud gasps everywhere in the room. Some cried out and tried again to speak, but I cut them off.

"Please, I implore you, let me finish this part, and then I'll answer your questions. The rest of the task force has picked up Io. She will be confined to a new compound the foundation owns on Salt Cay Island. Within the hour she'll be put aboard the black cabin cruiser now sitting in Provo's harbor—the one without markings—and removed to Salt Cay, along with her cats. Her personal possessions will be transported separately, probably by tomorrow.

"Her new accommodations are perfectly comfortable, well stocked with food and other necessities, and will have Internet connections available. But there will be an intercept on all communications to and from her compound. I can tell you also that the new facility will be under regular satellite surveillance. Moreover, there will be a permanent sea watch placed on Salt Cay Island to prevent her from leaving unless she has my prior permission. Adequate provisions will be shipped to her regularly, and anyone who wants to do so is free to go and visit her there."

At this point I could contain their outbursts no longer.

"Why, Hera, why? What could have been so serious as to justify these actions?" Tammy demanded.

I spoke quite deliberately now. "I'm coming to that. Before this meeting ends I will be asking you to signify whether you agree with what I have done or not. I want to recap what I said a moment ago, so that things are perfectly clear in your minds. What I did, specifically, was to give my permission for this private security group to enter our compound and escort Franklin and Io to new quarters on the Islands, using force if necessary. I also consented to an arrangement with the Islands' government under which the police and attorney general's office will not interfere in these matters. There is more, and I will get to those items later.

"Soon, each one of you will be asked, individually and by name, to signal your approval or disapproval of my actions, and I shall ask that there be no abstentions. A clear majority in favor is necessary in order for me to feel that I have the moral authority to carry on. However, if a majority of you disagree, I will have no choice but to leave this place and go my own way, permanently. My bags are already packed. If your decision goes against me, I will depart for the airport immediately and I will not return, ever."

"Hera," Rhea interjected, "we must focus on the most important issues first. How could these actions *possibly* be legal? What's to prevent either Franklin or Io from contacting the authorities here and asking them to lay a complaint of illegal confinement against you? And to launch a civil action in court? Surely you can't imagine that either or both actions would fail to secure their prompt release. Those of us in this room who may give our approval to these actions, as you have requested, almost certainly could be charged as accessories after the fact if criminal proceedings were to be launched. At the very least, all of us will be tied up for the foreseeable future in legal proceedings.

"I'm prepared to accept the fact that you believe you're acting in our best interests," she continued, "because I'm one of those who thinks that you have always done so. Like some others here, I was approached awhile back by Io who sought to enlist my support for unnamed measures to be taken against you. I refused point-blank even to discuss the matter. But now, I must admit to you and my sisters here, I am very worried about what the consequences of your actions might be."

"Let me deal with the legal situation first," I answered, "before speaking more broadly to the underlying reasons for these actions. I understand your concerns and you're perfectly justified in raising them. I'm afraid this is a rather high-stakes game, at least as I perceive it, and no mercy will be shown to me—or rather, to what I seek to protect in the foundation's future—if I lose. The short answer to your question is this: I can give you an ironclad guarantee to the effect that neither criminal nor civil proceedings will be filed in the courts of this country over these actions. And there is a specific reason why this is so.

"An advance detail for the security force that entered our compound today has been here on the Islands for the past three days meeting both with me and some senior government officials. They brought with them, and reviewed with us, documentary evidence prepared by US government agencies to the effect that Franklin and Io have been engaged in money laundering and securities fraud since we arrived here in the Islands. According to what we saw, arrest warrants are outstanding in Miami for both of them, listing charges that, if upheld in court, would see them spending a few years behind bars."

Hex leapt up from her seat. "Surely to God, Hera, you don't believe a word of that tale! Franklin? Money laundering? Securities fraud? That's absurd. No, insane! It cannot be true. I won't listen to such nonsense."

"No, Hex, I don't believe that the charges are fair, either," I said, very quietly and very slowly, "and I suspect they will be dismissed sometime in the future. But the evidence has been presented to government officials in this country by officials acting on behalf of the United States. The authorities in Cockburn Town have reviewed it and found it to be credible, and on that basis local arrest warrants have been prepared for the two of them."

"Then why all these elaborate preparations to house

them if they're just going to be arrested and carted off to jail in any case?" Percy asked.

"Because I've arranged to have the local arrest warrants suspended, that's why. Government officials here owe us many favors, as they are well aware. They also appreciate very much the economic activity we've generated on the Islands since landing here, including the set of reinforced embankments just built along part of the coastline and paid for entirely by the foundation. They agreed to suspend the warrants if I made sure that Franklin and Io were put under secure house arrest and kept that way indefinitely. Those warrants won't be executed unless either of them attempts to leave the sovereign territory of the Turks and Caicos Islands without permission. Since this is an overseas territory of the United Kingdom, British authorities have been informed, discreetly, and they have given their approval, although nothing is in writing."

"That takes care of the criminal side, but what about the possibility of civil proceedings?" Ari inquired. "What's to prevent them from going to a lawyer and suing us?"

"Pretty much the same reasons," I replied. "As you know, this is a very small country. When do you think was the last time it counted a distinguished Nobel Prize recipient among its permanent residents? Can you imagine any government officials wishing to see an action proceed, one in which the fraud charges inevitably would surface? So the officials have assured us that, if they get wind of any civil suits coming forward, they will have a word with the lawyer involved. No barrister on these islands can survive long in practice if he or she is cut off from government business. Nor will any civil actions proceed in the courts."

There were some expressions of relief in the audience as the prospect of arrests or lawsuits receded. I'm sure they knew they could accept my reassurances that the captives were safe and would be well cared for. Later, when they've had a chance to reflect on the day's events, I'm certain they will understand why things had been arranged in this fashion. I needed to find a way to put the two of them out of commission for a while in order to keep Franklin and Io from gaining legal control over the foundation and its assets. And to do this I needed a pretext to ensure that neither the authorities in Cockburn Town nor the local courts would interfere with their illegal confinement. And everything had to be done with a minimum of public fuss.

I used the opportunity of a lull in the commotion to return to the matter of the reasons for my actions.

"This is the point at which I must call in my chips with you. I've based these decisions largely on the intuitions I have about what Io's long-term objectives might be in taking control of the foundation and its very substantial assets. I believe she has convinced herself that what she calls the 'end of days' is fast approaching, the time of the Apocalypse, when the veil lifts and the Four Horsemen ride out, slaughtering the wicked over the face of the earth.

"I believe she thinks she has a special role to play in those events, that is, to engineer and breed a race of super-warriors to take part in the battle. The only point I'm not clear on is which side her forces will be supporting."

There was raucous laughter in the room at this remark, which helped to dispel some of the tension. "I apologize; I don't suppose that's very funny at all." I paused a few moments before continuing. "I really don't know why Io thinks she will be able to do this, but I am not prepared to let her use the foundation's vast expertise and resources to find out whether or not she can. I don't have solid proof of Io's agenda to lay before you today, but I do have some expectation that I might be able to supply at least some supporting documents by tomorrow. Nevertheless, a decision must be made now. It cannot wait. So I am forced to fall back upon your trust in me, to collect all of my outstanding

IOUs with you, so to speak.

"All of you here today have told me, at one time or another, in one form or another, either in Alberta, or here in Provo, or back in Tembagapura, that you are grateful for what I was able to do on behalf of the group. I do not seek any credit for what I did then. I did what I thought I must do—and what I was able to do. Now I need to ask you whether you retain the same level of confidence in me. I am going to call the roll."

Almost immediately Gaia rose from her seat. "There's no need for that, Hera, although we can call the roll if you insist. We who are here certainly don't think alike on everything, by any means. Yet I would be amazed if anyone in this room would disagree with what I'm going to say. You saved my life in Tembagapura. Then you risked your life for me in Jakarta when you took on Klamm all alone. I will speak for myself, and then let others have their say: I would follow you to the ends of the earth and back." She looked around at her sisters.

Tammy added, "Gaia has spoken for all of us." All except Themis got up from their seats and approached me, silently embracing me in turn as I wept.

Gaia, standing close, then whispered to me, "I know you still have much to do today. I have only one request. Let me choose a small delegation to go and talk with Athena. I think we can make her understand the reasons for your actions. I know that for a long time she worked very closely with you, and I for one hope the two of you will be reconciled before too long."

"Thank you, Gaia, please do that," I said, through my tears. As she was leaving I called her back. "And see if you can find Moira and Pan, too, and explain things to them as best you can."

A few hours later, just before the board meeting was due to begin, Gaia grabbed my arm. "I need a minute with you.

Moira and Pan ran up to me an hour ago and demanded to be taken to Salt Cay."

I directed us to some nearby chairs. "Actually, I suppose I'm not surprised. Pan has been very close to Io for years, and Moira spent a lot of time with Io this past summer. What's your view? We have to allow them to go, don't we?"

"Yes, of course. They're free to move around, just like the rest of us are—well, no, actually, the rest of us minus two." She said this with a twinkle in her eye; Gaia has an even temperament and a brilliant mind, and it was a great relief to me that she appeared to accept my reasons for sequestering Franklin and Io. "They'll find a way to get there on their own if we don't assist them, and besides I don't think it would be fair to refuse."

"I agree on both counts."

"Then I'll see to the arrangements. Perhaps this whole thing won't last long anyway."

The annual general meeting of the board of directors of the Sujana Foundation was convened by its president promptly at 3pm. "Let the minutes show," I intoned, "that the following directors are absent: Franklin, Io and Pandora. Four directors are present, which is a quorum, so the board may proceed to conduct its business. The first order of business is the letter from the president, announcing her resignation at the close of business this day. I now inform the board that I am withdrawing my letter. I ask for a vote of the board to continue as president with an indefinite term."

Gaia said, "So moved," and Ari was seconder. I did not vote. Tina abstained. Gaia told me later that their conversation had gone well but also that Tina needed more time to digest what had occurred. The remaining two directors voted in favor. I noted, "The motion is passed by a majority of directors present and voting." We agreed on a full slate of directors for the coming year; the four present were confirmed, and Gaia nominated Tammy, Percy, and Rhea to replace the three absent ones. We passed the usual enabling resolutions, and quickly adjourned the meeting. Fifteen minutes had elapsed.

§   §   §

From there I went immediately to an adjoining office where the three-person leadership group for the special security contingent was waiting.

"Just got off the phone with General Ziegler, Hera. I used one of our favorite phrases, 'I thought that went well.' And it did. The 'perps,' as we like to call them, are now installed at their new locations. We encouraged them to have a drink, or two or three, and take it easy."

"Thanks, Jessica. How did it go, in fact?"

She laughed. "Well, I would be lying if I said they were overjoyed to see us. But apart from that, what could they do? We took them totally by surprise, and given the amount of muscle we had on our side, 'resistance was futile,' as the saying goes. We got the most flak from your dad, of all people. The old geezer actually tried to take us on, so we had to give him a few gentle slaps to calm him down. We didn't have to use the needle. But he was in such a state that we cuffed him just for the hell of it."

"What about Io?" I asked.

"Now, that's one cool customer!" Jessica said, grinning. "When we introduced ourselves and told her where we were taking her, she just smiled and said, 'Silly me. I should have known. Round 2 to Hera. One more to go.' What did she mean by that?"

"Never mind now. I'll tell you sometime over a beer. I'd like to invite you all to our birthday bash, but I think I'd better not. That would require just too much explaining for one day. It's only late afternoon and I'm already drained. Let's review the ongoing arrangements and then I have one more appointment before I take my dog for a long walk. And by the way, did you find what I told you to look for in Io's house?"

"The semen sample? Yeah, we found an unlabeled vial in her freezer, which looks like it might contain such a substance; it's in the bag here, packed in ice. About the long-term arrangements: As I understand the deal from the briefing General Ziegler gave us, your own local security boys will take care of your dad. We'll put a permanent watch on the lady now ensconced on Salt Cay Island. We have small ships on constant patrol through the BWI, looking out for a whole host of nefarious activities. Ziegler has put the Salt Cay location on the watch list. That includes the satellite surveillance, too. Apparently he's linked up with your own people here, in the company with that funny name."

"Troglodyte Partners."

"Yes, that's it. The communications intercepts will be coordinated between them and us. By the way, we had a very pleasant chat with the girl we dropped off for a holiday on Salt Cay. What are you and Ziegler afraid of?"

"Like other people, I've been guilty of underestimating my sister Io in the past. Never again. Let's leave it at that. Ask Ziegler, and he'll tell you what he wants you to know."

"Fair enough. Well, we have to push off in our nice little cabin cruiser. I must say, your government folks here are very accommodating. There won't be a single record of our short visit to these lovely islands. I think I'll come back here for a holiday sometime."

"Look me up if you do, Jessica. And thanks again."

As I was heading out the door, she said, "Oh, by the way, here's the videodisc with all the nice pictures of the stuff we boxed up in Io's house, including the pages from her journals. Some of the boys on the team went bonkers at her collections of pornography and instruments of pleasure. It took all the authority my rank commands to keep them focused on the job at hand. We called the removal firm, as you directed, and they picked up the stuff at the perimeter gate. The old man's belongings have already been moved into his new house, and Io's will be in Salt Cay tomorrow; we let her take a suitcase in the meantime. We noticed that you had already stocked the place with food and drink. But we didn't sweep for drugs. I swear."

I thanked her and went to look for Marco. I found him in his apartment, sitting next to Magnus and listening to Mozart's *Abduction from the Seraglio.*

"I've been waiting for you," he said. "I knew you'd come looking for me. Tammy came over right after your meeting and filled me in. Can I ask you something right away? Was that group from the US working for General Ziegler?"

"Yes, Marco, good guess. I have a feeling we'll see them again, and next time you'll be there. I am so sorry, but I just couldn't bring you in on this one. I had to do it alone. I presume Tammy told you that nobody got hurt and that they both have comfortable accommodations?"

"She told me, and I think I understand why you had to keep it to yourself. What's going to happen now?"

"It's full steam ahead on all our files, Marco. You have the Colony and PathoGene."

"I'll have the first report on PathoGene ready in a week. I think everything's pretty much OK there, but after looking at the files I can see why you wanted somebody to keep a special watch on it. They're working on some awful stuff."

"Indeed they are. Did Tammy report to you what I said about Io at the sisters' meeting? Funnily enough, I think the rest of us are going to need the PathoGene technologies, in large part because almost certainly there are more people like your mother out there. I only hope that there aren't too many of them."

"Yes, she told me. Over the summer, while I was staying at Io's place, the two of us had a lot of long, late-night conversations. I knew you'd probably be interested in the content of those conversations, but I wasn't in the mood for running back to you every day and turning in a report on what I'd heard her say. Also, I knew you were still struggling with your own problems. But I can tell you now that I heard a lot of stuff that sounds similar to what you said. It was weird.

"She'd be sitting there very calm and composed, petting her cats, usually having a drink and smoking some *ganja*, pop music playing in the background; altogether a relaxing setting. But there were the strangest words coming out of her mouth. Always the same: slaughter, hellfire, the final battle, the Four Horsemen, the seven seals, demons, the angel Gabriel, on and on. And one theme over and over— the warriors she's designing and will lead into battle. Did you know that she's having a metal breastplate made to her own design?"

"No, I didn't know that. The security people took pictures for me of all of her personal effects as they were crating them for shipment. I imagine we'll find the design among them. Will you help me look through those pictures? Something tells me that I must try to better understand Io and what she intends to do."

§   §   §

(*Io's Journal, 16 September*) Unpacking on Salt Cay. What a dump. It was really nice of Pan and Moira to come over and keep me company. I can use some help trying to figure out how to escape, once we've sized up the situation.

I think Hera's serious, though. She means to keep us here permanently, on our own *Devil's Island*. She's even going to send over a small boat and our snorkelling gear so that we have lots to keep us busy. The nice people who escorted us here in that gorgeous cabin cruiser said something odd, though. When I volunteered that at least we were going to be closer to Cockburn Town and could have some fun there, they told me I had to have permission from Provo to leave Salt Cay, and that there are warrants out for my arrest that won't be served as long as I stay put.

Once again I failed to reckon with my dear sister's determination to maintain control over the rest of us. That's absolutely the last time I'll do that! I was sure I wouldn't find the semen sample when my things arrived here, and I was right. Thank the lucky stars there's at least one thing she can't find out about—for once I was smart enough not to leave any records laying around. No doubt she had the spooks snoop through my stuff before sending it over.

§   §   §

(Hera's Journal, 23 September) I finally found the time to pay a courtesy call on Franklin; Marco came along. He refused to talk to us, and referred to himself as a 'political prisoner'! That's rich, coming from him; he hasn't had the slightest interest in politics in his entire life. Apparently he did try to contact first the Solicitor-General's office, which told him in oblique language that there were unspecified legal complications to his case and no action would be taken by them. Then he tried a private law firm and got the same response. We've already arranged for his library and journal subscriptions to be sent to his new address. I'll just let him stew in his own juices for a while until I try again to reconnect with him.

I've been very pleased with the reactions of the biology group to September's events. These sisters are well-trained professionals now and they can separate our private affairs, including the situation of their father, from their scientific duties. Gaia was nominated by Percy and Rhea to replace Franklin as scientific director; above all, the three of them work well together as a team. They're confident that if the foundation decides to proceed with the Second Generation project, they can carry out the protocol from this point onward without Franklin's guidance.

Marco took it upon himself to go through the photographic records of Io's belongings. There wasn't much of interest there—other than the matters of prurient interest—except for some of her journal pages and the breastplate design. We copied the pages and circulated them to the sisters a week ago, but they hardly paid any attention. I think they found it so strange that they didn't know how to react.

I've devoted the time needed to repair my relationship with Tina. I think she realizes now how unwell I was when I lashed out at her that day. I asked her to assume the posts of senior vice-president of the foundation and chair of the board of directors, and she agreed. And the board officially appointed Marco to the post of vice-president, North America. He was so pleased.

Our primates are well; their numbers are up to 350 or so, and the hurricane shelters we built for them appear to offer sufficient sanctuary from the storms. Lucy seems happy with her tribe there and I've stopped bringing her to my place for visits, although I take a boat over to West Caicos Island every week and try to watch her from the observation platform.

§ § §

(Hera's Journal, 31 December 2044) In this year, after three decades during which we drew upon the immense strength of the circle's geometric form, the band was severed. A piece was cut out and the ends rejoined, but it can never be the same for us. This sadness will always be with me hereafter. Yet, although I regret the past, I dread the future. Something tells me there's worse to come.

Part Three

The Avenging Angel

JANUARY 2045, MARCO'S JOURNAL

Not surprisingly, the advance warning came from General Ziegler about a month ago; he seems to have the most sensitive antennae on the planet. When most people finally got the news yesterday, they misunderstood its meaning at first. What they heard was that another very large piece of ice had fallen into the ocean off Antarctica. Yet this has been happening regularly for more than fifty years and so everyone was used to it—or so they thought!

Well before the end of the last century the Larsen B Ice Shelf, part of the long, curving finger known as the Antarctic Peninsula, which used to stretch from the western side of the ice-bound continent toward the southern tip of South America, had begun to disintegrate.

Then during the last three decades huge pieces of the Ross and Ronne ice shelves have been periodically collapsing into the ocean in spectacular fashion, as duly recorded by satellite cameras and shown on evening television. Since these two areas were originally each about as large as France, the sheer size of the chunks of calving ice was unsettling to the public. Finally the message sank in that 'ice shelves' are similar to sea ice, that is, ice already afloat and thus displacing seawater. The bottom line is, when this type of ice breaks loose, there's no impact on global sea levels.

But as of now, things have changed for the worse. We were ready for this news because of the warning from Ziegler, but the rest of the world wasn't. About two days of consistent news reporting was needed before the average citizen could grasp why this latest occurrence is so different. For this event involves a piece of what's called the West Antarctic Ice Sheet, not one of the big ice shelves such as the Ross or the Ronne. The difference is that the Sheet is—or was, in the case of the piece that broke off—attached to the bedrock on which the entire continent rests, deep beneath the ocean surface. This news struck some as being a merely academic distinction, that is, until the pictures of newly submerged coastal areas around the world had been replayed endlessly on television.

The world's ice sheets, found only in Greenland and Antarctica, are in effect huge mountains of ice, but much of their mass is underwater, out of sight. An ice sheet, partially visible above the water line but anchored to bedrock deep below, is not floating, not sea ice. If a piece of it becomes detached from the rest and slowly slides into the surrounding oceans, that part of its volume that was originally above the water line will displace an equal amount of seawater. The subsequent sea-level rise is, for all practical purposes, instantaneous around the globe. The piece that just broke off happened to be a relatively small part of the entire West Antarctic Ice Sheet, so the amount of the rise was only about half a meter.

Along with the initial shock came the patter of legions of television commentators, utilizing brief snatches of interviews with scientific experts. One explanation for the event, which appeared to be widely supported, has to do with surface melt water that trickles down long crevices in the ice. While this has always happened, it has accelerated due to the persistent warming trend around Antarctica that began in the latter part of the previous century. The result was increasing instability in the enormous ice mountain—which is so large that it locks up more than 70% of the world's entire supply of fresh water—that is the continent of Antarctica.

The crevices eventually reach the bedrock thousands of meters below, and the surface water trickling down them infiltrated between the bottom of the ice mountain and the bedrock to which it's attached. When a sufficient layer of water had accumulated on the surface of the bedrock, the movements of the ice mass in the heaving oceans increased, and the fracturing forces being applied to the ice sheet multiplied enormously. The first piece broke off, rolling into the enveloping oceans as if it were riding on ball bearings. There's a lot more ice in the West Antarctic sheet that is still hanging on to its bedrock—for the time being.

The general panic that ensued was due not so much to the amount of new sea-level rise as it was to the uncertainty about how much more would be coming, and when. We watched the experts being hauled before the news cameras and government committees and asked to produce their scenarios for the future. Since people are by now quite familiar with weather forecasting using probabilities—the one that goes "there's a 30% chance of thunderstorms tomorrow"—the estimate of probabilities became the format they used for speculating on the chances of future ice-sheet collapses.

So for the past week experts have been debating their numbers for the likelihood of future occurrences—how likely it is that similar events will happen, the timing, and the possible magnitude of the pulses of water. A few citizens were overheard complaining in something like the following terms: "Why wasn't I told sooner that this West Antarctic Ice Sheet, if all of it becomes detached from the rest of Antarctica, is large enough to cause a six-meter rise in sea levels around the whole world? If I had known, I certainly wouldn't have bought that piece of expensive oceanfront property last year."

They weren't mollified by the rejoinder that news about climate change impacts had been circulating for a rather long time, only to be met by scepticism and disbelief from citizens much like themselves. Yet some of the people's instinctive rage was understandable, since their governments had been downplaying the risks, too, insisting on irrefutable proof that such events would happen. Soon those experts who had been calmly dispensing their wisdom and advice from higher-altitude locations, where their own property was out of harm's way, were unavailable for further media interviews!

§ § §

(Hera's Journal, 17 January 2045) Phil is flying to the Bahamas in two days and asked me to send Marco there to meet him. Sometime last month I finally confessed to him the truth about Marco's tender years. He replied that his only interest was in whether he could do the job, and so far there was no reason to doubt it.

§ § §

(Marco's Journal, 19 January) I've discovered that General Ziegler's Caribbean Surveillance Group has a very nice secluded villa on Cat Island. He had me picked up in Provo by a small executive jet; I've never flown in one before—not outside the womb, at any rate! The trip across the short strip of ocean separating us from the Bahamas was fast. Ziegler said that in the last two years, another 250 applicants on the waiting list had been accepted into the Vandenberg Colony and membership is now closed. Construction of the members' compounds in the zones adjacent to the air force base had been accelerated and was nearing completion.

This meeting turned out to be a get-together of the Colony's super-secret board of directors. I was amazed at being invited until later on when Ziegler explained why. The purpose was to receive and discuss an updated threat analysis from the board's security and intelligence advisory committee—presumably, this was occasioned by the recent global panic over the unexpected sea-level rise. A written report by the committee was distributed. No copies of any documents were allowed to leave the room, but I was permitted to transcribe certain extracts from it into my journal, including a précis of General Ziegler's comments for Hera's benefit.

THREAT ANALYSIS JANUARY 2045 (TOP SECRET)
SECURITY AND INTELLIGENCE ADVISORY COMMITTEE
THE VANDENBERG COLONY

The countries around the world bordering on oceans, as well as countries having inland seas and coastal river channels affected by ocean levels, include all of the most populous and important ones in the world. The recent events in Antarctica prompted the world's governments to refocus their attention on problems associated with sea-level rise for the foreseeable future. North America and Western Europe are still generally the most stable regions, since these two have the largest stores of technology and wealth with which to help their citizens adjust to catastrophic natural events.

Nevertheless, even here there are sub-regions showing severe impacts, including Florida and the Gulf Coast, parts of the east and west coasts of North America, as well as the whole Mediterranean coastline, where property losses are enormous. For all practical purposes there is no private insurance industry left in the world. Elsewhere, especially in Asia and Southeast Asia, coastal regions have long held some of the densest human populations on the planet. These populations are now on the move toward the interior, heading for higher elevations and destabilizing cities and rural areas further inland.

No one can predict how long it will be before the enormous pressure of population movements rolls on into areas that are still relatively intact. Since the European Union sits on the Eurasian land mass and is also easily accessible from Africa, the level of risk there is much higher than it is in North America. The US government has already helped Mexico seal off its land bridge with Central America, and we have stepped up our Caribbean patrols.

In an earlier threat analysis we predicted that additional destabilization caused by non-political factors, such as sea-level rise, would be exploited by terrorist movements. Our global intelligence networks are picking up signals to that effect in every region, indicating that new waves of attacks are being planned to take advantage of the recent redirection of government attention.

Finally, we were asked to do some projections of a longer-term future based on current trends. As a result of recent developments, we must assign a medium probability to the prospect of additional sea-level rises, occurring in pulses as a result of contributions from the West Antarctic Ice Sheet. When this trend is combined with probabilities relating to additional political upheaval, terrorist attacks, and use of biological warfare agents, the overall prognosis is for repeated periods of social and political disintegration—even on the continent of North America.

Ziegler then took the floor and read out the commentary on the threat analysis he had prepared for his directors:

COMMENTARY ON THREAT ANALYSIS JANUARY 2045
GENERAL PHILIP ZIEGLER

As a result of these new events, the executive committee of the board is recommending certain steps for your approval today. The committee believes that we should begin acting and planning on the basis of the worst-case scenario outlined for you just now. In other words, we should expect some level of socio-political chaos to take hold in the United States within the next ten years. The motions we're submitting today for your approval are based on this expectation.

First, we're going to expand as quickly as possible the outer perimeters of the Colony. Using our legal powers of expropriation, we'll be taking control of the entire Pacific coastline in Central California, on either side of Vandenberg Air Force Base, running north from Point Conception and south from Point San Luis. This stretch adds up to roughly seventy-five miles of coastline. We'll then gradually extend our eastern boundary inland, perhaps eventually right up to the foothills of the Sierra Madre and San Rafael mountain ranges.

The larger cities of Santa Maria and Lompoc, as well as the smaller towns in that area, will be legally reincorporated into the Colony, and the residents in the whole area will be brought under military authority. Access to the area off Route 101 will be severely restricted along the segment that runs southward from Avila Beach, just south of San Luis Obispo, to Gaviota, which is twenty miles west of Santa Barbara. I suspect that at some point we'll permanently sever Highway 101 at those two points, blocking off through traffic and using this section as an internal road only.

The bottom line is this: We're preparing a reasonably large territory within which our members will have a high level of security. If we must do so, we'll erect a perimeter fence around the entire length of our land borders and restrict access to authorized persons only. We have previously arranged a secure internal supply of basic necessities—energy, food, water (and wine!)—for all the populations under our jurisdiction, in the event that external sources of supply are compromised for extended periods of time.

Here I must thank our friends in the Caribbean, who run the Sujana Foundation and PathoGene, for suggesting an ingenious solution to the problem of assuring an indigenous food supply. They've spent some time in Alberta and got to know the Canadian scene quite well. In all of Canada's western provinces— British Columbia, Alberta, Saskatchewan and Manitoba—there are numerous Hutterite farming communities. After some more checking we found out that there are Hutterian Brethren in the Dakotas, Montana, Minnesota, and Washington as well.

Unfortunately some of their colonies, especially the ones in the Canadian prairies and the Dakotas, have been devastated by the persistent droughts there, so we've offered to resettle them within our territory. They'll supply agricultural produce to us under contract. The security we can offer is as strong an appeal to them as is the free land. They've often been persecuted over the centuries and are very much attuned to political stability. As for their own practices and beliefs, they aren't interested in converting you, unlike the many missionary sects. They just want to be left alone to carry on with their own traditions.

In terms of our overall level of security, the one thing above all that we fear, and against which we don't yet have adequate defenses, is an attack by an enemy using bioweapons that have been genetically engineered at a sophisticated level. Such pathogens could be infiltrated onto our territory either by air or through the external water supply. This one weakness seriously undermines the integrity of our otherwise impregnable fortress. This is our soft underbelly. We must protect it.

That's where our friends at PathoGene come in, and that's why you see in this room the firm's representative—a remarkable young man with whom I've been dealing for some years now. At my request PathoGene has agreed to relocate its main R & D laboratory to our territory. In addition, we will construct an adjacent manufacturing facility as a joint venture, so that we can turn out customized units on-site. You already know, from our existing contract with them, about PathoGene's proprietary technologies in the area of rapid DNA sequencing for identifying new microbes and engineering counter-measures against them. Just so the rest of you have an idea what the Sujana Foundation is up to, I'll now turn the floor over to my young colleague for a briefing.

I was told in advance by Ziegler how much to reveal about the foundation's work. He himself knew a lot of the story because by that time he and Hera had complete trust in each other's discretion. After our presentations, I was flown back to Provo, carrying an unexpected message from Ziegler to Hera: He would be returning to the Caribbean in a couple of months, and this time he needed to meet directly with her, preferably on Cat Island. He wanted to talk to her about Io.

§   §   §

(Marco's Journal, 23 March) Yesterday we were flown to Cat Island. Hera and Phil both seemed to be quite pleased at the reunion. I wonder if something's going on between them?

I must say that I've also become enormously fond of him in a short time. He's lean and fit and looks every bit the military officer in his uniform, but in other respects he doesn't match the conventional profile. He ignores routines of protocol and during meetings prefers to slouch in whatever chair or couch is readily available. He's always clearly in command—having been promoted to four-star rank recently—but eagerly seeks out the expertise of others, irrespective of their rank or standing. As I've learned, he's the child of two high-ranking soldiers and is himself a 'lifer,' as he enjoys saying, but unlike most of his peers he has a keen sense of politics, both domestic and foreign. In the time we've known him he's never explained to Hera—I asked her about this—why he became involved in the Vandenberg Colony project or what his own personal interests are.

I've been wondering about this because whenever he speaks of the Colony's members, which is not often, he can be sarcastic and sometimes contemptuous. "We have a fair number of drug lords, money launderers, corrupt officials, and *mafiosi* of every known type among them," he remarked to me once. "You don't accumulate that much money—in most countries around the world—by hard work or native smarts." I suspect that his main interest lies in the financing deal for the Mars mission.

Hera and Phil began by reviewing the contingency plans for evacuating us from the Turks and Caicos Islands. Hera said to him, "All our facilities, including our primate sanctuary, have been well shored up with protective embankments and are safe for the time being. But everybody around us is in full panic mode, and those who can are fleeing the islands. For the time being this makes life simpler for us— fewer neighbors to deal with."

Phil told her that, with her permission, he would be sending a logistics team to Provo soon to tour all the foundation's facilities and prepare emergency evacuation plans. He would also post transport ships on permanent standby duty in the Caribbean—he, too, had critical installations located there—that would be able to move in on very short notice to pick up people and property. No one could predict if and when another big piece of the West Antarctic Ice Sheet would detach itself and plummet into the seas.

"I must say," Hera continued, "that even our own small group on Salt Cay is getting a bit antsy. I received a handwritten note from Io the other day, asking if I intended to incarcerate her there until she drowned. I assured her that we have an emergency evacuation plan in place, and that the group there is covered by it. But I can't imagine why you've taken an interest in our dear Io, in view of all the other files you're handling."

"It happened accidentally," Phil replied. "You're quite familiar with our apprehensions about genetically engineered pathogens used as bioweapons. So one of the things we monitor is the movements of a little gang of rogue biologists who traipse around the world, looking for clients to sponsor their latest research schemes—you know, the ones that every reputable scientist in the world would shrink from in disgust. Well, recently we've picked up some communications traffic between a couple of these types who are currently hiding out in Asia. The other party in their conversations, we think, is none other than your precious sister."

"That's impossible," Hera interjected at once. "Both you and we monitor the incoming and outgoing electronic traffic on Salt Cay. We would have known if Io had established a pattern of messages to Asia." Then she paused. "On second thought, maybe not. The answer may be a single name: Moira. She's the member of Io's group who had worked with Troglodyte Partners, specializing in encryption routines. Ari said she was the best they'd ever seen. I'll bet that Moira has found a way to mask some of their communications."

"We assumed so. There's a fair amount of encrypted traffic in the world today, and we can't even record all of it, much less break it and read it. However, we can read the traffic on the other end, since these guys are just biologists who are using standard encryption routines that are easy to break. The one who does most of the messaging uses the pseudonym of 'Doctor Moreau.' But it's clear to us that the Salt Cay end is the one making the proposals. The biologists appear to be quite intrigued by what their new partners want to do, and they're impressed with the level of sophistication in molecular biology Io's team has."

"That would be Pandora. Gaia says she's very good."

"Anyway, these guys have indicated their willingness to relocate somewhere and to work for the new organization that's recruiting them, which goes by the name of Route 666. Even I know enough about some of the other crazies in the world to have twigged to that one—666 is the 'number of the beast,' that is, Satan."

"Yes, that sounds like Io. Did you say that the new organization was recruiting them, General?"

He leaned back in his chair and laughed. "For Pete's sake, Hera, as you well know, I'm Phil to my friends. Just because young Marco is sitting here with us, we don't have to fall back into formalities of address. And he's probably not as naïve as you imagine, either."

Hera glanced at me and giggled. "All right. I confess that I'm a ridiculously overprotective mother. But back to Io. Recruiting them with what?"

"Lots and lots of cash, apparently."

"But where would Io get her hands on big money?" She paused for a minute. "Oh God."

Phil and I leapt into the conversation with the same remark. "What's wrong? What is it?"

Hera waved her hand dismissively. "Relax, you two; it's actually not that important. I just had an idea of where Io got the money. Let me check something out and get back to you. If I'm right, the deed has already been done and there's nothing we can do about it in the short run."

"Actually," Phil remarked, grinning, "this may surprise you a bit, but I came here assuming that Io could not have much money at her disposal, so I was proposing to give her some. I have a fair amount of confiscated drug trafficking proceeds at my disposal." We looked at him as if he had become momentarily deranged. He laughed. "No, hear me out; I'm sure I can convince you that I haven't gone nuts. I have a new plan for your consideration. I think we should release Io and help her resettle in an out-of-the-way place where she can make her dream come true. Based on what we picked up from these rogue biologists, she wants to establish what she calls a 'hidden kingdom' and to create a class of invincible warriors."

"Phil, why on earth would we three help Io realize her mad dream? What she needs is a comfortable couch and a very good psychoanalyst, not a kingdom to rule. I've been heartsick about my sister, and worried about her visions, for a long time. I imprisoned her on Salt Cay Island just so I wouldn't have to be continually preoccupied with what she might be up to. Who knows what will happen if we release her and let her find a hiding place? And besides, *why* would we want to do this?"

"I'll know what she's up to, Hera; and I won't lose track of her, I promise. I'll keep her under tight surveillance, both satellite and ground-based. As to your second question: Because it's in our mutual interest to do so. Based on what you've told me, sister Io has few rivals in the world, in the genetic-engineering funny business, when it comes to ruthless determination. I think she can collect quite a few specimens from the ranks of the better rogue biologists at her hidden kingdom. *My* interest is in seeing all or most of them gather in one place and stay there for a while. It's much easier to keep track of them that way. And then, if it looks like they're going to disperse again, we can round them up. Or put them out of their misery."

"Sort of a sting operation, then," Hera muttered.

"Yes, you can call it that. Will you agree to it?"

"On one condition."

"Name it."

Her voice was almost inaudible when she finally answered. "I will agree to this plan because I already know that I can't keep her under lock and key on that tiny island for very much longer. Either I'll relent and invite them back to our compound in Provo or they'll try to escape—and one or more of them might die or be injured in the attempt. I will also give my consent because I'm convinced she's determined to do something like this anyway. But if and when the time comes to put your rogue biologists out of their misery, to use your words, you must promise to inform me in advance and you must promise to help me rescue any of my sisters who are there. No matter how much I fear the contents of Io's mind, I still feel responsible for her and the other two—who I presume will tag along if Io takes the bait. I want to have another chance to reach out to them and see if we can be reunited. No harm must come to them by our hands."

"Done. I give you my word."

"That's good enough for me."

"Where should we send her?" I asked.

Hera piped up at once. "Bali. She wants to go there. She wants to become a warrior princess in her mother's homeland."

"No problem," Phil replied. "Bali is as good a place as any. In fact, I also prefer Asia. There's a lot going on there that doesn't reach most people's radar screens. It's easier for Io and her friends to set up a secret facility, and for us to mount a surveillance operation on it, in a place like that as opposed to many other regions in the world. And you think she doesn't need any more money?"

"If my suspicion proves correct she already has as much as she needs. I'll get back to you after I check it out. If I turn out to be wrong, you can always help her stumble accidentally on a homeless hoard of drug cash. Are we done? When should we set this in motion?"

"As soon as possible. These rogue biologists are keen. I'd like to have them signed up with Route 666 before they get a better offer from some crackpot dictator or the Mafia."

"Well, that shouldn't present a problem. She's certainly anxious to leave Salt Cay. Will you escort them to Bali? And then just let them find their own spot for the hidden kingdom?"

"I'm not sure. I haven't figured out all the details yet. Right now I think it would be best if I work through an agent who pretends to represent someone else, say an Asian drug lord who claims to have met Doctor Moreau. There was a reference to such a person in one of his last messages to Io. The agent can pose as a prospective investor in the new facility, and that also gives me an excuse to dump some surplus cash on her. He can show up one night at Salt Cay with a very fast boat and some excellent fake passports. There are dozens of airports in the vicinity she can fly out of."

"This sounds like a good plan. We don't have to steer her to Bali. I'm convinced she will head there straightaway of her own accord. And, of course, your agent can have his associates tail her, just to make sure."

"Indeed. OK, that's a deal. I've got to go soon. By the way, we want to move PathoGene, lock, stock, and barrel, with its entire staff, to Vandenberg next month. Will you be ready?"

"Marco has been working very hard on the details. I'll let him answer."

"We'll be ready. We won't have to do very much in any case, because—given the rather sensitive nature of its products—your people will be handling the move."

"True, I wouldn't just send in a commercial shipper. And at the same time, we'll have another team there who will be doing the evaluation for the emergency evacuation plan for the rest of your operations—including your apes! How many are there now?"

I answered. "Close to four hundred and still increasing, both by procreation and additions from outside. We have all three subspecies of gorillas as well as bonobos, chimpanzees and orangutans. Even with our tunnel and cave network to offer them protection from the hurricanes, the increasing ferocity of the storms sometimes rattles them. They'll not be sorry to go. But we must have something suitable ready for them at the other end. We can't put them back into crates and small enclosures again, except for the duration of the sea passage. They're used to much finer amenities on West Caicos Island."

"I've already thought about that, Marco. When your mother can spare you for a few weeks, let me know, and we'll fly you up to Vandenberg and give you the royal tour. Bring some plans, if you want. We'll scout out a suitable site for your entire compound, and make sure the new primate sanctuary is sited where you want it to be. Hera has given me a list of the other facilities you'll need. No one can tell when the next big chunk of ice will hit the sea in Antarctica. We want to be ready for you."

§   §   §

(Hera's Journal, 23 March) As we were flying from Cat Island back to Provo, I reflected on how pleased and relieved I was about this recent turn of events. I knew, of course, that we were going to have to move again, perhaps very soon. And given what's been happening lately around the world, why wouldn't I worry about having a secure place for my tribe? I was relieved to hear Phil state clearly today that the deal was done for constructing us a new home at Vandenberg. There will be no safer place on the planet. Fate has been kind to us. And, for once, I didn't have to take care of every last detail myself! I now have both Marco and Phil to count on.

I'm pretty sure Marco suspects that Phil and I are more than business partners now. Our meetings on Cat Island and in Provo during the last six months have been wonderful times, although we both feel the need to be secretive about them for now.

I don't think I could invent another 'flight from Tembagapura' scenario if my life depended on it! When I look back on that period, I wonder, 'Who *was* that little girl who took charge then? How did she ever do it?' The only answer I can come up with is that she had the bravado of the young. She never even imagined that she could fail. I'm older now and a little less sanguine. I'm glad I have my two helpers.

Shortly after we returned home today I went to see Franklin. Last month we managed to start having a few short conversations again, although he is still consumed by bitterness and anger toward me. I stood on his doorstep.

"What do you want, Hera? I'm busy."

I knew he had nothing much to keep him occupied these days because, as I had been reliably informed by Gaia, who visits him regularly, he had stopped reading scientific journals, or any serious publications for that matter. Apparently he watches television or sits in his garden, daydreaming, rarely leaving his own house and yard. "I don't like being followed or having to wear an electronic tracker like a common criminal," he had complained to her.

"That's fine, I won't detain you for long," I promised. "Actually, I have only one short question for today. Did you give Io a large amount of money sometime last summer?"

He paused momentarily. "That's none of your business. What I do with my own money is my affair. Or do you intend to confiscate my personal property in addition to imprisoning me? Are there any other questions or will you be going now?"

"Look, if I want to spend the time I can come up with the answer myself, one way or another. Given the size of the foundation's asset base, our financial advisors are very accommodating. You use the same people for your personal investment trust."

"Ooh, don't we all know how very clever you are?! I can't stop thinking about that caper you pulled off last September. Who could have imagined you'd import some military-type muscle to rough us up a bit—your own family, no less—and put us in jail? And then get the local authorities to play along as if it was just a minor family squabble? It's not so bad for me; I'm old and don't have much time left. But poor Io, marooned on Salt Cay. Are you going to keep her on that godforsaken little stretch of sand until she dies?"

"I can tell you that we may be able to resolve her situation soon, so likely she won't be there much longer. Can we forget the recitation of old complaints and return to the point? Did you give Io some money from your investment trust?"

"As you said, you'll find out anyway, so what the hell. Yes. Or no—I didn't give her 'some' money. I gave her almost everything I had. She transferred 300 million euros into her own Swiss bank account. I have no idea what she did or plans to do with it. And I don't care."

"I suspected as much. Well, I can enlighten you as to what she plans to do with your money. She wants to team up with rogue biologists who are prepared to do genetic engineering experiments—including presumably on humans—outside the norms of the scientific research community. In her own words, Io herself would like to engineer what she calls a 'race of invincible warriors for battle on the day of judgment.' What do you think of that?"

"Why should I believe anything you tell me about Io? Undoubtedly you're prepared to invent the most implausible stories to blacken her reputation. And even if it were true, whose fault is it? Who imprisoned her on a miserable piece of land in the middle of the Caribbean Sea, with nothing to do except gradually go mad? So if it is true, we know whom to blame, don't we? Now leave me alone!" And he slammed the door.

Well, what does it matter now, I thought. If Io hadn't gotten her father's money, Phil had been prepared to bankroll her. The new chapter begins. Yet I can't delude myself into believing that I won't fret about Io and what exactly she'll be doing in Bali. On the other hand, how could I have justified keeping her locked up on Salt Cay for the rest of her life? My conscience would have demanded that I set her free soon anyway. And once free Io would do what her inner demons commanded. This sordid scenario will have to play itself out to the bitter end. I shuddered.

And speaking of Io! What had she wanted with Marco's semen anyway? What was that all about? Another one of her silly little games? Or something else? Io never does anything without a purpose. Until just now I'd entirely forgotten about the vial that was confiscated by the security force when they searched Io's house. I must send Marco to our clinic for a very thorough medical check-up soon.

§   §   §

(*Marco's Journal, 15 April*) "Look at these spectacular picnic hampers Roberto prepared, Marco!"

They did appear to be most appetizing so I asked, "May I keep one for myself?"

"Talk to Roberto if you want something for yourself. These hampers are going on the motorboat with Gaia, Tammy, Ari and Themis to Salt Cay Island. Among other things, they're delivering a message from me along with my gift of food—which is a traditional peace offering in human cultures, as you probably know. Io will be given a chance to return to Provo—or, alternatively, to relocate anywhere she wants. I've arranged for her arrest warrant to be quashed. I have to clear my conscience, even if it means adjusting somewhat the deal we made with Phil. Still, as I see it there's virtually no chance she'll come back here; I'm certain that Bali will be her destination."

Upon their return Tammy and Gaia went straight to Hera's place, where I had just dropped off Magnus following our late-afternoon play session, to deliver the news she was anxiously awaiting.

"We held some interesting conversations, I must say," Gaia reported. "Io kept pretty much to herself, as usual, but Pandora really opened up to me." Gesturing with her hand, she remarked, "Basically, Pan has had it up to here with what she calls Io's 'ravings.' She told me she refused point-blank Io's entreaties for her to participate in some bizarre long-distance communications about the genetic engineering of 'warrior prototypes.' Pan isn't going anywhere with Io; she intends to come back to Provo. Indeed, she would have returned with us on the boat, but she doesn't want to leave Moira behind."

Tammy added, "Themis spoke at length with Moira and said she appears to be wavering about what to do. On the ride back Themis told us that Moira is in really bad shape. But as we were embarking we were given a solemn promise from Pan that she would watch over her. I don't think we have to worry, Hera; Pan won't allow Io to railroad Moira into joining her on some madcap adventure."

I was watching Hera; tears filled her eyes. "I have to accept some part of the blame for the predicament Moira's gotten herself into. Tammy, will you do something for me?"

"Yes, of course, what is it?"

"Stay in touch with Pandora by telephone. Ask her to let us know immediately if she needs any help in getting herself and Moira back here safely."

She replied, "Will do."

"Gaia, did Io say anything at all to any of you?"

"Yes, she did, one sentence, at the dock as we were getting aboard. She had a kind of dreamy, far-off look in her eyes. She said, 'Tell Hera thanks very much for the offer, but I'll be making my own plans.'"

Gaia and Tammy each gave Hera a hug and walked off. She turned to me and barked an order, military-style. "Get on the phone with Phil. Track him down, wherever he is. Don't be put off by any of his flunkies. Io's just about ready to go, I'm sure of it. Tell him I want an intercept operation to be made ready. If Io tries to take Moira with her, she is to be stopped. I don't care if we blow the cover off our little scheme. She's not to be permitted to take Moira. Is that perfectly clear?"

"Yes, sir," I answered, saluting, as I reached for my cell phone.

(22 April) When I returned from Salt Cay Island with Pan and Moira in the boat, all of the other sisters were waiting to greet them at the compound's dock. After they left for the party Tammy had arranged at a downtown hotel, I said to Hera, "What's happening with Io?"

"She's gone, Marco. I just got off the phone with Phil. For better or worse, she took the bait and flew the coop at Salt Cay. She headed straight for Bali. I'm going to take Phil at his word on this one. I'm going to let someone else worry about sister Io for a change. He said he'd watch her. You and I have too much else on our plates at the moment."

§   §   §

(Io's Journal, 26 April) Home at last! These brave people have been calling to me all my life; I can sense it. This land has been waiting for me to touch down on it. Now I'm here and all is complete. But my imprisonment at my dear sister's hands delayed me. There's so much to do, and so little time left in which to do it. *(Sub-Compiler's Note: Some fragments of Io's journals from her Bali period were received by Hera in a manner to be explained later.)*

I feel within me the great sense of relief and satisfaction that's now spreading among all the peoples of the earth. They've been waiting for ages, and finally the blessed day is fast approaching. The waiting has been cruel for them, for they are believers, fervent and true, serving their many gods as best they could. They know they are bad, that they are pitifully weak and wretched sinners, but in their hearts they want to be washed clean again 'in the blood of the Lamb.'

They want to be cleansed, to be bathed and purified in Your blood. Why have You made them wait so long, O Lord? Many ages ago the ancient psalmist promised them—no, You promised them, through him—that 'the days of the wicked are numbered.' You told them that You saw how they were oppressed, You asked them to be patient, You promised them that one day they would 'look on the destruction of the wicked.'

Now that day is fast approaching. And so much remains to be done. The wicked have always held the upper hand on earth. That's how God wanted it, apparently, as a trial, to test the mettle of the good. He gave Satan a free hand on earth. In my mind I can hear God chatting with the Prince of Darkness, like two old friends, laughing and reminiscing. "Remember the fun we had with old Job, you and I? Give all of them a taste of that medicine, Satan. I want to see how their faith stands up to the test." What a horror show! All too many of them failed the test, finding it much easier to join the ranks of the wicked. The good have always been outnumbered. That's why God needs my warriors.

The good won't stand a chance when the last battle begins, not without my help anyway. Clearly God has been expecting things to go his way once the fighting commences. But I wonder whether He reckoned on Satan's outstanding abilities in recruiting followers to his side. I wonder if He realized just how tempting evil could be for all those weak souls. If God had it to do all over again, would He make the same mistake twice? Would He allow Satan to roam freely over the earth for thousands of years, marshalling his forces for the great showdown on the day of wrath?

I will come to the aid of God's outnumbered soldiers, *Inshallah.* I think that He knows that He needs my help. I will send my warriors to the places where there are many who long for martyrdom. These are the anxious ones, the ones seeking out others who will help them depart this earthly vale of tears as quickly as possible. My warriors will be happy to oblige them. It's not up to me to figure out what happens to them after they're dispatched to the hereafter. It's no business of mine whether they end up in Paradise, as they expect, or somewhere else. And we all know what that 'somewhere else' is, don't we!

As soon as I could after landing here, I made my pilgrimage to the city of Tabanan, which is not far from Denpasar. And there I saw it, shining in the sunlight: The statue of Sagung Wah, warrior princess. She's shown standing bold and upright, raised on a litter carried by her soldiers, bearing an unsheathed sword. She's dressed all in pure white and her hair falls loose to her shoulders, which, the legend says, means that she's ready for death. That is how I must dress from now on. Those who will be following me expect it.

Even here in this backwater I've seen many of the wicked; they don't seem to sense that the day of retribution is coming. The friends who contacted me when I was still on Salt Cay are arriving in Bali soon. They've been on this island before, it seems; they've suggested looking near the remote southeast coast, close to the Lombok Strait, to find a suitable gathering place for my flock. They'll like the warrior prototype I've sketched for them. It won't be hard to produce the copies. There's no point in getting too fancy!

After all, my warriors will be made in order to die. We'll start by suppressing the faculties of judgment in the prefrontal cortex with drug therapies. Later we'll have time to figure out how to switch these gene sequences off during embryonic development. What do holy warriors need such faculties for? All they require is the capacity to await my order and to strike where my sword points. We'll also supply them with enough extra testosterone so that they can enjoy their occupations to the fullest.

Which reminds me that I must write a letter to Hera. She must be made to understand that finally I have exposed the last of her many lies—the stories she invented in order to turn my sisters against me. By far the biggest of Hera's lies is that she risked her life, alone and unaided, to bring about Klamm's death. Oh, how my sisters revere her for that deed! And it's nothing but a sordid fib. Klamm isn't dead! I've seen him, alive and well. Here, in Bali. He's still following me. But he doesn't realize how strong I've become. That is a mistake he'll live to regret.

I'm going to have a great arena built within my compound. I expect many of the local people to beg me to shelter and protect them. They at least can see how strong I am. There is chaos everywhere they turn and they're looking for a little refuge. They'll find it here. I plan to stage great shows for them in my arena. And the main attraction at the opening gala will be Klamm's death. A slow and unpleasant death, at the hands of some local tribesmen I'll select; the fiercest I can find.

(09 October) Two weeks ago I ordered Klamm to be taken into custody, and he's been locked up in chains in my dungeon ever since. The arena is almost finished and ready for the shows to begin. Then, yesterday—what?! There he was, on the street again! I was furious that he had escaped and resolved to punish his guards severely. But they begged for their lives and said that I must be mistaken; no one could escape the underground fastness where he's chained to the wall. So I descended the steps to see for myself, and sure enough, there he was, bound and helpless. Then a little while later I saw him again from my window, moving around furtively in the alleyways below, watching me.

How stupid I am! Why didn't the answer occur to me at

once? Klamm has had himself cloned! Not one copy, but many, perhaps hundreds, maybe thousands. How could I have underestimated the depths of his fiendishness? My plans must be accelerated. There's no time to lose, for if I allow him enough time he'll multiply endlessly. This is exactly how the ranks of the wicked swell. I must hunt down and kill every last one of Klamm's copies. Otherwise I will have no peace. It must begin soon. Only when the last one is put to the sword will it be finished.

Then, finally, will my sisters know whom they have to thank. At last all of Hera's lies and make-believe will be unveiled for them to see. All my sisters will come to their senses and gather around me, congratulating me for saving their lives. Then they can help me decide what to do with Hera.

§   §   §

(Marco's Journal, 09 October) Just received the first report from the Bali Surveillance Team, forwarded by Phil. "The Hidden Kingdom has settled in on a 500-hectare property in the mountains east of Amlapura. There was an abandoned monastery on the site and a network of old buildings that are still habitable. The local people have been pouring in from the surrounding area ever since Io has had convoys of trucks start delivering food and necessities, which are distributed free to everyone inside her compound.

"Since she can pay good wages in hard currency, she's had no trouble recruiting the beginnings of a small army, who are already receiving training from some ex-officers of the Indonesian military. Construction is almost done on what looks to be like a crude arena, with seating for several hundred. Apparently, attendance at the coming events in the arena will be obligatory, for this is where the food rations will be distributed.

"Doctor Moreau and his colleagues also have moved in to a fenced-off inner compound. Two portable microbiological labs they purchased in Singapore were shipped to the nearest dock in Pandangbai, which is the terminus for the Bali–Lombok ferry. They were trucked onwards to the site. Other people presently unknown to us have taken up residence in the inner compound since the labs arrived. As predicted, it looks like a nice collection of characters is being assembled. Some of the locals appear to have been recruited to assist in whatever is going on in there, since we've seen them being admitted. But none of them has come back out yet."

Mᴀʏ 2045, Hᴇʀᴀ's Jᴏᴜʀɴᴀʟ

"Hybrid Sterility" was the title of a private memorandum that Persephone prepared for Marco and me, since neither of us is expert in biology. Marco had gone to our clinic for a full medical check-up before his trip to Vandenberg. At my suggestion the doctor requested a semen sample to be included as part of the full spectrum of analyses, including blood and urine tests. Then I had the samples sent to the biology sisters for a DNA scan, including a detailed examination of chromosomal structure. The memorandum was dated 12 May.

Mᴇᴍᴏʀᴀɴᴅᴜᴍ ᴏɴ Hʏʙʀɪᴅ Sᴛᴇʀɪʟɪᴛʏ
Pᴇʀsᴇᴘʜᴏɴᴇ Sᴜᴊᴀɴᴀ-Sᴛᴏɴᴇ

Hybrid sterility refers to a lack of reproductive success, in either the first or second generation of offspring, when two sub-populations within the same genus are crossed. The best-known example is the mule, the product of the mating of two species of *Equus,* the donkey and the horse. Mules are sterile—that is, no offspring will result if they are bred to each other or backcrossed with a horse.

The reason for the reproductive failure in mules lies in the fact that donkeys and horses, although they have a common ancestor, have evolved to possess a different number of chromosomes—32 in the horse and 31 in the donkey. The offspring of their mating (the mule) does not develop functional gametes or sex cells. Hybrid sterility is one of the main forms of what is called 'postzygotic' or post-mating reproductive isolation, because it is something that happens after successful fertilization of an egg by sperm, which creates a fertilized cell or zygote.

The example of mules shows us that the offspring resulting from such crosses can be perfectly healthy and, aside from being sterile, have a normal life for its kind. The big cats—lions and tigers—also can be crossed to produce hybrids, which occurs only in zoos, since the two species live naturally on two different continents: Where the male is a lion, the resulting cross is called a 'liger,' and where the male is the tiger, it's a 'tigon.' The crosses are usually infertile, but occasionally they can produce offspring, which are invariably only females, and the hybrid line stops in the second generation. Therefore, the so-called 'F2' or second generation of this type are cases of what is called 'hybrid inviability.'

More common is 'prezygotic' or pre-mating reproductive isolation, affecting closely related species, that results from differences in mating rituals or in physical size (morphological isolation)—or just from the fact that the two species mate at different times of the year. In all such cases, fertilization never occurs. In the case of geographical isolation, sub-populations begin to evolve separately because of topographical formations, such as rivers or mountains, that divide them. After sufficient time passes they can no longer mate successfully if they happen to join up again, because in the meantime morphological isolation, or some other cause for reproductive failure, has emerged.

I mentioned chromosomes when discussing hybrid sterility in mules and more should be said about this here. Chromosomes are the units within which sections of our DNA are compressed and 'packaged' when cells divide. Humans have 23 chromosomes (every cell has two copies of each, or 46 in total, except for gametes or sex cells, which have only a single copy). All our closest relatives among the primates—gorillas, bonobos, chimps, and orangutans—have 24.

Apart from this difference in DNA packaging, we great apes are remarkably similar genetically: 20 of our 23 chromosomes appear to be almost identical with those of the apes, with noticeable differences showing up only on chromosomes 2, 5, and 6. Even the change in total number of chromosomes (from 24 to 23) in our transition from the apes doesn't indicate a strong differentiation between them and us. When we put the two ape chromosomes that do not appear in humans side by side with our chromosome 2, we see that ours is just those two fused together! They are otherwise identical.

According to one theory, all of the large hominoid superfamily, going back to the common ancestor of humans and apes, have or had 24 chromosomes, including Neanderthal. The evolutionary change that resulted in the appearance of a single hominin species, *H. sapiens,* having a unique number of chromosomes (23), meant that humans were a hybridized variant that could not produce viable offspring with any other hominins. Thus, this small chromosomal anomaly that suddenly appeared in humans one day—the fusing of two chromosomes into one—could preserve their unique genetic structure.

This change was sufficient to produce first- or second-generation sterility after mating between humans and any other type of hominins. By preventing hybrid matings with other hominin species, this chromosomal change protected the unique genetic structure of human beings, allowing them to reproduce 'true to type' thereafter.

Many authorities believe that differences in the gross chromosomal packaging—that is, simply the total number of chromosomes—form the primary barrier to reproductive success among creatures that have become separate species. Such a difference indeed appears to be almost an absolute barrier to having offspring that can reproduce and thus carry on a distinctive line. In short, it is almost a guarantee that either hybrid sterility or hybrid inviability will result.

I will give just one example of how chromosomes in closely related species vary. Chromosomes show what are called 'banding patterns,' which offer clues to the types of genes present at different locations in each chromosome. There are notable differences in the banding patterns for chromosomes 2, 5, and 6 among the existing hominin species—humans and two of the three types of apes (gorillas and chimps), as well as greater variations in the case of orangutans. However, the patterns between humans and chimps are especially close. On chromosome 5, for example, comparing just the human and the chimp, there occurs what is called a 'pericentric inversion.' Pericentric simply means 'around the center.'

There is a place along the arm of each chromosome that is pinched together or indented, called the centromere. Two sequences on the chimp's chromosome 5 are, when compared with the human, inverted in position around the center point. The sequences themselves (the patterns in the banding) of the two sections that are inverted are the same. It's just that they have traded positions; *all* the other bands are identical.

So the chromosomal differences among us and two of the great ape species are minor. And yet we see, just by looking at them and their behavior, how unlike they and we are. So these small anomalies add up to immense outcomes in the developed animals. Since we share something like 99% of our most important genes with our closest relatives, the bonobos and chimps, scientists have guessed that most of the differences we observe between them and us are derived—on the genetic level—from variations in gene sequences and in gene expression. This refers to the timing whereby genes are switched on or off, or whether or not they are ever switched on at all. (Humans still carry the genes that can make a tail, but they are not 'switched on', except in the few cases where mistakes occur in the course of embryonic development.)

My conclusion: It is *possible* that offspring produced by mating 'normal' humans with us sisters, and with all members of the Second Generation, will be reproductively sterile starting in either the first or the second generation (F1 or F2) thereafter. In other words, it's possible that over time we could become a new race of hominin hybrids who produce fully fertile offspring only by mating with each other, assuming of course we have both sexes. For now we can produce offspring (such as Marco) by mating with 'normal' *H. sapiens,* but those offspring them-selves—if they were all like Marco—would display either reduced fertility or full sterility.

There is one other important point. It is also possible that only the male offspring would pass on reproductive infertility at the moment. There are technical reasons for this—associated with something called 'Haldane's Law'—which I won't bother to explain here. Female offspring resulting from a mating between us sisters or the members of the Second Generation, on the one hand, and normal humans on the other, *might* be reproductively viable. This could change later. In other words, even the females might eventually show the same type of hybrid sterility as the males did earlier.

This brings me to the case of Marco. Infertility in hybrids is not necessarily an all-or-nothing matter; it can range from none to complete. Analysis shows that his sperm count is far reduced from the human norm. This alone could account for reproductive failure. On the other hand, there could also be other factors involved. It's possible that something called 'gametic incompatibility' has occurred.

This means that the receptors on the surfaces of the sperm and the egg don't match up correctly—so what we call the 'lock-and-key' effect doesn't work. In other words, there is sperm transfer, and the sperm and egg meet up, but fertilization does not occur and thus no zygote is formed. As I said, the sperm's key didn't fit the egg's lock, or vice versa—it doesn't matter which way you phrase it. In technical terms, reproductive failure can be caused by a pleiotropic (multiple) effect of a gene alteration. But both of the explanations I have given here could be relevant to Marco's case. Either the first and second separately—gametic incompatibility or low sperm count—or both together could explain why his girlfriend didn't become pregnant by him. (We are assuming that in this case the problem is Marco's, since the report of the thorough medical exam done on his girlfriend included a reference to her having become pregnant a year before, with another sexual partner, a pregnancy that was terminated by abortion.)

Now, what could explain Marco's reproductive dysfunction? Could it have anything to do with the genetic engineering done on his mother? It is tempting to reply immediately: "How could it be that? The engineering was done on the genes that code for neural growth in specific regions of the brain. How could this possibly have anything to do with reproductive failure?" The answer is that it's entirely possible. Many genes have multiple functions in growth and development. This was discovered in a number of ways, for example in the creation of what are called 'knockout mice.'

Knockout mice are the laboratory animals involved in experiments in which scientists deliberately delete one of their genes, so that they can study what the gene did by observing what functions are absent by comparison with normal mice. Different genes are selected for deletion in these experiments. The odd thing is that many of the gene deletions caused various types of reproductive failure, even though the scientists had no intention of causing this effect! They were surprised, because they were working with genes that were not directly involved in the development of the sexual organs.

But there is a more direct relationship that is relevant to our case. Franklin's scientific protocol lays a heavy emphasis on modifying what are known as 'cadherin' genes. Cadherins are a superfamily of genes that encode cell surface receptor molecules. The protocol also emphasized the need to make heritable changes to the germline, so that our new traits could be passed on to our offspring. So some of the enhancements were carried out on the so-called 'protocadherin' genes (PCDHX and PCDHY), which are located on both the X and the Y sex chromosomes. The PCDH genes are known to be involved in both brain development and the determination of sex characteristics.

Therefore, it is entirely possible that modifying the cadherin genes, in order to achieve some intended effect on neurological development, had other, unintended consequences for the reproductive system of the organism. But you will remember also what Franklin once told you, that his scientific protocol called for a number of modifications of genes on the X chromosome. It turns out that the X chromosome has a major impact on male hybrid sterility.

Marco and his two cousins are special cases, since they are offspring of the first generation of sisters who have mated with 'normal' humans. We could say that they are the products of a 'backcross' with humans who were not genetically engineered—

at least, not in the same way as we were. Of course, Marco is the only one of them who has been genetically tested; as I understand it, neither of the mothers of the other children is prepared to allow this investigation to be done. So we cannot compare his results with those of the other backcrosses to see if there are similarities—and, especially, to determine if there are relevant differences between the males and the females in the group of children.

So, all we can say for sure at this time is that, presumably, if the females of the Second Generation also mate with non-engineered humans, the same type of reproductive failure might appear, at least in the males, immediately. If gametic incompatibility is involved, however, the failure will also show up in the females.

A whole other story is involved if we *wanted* to try to ensure our reproductive isolation from other humans. Prezygotic reproductive isolation normally takes a long time to evolve in nature. But in our case its development could be speeded up, hypothetically, in a number of ways. One way is for us just to isolate the second and succeeding generations from un-engineered humans and allow them to reproduce only among themselves—in technical language, *inter se*. After a few generations, full gametic incompatibility might emerge all by itself. Or we could try to speed up the process by further engineering a future generation with this specific objective in mind. This would involve attempted modifications to the gamete cell receptors.

Why don't you review this first with Marco? Then both of you can come over to the labs and have a discussion with the biology group.

§   §   §

I asked Marco to come to my house this evening, a few days

after he returned from his three-week trip to Vandenberg Air Force Base, so that we could read and discuss Persephone's memo together.

"I may owe you another apology, Marco, or perhaps a series of apologies. I didn't reveal to you earlier that I was the one who asked the doctor at the clinic to request a semen sample from you, nor did I tell you that I had the sample sent to the biology group for DNA analysis.

"My excuse is that I didn't want to upset you unnecessarily should all your results turn out to be normal, which is, of course, what I expected at the time. You must know that I made this request of the doctor only because I was troubled by a discovery I made some years ago, which again I neglected to reveal to you at the time. Hence, my remaining apologies. I'm going to come clean and tell you everything that's relevant to what we're discussing. I can only hope that you'll judge the reasons for my actions sympathetically."

"Hera ..." Marco started.

"Wait, let me finish. When Phil's team came in to apprehend Io and Franklin two years ago, I asked them to look for a specific item that might be found in Io's house. And they did find it. It was a vial containing a sample of your semen. You're probably wondering how I knew what to have them look for. You won't like this part of the story, I'm pretty sure, but I have no choice but to tell you. Let me get it all out and then you can be upset with me. I found out that Io had set you up with the young lady whose company you enjoyed during that year. In fact—this may hurt you, but it's time for the truth now—I also discovered that Io rewarded her quite handsomely for her services to you. I have proof of this if you doubt my word."

Marco interjected, "I've never doubted your word. Go on."

"Anything that Io was doing in those days—and does in these days as well, frankly—made me suspicious. So I sent my security agents to interview your girlfriend. She told them, and they reported to me, that Io had asked her to get a semen sample from you and had given her a device in which to collect it after intercourse. Anyway, the team found it and handed it over to me. Then in the excitement of the moment I put the vial in a refrigeration unit and promptly forgot all about it. Until earlier this year, just after you and I came back from Cat Island, where we made the plan to release Io. All of a sudden I remembered. That's how this all happened. Are you terribly angry with me?"

"No. And you'll know why in a moment. It was when the reference to backcrossing came up in Percy's memo that I realized I, too, had something to get off my chest. The reason I can't be angry with you about keeping a watch on my liaison, even if I wanted to be, which I don't, is that what I'm about to confess is probably more serious. There's no good way to sugar-coat what I'm about to tell you, so I'll just say it. That liaison was not my first sexual experience. Sometime earlier I had been seduced by Io."

I gasped. "Good Lord! Are there no limits for her? What is she not capable of? Her own son! When did this happen?"

"It started early last year, just after you left on your long trip abroad. I guess she thought she'd have a better chance of carrying out her scheme when you weren't around. Of course that was before I knew she was my mother. But still, at that point I considered her to be one of my aunts, so it's bad enough."

"Marco," I said as gently as I could, "you mustn't feel as if you did something wrong. Please. Promise me you'll try not to. You were about thirteen-and-a-half at the time. Your testosterone levels were shooting up, I'm sure, like those in any young male your age. I'm convinced that what she did with you was a calculated seduction planned to the last detail in advance. You were no match for her! I wouldn't be surprised one bit if we learned that she had administered some drugs to you. But none of that is relevant anymore.

"In fact, I think it's better that you relate no more details to me now. Reliving it will bring a lot back to mind that you may have been trying to repress since then. Leave it there. It doesn't matter now. Unless, of course, you're having psychological difficulties because of it. If so, then you should see a therapist and find out if that helps. But I can't help you, and I don't want to make things worse for you."

"No, I don't think I need any therapy. It's over. I actually had a very nice relationship with the girl whom Io apparently procured for me, and I was sorry when it ended. So I really don't care if she was paid to be with me. Since then I've become almost as absorbed in my work as you are in yours. Let's assume everything's OK for the time being."

"Fine, we'll leave it at that. Then let me give you one more piece of relevant information. By the time my security people got to your girlfriend, you had been having unprotected intercourse with her for four or five months. I know she told you that she was on the pill when she first met you, but in fact she wasn't: That, too, was part of Io's ploy. By the way, I assume that Io didn't have you use condoms with her." Marco shook his head. "She was up to something. First she tried to get herself pregnant by you. Unless I miss my guess, she timed some of your liaisons so that she would be at the height of her fertility cycle. She was puzzled when it didn't happen, I'll bet. Then she devised Plan B and recruited your new lover. That woman didn't get pregnant either, even though, as my agents found out, she had had an earlier pregnancy with another partner."

"Are you thinking what I'm thinking, Hera?"

"Yes. I think you may be a case of hybrid sterility."

§   §   §

(17 May) Marco and I reviewed with Persephone and the

other biologists the conversation we had. The others—Gaia, Pandora, and Rhea—concur with Percy's preliminary analysis and will help her to do some further investigation. They believe they may be able to be more precise about the possible explanations later, but even if they are, it's likely some uncertainties will remain. We agreed that this information should be treated as top-secret among the six of us.

I've hardly been able to sleep since I read Percy's memo. *Everything changes* if this is true! Everything changes if we are indeed hybrids who may be reproductively infertile with normal people. What shall I call *them* now? What terminology should I use? *They* are known in the parlance of scientific anthropology as *H. sapiens*. If we are a new species, then what are we to be called? Whatever we are, this is the essential truth: If we cannot mate with them, but are ourselves fertile *inter se*, then we are a distinct species of the genus *Homo*.

I need a provisional name even to be able to set down my own reflections. We were conceived and born of a European scientific tradition in the shadow of New Guinea's Carstensz Pyramid, which is the highest point of land between the Andes and the Himalayas and was named for a seventeenth-century Dutch explorer. I will call our kind—for now—*Homo carstenszi*, sp. nov. It almost makes me giddy to add that Latin abbreviation "sp. nov." to our name—*species novum* or new species, the designation used by biologists to report to their peers the discovery of a previously unknown type of organism!

What does this mean for *us*—my kind—and for our descendants down the line, if we are to have any? But there is a prior question that dwarfs all others: What will *they* do when they discover the truth about us? Perhaps it wouldn't matter to them as long as we are just a bunch of unique women who mate with regular guys and sometimes have children by them. So they might not find out about hybrid sterility until later, maybe in the next generation, when all the females in our line turn out to be barren when mating with normal humans, and scientists start looking closely at our DNA, and figure out what happened back in time when Franklin did his work. If they ever discover the truth about us, we'll just become biological curiosities to them, I suppose. No doubt they will want to study us and write learned papers in scholarly journals about their findings.

Everything changes again, however, if the members of the Second Generation were to be made up of both males and females, who would then interbreed and do so successfully. Of course, since the genetic modifications to us and to them are basically similar, presumably we also would have been reproductively compatible if our group had been composed of both males and females. In such a case, of course, Franklin would have used eggs and sperm from a varied set of parents instead of just Ina's and his.

If we're able to breed among ourselves true to type, at the same time showing hybrid sterility in crossing with humans, this would mean that we are a biologically distinct or isolated species of hominin. In that case I'm certain I know what they'll try to do to us if they find out. They'll adopt the strategy that worked so well for them with Neanderthal: Wipe us out. Neanderthal is not the only animal species to learn the hard way that *Homo sapiens* brooks no competitors. They might, if they were feeling unworried, put the last few of us into zoos or circuses. But they're plenty worried these days. So it's more likely we would go the way of Newfoundland's aboriginal people, the Beothuks—hunted down and shot, our corpses publicly exhibited to reassure the population that the extermination campaign was going well.

God be merciful! Did I not say to myself, only a few months ago, that finally I could stop worrying so much about the sisters, the Second Generation project, and everything else? That soon we could all allow ourselves to be folded gently under Phil's protective wings and relax among the most secure people on earth? Had I not also fooled myself into thinking—be honest with yourself for a change, Hera!—that he and I might someday live together as lovers and partners?

Why shouldn't I be allowed to imagine such an outcome for myself? Why should I, too, not rejoice in having the burden of responsibility, which I've carried for as long as I can remember, lifted at last from my own shoulders? Why couldn't I, too, just allow myself to be happily in love and forget for a time that the rest of the world exists?

I've had only a year or so in which to indulge myself in such 'girlish' fantasies and foolishness, after we discovered, at one of our meetings on Cat Island, that we were interested in each other and became lovers. The time we've spent together since then during our brief visits with each other on various islands in the area has made this the best year of my life so far. But now I'll have to banish all this from my mind again, for good. Because Phil is one of 'them.' He's spent his whole life—the life into which he was born—protecting his kind. I cannot breathe a word of this to him. What would he say if I did?

I can just imagine what his duty would compel him to say. "I'm sorry, Hera, but the deal is off. I serve a bunch of very rich clients who are frightened of their very shadows now. They think that the private territory I've established for them, and which I promised them would be impregnable, is the last place on earth where they can hide and hold onto their assets and families. Do you think I could announce to them one day, sort of as an afterthought, that I've admitted a tribe of genetically engineered mutants into their midst? I'm sure you understand why we have to cancel the plan to relocate you and your operation to Vandenberg."

So be it. There's no going back for me in any case. I've been through my own personal hell and still I've emerged whole. "Yea, though I walk through the valley of the shadow of death I will fear no evil." I've passed through that valley and emerged at its distant end, without fear. The darkness has no hold over me anymore because I now know what I've been put on this earth to do: I am to secure the foundations on which later generations of our kind will flourish, be fruitful and multiply. I'm here to make certain that humans will not succeed in hunting us to extinction. *Homo carstenszi* will not go the way of Neanderthal and the Beothuks. This will be my doing. And if need be, I shall do it alone.

I must talk to Gaia and Percy immediately about rethinking the Second Generation project. And to Rhea as well: Thank goodness she carried on and finished the last stages of the surrogate mother screening steps a few months ago!

§ § §

(21 May) Except for brief catnaps I haven't slept for days. But at least I think I understand my own dilemmas about the Second Generation project a bit better now. I was hesitating—reluctant to give approval for the final go-ahead—for two reasons, primarily. First, I just didn't agree with Franklin's ultimate objectives, the goal that lay behind the rationale worked out in the original *Memorandum to the Group of 300* way back in 2021: The idea of using the children as instruments in a grand design worked out by their parents before their birth. This was, in effect, a brand-new creation story, a rival to the Book of Genesis, as it were.

There are at least two major objections to this rationale. The most important is that it cannot *ever* be right for some people to engineer others for a specific goal, no matter how noble or urgent the goal appears to be in the eyes of its beholder. This is true, as far as I'm concerned, even if the new design affects only their bodies, as in the case of the super-athletes who have been produced for some time now.

But it's much more compelling when the mind is the subject of the design process—although some people try to finesse the argument by referring to the brain as nothing more than another bodily organ.

This is just an evasion, however; in humans, and as I believe in all the higher mammals, including my beloved dog, the brain generates a mind, an entirely new organ in biological life, one giving rise to an awareness of feeling and experiencing the world. Our highly evolved minds are organs of great subtlety. One could surmise that we've only scratched the surface in trying to know our minds—so what exactly do we think we're doing, fiddling around in there? It's like trying to repair a defective light switch in a pitch-black room: There's a good chance of blowing the fuses and getting electrocuted in the process.

As to the second objection: It was a great revelation to me when Franklin confessed, on our flight from Heathrow to Miami years ago, that the children of his project were not supposed to become aware of the purposes they were created to serve. Only the accidental disruption of the original scenario, as a result of Klamm's attempt to hijack the experiment, caused Franklin to uncloak his design to his girls. This is why I felt I had to confront him with the Book of Genesis because there, too, the creator's design is and remains an external reality, as far as the created beings are concerned. For those who carry it in their genes as the sign of fate, that design represents a violation of the very possibility of an autonomous, self-directed future, which is what we associate with an authentic human life.

However, what the designer of my own kind most certainly *didn't* intend was to create a new species of hominin! And in that accidental happenstance is our freedom! We have been given the power to seize our fate, to take our destiny into our hands and turn it into our own authentic project—provided we have the courage to do so. Deep down inside, I think I always knew that we were, somehow, not just improved versions of the other people around us, but truly, *radically* different from them. But we can 'become what we are,' so to speak, only if we understand and accept our own fate. What this means is simple, really: We must reject the goal set by those who generated us, my parents— namely, to diffuse our new genetic structure into the human population, to blend our superior genes with theirs, like the chef who adds cream to her sauce in order to enrich her culinary creation.

We will not do this. We will stand apart and preserve our difference, and in this way we will realize our destiny. Seen in this light the impending creation of the Second Generation has an utterly new meaning: It is an act of *self-generation*, symbolized by the fact that we will include both males and females in the mix who will eventually interbreed with each other, exclusively. But the new children are—and are meant to be—just exactly like us, in terms of essential characteristics. When Franklin and his acolytes revised his original protocol, they weren't trying to start all over again, but just to use the new results in neurosciences to better avoid the chances of accidentally creating psychological disorders.

We are thus unlike Victor Frankenstein's miserable creation, who pleaded with his begetter on bended knee to grant him the comfort of having a mate of his own kind. The scientist who made him dismissed the creature's pathetic entreaty with scorn. Later Victor said to himself: If I do this, they will want children. Interestingly, he was assuming that upon mating, his creations would reproduce true to type, that in procreating they would bring forth children like themselves, 'a race of devils,' not ones similar to normal humans.

Yes, of course they would want children, and why not? Mary Shelley portrays her protagonist's anguish vividly, but it seems to me that she glosses over his heartlessness toward the fully self-conscious being he had brought into the world and then summarily abandoned. Simply put, he refused to take responsibility for his own actions. The project he had undertaken was over and done with, there was no turning back, and the consequences of the deed had to be played out to the bitter end.

Yes, what's done is done. My parents' design is their handiwork, not ours—but we shall now appropriate it for ourselves and redefine this particular project. We sisters came into being, we exist and know ourselves to be a unique kind, and now we want to perpetuate our kind, just like all other natural entities strive to do.

§ § §

(Gaia's Journal, 24 May) "So," I said, "collectively we twelve sisters shall become the 'mitochondrial Eve' for our species—metaphorically speaking, of course."

Hera asked, "What does that mean?"

Percy replied, "The mitochondrion is a specialized organelle inside every living cell, and in simple terms it is the cell's energy factory. Mitochondria have DNA strands, like the cell nucleus does, but they're in a different form. They're not divided into chromosomes, for one thing; for another, they're slightly different from the regular DNA that we carry."

I added, "My reference to Eve refers to another peculiarity: We inherit our mitochondrial DNA only from our mother's side. That's why it can be used to trace our matrilineal evolutionary lineage, and why we know that, somewhere in the murky past of *Homo sapiens,* there was one original mother from whom all living humans ultimately are descended."

Percy looked at Hera and said, "The biology group spent ten years sitting at Franklin's feet and learning their trade. During the latter part of that period we participated in iden-

tifying the changes we needed to make in his original protocol. We believe that we'll have good results and we're
anxious to proceed."

Rhea commented, "There are 1,200 women, scattered
around all the islands of the Caribbean, who are ready and
waiting for our call. The multiple levels of screening procedures we put them through were exhaustive—literally, on
both sides. But where are we going to house them?"

"Marco proposed a solution to me the other day," Hera
replied. "Contact the women and tell them to pack their
bags. I'm going to call a foundation board meeting. It's only
a formality but we need to get the paperwork in place."

§   §   §

(Marco's Journal, 22 May) The Buccaneer Resort Hotel in
Provo declared bankruptcy a month ago, its remaining clien-
tele having deserted it after a line of concrete embankments
appeared all along the beachfront. Hera told me to go and
make an offer to the receivers to lease the facilities on behalf
of the Sujana Foundation. The group of surrogate mothers
will be moved into its luxurious rooms as soon as I've
arranged for a security fence to be erected around the
perimeter.

§   §   §

(Hera's Journal, 31 May) Yesterday the board of directors gave
final authorization to proceed with the creation of the
Second Generation. We've buried the *Memorandum* for good
and are ready to set out on our own great adventure.

During the meeting Gaia remarked: "As you know, we've
prepared only female embryos. However, we still have a
good stock of frozen eggs and sperm. Our team will need
two or three months to carry out our procedures and create

a group of male embryos. How many do we want to have?"

With respect to gender proportions, I argued against a 50-50 division of males and females, because we won't be setting up shop somewhere as a group of nuclear families in our own little suburbia. In order to protect ourselves, we must live in a close-knit collectivity for a long time to come. But we must also 'increase and multiply,' as the Bible commands, as quickly as we can.

We had a good discussion and in the end we opted for one-quarter males and three-quarter females. I asked the others not to reveal this new strategy to Franklin until some-time later.

§   §   §

(Marco's Journal, 31 May) What's happened to Hera? It's as if she has touched the earth, Antaeus-like, and rebounded with ferocious energy. Yesterday, she looked me up because we hadn't yet managed to discuss what happened on my trip to Vandenberg.

"It's quite amazing. They're building a little principality there in central California all for themselves. It reminds me of what I've read about the medieval Italian city-states. Money appears to be no object—they're installing the best of everything, and we're invited to join the party. I showed Phil my complete set of photos of the primate sanctuary on West Caicos; he said they would try to duplicate the layout and that at least some of the vegetation will be similar to what we have here. Our apes will feel right at home when they move in.

"As for the rest of us, we'll have our own private territory, just as we do here, situated in a lovely valley just south of the air force base. We won't be mixing with the rest of the inhabitants except on our own terms. Of course, like everyone else there, we'll be subject to military authority. But all of you sisters and I will be part of the Colony's senior administrative complement and will have the equivalent of officer rank. Basically, we're to tell him what we need and he'll see that we get it."

"I thought it might be like that, Marco. But since you returned, our situation has changed, and I've been giving this a lot of thought. Despite the fact that you and I feel a close personal bond with Phil, it's still basically a business relationship that we have with him, at least so far. He needs us and we need him. I've concluded, after mulling things over for a few weeks, that we don't have any other good options. We can't stay on the Islands for very much longer; that much is obvious. So where would we go? There's turmoil everywhere on the planet.

"You may think that I'm cracking up when I tell you this, but here goes: I even thought of maybe going back to Tembagapura! Franklin chose it in the first place because he could hide us away and not have to worry about people finding out what he was doing. And it all might have worked out as he had planned if it weren't for Klamm and his awful scheme; I'm sure Franklin would have responded to our complaints about its isolation and moved us out into the world within a year of receiving his Nobel Prize. But I realized almost immediately that the idea of going back there is ridiculous. The remoteness of the place drove us crazy as youngsters, so just imagine how it would affect us now!

"Next I thought about returning to the Highwood River valley area in Alberta. Then I said to myself, 'If we're going to end up in North America anyway, we might as well take advantage of what the Vandenberg Colony has to offer.' This is all quite silly, I know. We can't go back to either place, because things wouldn't be the same for us now as they were then.

"In a way what we've learned recently about hybrid sterility has set us back in time, however. That's why I thought about Tembagapura again. We're back where we started in the sense that we're still in the launching phase of a secret project, and we don't know how the rest of the world will react to it. So this is what I finally figured out. We're back at square one. And we need protection. Only Phil can offer us that, at least for the time being. But I have to tell you that I regard this as a temporary relocation. Once we're settled in there, I'm going to be exploring other options. We're just renting space, so to speak, and I want to own my own home, once I can find a suitable location.

"So we'll go to California as planned. We have to keep our little secret to ourselves, at least for now. I considered whether this would be a betrayal of our relationship with Phil, and came to the conclusion that it isn't. We're not privy to all of his secrets either, not by a long shot. For example, we don't really know what the Mars Expedition is all about or who's supposed to be involved. So we'll both keep our secrets for a while longer."

"That's fine with me, Hera. I surely don't believe that we know everything about the Vandenberg Colony. After we're there for a while we can re-assess our situation and decide if it's time to trade more secrets with Phil."

§   §   §

(Hera's Journal, 01 October) The last of the embryos was implanted today. The final count is close to twelve hundred. Because we took such great care with the screening process, the surrogate mothers are a group of women with sound genetic histories and excellent health. Therefore, Rhea estimates, we can expect at least one thousand healthy babies to be delivered.

In nine months the real work will begin.

06 DECEMBER 2045, HERA'S JOURNAL

Today's was by far the best in my series of one-on-one meetings with Franklin at his apartment, which I initiated back in mid-October. I'm doing my best to repair the damage. About a week after Io had been allowed to escape from Salt Cay Island, I sent Athena to Franklin's house with an offer to release him as well. After directing a brief outburst of vitriol at me and indulging himself in some grousing, he agreed to be relocated back into his apartment within the compound. He was no longer forced to wear an electronic bracelet when moving about the Island. But his passport was not returned to him and the security detail continued to keep an unobtrusive watch on his movements outside the compound. I was determined that he would not end up in Bali.

He seems changed, too. He's aged a lot recently—no surprise, I suppose!—but, actually, not all of it is for the worse. He's much calmer and more reflective than he used to be. Mostly we talk about the old days, those strange years in Tembagapura. But I've also been pressing him to retreat further into memory and tell me stories about my mother and him, about their lives together both in the laboratory and in the wider world outside.

That's when unmistakable signs of joy return to his face and voice. Strangely enough, during all those sessions he never once asked me about the Second Generation project. Finally I raised the subject and told him that the implantations had been carried out. I said that some changes to the plan had been made at the last minute, and that I would like to discuss them with him this evening.

That night Franklin, Marco, Tina, Gaia, and Percy showed up together on my doorstep. I asked Roberto to make another special effort with the dinner and the wine selection, and again he didn't disappoint. Percy opened the after-dinner conversation and, on my suggestion, omitted most of the details concerning why she had pursued her investigations in the first place. Franklin was informed only that she just decided one day that she wanted to have a look at Marco's sperm as a matter of interest, in the context of a thorough medical examination.

All of us present were well aware that the failure of his daughters to procreate within normal family contexts had preoccupied and tormented him. He had clear evidence that his daughters—at least some of them—were capable of conceiving and bearing children, and so it had never occurred to him to worry about the more general problem of reproductive failure in later generations.

I had guessed what Franklin's first reaction might be once Percy was through briefing him on her analysis of the possibility of hybrid sterility in our line, and I was correct.

"I was pretty sure this wouldn't happen, Persephone. That is, if it's true. You emphasized that there are some outstanding uncertainties still to be cleared up. But let's assume it is true, for the sake of argument anyway. This is, of course, an utter disaster for the Second Generation—providing they are similarly afflicted.

"I must speak bluntly here. You sisters are rapidly approaching the age when the chance of delivering healthy offspring starts to decline. I still see no signs of marriage and family building among you. So it's the future offspring of the Second Generation we must focus on. Again, for the sake of argument, we must assume it's possible that all, or at least many, of them could be incapable of producing a fertile line, extended into the future."

Percy responded, "That is indeed my assumption, namely, that this is a strong possibility—barring evidence to the contrary, of course."

He spoke quickly, animated now, with the air of the scientist I imagined he once was, back in the days when he had risked professional ostracism, and perhaps worse, for the sake of his pet project.

"Let's approach this problem systematically, shall we? First, have you run any genetic tests on the other sisters' children yet? That's one way to find out if this is a general problem or something limited just to Marco. If you haven't, let's get that done right away."

I intervened immediately. "I'm sorry, Franklin, but that's out of the question. The mothers are unwilling to have their child become part of any kind of experiment—even indirectly, and however noble its aims." I smiled at him. "I thought of doing such testing myself, as soon as the results on Marco came back; I wanted to find out the same thing as you do. So I made my inquiries, and I was honor-bound to disclose to them why I wanted the genetic information. They refused without a moment's hesitation. In fact, I was told that if I did not swear on my mother's grave, right there and then, not to do this, they would take their children and leave our compound at once. They are fiercely protective, like most mothers. Perhaps they fear that one request will lead to another, and before they know it, you or I will be asking to make a few 'improvements' to their children. Whatever their concerns, they will have nothing to do with such a proposal."

He pondered this for a moment. "Yes, perhaps now I do understand why they might take that position." Ever alert to the smallest nuances of expression where Franklin was concerned, I looked at him again, tenderly; he's been thinking some issues through, it appears. Good! He had paused briefly again before resuming. "All right, then; the other solution to our problem is clear. We must cut our losses and start over. What I mean is—I suppose it's obvious—that we should waste no more time on the future of the Second Generation. Given how much effort we must still invest in that group, we can't take the chance—even if it's a small one—that the supposition of hybrid sterility or inviability will turn out to be correct. Certainly I also mean that we should support those children fully after birth, raising them in a good, healthy environment, and later giving them the best education that money can buy. We could even contact their natural parents to see if any of them would like to take and raise their child.

"The foundation's resources are more than adequate to discharge in full our responsibilities to the Second Generation and also to commence work on the Third. We can do both simultaneously, because the first takes no special skills. Even if we wind up keeping under our wing every one of the new children we're expecting, we could just hire however many people we needed, in the way of support staff, to care for them. Then we—the biology group—could turn our full attention to overcoming the possible problem of infertility.

"I'm sure we can either solve it or, alternatively, put it to rest as a concern after further study. If necessary, we can bring in outside specialists in reproductive biology to assist us. We *must* do this. Everything that I and some of you have labored on these many years—going on forty now—hangs in the balance. How could we refuse to try? To do so would be tantamount to saying that we've been wasting our collective time for nearly the past half-century."

I surely did not miss his use of 'we' as including himself. Despite the fact that he had turned seventy-two this year, he was going on excitedly, reminiscent of his younger self, keen to be back in the thick of things scientific. I didn't mind at all. On the contrary, I found it heartwarming. Yet it might make my task tonight all the more difficult. So be it.

There was no point in postponing the discussion we needed to have. "Franklin, there is an alternative option, isn't there?"

His mind was still lightning-fast. "Of course there is—or there might have been, if we had produced males as well as females in our cohort. You mean, obviously, that we could defer to the other possibility, that our progeny show hybrid sterility or inviability when crossed with 'outsiders' but would be fertile *inter se.* I have always assumed that such an option would never be on the floor for consideration among us. In effect, were we to allow this option to prevail we would be acceding in the formation of a new and separate species of hominin!"

"I'm not at all surprised at hearing the view you just expressed. And I agree that a strong case could be made for choosing the first option, the one you preferred from the beginning. Because doing so would simply be reaffirming the intentions of the original project, out of which both we sisters and the entire Second Generation were conceived. So it seems almost like simple common sense to say, 'Let's find the reproductive flaw, repair it, and get on with creating the Third Generation while we still have the time and resources to do so.'"

"My sentiment exactly. I think we shouldn't lose a minute more. We should start tomorrow along the path you just summarized. If you want, I'll get in touch right away with some experts in reproductive biology who can help us. I'll find a way to pose my questions so that we don't reveal what our problem really is."

"No, please, there's no need to do that just yet." I paused momentarily but kept my gaze fixed in his direction. "I'm well aware that in all likelihood you won't like what I'm about to say, but here it is: We've already decided to proceed with the alternative option."

There was an audible stirring among the other parties in the room as they waited to see what his reaction would be.

In his younger days and in similar circumstances it's likely he would have exploded with rage—and, an instant later, a younger Magnus would have leapt to his feet, looking for the source of trouble. Both are older now. I could detect Franklin's inner agitation, clearly written on his face, but his expressed emotions were muted. During the silence Magnus just picked up his head for a moment, looked at me, observed my state of perfect calm, and with a deep sigh, relaxed again on the couch, where Marco was also sitting.

He appeared to be concentrating on his own ruminations and didn't say anything, so I carried on. "Let me back up a bit in time. It was about thirty-five years ago when you and Ina first began to formulate your bold plan, as I recall. At the time it wasn't at all unreasonable for you both to believe that a new type of person, genetically modified according to your protocol, could be ushered out of your laboratory and onto the world stage. You knew, of course, that isolated genetic mutations can't spread very rapidly throughout the wider human population.

"That's why you envisaged enlisting the help of your colleagues and creating a series of larger batches of modified individuals, starting with a thousand at a time. And, of course, a basic requirement for the success of your plan was that the new individuals would interbreed with other humans and pass on their modified genes to their offspring.

"Under this plan it was at least plausible to imagine that there might be enough time for those modified genes to be disseminated far and wide through the earth's population. You thought that, if all went well, your 'good people' would appear soon enough as leaders on the world stage, helping to head off the impending chaos in human societies. If events had unfolded as you and Ina envisioned they would, first in your planning with her and later in your 2021 *Memorandum to the Group of 300*, perhaps as many as a thousand men and women from the first generation might already be in leadership positions, in every corner of the globe, and there would also be thousands of their offspring being raised, eventually to spread further your modified genes."

"Indeed," he said, not looking at his companions seated around him, his head bowed, his voice hushed, "that was exactly what we had hoped would happen."

I waited a moment and then continued, speaking softly and looking directly at him. "I'm truly sorry, but I think it would have been pointless for us to try to follow your original plan anymore. It's too late. The forces of chaos and destruction have been gathering strength with each passing decade. Now the panic induced by a series of sea-level rises adds fuel to their fires. Even more relevant to the issue before us, the numbers of competing genetic experiments on humans have exploded in the past thirty years. We're reliably aware only of the publicized ones being done according to approved protocols. If we just consider that set for a moment, we see that almost every human trait under the sun is being tinkered with. Percy reeled off a list for me one day last week."

"Well," Percy chimed in, "from what I've been able to gather, there are modifications for longevity, for all different versions of what people think of as beauty, for height and skin color, for musculature and physical enhancements of every conceivable type, for mood and temperament, and for the skills considered to be useful in specialized professions. There are therapeutic interventions for every kind of disease, for changing the outputs of the endocrine glands, for strengthening the immune system, and so on. All involve germline modifications in the genome.

"More relevant to us, however, are the interventions relating to almost every facet of brain function—memory, cognition, affect, information processing, you name it—that started being investigated in earnest about forty years ago. At first the point was to treat people who were sick, but soon healthy people started demanding treatments to give them souped-up brains, not just mood enhancers but boosters for cognitive functions as well. Neuroscientists even coined a term for it: 'cosmetic neurology.' Along the way, every steroid hormone, as well as every neurosteroid and neuro-transmitter, has been synthesized, manufactured and distrib-uted widely as a pharmaceutical product, being administered in various doses according to one or more therapeutic protocols."

"But that's just the applications we know about," Gaia added. "How many half-trained scientists are there in the world like our dear Io, who have their own private agendas and who scorn ethics controls? We know that human cloning experiments went ahead full steam a few decades ago, even in the face of criminal penalties and full knowledge of the risks of gross deformities. If there's money to pay for it and a country to host it, it's going to be done, usually sooner than predicted. Who knows where this will all end? Who knows when a truly monstrous modification of the human type will suddenly be sprung on the world?"

Now he looked up to face us again and spoke softly. "Precisely, my dear daughters. That's exactly why we must throw ourselves back into the breech. We're on the side of the angels. How can we just concede the field to the other side without a fight? How can we justify such a choice to ourselves?"

I smiled, looking directly into his eyes. "Do you remem-ber a rather animated conversation between us, some years ago now, pretty much along those lines? We didn't get very far, you and I, did we? You found my way of reasoning too—what did you call it?—theological or metaphysical. Remem-ber my analogy of the train, which you disliked so? Perhaps you don't recall it, but I do. Only the analogy has shifted somewhat. Back then I suggested that you, a representative of human science, should stop the train and jump off. Now I propose a completely different strategy: I suggest that we all jump off, while the train's still running full steam ahead, and board our own train, one heading in a different direction altogether."

He remained silent for a full minute. I waited patiently for his response because I wanted him to become fully engaged in the subsequent dialogue.

Finally he looked around at all of us, wearing a broad smile on his face and suddenly seeming more animated, and said, "You're serious, aren't you? Anyway, let me take it that you are, which is always a safe assumption where you're concerned, Hera. You wish to propagate a new hominin species on planet Earth, don't you? By the way, just out of curiosity, have you named it yet?"

"We have," Gaia remarked, also smiling broadly. "Its provisional scientific name is *Homo carstenszi,* sp. nov."

He laughed heartily. "All right, then, let's go down that road a bit and see where it leads. There's no point in trying to compete with humans if you think you'll be creating a type that's inferior to them. So you must regard your kind as superior to them in some important respects."

Tina interjected, "If we are, it's entirely your doing, remember."

"*Touché.* I have to concede, you're at least superior to the norm in certain specific traits. That was, after all, the whole point! So what do you intend for your new race of superhuman beings, my daughters? Will they rule over the rest of us like gods? Now I recall one of your other stories, Hera, the one about 'new people' and 'old people.' Will you show the rest of us the whip if we get out of line, as I recall you saying then?"

"I have two answers to your questions, and I'll cover them

in turn. No, I want no new gods. In fact, it's precisely because I fear those who cannot resist the urge to become 'like God'—remember the serpent's promise to Eve?—that I've chosen the option I now defend to you. Is it possible you don't see the paradox lying before our very eyes, Franklin? Who among us—sitting around this room tonight—is the one who first dared to cross the line between created and creator? It was you.

"You—one of the sterling representatives of modern science, praised and celebrated by your peers and governments everywhere, honored with their highest awards— decided to engineer my sisters and me. We're the product of an exquisitely crafted plan formulated by you and Ina and then realized by you. You humans did become gods, just as you so urgently wished to be. You designed us as an improvement over God's handiwork; you gestated us, nourished us, educated us, and when you were around, you nursed me through the days and nights of my worst headaches."

"I don't think what Ina and I did necessarily must be described in those terms, although I will grant you that many followers of established religions might see it in such a light. But few, if any, of them—including religious leaders and theologians—complained when we showed them what great benefits might result, say, from correcting the genetic flaws that cause terrible inherited diseases such as Huntington's chorea."

"Indeed," Tina chimed in, "humans always love having the best of both worlds—science and faith—don't they? Partly it's just a matter of seemingly harmless steps happening in small increments. A little snip here, and we've excised the erroneous stretch of nucleotide triplets that causes Huntington's disease, with its sentence of an unavoidable and miserable early death. Change another mistake, a single nucleotide polymorphism hidden deep inside the sequence of 2.9 billion base pairs in the human genome, and we've eliminated the French-Canadian variant of Leigh's syndrome. A few different excisions or manipulations at other places on the genome, and we could remove or switch off the breast cancer genes.

"And so it goes, because, of course, people couldn't stop there; they then wanted traits to be added as well as subtracted. 'Oh,' they begged and pleaded, 'just some minor, inconsequential changes, really—a different hair or skin color, a few more points on the IQ scale, a little more muscle mass, a smaller nose, on and on. What's the big deal? God did a fairly good job with the basic design; we're not faulting Him for that. We just want to upgrade the accessories.'"

"I do see where you're headed, Athena," Franklin responded, "and again, I can't disagree with you in principle. It all starts to add up after a while. When we get to the matter of mental functions that are critical not only to personal well being but to social organization as well, we've begun to tread on far more dangerous ground. That's what your mother and I did, right? I concede your implied point, that on this plane the type of modifications we attempted could, accidentally or purposefully, yield some very bad outcomes."

"Absolutely!" I responded, laughing merrily. "Dear father, I've waited a very, very long time to hear you make that modest concession. Let's go back to us sisters, to the case at hand, as it were, because the intensity of self-interest we must feel—on both sides, yours and ours—makes the nature of the stakes more apparent. The core of the problem here is that you—the engineer—were in no position to criticize us if we failed to fulfill your expectations. None of us asked to be made in quite this way, did we? In fact, precisely your act of engineering us itself—understand me, not the outcome, which as you've discovered you can't necessarily control, but the act itself—is what I referred to in our earlier conversations as the loss of innocence.

"Although so far I haven't been able to find a way to make you grasp my point, I want to try again. But first let me say something else: It's become more and more important for me, Franklin, to try to reach you with my arguments. Not necessarily to convince you to agree with me, that's not what I mean. Just to have you take them seriously and engage me in a dialogue about them.

"Despite the bitterness that came between us for a while, and the intensity of our arguments, the plain fact of the matter is that you and mother created us. How I would have loved to include her in these heated conversations, father! You're not the only one here to have suffered so on account of her absence. How often I have longed to have been able to test her, too, to see perhaps if even a small part of the division between you and me was gender-based, for example. It was not to be. But I want the two of us to understand each other better before it's too late. It's as simple as that."

For the first time in many years I reached out to touch him. I took his hands in mine and held them for a moment, and a look of peace, which his daughters had not seen on his face in many decades, came over him. "May I go on?" He nodded.

I turned back to face my small group of listeners. "I have to refer to the idea of a moral order so that I can get my main point across. A moral order defines relationships within a community or among different communities. It tells you what's right and what's wrong among the choices you might make, or what's permitted and what's forbidden. It creates a moral community, including—at least for some of us—one encompassing not only our own species but our relations with all other species as well. I'm concerned with the latter kind, the one connecting *Homo sapiens* with the rest of creation.

"I'd like to start by focusing on the moral community that

was created for humans as a result of their expulsion from Eden ...." I stopped abruptly when Franklin interrupted.

"Wait, Hera, please. I must ask this before you go on. I've never understood why you keep returning to the myth of Genesis. For many of us non-believers as we're called, that's just ancient history, so to speak. It's just not relevant to people like me who think that the moral community is a purely secular creation. Our notion of upholding the difference between right and wrong simply doesn't depend on the support of a religious framework."

Gaia broke in. "I think I can answer that, because Hera and I have discussed this many times over the years. We look around us and observe how most humans behave, and our conclusion is simple: The religious framing of experience remains extremely powerful, even in our modern world. Whether it's Christianity of various stripes, or Islam—Sunni or Shia—the Jewish faith, Hinduism, Sikhism, or even the remnants of animism, the form of faith doesn't matter. What matters is that most people in the world need an organized religion. Where this need has been repressed, as it was in Soviet-style communism, we find it re-emerging as soon as the anti-religious regime is overthrown.

"Even though we sisters have never felt this need for organized religion, we aren't bothered by other people's preferences. No, what bothers us is what might be called the collateral damage done by most forms of religious belief. I'm referring to the endemic, ferocious hatred each faith expresses for all others—even when they're the same basic type! The world created by organized religions is like an ever-simmering cauldron that threatens to boil over at any time, sending the faithful into orgies of slaughter and mayhem. In contrast, those like you, father, the secular moralists, are pitifully outnumbered and usually wind up being swept away into the maelstrom when it arrives."

"All right, Gaia, I take the point. That much is obvious,

even to one like me, who has spent his life bent over a laboratory bench, isolated from the turmoil outside. I agree that a lot of the world around us is pretty much as you describe. But what I still don't understand about Hera's line of argument is the connection she wants to make between the old heritage of religion, on the one hand, and what modern science tries to do, on the other. For me they are opposites, not partners."

I rejoined the discussion. "I'm glad you made those last remarks, Franklin. I'm going to end up exactly at the point that still confuses you, because obviously I haven't made my arguments sufficiently clear. So if I promise to arrive at that point before I'm finished, will you allow me to return to my starting line?"

"Of course."

"Good. Now, back to the beginning. The key element is that God allowed Adam to retain his dominion over the earth and all the living things thereon, even after the expulsion from Paradise. This is the dispensation that taught them to regard themselves as superior to all other beings: No other creature has been set above you. Humans have the moral community all to themselves, for all other living things are excluded. Under the sway of this divine dispensation, humans are entitled to do whatever they wish with the rest of His creation, including inflicting torture, mayhem, and slaughter unto extinction, in pursuit of benefits for themselves.

"Only their religions, not their science, tell humankind that they are *morally entitled* to rule all of creation. This is why we have to speak in religious terms. Now, here's the catch: They're the sole beneficiary of the moral order established by God, the only beings who will be 'saved' at the end of days, *but they're not entitled to change it,* because it was a gift to them and was not of their own making. If they do change it, as they have done, its rules are no longer viable.

"No one compelled them to go this far, because they're top dogs, aren't they? They did all this by themselves—and to themselves. Those humans—I refer to what's called modernity, that is, the age of the science-dependent world-view—and no one else brought the old moral order to a close. They overthrew it and set up one of their own devising in its place. This new one teaches them that they have the right to rework the entire labor of creation.

"The old moral order, where humans have wrestled with the play of good and evil in their souls, represented God's second-best solution for humans. His preferred choice was the first one, the state of innocence. Probably that had been His first choice because He had an inkling that His humans wouldn't fare very well if they had to resist evil and temptation! So the second-best solution was a kind of experiment, or game of chance, with very high stakes. And whatever happened this time, there would be no third option.

"Once this new experiment was launched and started to run its course, following the expulsion from the Garden of Eden, He could not thereafter change its terms again—ever. That's because of the type of second-round experiment God was running, where it was up to His humans to make their own choices, about resisting evil temptations and seeking the straight and narrow path of the good.

"God couldn't intervene again to halt the game some-time later, perhaps to tinker with it again, because doing so would violate the terms of the experiment, which had laid the primary responsibility for achieving salvation squarely on this very special species He had brought into being. For if He had done so, even for an instant, He could never have known for sure whether or not it was His new intervention, and not their own authentic choices, that had shaped their behavior thereafter. And this is, if you will, my theological variant of Heisenberg's famous uncertainty principle—the one that says we can't measure with precision, and simultaneously, both the position and momentum of an electron because our attempt at measurement changes the system we are trying to examine. It applies to God as well, you see!

"In any event, modern humans, deploying their all-powerful science, have given Him their own, much shorter evaluation, of His original experiment: It was a failure, they declared. His handiwork needed improvements, they had decided, and moreover, they knew exactly what kinds of improvements were required.

"Thus by their own hand the old moral order passeth. Our new species—*Homo carstenszi*—represents a fresh beginning on earth. Those other humans are no longer supreme and unchallengeable on this planet. They can no longer dictate the rules of the game to all other species because we now exist, and we don't intend to submit to their rules. My sense is that our kind will seek to establish a radically different type of moral community, one in which every existent species is deemed to have the same right to exist as any other.

"Subject to the prevailing environmental conditions applying to all—the ecological rules of the game—each has the same right to seek to flourish for its allotted time on this earth. This doesn't mean something silly, like having us manage the affairs of all other creatures. No, all it means is that we'll leave enough untouched space on the planet for the others by limiting our own numbers and permanent settlements."

He asked, "Wait a minute, Hera; may I comment on what you just said? Let me accept all of your premises for the sake of argument. Why is it not simpler then to assume that your kind will take over the role and place formerly occupied by ours? That you'll now be top dogs? And that humans will just have to get used to it? Well, I see there's only two small problems with this nice little scenario. The first is that humans won't go down the species hierarchy without a fight. The second is, we'd appreciate just a little effort on your part to justify yourselves. How have you earned the top spot?"

"No, I don't think we have to accept your analogy with human social organization—top dog and all that stuff," Tina replied. "That expression is just the old Biblical doctrine of human power over other species peeking out again. On the other hand, our perspective is that of natural evolution—the chance appearance and disappearance of endlessly varied species. In this perspective our kind is, just like humans and all other species, its own justification. None of them asked to be created—speaking metaphorically, of course. Remember your Milton: 'Did I solicit Thee / From darkness to promote me?' My sisters and I certainly didn't.

"It seems to me that this is where the special arrogance of modernity comes into play. Did you or any of your peers ever imagine for a second that in tinkering with your genome you might accidentally produce a variant who would rule over you? Or, alternatively, a variant who would just choose to keep itself apart from you and demand an equal right of existence, a right to share the earth on fair terms?"

Franklin again paused for a moment before replying. "Speaking for myself, Athena, I can say with complete confidence that the answer is no; I never even imagined this as a possibility. Obviously, in view of the present conversation, I made a big mistake!" He said this without sarcasm, almost jocularly, which pleased me no end. I didn't want this exchange between us to become a battle royal, like earlier ones had been. Rather than humiliation or further estrangement between us, I was seeking reconciliation.

"My guess is that by their very nature, humans cannot imagine they would ever have to deal with another reasoning being who is their equal or better," Tina added. "Not seriously, anyway, not outside the bounds of science fiction literature and the Hollywood movie versions of the same. It's so far outside the scope of their *political* imagination as to be, literally, unthinkable. Why? Because of their religions, most of which flatter them into believing that they alone are special among created things, that they are entitled to use everything for their pleasure and to be used reciprocally by no other being.

"It's on this point that their religion and their science are perfectly in tune. Both reaffirm the absolute dominion of humans over all else. These two are also alike in the passion they evoke in people, in the motivations fuelling their behavior. I have to confess, this is to me the oddest of all the many odd aspects of human traits. I sense the strong passion in you and others for your scientific work. I feel equally strongly the selfless devotion of genuine believers to their religion, for example, among the people we came to know in Alberta. But you're all part of the same integrated social order. What I can't figure out, for the life of me, is how humans hold those two passions together.

"One of the two—religion—demands that you eschew the things of this world and seek only the salvation of your immortal soul, which depends in no way on accumulating earthly benefits. The other—science—says to you, 'I can teach you how to make nature serve your slightest whim, so that She piles up unlimited riches at your feet.' And yet, somehow, they have persuaded themselves that they are entitled to have both, and moreover, that one does not contradict the other. What amazing logicians they are! What subtle metaphysicians!"

Franklin spoke, softly. "Most of us, I think, feel the promptings of one of these two—science or religion—more strongly than the other. It's rare to find someone equally motivated by both."

"Yes," Athena responded. "That's perfectly true at the level of the individual. But all such individuals, driven by either of these two, are then summed up in one body politic. The human collectivity reflects the passions of both and

somehow holds it all together. For a long time the best illustration of this kind of society has been the United States—
the world's leading science-driven nation and,
simultaneously, a hotbed of religiosity and belief in a
personal God. For goodness' sake, three-quarters of them
claim to believe in the reality of the devil—and the churches
in which they profess this belief are just around the corner
from the lavishly funded science departments in their
universities!"

Marco piped up at last. "When I visited the United States
not too long ago, I watched a lot of evening news broadcasts.
The sheer numbers of people who were talking about the
coming of the Apocalypse and the 'final battle between good
and evil' just stunned me. They were deadly serious, if you'll
forgive the pun. They believe it's actually going to happen,
and soon, pretty much exactly as described in the Book of
Revelation. They're preparing for it."

"Marco, you're right," I put in, "but I'd like to come back
to my main point, which I don't think has been made clearly
yet. Let me try again. The problem, as I see it, is not *either*
apocalyptic religion *or* all-powerful science. It's the combination of the two that's lethal. What is so awful is the fact that
people today have both weapons, one in each hand, and that
each weapon supports the other. Religion supplies the
scenario, science the firepower.

"In their purest form religions are just harmless stories
that humans made up once upon a time and retell to each
other regularly when fear of the darkness comes over them.
And in its purest form, modern science expresses humans'
wonder at the intricate structure of the natural world and
their irrepressible desire to know how it works. However,
these two don't play out together in their pure forms, rather
in the actions of living, breathing humans, formed into
social groups. On one block the fiery preacher thunders,
'Annihilate the unbelievers and the wicked.' Meanwhile,

over on the next block, the mild-mannered scientist whispers, obligingly, 'Here are some new powers you can use in achieving whatever goals you have in mind.' What a lovely combination!"

"I remember you mentioned to me once, Hera," Percy interrupted, "that this insight—about the lethal combination of science and religion—occurred to you while you were reading about what happened on September 11, 2001. In retrospect what occurred then is still a signal event for our times, because so much of what is now going on around us seems to originate there. You recall that people were puzzled by the reference to the 'tragedy of Andalusia' in Osama bin Laden's communiqué after September 11, until they realized he was referring to the final expulsion of Islamic rulers from Spain in the late fifteenth century! You remarked that bin Laden's philosophy of action combined the eighteenth-century religious fundamentalism of a primitive desert sect with twenty-first-century science and technologies of mass destruction. You said that what struck you especially about this philosophy was the apparent ease with which its two dimensions were integrated within a single mentality."

"I remember that conversation, Percy. What had struck me then, and still bothers me, is that humans can vacillate so apparently cunningly between their religion and their science—but it seems to me that in doing so they fool only themselves. For example, their religion, if it were to be taken seriously, tells them that their scientific worldview is blasphemous, for it has no gods in it. Religion tells them that it's not their mission to seek to create a paradise on earth—for Paradise is God's handiwork, not theirs. Religion tells them not to meddle with the reality of death, for that, too, is exclusively God's domain.

"Religion tells them to welcome death. Marco, do you recall these lines from the first *Recitativo* in Bach's beautiful cantata, *'Ich habe genug,'* that we enjoy every so often?

> *If the Lord might free me from the body's chains*
> *Where I am constrained!*
> *If my farewell I could foresee*
> *I'd say with joy, O World, to thee*
> *I now have enough.*

"This is what believers used to pray for, before their science seduced them, whereupon they began to hope instead that death be could postponed and ultimately defeated.

"Your Enlightenment forebears, Franklin, at least had the courage of their convictions. They regarded religious belief as mere superstition and longed for the day that faith would be replaced by the scientific ethos. After a while it seemed that the proponents of this idea simply were wrong about how long it would take to achieve this goal. But now it's clear that this is not the difficulty at all.

"Humans simply cannot give up their religions because they need religion to give them the courage to face death, and the godless science that modernity brought them is useless in that capacity. They cannot live solely on the promise of figuring out how the cold and lifeless universe really works. They need the comforting presence of a personal God and the promise of salvation to make it through the night."

I was animated now. "They can search forever in the extensions of matter, in the unfathomable distances of outer space, or in the unimaginably small bits of subatomic particles—but they'll not find their God in any of these places. Nor salvation, redemption, forgiveness, nor 'the peace that passeth all understanding,' which are the things that men and women seek when they lie upon their deathbeds, regretting their lives.

"No, as they observe the universe they'll hear only the eerie hum of radio waves and X-rays, and the faint yet unmistakable B-flat chord of the Big Bang, still somehow reverberating after fourteen billion years. There they'll discover only the impossibly immense architecture of empty space, cold dust, and fiercely hot gases. Imagine if you will the Eagle Nebula—a column of gas and dust extending almost *ten trillion light-years* in space. One light-year is a distance of 59 trillion miles, so we're talking about a span in miles represented by the number 1,000 followed by 24 zeros. And the Eagle Nebula occupies just one tiny little corner in the universe! Well, they can scour those vast spaces all they like; they'll find no spirits there, and no consolations."

"I for one don't need those consolations," Franklin remarked suddenly. "Yet I'll freely admit that when I look at the world around me as it is today, with my scientist's eye, I'm amazed at the degree of religiosity among my fellow human beings. I'll admit this to you now in front of this little gathering. You'll undoubtedly remember how I used to become so upset whenever you turned your argument from science to religion.

"Well, I've learned something during my period of enforced incarceration at your hands, which you can guess is rather hard for me to admit. On the other hand, still being able to learn at my age should be a source of joy, right? Anyway, I began to watch a lot of world news and I couldn't believe my eyes. What's happened to the modern world? Everywhere I look religious adherents march in the streets shouting, 'death to unbelievers.' In the country next door, one hears the same cries, from the same type of people, but one soon realizes that each party is referring to the other! You're right, Hera. The Enlightenment dream is finished. I fear that some day our science will be returned to the control of mullahs and bishops, as it was in the Middle Ages."

Gaia said, "I think it's much worse than that. I fear something else far more than I do the resumption of control over science by religious dogma. Remember when in 1633 Galileo—who was then an old man, nearly seventy and half-blind—was hauled before the Inquisition, and forced under threat of torture to defend his scientific views against a charge of heresy? He had very little to offer his opponents, other than a theory about the movements of the heavenly bodies—a theory they didn't much care for at the time. Part of the reason they didn't care for it, quite frankly, is that they didn't see how the organization they represented—the Holy Roman Church—could derive any benefit from adopting this theory.

"The Catholic theologians of Galileo's time couldn't imagine then how switching their belief about planetary orbits, from one system of ideas to another, would yield any further advantages to them in solidifying their power on earth. But later on, they did just that. As you know, on the many occasions when the highly flexible and inventive brains of theologians did perceive such benefits, switches in dogma happened readily enough.

"Things have changed so much now, more than four hundred years later. After science was liberated from dogma, the church authorities observed the immense increase in earthly power that an unfettered science could extract from nature. And religion always finds uses for secular power, doesn't it? Think of the close cooperation between church and state during the struggles over religion in medieval and early modern Europe. The church defined the crime of heresy and also announced that God permitted the confiscation of property belonging to heretics. The state then arrested, tortured and killed the heretics; thereafter church and state together divided up the heretics' property for themselves. A lovely little racket.

"Returning to modern times then. So now the legions of believers, who live on nothing but pure hatred of the other, take whatever scientific and technological marvels they find at hand and turn these powers against those who invented them—those who believed so naïvely but with equal passion that their devices would bring peace and prosperity to all the peoples of the earth. I include the powers over genomes handed to them by the molecular biologists. The same fundamentalists who loathe and despise the secular spirit of modernity, and wish to extirpate it root and branch, gleefully adopt its technologies so as to be able to slaughter their opponents with greater efficiency."

"Do you remember, Franklin," I broke in again, "when you used to insist on throwing back at me what I regarded as that tired cliché about the innocence of knowledge? You know, the one about the purity of the instrument that may be subsequently wielded either for good or evil ends? All of which conveniently presupposes that somebody is in control of the applications? Once again, in this respect, too, humans somehow came to regard themselves as gods in their delusions about their disposition over power.

"*Now* I can get back to where I started in this conversation, to pick up the main thread again. Tempting humans to believe that they *are* godlike, in control of their ultimate destiny: Isn't this what really happened in the Garden of Eden? Satan insinuated to Adam and Eve that they would be capable of managing their experience of good and evil. He suggested that they could just taste the fruit—monkeying around with God's plan—and then find their way back again to the good. What they missed was how audaciously cunning Satan's plot really was: For on the road through evil and back to good they would encounter a final temptation, namely, *to alter the rules of the game of life itself,* the game that God had commanded them to play by His rules. Satan set them up. And they took the bait. They bit into the apple.

"God's plan was that sinners would find their way through evil back to Him—and nothing else. But Satan guessed the truth. He encouraged humans to believe that they need not make such an arduous and self-denying journey toward redemption after all. Satan guessed that if he told them they could short-circuit the process, so to speak, by putting themselves into God's shoes, thus becoming 'like God,' they wouldn't be able to resist such a temptation. And he was right. He also guessed that once they had embarked on this journey, they would find the exercise of godlike powers so thrilling that they wouldn't be able to stop. And he was right about that, too.

"It seems that many are persuaded that they must go down this road because people have gotten themselves into such a mess with what they've already created. More powers are needed because the more they try to solve their problems, the more the problems seem to increase—more food, more hunger; more farming, more erosion; more wealth, more poverty. And so they think that if they can just get their hands on one more little increment of power, such as the power to rule the world's DNA, this will do the trick.

"One additional increment would allow them to avoid the embarrassment of conceding that they aren't such an intelligent species after all. But looked at coldly, is it not more reasonable to conclude that more power in their hands just means that much more trouble? Science and technology create utilities, but these are not themselves solutions, only means to the ends people seek. Now they seem to be addicted, not so much to the actual utilities themselves, but to power over nature, as such. They simply cannot get enough of it. If they continue down that road much longer, Franklin, I fear that it will be the end of them."

I paused abruptly and turned to Marco, still sitting on the couch next to Magnus. "I'm terribly sorry to carry on like this. Are you incredibly bored?"

Out of politeness or apathy, he replied with a grin, "No, it's interesting to me."

Franklin picked up the thread of conversation again. "Well, Hera, you did say a short while ago that a species will do whatever its nature compels it to do. Maybe humanity will engineer its own demise as a species. Yet I sense that some other argument altogether is being built here. I get the impression that, lurking somewhere in the background, you have a solution to the problem about humans that you have diagnosed. And that this solution has something to do with what you call your new species. Am I right?"

"You weren't awarded a Nobel Prize for nothing!" I laughed heartily. "I knew you could figure out where I was going. You realize, don't you, that things could be much worse for humankind? I find in myself no wish to dominate humans, although I do, like all creatures, have a will to survive and propagate my kind, which I intend to arrange, if I can.

"But just imagine that through genetic manipulation some scientists among your peers create, either by accident or design, a true master race that replaces humans at the top of the food chain. And imagine that this race enslaves humans, domesticating them as humans do their horses and cows. If I were an observer on a distant planet, I'd say, 'Well, they did this to themselves, didn't they? They have no basis for complaint, and anyway, they have nobody to lodge a complaint with, since they overthrew the God they had some time ago.'

"I sense that my kind is not like this. I believe I'm willing to live and let live, as long as this sentiment is reciprocated by humans. But I also believe that I and my sisters, and the new generation we are now raising, are at extreme risk from what humans may yet do with their potent science and their desire to become 'like God.' We're not observers sitting on a distant planet, obviously. If humans should discover that we might be, as Gaia and Percy have suggested, a separate species of hominin, they would almost certainly try to re-engineer us in some way, or failing that, annihilate us."

Now exhausted, I lapsed into silence, and Gaia picked up the thread. "Or they might, if they continue fooling around with their own genome, create a monster race that would enslave our kind as well as theirs. So you see, it's not just a matter of where their kind and ours stand today in relation to each other. It's what else they might do or try to do in the future that frightens me to the core of my being. We cannot allow this to happen, for it's a matter of our self-preservation, and all beings have an equal right to strive to preserve their kind.

"If they set out to annihilate us, as they've done to other species many times, we must stop them. If they try to re-engineer us, we must seek to prevent the attempt. Even if they just keep fiddling with their own genome, we must figure out how to block these trials. We may fail, but I think you can understand why we have to try. Either we'll succeed or we won't—and in the latter case we will disappear. In any case, for us not even to try is unthinkable."

Tina interjected. "None of these things has happened just yet—so far as we know! But we're in no position to find out what may possibly be in the works in other places on the globe. You hid away high atop a mountain in the remoteness of the New Guinea jungles to create us, Franklin. How many of your fellows are now doing the same among the many nooks and crannies on the earth?"

He rose to the challenge. "Maybe my kind can change, daughters, just to follow the logic of your own argument. Perhaps you could convince us to change. Are you willing to try this course of action?"

Tina paused before replying. "In principle, I'd have to say yes. But in practice? No, I cannot imagine that the chances of success for this re-education program would be very high. It's much more likely that we'd all end up being burned at the stake somewhere."

"All right. Let me grant you that point as well. But you still have a problem, don't you, and a serious one at that. Your kind may very well be in mortal peril as soon as the truth about you is known among humans. So if you can't re-educate humans, what exactly are you going to do? Surely you can't just sit around and wait for these horrible things to happen?"

I looked at him. "What I would do, assuming that somehow I had been granted the power to do it, is to take their science away from humans for a time, both to protect my kind and, indeed, the future for humans as well. Some of them might even be grateful for this if they ever became aware of it."

There was complete silence in the room. A younger Franklin would have burst out in scornful laughter at this point. Not now. Gradually the entire weight of the evening's news about hybrid sterility had been sinking through the layers of his consciousness, being absorbed and processed as the conversation went on. He was silent but alert.

Encouraged by his tacit acquiescence, I went on. "The vast majority of humans cannot endure without their religions. I cannot even imagine trying to take those away from them, for the simple reason that they would have to re-invent them at once. But if I could take their modern science away from them, at least for a time, and hide it away with such skill that they could never rediscover it unaided, I would do this. My successors could decide when and if they could have it back again."

Now Franklin was ready to engage me once more. "Fine, Hera, let's follow your train of thought, and let's just stick to the practical side of things for now. We humans discovered our science once and can do so again. Therefore your mission is futile."

I was truly delighted that he had re-entered the dialogue. "Perhaps. But remember that social evolution, like its natural analogue, is largely a matter of chance. There is only some indeterminate probability that, once deprived of it, humans would find their way back to the scientific worldview they know today. But no matter. If by chance they did find their way back to it, and in the opinion of my kind they were still not ready to use it wisely, we would have no choice but to take it out of their hands once again, always presuming, of course, that we were actually in a position to do such a thing."

"This has been quite an extraordinary conversation for me, Hera. I know you well enough to realize that you're serious. For me personally, what has happened this evening also has been most unusual. I understand myself much better now than I used to. It's the result of my period of enforced isolation, and I'm still humble enough to admit to you that this time for self-reflection was very good for me. I've changed my views completely with respect to one important point. I now know in my heart, not just in my mind, that you and your sisters are the result of my intention and acts.

"I made you. I'm responsible for the fact that you exist and think and feel—and hope and fear—in the ways that you do. And if I encounter you now, as I have, and you tell me what your deepest feelings are, I believe I must accept them. We both have all the requisite faculties of intelligence and judgment. I cannot say to you, 'You are insane or delirious, see a doctor and get those thoughts out of your head.' For what would prevent you from turning this statement around and redirecting it at me?

"I accept you, and Gaia, Percy, Tina, and Marco, too, and all the others, as you say you are. I really have no choice, as I see things now. I must also accept Io as she is, poor soul. I don't know what she's up to now, but during the time I was under house arrest, Gaia visited me frequently and told me some of what you knew then about Io's state of mind. I'll confess to you that if I had realized in the summer of 2044

449

what I learned later, I wouldn't have showered her with my remaining fortune. It's too late now, but I wanted you to know how I feel anyway. I was a pathetic fool and she used me. I'm sorry for what I did then."

I went to him and embraced him, and we held each other for a long time without speaking. We were both shedding tears of happiness. When I was finally able to speak again I did so softly and with warmth, looking directly at him.

"Listen to me carefully now. Above all, father, my sisters and I are the authentic products of your own great intelligence and skill. And as such we're also the authentic products of the entire trajectory of modern science, from its beginnings in the seventeenth century to the latest discoveries in neurogenetics, which you used to create us. You brought us into being. True, we're not quite what you expected. We do not, for indeed we cannot, express the intentions of your original plan. But you now understand that the possibility of such a deviation was inherent in your own act of creation. From your standpoint we turned out to be mistakes."

He started to speak but I rushed on. "No, don't protest, not the slightest criticism of you was meant in that remark. I'm simply referring to the obvious discrepancy between your intention and the final outcome. Remember your instantaneous reaction to the news of hybrid sterility tonight: You wanted to correct your mistake at once.

"Whatever you think about us, from your perspective as our creator, is, of course, entirely legitimate. However, you're also wise enough now to see that if we must be regarded by our creator, at least in part, as incorporating certain mistakes, we ourselves cannot possibly hold the same view. For the same reason as you, we, as the created beings, must have our own unique perspective on what we are. If I can put it bluntly, we could not possibly regard ourselves as the result of a programming error on your part!

"We exist as we are and as we were made by you. As such we wish to persist, now that we believe that we may be a viable, independent species. Something else, vitally important, also flows from the fact of our existence and from our very being on earth: We must, if we can, put an end to these genetic manipulations by humans—at least for the time being, until we are quite convinced they are capable of managing responsibly such awesome powers.

"I'll try to explain what I mean first in the technical language of philosophy, which I was forced to delve into in order to understand myself and my feelings fully. If you find this rather off-putting, Franklin, please try to remember that you natural scientists have many rather complex technical languages of your own! Then I'll try my best to translate what I say into jargon-free terminology. I've tried this out recently on Marco, and he at least pretended to agree that it made some sense—although I concede he may have been humoring me!"

Marco remarked, jocularly, "Over the years my mother has turned me into an excellent sounding board."

"In what I'm about to say, I'll use the pronoun 'I' to stand for me, my sisters, and the entire Second Generation cohort—all of those in our midst who have been engineered to the specifications of a plan. I'm not referring to me alone; it's just a more dramatic form of referent. Here goes.

"I already said that I'm the authentic product of the entirety of your modern science, which is itself grounded in the will to dominate nature. That will expresses itself in purest form in your acceptance of your right to re-engineer all living things, including, of course, yourselves. We've been over that ground already.

"And here comes the new part: Inasmuch as I am the authentic product of this will and this science, I am also and at the same time its authentic self-cancellation and self-transcendence. No, let me restate my thought with more preci-

sion: Insofar as I am the product of a purely internally generated process of discovery and innovation, within the scope of
modern science itself, and inasmuch as I preserve that
process in my being, I am also its own internally generated
self-cancellation."

"I can't speak for our resident sounding board, Marco, or
the others here," he remarked, laughing. "Maybe it's my
advancing age or just the lateness of the hour. But I confess
I haven't the foggiest idea of what you're talking about!"

"I was ready for you, Franklin," I replied, laughing with
him. "So here's the plain language version. You have no difficulty with the first part, I'm sure: Modern science evolved
after the seventeenth century as what is sometimes called an
autonomous institutional subsystem within modern society. I
think we discussed this on another occasion. Science made a
bargain with society, or, more specifically, with the church
authorities who then controlled such matters on behalf of
the secular state.

"The terms of the deal were as follows. Scientists said to
the church, 'Leave us alone, as we go about creating a new
representation of the laws of nature. Don't bother us about
whether or not our view of how nature works is consistent
with your religious dogma. Let's just co-exist together as
independent subsystems within the framework of a larger
social order. If you agree to do this, we'll promise in turn not
to overtly challenge the bases of your faith.' We shouldn't
worry right now about why the other side—the church—
agreed to this deal. Basically, as far as I'm concerned, the
churches had figured out early on that they could hold onto
their flocks of believers because the believers wouldn't be
able to find in a soulless science the kind of solace that faith
brings them.

"Anyway, the only relevant point here is that modern
science succeeded in freeing its system of ideas from outside
control. That's what I mean when I say that it became—

within the larger society—an autonomous subsystem. So now fast forward to the early twenty-first century and observe young Dr. Franklin Peter Stone hard at work in his laboratory. In his labors he is constrained by only one set of rules—the principles and methods of scientific investigation that have withstood the ongoing examination that he and his peers, and their predecessors and successors, have imposed on themselves over the course of a period of development spanning four hundred years.

"They're autonomous, these scientists. The discoveries and products that emerge from their workplaces are the authentic products of their system of knowledge, in the sense that no one else—no one who does not share their principles or concepts—has been allowed to interfere with their work. I am one of those products—an authentic product of your science. I literally incorporate in my body the results of that science. Thus I preserve it within me, in my very being as a biological entity on this earth. This is what I mean by saying that I am the authentic product of modern science. And the Second Generation—we very much hope—will pass on the traits you engineered in them and us for as long as our kind persists on earth.

"So far, so good. Here comes the harder part. Now I exist—as a self-conscious being. And suddenly I say to you, 'Stop! No more. The party's over. I don't accept your right—neither on practical nor ethical grounds—to attempt to change me again.' Note very carefully that what I've said is not just an *argument*—a logical sequence of theses—that I wish to put to you in order to see whether you'll accept either my reasons or my conclusions. For me, it's not only or even primarily a *proposition*, a syllogism that can be alternately defended and refuted by a skilled dialectician such as St. Thomas Aquinas. Rather, this is primarily a statement about my *being*, about what I *am* in and for myself, about my actual existence as another hominin who thinks and reasons much as you do, but who sees herself as a separate and distinct species.

"But you may say, for the purposes of discussion, 'Fine. I agree not to change you any more. But surely you have no right to object if I continue to introduce new manipulations into my own genome. Surely that's none of your business.'

"To which I would reply, 'Ah, but it is indeed my business. As some of you continue tinkering with your own genome, you may—accidentally or purposefully—bring into being another species, different from both of us. Remember, there isn't anyone exercising general control over all the experiments taking place on the planet. And this newly moulded creature may wish to dominate both you and me, and you may have given powers to it that enable it to do so. This I cannot permit.' The key to my argument is this, Franklin: What you and mother created were not new kinds of rats or rabbits, but rather a new order of *thinking, reasoning, self-conscious* beings! Now, using my reason and reflecting on my own being, I find in myself the urge to go my own way, separate from your kind. You didn't intend this to happen, of course, quite the opposite! But it did, somehow.

"And so I must, if I can, try to take your science away from you and put an end to your experiments, at least for a time, because, potentially, they pose a mortal threat to me. So in wishing to do this, father, I *am*—in the very essence and existence of my being as such—the self-cancellation of humanity's project to dominate nature through science.

"Think back to Milton's line again, which Tina recalled earlier tonight. Your science brought me into being; you formed me out of matter, as God did his Adam; you called me forth out of the nothingness—that's Milton's 'darkness'—into the light of existence and self-awareness. And now you have to deal with the consequences! Of course, by saying 'you' I am really referring to the human species as a whole. Our existence changes everything for you, as far as humanity's conception of the moral community is concerned.

"Now you are no longer alone on earth, undisturbed in your arrogant claim of rightful dominion over all other creatures. There's a competing self-conscious will set against *Homo sapiens*—as that species so modestly designated itself—by virtue of the existence of *Homo carstenszi*. And we're not intending to make you the same kind of overly generous offer that Frankenstein's monster proposed to his creator: 'Just grant me a mate of my own kind and the two of us promise not to bother you anymore; we'll disappear forever into the deserts of the new world.' We can't afford to be so humble in the face of your delicate sensibilities because we're deathly afraid of your well-known penchant for exterminating those who might compete with you.

"The fact of the matter is, your science—or at least what I fear that some of you may do with it—imperils my kind, so I must try to somehow neutralize that threat. Yes, Franklin, I'm well aware what the reaction would be should I go out into the central square in one of your great cities and proclaim this news to the stunned populace. Undoubtedly most of them would reply, 'We've got a simple solution to your little dilemma, lady. We'll snuff you out. End of problem.' Well, maybe they can, and maybe they can't. We'll see how it all turns out, won't we?"

I stopped, exhausted again by my long disquisition. Then I looked up and smiled. "I'm well aware I've built a pretty complicated argument for you tonight! My only excuse is that the stakes in this business are very, very high for us—quite simply, these are matters of life and death for the wonderful children of the Second Generation that we'll be raising soon. So I'll just recap the bottom line and then stop.

"Here it is. Because I am—in and for myself—the authentic product of the internal process of self-development within your science, as I said earlier, I preserve that process within my own being. On the other hand, and at the same time, my *being* demands an end to this process. Because it originates in me that demand is also the authentic, internally generated product of the science that created me. Therefore, I am at one and the same time both the self-preservation as well as the necessary self-cancellation of that project."

We were sitting close together on a couch; he touched me and said, "Hera, I do believe that I understand, at least partly, what you're trying to get at. Not fully, not yet. And please don't ask me whether I agree with you or not! I promise to mull over what you've told us. And then we can talk again. I'd like to do that, really I would! But let me just add one further comment, and then I really must go and get some sleep. Nothing exhausts me more, it appears, than your artful confabulations!

"Okay, I could, for the sake of argument, agree in principle with what you say. But you face an eminently practical reality. Your kind soon will amount to about a thousand in all, mere babies at that. Its numbers will not increase for another twenty years or so, more or less. We humans count ourselves in the billions, although the total seems to have peaked two decades ago. Whatever; the figures speak for themselves. You face overwhelming odds. You can't possibly succeed in your mission, purely as a practical matter."

I took his hand. "And here my final comment for tonight will be that I agree with you. I cannot even imagine how we could possibly succeed. Our chances are so vanishingly small as to be off the scale of probabilities. Almost certainly my kind is doomed. Like Icarus we may soar to the heavens on the wings of the special abilities you engineered in us, but like that foolish flyer we will be carried by our talents too close to the sun's heat. Our golden wings will melt and we will plunge to our deaths. This is what I see. Only one thing is as certain as our fate. And that is, that we must try to avoid it, however hopeless that endeavor seems to be.

"There is one more extremely important point: These conversations must be kept in absolute confidence among the six of us, until we agree otherwise. Our very lives may depend on it. Are you all willing to take such an oath?"

They all nodded and Franklin spoke. "Hera, Gaia, Percy, Athena, Marco—I am on your side now. I fully accept everything that flows from my role as your creator. I must draw the necessary conclusions from that acceptance, and I have. I will do whatever is in my power to help and protect you. I will keep your secret and take it to my grave."

"Thank you so much, father dear," I said, embracing him as everyone stood. "And now good night to you all. I have abused my own hospitality shamelessly in forcing you to endure this grim conversation. Tomorrow is another day. The sun will be shining. And at least for tomorrow we'll resolve to avoid approaching it too closely."

§   §   §

(07 July 2046) During the last three weeks the doctors have delivered well over a thousand live births of healthy children. The biologist group and the complement of nurses they're overseeing have been incredibly busy!

11 AUGUST 2047, MARCO'S JOURNAL

The storm-driven sea surges were particularly severe throughout the long hurricane season last summer and fall. Our main primate sanctuary, built on the leeward side of West Caicos Island, had good protection from the howling winds, but the margin of safety for all our installations here has been eroding with each passing year. The human populations, including those under the Sujana Foundation's care, were quickly coming to the same conclusion as the apes: It was time to consider new quarters on higher ground. Unlike their human counterparts, the apes were not spending a lot of energy arguing whether the blame for climate change should lie on their own shoulders or those of Mother Nature.

The message came from General Ziegler's office forty-eight hours ago: "Be packed and ready to move in three days." He'd had advance warning of another possible ice-sheet collapse that could occur anytime within the next six months. Further delay in getting off the Islands could not be justified. We were ready by the deadline since most of our personal belongings and office records were already crated. Dozens of shipping containers and trailers had been leased and stored on the grounds of our two main compounds, and the crates were already packed inside them.

Yesterday two ships arrived, a freighter and one of the smaller cruise ships. The latter can be picked up for next to nothing in the resale markets these days, since few people want to go anywhere near the oceans if relaxation is their objective. All of the foundation's personnel fit nicely into its comfortable cabins. The freighter's last stop, after taking on the cargo and the horses, was West Caicos Island, where the primates were grouped in large pens ready to be loaded by a crane onto its deck.

The younger and livelier ones had been mildly sedated for the first phase of the trip. I watched over everything, admittedly nervous should anything go wrong, and I was greatly relieved when it didn't. I kept a lookout for the western lowland gorillas as one by one the loaded pens swung by me on their way up. I think that among all creatures upon which humans had ever bestowed scientific names, these apes own the best: *Gorilla gorilla gorilla.* And I gave special greetings to Lucy as the pen holding her and her group of bonobos settled on deck.

Hera, Tina, Gaia, Magnus and I stood together along the deck railing as the cruise ship sailed out of Providenciales harbor. The place and the people of the Turks and Caicos Islands had been good to us, as had those of southwestern Alberta. As we steamed away, the United Nations officials were just landing at the airport, there to negotiate the final stage of population resettlement off the Islands. All of the low-lying Caribbean island groups would be swept clean of their last remaining human and animal residents over the course of the coming months.

Alas, Franklin was not with us. As I stood at the ship's railing I thought back to the time, about six months ago, when he finally succumbed to the effects of his second severe heart attack. Hera had waited at his bedside in the hospital as his last days slipped away. He was semi-comatose much of the time, and for the periods when he was awake and alert, Hera sat by him, holding his hands, talking mostly of the days in Tembagapura. When Franklin answered he spoke of nothing else except his too-few years with Ina, the excitement of their joint scientific discoveries, the beginnings of their great idea, and her tragic death. I think that Hera felt she and her father had achieved peace with each other. He died one night in his sleep, and Hera had the urn with his ashes—as well as another holding her mother's ashes, which Franklin had given her before he died—among her belongings below deck.

Hera had Troglodyte Partners send a note into the electronic void to Io about their father's passing, never expecting a reply.

§   §   §

(Hera's Journal, 14 August) I didn't sleep a wink last night. Late yesterday afternoon, just after we had embarked, the Troglodyte girls delivered a note to me—from Io. My worst fears have been confirmed. I called Phil on the satellite phone and read it to him. He didn't say much, except to reassure me that his team was maintaining a round-the-clock watch on the Hidden Kingdom. He appears to be satisfied with how his plan is playing out, since, as he put it, a fair number of the world's rogue biologists had decamped to Bali since Io set up shop there and issued her call to them.

Of course, it cannot be the same for me. My sister is being used as bait in a trap! Shouldn't I have had her institutionalized instead of allowing her to think she was escaping from Salt Cay? But on what grounds? A few pages of madcap scribbling out of a journal for which she could have denied authorship? Is it still my responsibility to decide these things? No, not anymore. I can let go now. Still, the note is so awful I can't get it out of my mind.

"Dear Sister Hera: So, father is dead. I know that he wanted to accompany me when I was delivered at last from your island prison, but you managed to stop him. He would have been happy here with me. After many years of listening to your lies about me, he was finally able to connect with me during our last summer together, before your little *coup d'état*. With my help he was finally learning to see how you were busily destroying his life's work, but it was too late; he couldn't prevent it. I suppose you had him burned up in some sordid little crematorium in Provo. If he had been with me, he would have had a great funeral pyre; many would have gladly sacrificed themselves at my request to accompany his soul through the underworld. My people are happy to do these things when they know I wish it.

"PS: You may be interested also in the attached note, which I am sending to all my sisters who are still held in captivity by you in the Caribbean."

"My Dear Sisters: The time for lies is over. Of all the falsehoods we were fed by Sister Hera over the years, the greatest is the one that told of Max Klamm's death. How happy we all felt when the news came! How grateful we all were to her for delivering us from the hands of this dark lord! But you must now have the truth: He is not dead; Hera didn't have him killed after all, despite what she told us. He is here, in Bali, still searching for me, still seeking to harm me. And not just one of him. He has cloned himself; there are dozens, maybe more, all the same, all wicked. But he failed to reckon with my power.

"Each week one of his copies is brought bound in chains into my arena, where my people gather to worship me and watch me deal with the wicked. My warriors make sure that he dies slowly, that he suffers as he has made me suffer. Then the next week, and the next, we bring another one of the copies we have captured, and the process is repeated. Years will go by, but slowly we will take into custody every one of the copies, until the last one appears before me, and begs for mercy. That one I shall dispatch with my own sword. Then it will be over."

Both notes were signed, "Princess Sagung Wah."

Gaia was standing on deck, reading the two notes with me. "What is she raving about?" I asked. "There is no way that Klamm escaped his captors. What is this business about cloning?"

She put her arm around me, tenderly. "Think it through. Io is psychotic, Hera; she's hallucinating, and I don't think it's being caused by the cocaine and other stuff she's undoubtedly ingesting. These are signs of paranoid schizo-phrenia, which among other things causes distorted percep-tions; its victims often substitute, in their minds, imaginary persons for real ones. Paranoid schizophrenics have been known to murder the long-suffering parents who are caring for them, thinking them to be imposters."

"Oh my God," I screamed, and ran to my cabin.

§   §   §

(*Marco's Journal, 24 August*) We docked a few days ago some-where near Vandenberg Air Force Base after a pleasant trip through the Panama Canal and up the west coast. Our compound and the new primate facility are both located in an incredibly beautiful area at the head of Jalama Valley, situ-ated a short distance south of the town of Lompoc. This valley winds about fifteen miles west off Highway 1 toward the nearby ocean, and along the valley floor there are rich agricultural lands for farming and grazing assigned to one of the Hutterite colonies. As promised, Phil has done a wonderful job on the apes' new home, located deep in the ravines on the protected hillsides of our secluded spot. Our animals tolerated the sea passage well—it was nice and calm the entire way—and they appear to be delighted with their new digs. Their numbers are approaching 450, but we have lots of space into which they can expand.

We're located in an area known as the Central California Coast Ranges, which has abundant precipitation and a wonderfully mild climate, averaging 55° to 65°F year-round, thus making possible a long growing season. The vegetation is a mixture of open woodland, including coniferous forest—pine, blue oak, and juniper trees—shrubs, and meadows. Settlement in this area has been tightly controlled for many years, so there are lots of wild fauna about, including the California condor. Humans have been using the area for eight thousand years in total, and the prehistoric way of life among the Chumash tribes is shown in the area's famous rock-art paintings.

The sisters' private quarters are nothing short of spectacular—a series of two-story buildings, connected by walkways, done in the white stucco and red-tiled roofs of the area's Spanish heritage, and emplaced along the top of the last ridge in Jalama Valley, which overlooks a beach and the Pacific Ocean. The babies and their nurses are set up in some larger buildings nearby, lower down, close to the Colony's private, narrow-gauge railway that runs along the coastline. We and the apes are the valley's sole occupants, apart from the Hutterites; Phil wanted to create a large buffer zone south of the air force base, populated only by people he knows and trusts. Lucky us!

Our entry into the US was a smooth one, especially since the Vandenberg Harbor is on private property. To take care of the legal formalities, Phil had the Sujana Foundation declared a 'special member' of the Vandenberg Colony. Everyone on the foundation's list of personnel is covered by that membership, and we have all received our diplomatic passports, entitling us to move about freely anywhere in the United States if we so choose.

But Hera wants us to stay put for the time being, and there is certainly enough to do in getting resettled here. Gaia was named president of PathoGene—to 'keep an eye on things there,' as she put it. The corporation's dedicated space, including the joint-venture manufacturing facility, is now many times the size of what it was in Provo. The firm has completed its customized version of the microbial DNA sequencer that will be taken aboard the spaceships to Mars.

(19 October) Thank goodness we got off the Islands when we did! Two days ago the latest big piece of the West Antarctic Ice Sheet hit the water, and global sea levels rose again, virtually instantaneously. Adding up the totals over the last fifty years, sea levels around the world are more than one meter higher than they were at the beginning of this century. In the period since the last ice-sheet collapse in early 2045, some people had been creeping back into the coastal areas abandoned by the more timid, and this movement had been accelerating recently. Now they are on the run again, all around the world, and others further inland are joining them, not wanting to wait to be washed away instead.

Responding to the new waves of panic, Phil's command sealed off our entire area by closing Highway 1 at the termini of our perimeter fence, which are located at Pismo Beach on the northern end and Las Cruces on the southern. The land between Highway 1 and the ocean now falls under the quasi-military administrative authority of the Vandenberg Colony. Soon we will begin erecting a continuous security fence running along the far side of the highway and around the entire land perimeter of the Colony, with electronic monitors and computer-controlled cameras along its entire length. Our section of the highway needed only two small stretches added at either terminus, to take the perimeter wall right to the ocean. There are daily sweeps by jeep convoys along the highway, matched by periodic gunboat patrols along the oceanfront bordering on our territory. We are hunkered down in a true medieval principality, symbolically walled off and secured.

The last of the remaining members' families to assemble here are arriving daily by air and sea with their movable property and assets in tow. In addition to the Hutterite colony in our Jalama Valley, four other colonies are located within the territory and assigned to the former vegetable and flower-growing sections around the towns of Lompoc and Guadalupe. On the other hand, the vineyards near the town of Santa Maria remain outside our perimeter fence, which does not extend that far, but their owners have been made very sweet offers of protection, inducing them to stay put and continue their important activities.

Many governments around the globe continue to disintegrate under the twin pressures of terrorist-driven attacks and the impacts of sea-level rise. Huge population movements are continuing in the direction of any region still maintaining a modicum of political stability. At this point, there are almost no functioning national governments in much of Africa, Southeast Asia, the Middle East, Central Asia, and South America. China, India, and Russia are all under martial law. Japan, Australia, New Zealand, and some other still-functioning island states have 'no-go' zones under constant patrol at their 200-kilometer offshore perimeter lines, with standing orders to sink unauthorized vessels without warning. North America is sealed off near the Yucatan Peninsula.

Inside the United States and Canada, much of the central-western interior has been largely emptied out by persistent droughts. Many among the populations of southern and central California, squeezed between the rising seas on one side and the steaming deserts on the other, are moving northwards. Those that remain are being forced to consolidate into self-defense units in response to the first appearance of roving gangs of the hungry and dispossessed. Wherever a military base is still functioning, civilians are crowding up against its perimeter fences in search of protection. Cities are under siege as established residents try to fend off the swarms of the newly homeless.

(02 June 2048) This was one of the saddest and most difficult days of my life, because Magnus was put to sleep by the vet today. For me it was like losing a brother. He was diagnosed with cancer only a week ago and nothing could be done. Thank God there was a litter of his puppies a year ago. We're well into the training regime for Magnus Junior.

Phil had me named as his executive assistant last week. Recently I've had a chance to observe the comings and goings of the members' families, since Phil has been including me on his rounds and taking me to briefing sessions. I must say, I don't much like what I see, especially among the younger crowd, the idle sons and daughters of the patriarchs whose vast fortunes are represented here. There's already a fair amount of friction between them and the local resident population, who have been persuaded to stay on here after being offered security in return for what amounts to joining the ranks of servants. In their countries of origin the younger rich are used to treating their servants and the rest of the population as just one notch above insect life, and nothing has changed now that they're here.

A group of teenage males from members' families has taken to calling itself the 'Chumash Warriors,' after the name of the aboriginal tribe whose land this was before the Spanish came. Everyone in the military here holds them in contempt, since the only actual warfare they engage in is the one they wage nightly with chemical mixtures against the neurons in their own brains. They've already killed some farm animals and injured a couple of youngsters by speeding around in their expensive sports cars at night, drunk and high. There's been one extremely ugly incident involving a Hutterite teenage girl, where the alleged assaulter wound up impaled on the side of a barn with a pitchfork put through the flesh of his upper arm by the girl's father. Strenuous re-education efforts were necessary to impress upon the wastrels the fact that some people take their religion seriously.

But it's the drug business that's shaping up to be the first big test for the Colony's senior administration. A number of the members are themselves former representatives of some of the most active drug cartels on the planet. As I understand the way things work in their home countries, most of the younger generation who moved here were accustomed not only to easy access to all the drugs of choice, but complete immunity for their actions from the authorities as well.

Phil's security apparatus assumed that large quantities of the whole spectrum of natural and man-made psychoactive substances would be trucked in with the members' household goods. They were prepared to look the other way at anything taking place within the borders of a member's own private compound. They even resolved to tolerate the occasional appearances of fast cigarette boats pulling in from the coastal waterways at the territory's more remote beaches. But they drew the line when light planes were commissioned to search out new supplies in the surrounding communities and ferry them back to the Colony via the base's runways.

After Phil's detail confiscated the third lot of chemicals from the holds of a small plane, an emergency board of directors meeting was called and I was asked to attend. It seems that the original slate of directors still make up a slight majority on the board. Most of them have known Phil for a long time and had in fact recruited him as leader of the Colony. None of them was drawn from the ranks of the drug lords or even of the newly wealthy. They all represent various forms of old money and know how to pursue their vices with discretion, out of the limelight. They're solidly behind Phil and gave him the vote of confidence that he demanded. He thanked them but insisted that they rein in the Chumash Warriors, and they agreed to do so.

(18 July) There was a serious incident about ten days ago. The base security detail apprehended a group of the Chumash Warriors in the act of collecting a large supply of drugs air-dropped into a remote corner of the Colony's territory. They were arrested and thrown into a military brig, and on Phil's orders their families weren't notified as to their whereabouts for about three days. The basic problem is clear to everyone. Although the members of the older generation are extremely grateful to have found refuge with the Vandenberg Colony, the younger ones, used to roaming their own countries like feudal lords and jet-setting to every pricey resort on the globe, began to develop acute boredom within a week of arriving. Although some of them still fly out to entertainment spots around the world, the fact that murder rates have been rising steadily wherever the rich congregate relatively unprotected keeps most of them close to home.

So the more timid among them have had a series of nightclubs constructed within the territory where, apparently, anything goes during all-night revels. The authorities tolerate this as long as the excesses are kept indoors and do not involve anyone from the Hutterite colonies. They regard the regular deaths from drug overdoses as strictly a family affair, confining their own responsibilities to collecting and delivering the bodies in the morning. Phil told me that if I needed help imagining what occurs in these buildings I should go on the Internet and buy a copy of *Satyricon*, an old film by Federico Fellini.

These recent events led to a nasty blow-up at another emergency meeting of the Colony's board a few days after the Chumash Warriors were released from the brig. A couple of the directors representing the members have rotated recently, and the new ones are drawn from the ranks of the less-refined elements among the wealthy. One had a son among the group that was arrested. They attacked Phil for his handling of the incident and demanded assurances that it wouldn't happen again.

Phil put his resignation as president on the table in reply. This scared the rest of the directors sufficiently and the board again passed a motion of full confidence in him. But it wasn't unanimous this time, and the losers vowed to continue their campaign for what they called 'reform' of the Colony's legal structure. My guess is that there's trouble ahead for everyone.

§ § §

(*Hera's Journal, 23 September*) Phil and I met today for the first time in weeks; both of us have been impossibly busy. He insisted we take the day off and announced that our schedule of activities would be a surprise. So early that morning, with Phil at the controls, I climbed into the co-pilot's seat of the vintage P-61 Black Widow fighter aircraft that he had helped to restore. He said he would have preferred to show-off for me in one of the US Air Force's newest fighter jets, but in that case I would be flying so high and so fast I wouldn't have seen anything except the radar monitor.

We flew east and north, first over the Sierra Madre Mountains, then past Bakersfield, over the Sequoia National Forest and on into desert country. As we were dropping down in altitude on the southeastern side of the Sierra Nevada Mountains, he pointed out the route of the Los Angeles Aqueduct, running almost 300 miles along the eastern slope of the mountains on its incredible journey from Owens Valley to the distant thirsty city. When the watercourse began to be sabotaged and water was diverted at many points along the way over the last five years, the City of the Angels had begun to slowly unravel backwards in time toward its origins, like a movie run in reverse. We flew on over Death Valley National Park and into Nevada, where he circled a mountaintop close to the state's border with California before landing for refuelling at Nellis Air Force Base, located outside Las Vegas.

"That was Yucca Mountain we circled, Hera. I've just been handed responsibility for exploring the creation of a public-private partnership to manage the facility located there. It seems that success breeds only further duties. People in Washington, DC, like the model of the Vandenberg Colony and want to recreate something like it here in Nevada. Of course, the fact that revenues from the Colony make such a nice contribution to the air force budget each year may have something to do with the desire to repeat it. The people at Nellis, who provide standing air cover for the Yucca facility, want to get on the gravy train."

"What on earth could there be of such value inside that mountain? All I saw were a few roads and a railroad line leading in and out of it, apparently going underground. Are they mining gold or something there?"

"It's not what's coming out of the mountain, but what's been going into it that's of high value. I surmise from your ignorance about this well-publicized project that you've been otherwise preoccupied during your life. In underground caverns beneath that mountaintop is the largest single repository of high-level nuclear waste in the world. Stuff that the US government says needs to be hidden away in secure storage for about 100,000 years."

"Will you have to relocate to Nellis for this new assignment?"

"No, at least not for a while yet. There's far too much still to do at Vandenberg. And there's a lot of pressure on me to get the Mars Expedition off the ground, so to speak. The logistics are rather daunting, as you can imagine."

"I've never asked you whether you're leading the mission to Mars. I'm not sure I want to ask even now."

He looked at me and smiled. "I've always been scheduled to go. But I'm not getting any younger. You know, it used to take anywhere from one to two years to get to Mars from earth, depending on the launch trajectory and the alignment of the planets. Now the journey can be done in about three months, thanks to the fast nuclear-powered space shuttles that take off from and return to the huge international space station orbiting the earth. But I can't get the mission into space in less than three years at the earliest. I'll probably be too old to join them when the rocket finally blasts off."

Good, I thought to myself, and quickly changed the subject. "What kind of partnership will you be looking for in the case of Yucca? I can't imagine that a bunch of rich folks will want to be plunked down in what looks pretty much like a wasteland from the air. Some of your new friends appear to be having trouble getting adjusted to life on the Central California coast. I'm not sure why. I think it's lovely there."

"So do I. As for Yucca, obviously only a very special sort of people might be interested. The government thinks it needs some kind of settlement to be established there in order to babysit the waste over a very long time. It's the same kind of deal as Vandenberg, essentially. The federal government spent a king's ransom on the waste repository over a period of about fifty years. They'll be emplacing the last few shipments inside within the next six months.

"But there is absolutely no more government money left to create an infrastructure for a settlement. That's where the partnership comes in. In return for a guarantee of air cover from Nellis—we pledge to blast the shit out of anyone who comes near the place uninvited—the private partner builds a permanent settlement and gets first dibs on water rights in the surrounding area for irrigation. All the legal niceties will be taken care of in return for cash."

"An interesting proposition for someone who needs a lot of solitude. What's the time frame?"

"I don't have a decision yet on that. There's not a big hurry, since we're here in the forbidding desert, and there's not a lot of foot traffic anymore, or even vehicle traffic for that matter. In any case, more on that later. We'll have a drink here at the base with some of my friends and then I have to get back."

§   §   §

(Marco's Journal, 10 November) The P-61 Black Widow is the only fighter plane ever made to seat three people, and clearly Phil loves to fly it. Two weeks ago he took Hera and me out at the crack of dawn one morning and flew us over almost the entire length of the Sierra Nevada range before landing at a restricted military airbase east of Reno, Nevada. There he picked up a jeep and a picnic hamper and we headed out into the surrounding hills. After lunch he turned to Hera and said, "I think it's time we put the Hidden Kingdom out of business."

I knew what was coming because he had raised the subject with me a week earlier and gave me some recent surveillance videodiscs to watch. His team had been set up for the last three months in a hideout on a neighboring mountain overlooking Io's encampment. Their long-range camera lenses were the best that money could buy, and they had photos from the orbiting satellites as well. Earlier they had installed sensitive listening devices in the dense forest near the compound and the arena. The sound and visuals they recorded showed the proceedings almost as clearly as if they had been shot by a spectator at the arena. I took a copy back to my apartment to play it.

The ceremony at Io's arena that evening had begun at nightfall. There were flaming torches ringing the arena itself and on the stage that was set at one end. After the crowd had filtered in, already drunk or high or both, filling every seat and the standing areas as well, Io's procession entered from a doorway hidden somewhere behind the proscenium. Her entourage preceded her, dressed in blood-red costumes.

Then finally, born on a litter by a half-dozen male attendants, Io herself entered, dressed in sumptuous white garments, her hair long and flowing loose down over her shoulders, an unsheathed sword lying before her. She was no longer the Princess Sagung Wah; the standards carried alongside her litter identified her now as Durga, the Hindu goddess of death and disease, whom the ancient Balinese culture had adopted from India along with the religion. Io was then seated on an elevated white throne placed on the stage, while lower down her attendants were arranged in a semicircle in front of her.

Teams of dancers in garish costumes entertained the crowd for an hour or more. At a signal from one of the attendants, the first beast came through another portal in the arena wall. My God, she's scripted this literally from the Book of Revelation! I thought to myself as I watched. It was an enormous black bull, carrying over its shoulders, just behind its great horned head—which was bleeding from a wound—a large wooden sculpture representing a creature with seven heads and ten horns. It was followed by a ram, also bloodied.

There followed a procession of four bound men chained in a row, each bearing a painted image of the bull. When I stopped the disc for a moment and looked at a close-up shot of the men, I saw that each bore the number '666' on his forehead—it looked as if it had been freshly carved into the flesh. The chained men were forced to kneel behind a post placed in the ground in front of the stage. Another man, bound separately, was dragged out and secured to the post. Pointing to him, Io intoned, "This is Klamm, the Devil's servant. Tonight he will die."

At another signal from the stage, a second and larger group of men entered, loosely linked together at the waist with a rope but with their arms free, carrying machetes. They were large men and appeared restless or agitated, with a look on their faces that could only be described as a mixture in equal measure of pain and joy. Io announced, "Greet the Warriors of Durga." The crowd, supplied liberally with additional drink since taking their seats at the arena, howled in anticipation.

The warriors shouted and saluted Io. She raised her sword. When she lowered it, they advanced, screaming, on the man called Klamm and the others who bore the sign of the beast on their foreheads, and slowly butchered them.

As I watched the proceedings, the strains of Verdi's *Requiem Mass* passed through my memory, so I dug out my favorite recording of it. The first section, *"Requiem,"* ends slowly and very quietly, the chorus' voices barely audible as it closes. After a short pause the massed strings of the orchestra enter at full volume, a single note is repeated four times, then the full chorus joins the orchestra with matching intensity. Suddenly the massive kettledrums are struck, four thunderous beats in succession, each separated by a note from the strings, as the *"Dies Irae"* unfolds. The chorus sings:

> *This day, this day of wrath*
> *Shall consume the world in ashes.*
>
> *What trembling there shall be*
> *When the judge shall come*
> *To weigh everything strictly.*

*Death and nature are astonished
When all creation rises again
To answer in front of the judge.*

In the *"Liber scriptus,"* the chorus continues with the Latin text of the mass:

*When the judge takes his seat
All that is hidden shall appear,
Nothing will remain unavenged.*

The passage where the fearful striking of the timpani resounds four times returns at the end of the *"Confutatis,"* and for a final time toward the end of the mass in the *"Libera me."* The line "Nothing will remain unavenged" recoiled through my mind as those terrifying drumbeats sounded. I found myself thinking, 'Is there anyone who cannot hear there the cry for justice from the nameless victims of history's stupendous crimes, or the sense of satisfaction at the Bible's promise that revenge will be exacted on the perpetrators at the end of days?'

As I put the memory of those dreadful scenes out of my head, Phil said to Hera, "Marco has seen a recording of a recent ceremony held at the arena. Io presides at these ceremonies, which occur every other night. I don't think you should watch it, but you can if you want to. It's pretty ugly."

She replied, almost inaudibly, tears streaming from her eyes, "No, I don't want to watch it. My imagination will suffice, thank you. I think I'd prefer to remember Io as she was in Tembagapura, the beautiful child with the flashing intelligence, witty, quick-witted, her mind racing across bodies of knowledge, the entire universe open before her. Even then there were unmistakable signs something was not quite right. She absorbed everything, and yet simultaneously boiled it down, reducing the mixture to the simple opposition of elementary contrasts—black and white.

"Everything she transcribed into her mind simply made that one pattern reappear more vividly. I argued with her, 'Io, listen. I've read that the truth is colored in gray on gray, not in black and white.' And she answered scornfully, 'That's ridiculous, Hera. How could ordinary people see the truth if it were presented to them in shades of gray? They need the unmistakable contrast of black and white. They don't have time for subtleties. They need to grasp the truth quickly and then to follow the correct path, almost without thinking.' Perhaps I should have tried to help her more then. But how? I was only a child myself; I didn't even understand what was going on in my own mind, so how could I try to fathom hers? I have to close that book for myself now. Done!"

She lapsed into silence. I thought I could imagine what was going on inside her head because for at least a year she and I had hashed out the 'Io problem' to the point of mutual exhaustion. I suspected she was wrestling again with her guilt, and that it concerned not Io so much as the innocents who were allowed to fall into her hands. I imagined she was asking herself why she had agreed to that risky plan of allowing Io to escape to Bali in the first place. And I knew the answer she gave herself as well. Hera had hoped against hope that Io would just go to Bali and find some private amusements to occupy her for the rest of her life. Some of the locals paid a heavy price so she could indulge herself in this illusion for a while.

I looked at her. "Sometimes I wonder if the names bestowed on us are more meaningful than we think. Did you know, mother, that Io is the name given by astronomers to one of Jupiter's four moons? More to the point, Io is the most volcanically active body in our entire solar system, a seething cauldron of violent heat and energy. Strange, isn't it?"

She didn't answer. Then Phil remarked, "The so-called Warriors of Durga appear to be a rather crude piece of engineering, but we don't know what else is going on inside those laboratories. It seems we've pretty much succeeded in collecting in that spot all the rogue scientists who are likely to make the pilgrimage to the jungle outside Amlapura. In all good conscience, we cannot allow Io and her helpers to go on playing with their experimental subjects and staging those shows in the arena."

Hera appeared to be resigned, sad and relieved in equal measure. "No. You can put an end to it if that's what you want to do, Phil. But get Io out of there first, as we agreed. Please have her taken to the house in Tabanan we've prepared for her and keep a close watch on her there. Now let's fly home so we can get Marco ready for his trip."

We flew back to Vandenberg by a different route, first west and south until we were overhead Monterey, then turning due south, flying high above the topline of the Coast Ranges.

Upon landing Hera and I at once put in motion the rescue plan we had scripted. I collected the psychiatric specialist and nurse—medical staff under contract to the foundation—we had briefed earlier. The three of us packed our bags hurriedly and caught a military flight headed out of Vandenberg on a routine mission to Jakarta, where we transferred to a commercial flight for the short trip to Denpasar. Once in Bali we made a beeline for the town of Tabanan where we relieved, with thanks, the minders from the surveillance team. They had been keeping Io under observation since slipping into her compound under cover of darkness, sedating her, and flying her by helicopter out of the jungle that very morning.

At our briefing meeting with the medical staff, Hera handed them a document. "Inside is a long handwritten letter from me, addressed to Io. In it, I ask her to allow herself to be put under your care and taken to a private clinic in Denpasar for observation and treatment. I have described some of her symptoms to you, and you suggested she would benefit from anti-psychotic medication; of course, this is subject to confirmation through a proper diagnosis once you've had a chance to examine her. If she cooperates, then prescribe a course of treatment to be carried out at the clinic. I have informed her in my letter that when she is well enough to leave the clinic, she is welcome to travel to the Sujana estate in the countryside, where the family will be awaiting her and where she can stay in their guesthouse for as long as she wants. I ended by saying that it was my fervent hope she will rejoin the band of sisters in California just as soon as she feels well enough to do so."

When our trio arrived at the little cottage where she had been taken, Io was still semi-comatose, undoubtedly the result of the sedatives combined with whatever other drugs she had ingested recently. I dropped off the doctor and nurse, who started to work immediately on their patient, and returned by helicopter to the surveillance team's base a few miles from the encampment. The team reported that everything seemed to be calm there, and that her colleagues were probably unaware that Io was even gone, since on earlier occasions they had seen her disappear from public view for days at a time.

On the following day in early morning, while the Hidden Kingdom still slept, recovering from the previous night's debaucheries, I was a passenger in a small military spotter plane circling high above the camp, marking the precise location coordinates of the fenced-off compound, reserved for the group of rogue scientists, that was set some distance away from other dwellings and the arena. The coordinates were radioed from our spotter plane to the submarine moving slowly through the Lombok Strait. The salvo of Tomahawk missiles it launched struck the target compound without warning. The local people in the nearby huts fled at the first explosions. Later, when the fires had died down, the recon team slipped back in to inspect the ruins, finding some records in a fireproof container that were then carefully preserved and sent to Hera through Phil's office.

§   §   §

(Hera's Journal, 23 May 2049) A few months ago I asked Phil to move into my suite overlooking Jalama Beach, and I was overjoyed when he agreed. Now I must tell him everything, make a clean breast of things, and hope for the best.

Early every morning we take the feisty Magnus Junior on long walks back and forth along the beach that stretches for about a mile along the shoreline below our compound. I asked him to listen to my whole story, starting with my parents' dream to engineer superior humans to help save the world, through our childhood in Tembagapura and the revelation about Klamm's awful scheme, then our flight to Alberta and the years at the missionary college there, right down to collecting my father in England and setting up our operation in the Turks and Caicos Islands. I told him a little bit about my father's scientific protocol, but he didn't seem interested in the details.

"I'm a military lifer, Hera. I don't know anything about neurobiology and am unlikely ever to learn. I like you the way you are, so whatever your father did couldn't have been all bad."

I stopped there and waited until he had reciprocated with his own life story, although he had tried to evade doing so by maintaining that it was horribly boring by comparison with mine. But I insisted and he complied. In a way he also was the victim of a dream that had soured. He started out by conceiving a plan to build a fortress somewhere, amidst the enveloping social chaos, that would be strong enough to preserve some important human values while the world went through its paroxysm.

But for reasons he couldn't quite articulate, his project started to veer off-track and he could never right it again. By the time the members started piling into their compounds at Vandenberg, he realized it was not going to turn out well, but at that point the project had its own momentum and he couldn't deflect it. Under some duress he had agreed recently to stay on as a member of the Colony's board of directors, in return for a confirmation of our entitlement to occupy the Jalama Valley area indefinitely.

"It's great that we can stay here in this lovely valley, Phil—I've been counting on that—but I'm afraid it doesn't serve all of my own purposes or those of my foundation in the longer term. I and my sisters and associates are very grateful to you, of course, for plucking us out of the Caribbean just ahead of the rising waters." I paused briefly, but not long enough for him to say anything. "I've been waiting for a good time to tell you this, Phil. I want to buy into the Yucca Mountain facility as the private partner and build a secure settlement there for my tribe.

"I want to move most of my entourage there, including some of the apes, although we'll have to protect them and us from the extreme heat. If my plan works out, most of the apes will stay in Jalama Valley indefinitely with the professional staff who care for them. As long as things remain relatively peaceful in this vicinity, we could take the whole group of children back to Jalama from Yucca for the hottest part of the year—June through September. However, I have a feeling we'll be most secure at Yucca Mountain, so the rest of them will just have to get used to being in the desert for good at some point. I've been doing some reading about that general area. It seems many of the aboriginal peoples found that cave dwellings carved into the mountainsides provided quite comfortable abodes in that region. Maybe I can follow their example for my own settlement.

"There's one more thing. I want you to come with us

and live with me there."

"If I stick with my new assignment at Nellis, Hera, which I'm inclined to do, since I'm not quite ready to retire, nobody is going to object if I live off the base nearby."

"I hoped you would say that and I also hope that you won't change your mind when you hear the final chapter of my story. I have to be honest, I'm afraid you might. But what can I do? I can't alter my own course now, as you'll see when I've related the story. Let me tell you the whole thing before you react, OK?"

"I can't imagine what could be that earth-shaking, but I'll hear you out."

So I told him everything, about discovering hybrid sterility, and about the decision I made to nurture a separate species who would keep themselves apart from humans, while demanding both the right to exist and the right to share another hominin's fair portion of the earth's resources. I told him why I feared what humans might do in the future with genetic engineering. I even confessed to him my silly illusion about being able to take science away from humans for a while, perhaps a long time, before restoring it to them. I told him these were all the reasons why Yucca Mountain was the perfect place for me to be. And I concluded by saying I hoped it wouldn't make such a difference to him that he would feel it necessary to rescind his agreement with me to share the rest of our lives together.

"I'm a practical person, not a theorist. I might have given you a different answer if I hadn't been through the experiences of the last few years at Vandenberg. I was always pretty much a naïve optimist about human nature, even as the world was descending into chaos and I was trying to figure out how to seal myself and my associates off from the decay. But I hit bottom in the last few months. I came face-to-face with some of the ugliest aspects of the human temperament on view anywhere. And that includes the escapades of your poor sister Io and her friends.

"The bottom line is if you think you have even the remotest chance of bringing something better into the world, why should I refuse to help you? You said that you don't want to go on the warpath against the rest of us, just to be left alone until you can deal with us on a more equal footing. And you admit that even with all the luck in the world you have only the barest chance of succeeding, because the mismatch in numbers is so overwhelmingly against you. That appeals to me, since I've always enjoyed a challenge.

"I can't actually help you very much, apart from putting the deal together to create the partnership with Nellis AFB. But I'll do what I can. And I want to be with you. I know all about your legendary determination. So if I want to live with you, I guess I'll have to inhabit a cave on Yucca Mountain. I've done lots of different things in my life, but cave dwelling is not yet one of them. But I do like new experiences. I'll be there."

§   §   §

(Hera's Journal, 20 December) A few days ago Phil presented me with a belated moving-in gift and early Christmas present. It was delivered by truck, and the gift turned out to be the entire truckload! He had heard me say that I wanted to build a safe storage vault at my Yucca Settlement for something special—the huge videodisc collection, issued by the Library of Congress, containing the complete record of modern science—all the journals, books, and detailed blueprints for scientific instrumentation. Only a few copies had been made available to private organizations. And now I had one of them.

This holiday season has also brought me a piece of very good news. Io has been discharged from the clinic and has traveled to the Sujana family estate. Our foundation's doctor has kept in regular contact with the clinic staff and flew to Denpasar for the examination that confirmed she was ready for a new phase of rehabilitation. Our nurse has been with her the entire time and will stay with her at the guesthouse. For the first time in many years I can begin to entertain the hope that we will be reunited with her in the not-so-distant future.

§   §   §

(Marco's Journal, 27 August 2050) Phil had been telling his staff for months that more delays could be expected before the Mars Expedition would depart. Some experiments being conducted on the orbiting space station, dealing with forming metal compounds in weightless conditions, had not yielded the desired results and would have to be redone. Recruitment of the prospective colonists from among the member families was also turning out to be a far greater problem than anticipated. Only by varying the allocation of the quota among members was it possible to put together a preliminary list.

Today he surprised them all by removing his name from the roster. "I'm well past my prime, as you all know," Phil announced after his staff was assembled, "and this expedition is going to need a full complement of the most energetic people that we have. I'll be canvassing for a replacement for myself over the next few months. If anyone here is interested, get your name on the list."

I'm interested, but I dare not tell anyone yet, especially not Hera. But I'll have to put my name down before the list closes.

§   §   §

(*Hera's Journal, 04 March 2051*) Today I signed the deal to become the private partner of Nellis AFB and to build a permanent settlement around the base of Yucca Mountain. I expect it will take four or five years to get everything built and us relocated, including one or two of the Hutterite colonies that will accompany us. I will transplant huge groves of mature trees—shade and date palms, citrus fruits and avocados, nut trees of all types, and cottonwoods—if I can get my hands on enough water for them. I'm working on this. On the whole, thank goodness, everything seems to be going well, so there's lots of time to plan carefully and get everything in place for reasonably comfortable habitation before we actually move to that hot place.

Just as I was finishing these relaxing thoughts Phil came to me with the news that Marco wants to join the Mars expedition. What a little coward he is that he couldn't tell me himself! Phil obviously felt awkward about being the news bearer, but actually, I shouldn't have been surprised. Marco hasn't been at all happy with the thought of moving to the desert, no matter how much I try to convince him that people have lived in those places for a long time. Maybe he's not really serious about this space travel plan, and is just trying to get back at me for planning to uproot our tribe from this lovely valley.

Part Four

To the Deserts
of the New World

19 JULY 2052, HERA'S JOURNAL

"Please come with me. Right away."

I had been waiting for Marco and Phil in Marco's office at the base's administrative center. Phil had flown in from Nellis that day and, after doing some business, was going to fly Marco and me from Vandenberg Air Force Base to the Yucca Mountain area for some site planning discussions. I was expecting the two of them to return from a meeting with some of Phil's former colleagues, which had been delayed due to Phil's late arrival, when the stranger suddenly appeared in the doorway.

To tell the truth I had been growing uneasy even before this encounter happened. For reasons I can't quite understand, my personal security instincts, which had never once failed me over a period of almost forty years, had counseled me not to meet up with Phil and Marco that day. But I relented. After all, I had reassured myself, no one's going to mess with the special friends of a four-star USAF general, are they?

Behind the stranger stood two armed members of the Colony's private security force. I was frozen in place.

"I'll say it just once more. Come with me. Now, please. Don't make me ask my friends to help you to comply." He then entered the room and took my arm, quite gently, and walked me down the corridor and out the building, where a number of vehicles were parked, their engines running. He opened the rear door of a black limousine with tinted glass, deposited me inside, and remained outside as he closed the door again. As soon as he did so, the vehicle accelerated. There were no interior door handles, and the driver was hidden behind a partition.

"I've just been kidnapped," I said aloud, although there was no one to hear.

The ride in the car took about half an hour, then I was blindfolded and whisked onto a waiting helicopter that flew for quite some time, more than an hour I supposed. Later I found I could no longer remember exactly what wild thoughts raced through my mind during that period. I'm sure they included fears for Marco's safety, and Phil's, as well as sheer bewilderment at this wholly unexpected turn of events. We were on Phil's former home territory. What on earth was going on? Then anger arose, directed at myself, for the sheer folly of leaving my secure sanctuary at Jalama in order to take the flight with Marco and Phil this morning. The copter finally landed, the door flung open and my blindfold removed, and there he was again, reaching inside to pull me out. He said nothing while he frog-marched me into a low building and then into a windowless basement office, closing the solid door behind us.

He pointed to some chairs and we both sat before he finally spoke again. "I've uncovered your dirty little secret." My gaze was impassive and, I'm quite sure, betrayed no reaction to the stranger's remark. He was smirking, I thought, the little asshole, just like a teenager recounting a first sexual escapade to some of his lowlife friends.

"You're intending to create a distinctive human subtype, aren't you?" the stranger blurted out. "Don't try to deny it. You won't allow your little tribe to interbreed with the rest of us. You want to isolate yourselves genetically until other people *can't* breed successfully with you. Even if we try to do so, and even conceive children, they'll all be sterile, just like mules. Am I right?"

I was absolutely certain I had never before laid eyes on the man who now sat opposite me. "Apparently, whoever you are, you don't believe in common courtesy," I replied, adding as much contempt to my voice as I could muster. "Most people introduce themselves to others they've never met before hurling bizarre accusations their way. Even kidnappers."

"Oh dear, please forgive my rudeness. I was just so excited to meet you at last that I couldn't help myself. I'm Dr. Jerry Bild and I'm a geneticist employed by some people associated with the Vandenberg Colony. But I already know who you are. You're the famous Hera. I've always been impressed by people who go by only one name, something that used to be common in Indonesia, where your mother comes from, I believe. You were plucked out of the Caribbean Sea some years back by General Ziegler and brought here with your curious broods of children and great apes. What a strange menagerie! Did you really think you could now just disappear into the desert with no one being the wiser?"

I sat there and looked at him for a few moments while I was trying to guess where all this banter was leading. "You've just kidnapped me and are restraining my movements by force. How do you know who I am? I don't see what business it is of yours what kind of entourage I have or where I choose to live. Since I don't intend to answer any of your questions, what is the point of this little exercise?"

"Ah, I was warned that you're a tough nut, just like your namesake, the ancient Greek goddess, who didn't tolerate being trifled with by Zeus, even if he was king of the gods!"

In the background my mind was racing. 'Where was Phil? How did this Dr. Bild know I was going to be at Marco's office today? How did he know about the circumstances of our arrival at the Vandenberg Colony and our planned move to Yucca Mountain?' Then I abruptly stopped that chain of thought, running in my interior voice. 'No, don't bother with those questions,' I said to myself. 'Somehow, he's discovered the only secret that really matters—my plan for the future of my kind. And his cocky demeanor shows that he believes he has the upper hand. Which can mean only one thing: Something has gone wrong and both Phil and I are in trouble. Serious trouble.'

I focused again on the stranger sitting opposite me. "Since you refuse to stop annoying me, can we get on to what you want, please? Surely you can't think that I'm at all interested in your display of familiarity with Greek mythology."

"Fine, why not? I represent a company founded by some of the wealthy members. They want to improve the overall genetic endowment of their future grandchildren, to give them a better chance of surviving and prospering in the chaotic world around us. I'm responsible for finding the most promising genetic manipulations for their project, and, of course, I've studied carefully your father's published scientific papers. But I didn't stop there. I guessed—I'm not even sure why—that he didn't just design gene therapies for mental disorders, which is what made him and the investors in his company, Wollstone Corporation, very rich indeed.

"I think he achieved much more, and that he did that part of it in secret because his scientific peers wouldn't have approved of what he did. If they had found him out, there's no way he would have been awarded a Nobel Prize, that's for sure. Anyway, I'm certain that he engineered you and your little tribe. I don't know where he worked on you and the other women in your cohort, whom I assume are your sisters or cousins. But I'm pretty sure that he engineered the big group of kids down in Jalama Valley—how old are they now, about seven or eight?—at your hideout in the Caribbean. That's where he died, right?"

"Cut it short, Dr. Bild," I said, with as much rudeness of my own as I could muster, attempting to cloak my state of extreme anxiety. "What do you want of me?"

"Right, then. It's simple. I want the scientific protocol that your father developed to create you and that big batch of kids—the one that he never published. That's all."

"There's no such protocol, and none of us was engineered, to use your word. You don't know what you're talking about. Now, will you take me back to where you found me?"

Bild laughed loudly and his tone changed at once. "Don't toy with me, Hera. Believe me, it'll be far better for you to cooperate fully with us. I'm sure we can come to a mutually beneficial arrangement, as they say. We don't expect you to help us without offering you some inducement or compensation in return."

I, too, changed my tone. "I want nothing whatsoever from you. This conversation is over."

He paused. "Of course, I anticipated that you would react like this. Tell you what, I'll give you a day to think it over, and we'll talk again tomorrow."

"Unfortunately that won't be possible," I shot back. "I'm leaving later today and I won't be back. Perhaps you'd like to write me a letter?"

"Unfortunately, as you put it, you'll be staying here awhile longer as our guest. Too bad we couldn't include that handsome lad Marco, too. By the way, is Marco really your son? I've picked up conflicting stories about that angle. In any event, you won't be leaving until I say so."

There was no way I could prevent my rising sense of alarm from inflecting my voice anymore. "Where is General Ziegler?"

"I don't know, actually, probably with his friends somewhere on the Vandenberg base. I'm sure he's fine. I'll try to arrange to put you two in touch with each other by phone—but not until you've come to your senses and agreed to cooperate with us."

So I reviewed my limited set of options while Bild watched and waited, since it would have been obvious to anyone what was running through my mind. Only two choices presented themselves. One was to refuse to engage in any more banter with my host and simply wait until I was rescued, either by Phil or someone else—assuming, of course, they knew where I was being held or could find me. But if that assumption proved wrong, I could be in for a long wait. The other was to cooperate—up to a point—and see if this approach actually would secure my freedom. If making the second choice resulted in some damage to the foundation's interests, perhaps I could figure out later how to mitigate that damage. I had already decided that I would agree to no terms that put anyone else in my entourage at risk, no matter what the personal cost turned out to be.

I returned his gaze. "All right, I know when I'm beaten. I'll give you what you're after. But I have to admit that I'm just a little bit curious, too. How did you find out about us, if you don't mind my asking?"

"Excellent! I knew you'd see reason." Clearly he was pleased with himself and couldn't resist a bit of boasting. "It was simple, really. As you are aware, some of the large staff contingent you've employed during your stay at your private camp in the Jalama Valley have drifted away over the years. Obviously, you couldn't compel them to stay with you. After I guessed what your father was really up to, I figured that the best way to explore my hypothesis was to find some of your ex-employees and interrogate them. I don't think my associates had to do much more than scare the shit out of them before they agreed to open up to me. You know how it's done—just let them know we've kidnapped their kids and will start experimenting on them unless they cooperate."

"What charming people you are," I remarked bitterly. "Didn't I hear you say that your clients want to improve the genetic heritage of their grandchildren? What's your plan, to make them better torturers and child molesters?"

"Very funny. Actually, we didn't have to do anything at all to the kids in order to make the parents sing. When I was finished talking with them, I was certain my guess was right. If you and your brood weren't engineered to be special, why the need for all the secrecy? Why segregate them from everybody else? Why give them special medical treatments during their early years, and a highly sophisticated learning environment? Given what your father was up to as a genetics researcher, no other hypothesis made sense."

I was about to speak when he rushed on. "But it was your new plan to pick up and move to the desert near Death Valley, lock, stock, and barrel, that convinced me there was something more going on. Why leave beautiful central California for that godforsaken wasteland? And why choose, of all places, a bloody high-level nuclear waste site for your new home?

"I drove out there once and got as close as I could without setting off any alarms. The whole periphery is plastered with scary signs! You don't want anybody coming within 100 miles of you. Why? The answer had to be that you intended to cut yourself off completely from the rest of us. And just interbreed among yourselves, creating your own little gene pool. Well, when I put two and two together, I decided I just had to dip into that pool for myself and my clients."

I held up a hand. "All right, you can save the full recounting of how clever you are for your memoirs, Dr. Bild. I've already told you I'm willing to make a deal. Let's just discuss your offer. I'm prepared to hand over my father's scientific protocol to you providing the terms are fair. Why not? You want to make more people like me. Why should I object to that?"

"Precisely. I'm glad you see it that way. So let's get down to brass tacks, shall we? There are secure communications facilities in this room. You can contact your base at Jalama

Valley and arrange to have the protocol delivered here. In the meantime we can complete our discussion of terms. I'll step outside so you can make the call now."

"Don't be ridiculous. I don't know what other demands you might make after you have your hands on the protocol. So I'm afraid I'll need to negotiate the terms of my release before I place any call."

"Right. I didn't really expect you to pick up the phone, but I thought, why not try it on? Anyway, I've already worked out a plan. And here's my proposal. You have the documents sent right away to Ziegler's office at Vandenberg while you remain here as our guest. Then tomorrow morning you and I, along with an armed security detail, will go to a rendezvous point where he—or someone he designates—can meet up with us. I'll have two attack helicopters and four heavily armed guards with me. Your people can bring exactly the same type of security detail so that we'll be on an equal footing. After we've done the exchange we can both be on our way. By the way, you should advise your people not to try anything funny—I'll have air cover from Vandenberg protecting my little fleet."

"You've neglected to mention my compensation, I believe. What do I get in return?"

Bild opened his briefcase and extracted a piece of paper. "I assume that, like everyone else in these troubled times, you prefer gold bullion as payment. We're prepared to offer you a stack of very nice gold bars, which we have with us in our helicopter. At the going rate of about 5,000 euros per ounce, they're worth about 9 million euros. I think that's an eminently fair price for Nobel-quality research, don't you?"

I let some time elapse before replying. I didn't want him to think I was too eager to end the discussion. "Make it an even 10 million and you've got yourself a deal."

"Done. Can we shake hands on it?" We did. His cell phone beeped; he chatted briefly and disconnected.

"Ziegler's apparently been spotted looking for you in the building where I picked you up. We'll have him paged and tell him to call the number of the cell phone that's on the desk there. I'll step outside and give you some privacy while you chat with him about the arrangements. Then I'll take you to the very comfortable suite reserved for you right here in this building, where you can relax until we leave for the rendezvous in the morning."

The phone rang a minute later and I answered.

"Hera? Where in God's name are you? Are you all right?"

I reassured him that I was, then related the first part of my story.

"Son of a bitch! It's the Colony people again. They must have bribed some officials to get passes for access to the base. I wonder if this is revenge against me for what I did to the drug-smuggling rings run by some of their kids?"

"I don't think so, Phil. It's about me. They want something from me, and I've already agreed to give it to them." I told him quickly about the bargain I had made, and the conditions of the arranged rendezvous.

"Is there no other option?" As he said this he realized that electronic eavesdropping equipment must be picking up our words. "Sorry, our communication is certainly being bugged, so forget I asked."

"Under the circumstances, I don't think I have a better option. I don't have a clue as to where I'm being held. If I survive this, I'll never forgive myself for my own stupidity. Anyway, I've already agreed to the deal and I'll live up to my part of it. I just want this ordeal to be over so that I can get safely back to Jalama. I'll send an encrypted e-mail message right now to Athena, who will open our vault and retrieve the videodiscs and documentation dealing with the protocol. Make sure the materials arrive at your office by this evening. I'll be fine. Our Dr. Bild said you should expect me to call you on your satellite phone very early tomorrow morning with the exact place and timing of the rendezvous. By the way, we'll be transferring about a quarter-tonne of gold bullion to one of our copters." I hesitated. "Phil, is Marco with you?"

"Yes, Hera dear, he's right here. Do you want to talk to him?"

"No, I'm too upset, and I'm afraid I'll burst into tears if I hear his voice, and I really don't want to do that right now. Just tell him I'm OK."

"I understand. Look, I'll take care of everything on this end. Try not to worry. Things should be fine, since you've agreed to give him what he's looking for."

Bild returned as soon as I rang off. "Everything arranged?"

"Yes. Now I need to send an e-mail message."

"Great. You'll find the facilities you need in your suite. I'll escort you there now."

Later that night, as I sat alone and afraid in my rooms, it occurred to me that I was separated from my main band of sisters for the first time in more than twenty years. My mind quickly took me back to the fall of 2031, when I had journeyed from Calgary to Jakarta to face my deadly duel with Max Klamm. How many perils did my little group surmount together in those years? And now this. What a fool I was to get myself into this trap! We'll never be able to survive in their midst. They'll find us—I've got proof of that now, and surely it'll happen again—and when they do, we'll be overpowered.

I knew that I wouldn't sleep that night. So after e-mailing Tina again to reassure her that things would turn out all right, I turned on my portable music player. There was a piece I needed to hear, right then and there, even though I've listened to it frequently for most of my adult life. I found the recording I loved most, featuring the Canadian tenor Ben Heppner. Then I waited as the opening notes of "The

Drinking-Song of Earth's Sorrow," the first section in Mahler's *Song of the Earth*, obliterated the silence, and I listened for the stanza I had just remembered:

> *The firmament is forever blue and the earth*
> *Will long endure and blossom each Spring.*
> *But you, Man, how long will you live?*
> *Not even a hundred years may you revel*
> *In all the rotting trinkets of this earth!*

Let them lust after expensive baubles in the marketplace, I thought as I listened, those pathetic signs of their superiority over others that are so longed-for on one day and then discarded indifferently on the next. Let them monkey with their genes, trying to prolong their life spans for a few decades or even a century longer. What will these few years count against the eons during which our beloved earth labored mightily to create a lush welcoming nest for its living creatures?

Later, when the last chords from the final song in Mahler's work had faded away, I knelt and prayed for the safety of my family sequestered at Jalama Valley. I had begun to do this on occasion in recent years, without even knowing why. But whenever the need came upon me, I was aware that the entity whom I addressed in my prayers was not any disembodied and vengeful deity from the pantheon of the world's great religions. Mine was the spirit of the earth, source of all beings, who sheltered them in her warm bosom against the dark and bitter cold of the infinite spaces all around them. Why would one need any other god but her?

If things go wrong tomorrow, I will be prepared for what I will have to do. The suicide apparatus I always carry with me will ensure that I could not be held further against my will or be forced to cooperate with some other, deadlier scheme. But if by some miracle I am delivered from the hands of my enemies and returned safely to my tribe, I swear I will never again make a similar mistake. I will not set foot outside my own secure territory hereafter.

§ § §

It was not yet mid-morning and the air was still cool when the four helicopters touched down at Panamint Flat Dry Lake, just outside the hamlet of Ballarat, on the western edge of Death Valley National Monument. I realized at once why Bild had chosen this remote spot for his rendezvous: There was excellent visibility in all directions. At first the two support teams approached each other warily, but Bild and I both tried to put everyone at ease, relaying a greeting over the radio that explained this was an exchange for mutual benefit. Then I saw Phil disembark and my heart soared. I recalled that in our phone conversation he didn't promise to be on this mission, and I understood why—the whole episode might have been designed to ambush him, with me as the bait. I remained with Bild; three of his armed guards stood outside while the fourth started to help Phil's group transfer the gold bullion. Other aircraft could be heard in the vicinity, and I assumed this was the air cover that Bild said he had arranged.

Phil, who had walked over to the copter where we sat and casually tossed a satchel inside to Bild, didn't attempt to make eye contact with me, which strangely enough set me at ease. While I watched, willing myself to stay calm, Bild opened the satchel and removed a videodisc that he put into his reader. He then scanned the hard-copy documentation, quickly ascertaining that the scientific protocol before him was indeed Franklin Stone's handiwork. At this point he indicated with a wave of his hand that I could exit and move to one of Phil's helicopters, and I was then once again under the protection of my own security personnel.

As I crossed the ground between the two machines, Phil neither approached nor even appeared to pay the slightest attention to my movements. He seemed to be quite engrossed in verifying the count of gold bars. How odd! A few minutes later Bild sent one of his henchmen over with a message, saying that he made several copies of the videodisc and was returning the original to me—with a message that his team was ready to depart according to the routine previously arranged. Meanwhile, the entire cache of bullion had been reloaded into our second machine.

Phil boarded our helicopter and, before I could say anything, motioned for me to stop. He took the co-pilot's seat without saying a word and put on his helmet. One copter on each side stood guard, with its missiles ready to fire, as the other two, carrying Bild in one and Phil and me in the other, took off and turned in opposite directions. As soon as we were airborne, Phil was on the radio: "Desert Fox to Viper's Nest. Come in please."

"This is Viper's Nest, Desert Fox. What can we do for you?"

"Take them down. Now."

"Roger. Over and out."

He said to the pilot, "Turn around and put us back down at the rendezvous point." He turned in his seat, smiled at me and gave me the thumbs-up sign. "Sorry, I have to monitor the rest of the radio transmissions. I'll explain everything in a few minutes."

We landed again and disembarked. After helping me out, he held me, tightly, in silence, for what seemed like a full minute. Finally he looked at me and said, "Your friend Dr. Bild has stumbled into a very nasty nest of vipers, I'm afraid. But they're not going to bite him, not yet anyway. He'll be coming back here for a chat with us in a few minutes."

I stared at him wordlessly. Then I collapsed on the ground and broke down; Phil sat next to me and held me as sobs wracked my body.

"Let it out," he said softly. Then he looked up at the sound of approaching helicopters.

As the first copter landed Phil ran to it and greeted the soldier who hopped out. They stood talking as the second machine touched down. Phil opened the door and roughly pulled at the figure inside, who tumbled out the door onto the ground. He couldn't break his fall because both his arms were bound tightly to his sides. He yelled as he hit the earth. Another figure still inside threw the satchel to Phil.

"Here's the loot we took from him. Is there anything else, or should we be going?"

"That's all for now, thanks, Katy. I'll talk to you later."

Phil hauled the bedraggled figure of Dr. Bild to his feet and marched him over to me. "Is this the culprit?"

"Yes."

He handed me the satchel. "Look inside and see if everything's accounted for."

I opened the bag and glanced at its contents. "It seems to be all here."

Finally Bild spoke. "I demand to be released at once. You have no authority to detain me. And when you see the size of the lawsuit I'm filing, your mood is going to change considerably."

Phil cuffed him on the side of the head, none too gently. "Shut up. Don't say another word until I tell you to." He turned to our crew. "Blindfold him and take him to the place I told you about on the way up here." Then he turned to me. "Let's go home."

§   §   §

Around dinnertime my fear had finally dissipated, and I was sitting on the veranda outside my suite at Jalama Beach with Marco, Tina and Gaia when Phil found me again later that evening. After we had touched down on our landing pad earlier, he kept the engines running and prepared to take off again, saying he would have to spend the rest of the day in the communications room back at Vandenberg. As soon as he walked in, I jumped up to hug him. "Please, I want the whole story. Right now. But help yourself to a drink first."

"You will have a full report, but I'll have to go back to the beginning and fill you in with some background." With drink in hand, Phil sat down in the chair next to me. "I was so uneasy about who at Vandenberg might have been involved in your kidnapping that after receiving your package, Marco and I flew back to Nellis. I spent all of last night on the videophones, mostly with Washington. Others besides me have been warning them for years that these privatization deals with the armed forces—such as the Vandenberg Colony, which is the biggest of them all—were going to blow up in their faces. Last night we brought it to a head. What happened two months ago in Florida really scared them, and this little episode finally tipped the balance.

"In Florida we narrowly averted a full-scale firefight between some heavily armed US marine battalions that had been seconded to a couple of large American corporations. The companies got into a bitter contract dispute over some lucrative work in the Caribbean; things escalated, and before anyone knew what was happening, the troops were being mobilized—against each other! At Vandenberg, as it turns out, for some time already some of the wealthiest members had been busily turning the base and its personnel into their own little private army. Among other deals, special passes to high-security areas on the base had been issued to the Colony administrators, which is how Bild managed to kidnap you. And he really did have air cover arranged for his helicopters."

"How did you manage to spoil his fun, Phil?"

"By midnight I had a commando team on the grounds of the Colony's administrative center; they were trying to trace your movements and figure out who had been involved. While they were on their way, I started dealing with Washington. At about 2am or thereabouts, just after I threatened to send a squadron from Nellis to bomb and strafe the Colony compound, everybody started looking for solutions. The prospect of an aerial dogfight between fighter wings from Nellis and Vandenberg concentrated everyone's mind in a hurry.

"Isn't it ironic? Think about it. You're now the official private partner of Nellis Air Force Base—a most important contributor to its financial bottom line—and you had been kidnapped by none other than people working for Vandenberg's private partner! A rather ugly mess, don't you think? I made it clear I wasn't going to wait around for a few years while expensive lawyers on both sides sorted things out. In fact, I wasn't prepared to wait for more than a few hours before putting my pilots into the air.

"To cut a long story short, just before dawn the base commander at Vandenberg AFB was summarily relieved of his duties and charged with accepting bribes. You're looking at the new head of the Joint Southwestern Air Command, comprising both bases and everything in between. Right after we had succeeded in rescuing you this morning, the Colony's entire administrative staff was put in detention by my commandos. They'll stay there until I have time to sort things out. Something tells me other priorities will keep me from attending to that task for some time yet."

"So your staff already had control of the airspace we flew through by the time Bild's helicopters left for the rendezvous this morning?"

"Yes, Hera. Once I had taken control of the entire military contingent at Vandenberg, it was far safer just to let the original plan proceed, rather than trying to locate and rescue you where you were being held prisoner. For one thing, we weren't sure exactly how many private security guards were watching you. Besides, I had what Bild wanted, so we were pretty sure he'd be coming to collect it, with you in tow. But I'm terribly sorry that I couldn't shorten your ordeal."

I reached over to hug him again. "Don't be silly. You rescued me. I'm back safe and sound. I'm not so ungrateful as to berate you for not doing it sooner!" I paused. "By the way, where is Dr. Jerry Bild at the moment?"

"Under lock and key in our own little detention center in Lompoc. He's going to get a little lesson in the downside of privatization. I didn't want to have him taken to one of our bases, where I have to watch the rules. Around here you and I make the rules. I'm guessing you'll want to have him inter-rogated, so as to find out what he knows—or thinks he knows—about your operation, and who else might have been in on this sordid little scheme."

"Yes, I want to find out what he knows. But I don't want to think about that right now."

"Fine, he's in no hurry. Just let me know when you're ready."

The five of us sat in silence for awhile. When my sisters got up to leave, I walked with them to my doorway. "Let this be a lesson to us. We were lucky this time because this person wasn't especially clever. But there are others out there who will test us more severely. The genome wars have begun for us. It's true that we can rely on our defenses here for now, but only as long as we hunker down inside the perimeter. We're safe for the time being on our own territory, but it's still a big prison. At some point we'll have to break out.

"I think you all know what I'm getting at. We're secure here for the time being, but we're also extremely vulnerable because we're concentrated in one spot. A single deter-mined effort could render our kind extinct. So the urge for self-preservation will impel us to venture out at some point. But not before we figure out how to do it on good odds."

01 April 2053

(Hera's Journal) Marco told me not long ago he's been thinking back to the end of the period we spent in the Caribbean,
and especially to what he heard me say during that last, long
evening conversation I had with my father and a few of the
sisters. He realizes that my plan to construct a permanent
settlement for us in some remote place like Yucca Mountain
began there, when I came to understand we no longer
should regard ourselves as full members of what's called the
human race, but rather as a breed apart—literally, not figuratively. He told me he wants me to go over that idea with
him again because he has trouble understanding why I came
to those conclusions.

§   §   §

(Marco's Journal) We were seated on the veranda of her suite
in early evening, listening to the waves roll in at Jalama
Beach. When we had settled into our armchairs, with
Magnus Junior dozing on the futon next to Hera's chair, I
said, "I want to understand better, mother, why you're so
sure you must isolate our group from other humans, why we
must never again allow ourselves to interbreed with them.
You do realize why I have a rather keen personal interest in
this topic? If your scheme succeeds, I'll be one of only a few
products of such 'backcrossing.' Also, despite the detailed
exposition you gave to your father that night, I never really

grasped what you were getting at when you talked about your kind being the 'self-cancellation and self-transcendence' of modern science.

"How could any small group of people, even if they were engineered using the science of molecular biology, represent such an idea? What about all the others who have been engineered in the meantime? Are they also part of this self-cancellation? Why are you so special, if I may put it that way?"

She laughed. "My goodness, Marco. Have you been brooding on that last serious conversation I had with my father for all these years? Why didn't you say so earlier? Oh, I know why—you were too obsessed with your own little scheme in the meantime, planning to sneak off to Mars without telling me beforehand, then sending me a radio message from space after it was too late for my opinions to matter. Apparently I was supposed to regard your little trip as something akin to taking a hike in the Sierra Nevada mountains!"

"Now, let's not rehash that old business again. I freely confess I was very upset about the move to the desert as soon as you announced it. I'll also admit I had been enjoying myself immensely once we got to the Vandenberg Colony, especially after Phil appointed me as his executive assistant, which meant that I was at the nerve center of all the activity. The fact that there were repeated crises made it even more interesting and exciting. I was afraid I'd just end up sitting around in a cave with all the other yuccans, hiding out from the fierce heat and playing video games to pass the time."

"Have you forgotten that some of us could have died during one of your interesting crises?"

"No, I haven't, but you must remember, I was in a different space then. I wasn't thinking about the long-term, as I know you always are. I just didn't sense at all what was uppermost in your mind, the fear of humans you carry with you, and your overpowering need to find a secure hiding place for our group."

"Ever since that first moment, Marco, back in the Turks and Caicos Islands, when the thought first came upon me like a flash of lightning—that we were different from them, different enough to want a divorce, so to speak, and compelled to go our own way—I've had to suppress a feeling of stark terror inside me. I was so afraid at first that I fought against my own idea, and for a while I convinced myself that we should stay faithful to my mother's and father's original concept of our mission in life—to mix our genes with those of other people and over time try to improve the human lot. But in the end I capitulated to my new way of thinking.

"You know how it is, I'm sure, when you have the very first apprehension of a great idea, and in that same instant you know that it must be true? At that point you can't fathom your sense of absolute certainty, or adduce any reasons to explain to others, if challenged, why you are so utterly persuaded in your mind that it has to be so. You're just convinced that there's a compelling logic lying behind the idea somewhere, which is hidden from you now, but if you persist, you'll be able to find it. It's almost like when you work on a mathematical proof and have figured out what the solution is, although just then you're not able to write it out in logical steps."

"Still, what's interesting to me is that you really did have a choice, didn't you? I remember Gaia and Percy saying that maybe the problem of hybrid inviability or sterility was just confined to me, that they couldn't rule out that possibility entirely. Or you could have allowed your father to search for the genetic flaw that produced the problem—if, in fact, that flaw actually existed in our Second Generation's genes, by the way! If it did exist, he may have been able to detect and correct it for future generations. Then the foundation could have reverted to its original plan for spreading your father's genetic manipulations into the human gene pool.

"If you had chosen that path instead of the road leading to separation, you could have found persuasive reasons for dismissing your great idea—founding a separate species of the genus *Homo*—if you had tried hard enough, couldn't you? After all, occasionally we're convinced in our own minds that something we've intuited is a truth, yet later it turns out not to be so; our intuition was misguided. Surely that's happened to you as well? I'll be blunt, since you always speak frankly, too. Isn't it foolish to set out on such a perilous path merely because this mental flash appeared to you once upon a time? What if it was just a bad idea to begin with? Or a bad day you were having?"

"*Touché*, Marco. I grant the objection and concede that a rejoinder is required, so here it is. Starting when I was about six years old, I began to discipline my mind in my own way, being already convinced then that I would become responsible someday for ensuring my sisters' safety. I started preparing myself for that role. From that point on I never stopped trying to tame the extraordinary faculty of intuition I'd been given, honing and training it until it was an instrument I could rely upon to find the right answers to dangers and challenges of every sort.

"It's not infallible; nothing of this kind could be. But on the other hand, few others, I suspect, have ever devoted as much time and energy as I did to disciplining the faculty of intuition. I did this, in part, by forcing myself to take its sudden flashes of insight as a starting point rather than the last word. I insisted to myself that later I would have to construct a foundation in logic and reasoning for the conclusions that had leapt out at me earlier.

"And you know what happened? Over time, the results of my strict training showed themselves. I found that the strongest intuitions I had could be reassembled bit by bit into logical chains, more and more readily, as if one part of my mind knew that another part would be expecting this demand to be satisfied."

"So the bottom line is, you found that you could trust your intuitions. OK, now I'm ready to hear you restate the reasons why you believe you must separate your kind from humans, permanently and for all time."

"Wait, Marco; there's one more important part to this puzzle. While I was becoming aware of my mind's abilities as a young girl, growing up in that amazing learning factory my father had constructed in remote New Guinea, I was influenced by something else—my sister Io. This is why I emphasize so strongly the self-disciplining exercises I imposed on myself. Because I do concede fully the point you raised when we started talking, namely, that intuition can be unreliable and perhaps dangerously so. Indeed, think of the many examples we have where groups have been misled by the visions of prophets and the delusions of madmen: Are these, too, not intuitions? Of course they are.

"Io is very much like them; her way of being is that of a prophet. I didn't realize this until it was far too late to try influencing her, but perhaps nothing I could have said or done would have changed her anyway. After all, she's exceptionally bright, brilliant even in her intellectual capacity, her mental quickness and powerful imagination—also strong-willed, profoundly so. She has the prophet's capacity to attract dedicated followers by the sheer force of her personality, even amidst the dreadful phantasmagoria she created at her camp of horrors in Bali."

Hera paused and seemed shaken.

"What is it?" I asked.

Finally, she answered. "I cannot think of Io's trajectory in life without horror and regret. Even now it's hard for me to remain convinced that I did the right thing in allowing her to set up shop there in the jungle in the first place."

"What's done is done, mother, and it's over now. Maybe it

would help if you watch the videodisc with me. At least you would see that you made the right decision in shutting it down."

"Perhaps. Still, I dream of bringing her back here some day and being reconciled with her."

I tried to change the subject slightly. "You thought of Io just now because she, too, had strong intuitions, but there is a difference between you two—you tried to keep your intuitions in check by forcing yourself to examine them critically and sceptically. Am I right?"

"Yes. So, I guess that's also the answer to the question with which you started this line of conversation. Indeed, many other humans have become products of genetic engineering in the last fifty years—that is, if we consider just the ones we know about. I'm absolutely convinced that there were and are many more, tucked away in isolated encampments here and there around the world. Many of them are the result of germline experimentation, too, which means that they could—and undoubtedly have—passed on to their offspring the genetic modifications that were done on them, launching their novel traits into the gene pool of the species as a whole.

"To answer your question directly, then, yes, I do think that what I call my kind is special, in a specific way, in relation to all the others who have also been experimented on by geneticists. That's because something happened in our sense of empathy that my parents didn't foresee. And yet, since my father was such a brilliant scientist in his field, I had the sense after the conversation that night long ago in Provo, that he had indeed half-anticipated such an outcome—not its specific form, of course, because even he couldn't have done so. Really, is this so surprising? What should one expect when one sets out to rejigger something as unimaginably complex as the human brain?

"Especially when one decides to take a crack at precisely

those specific functions in the brain that are crucial to human uniqueness. I'm referring to the language and reasoning skills that set us so far apart even from our closest animal relatives, the great apes. It always amazes me, no matter how many times I think about it, how *subtle* the genetic differences are that mark us off from the apes. At the level of the most important genes in the genomes of us and the chimps, those differences don't add up to as much as 1 % of the total! It's almost impossible to imagine—even for us who believe that DNA is the book of life—how such small differences could have such immense and fateful results."

"Our relation to the apes is very important to you, isn't it, mother?"

"Indeed. This sense of a close kinship with the apes once came upon me like a sudden flash of insight some years ago. As you know, when my parents designed their protocol for the modification of our brains, their intention was to strengthen what's labeled the moral center, where the feeling of empathy is supposed to arise in humans. Empathy is sometimes called 'fellow-feeling,' an innate sense of sympathy for one's kind. Other higher mammals possess such a capacity, too, of course, most famously female elephants, who collectively welcome newborns into the herd and also grieve over their departed kin, standing watch over their fallen bodies sometimes for days on end.

"My parents' purpose in engineering our sense of empathy was to give us a much more powerful bond with our own kind, with humanity as a whole, so that we could help lead them to a state of global peace and tranquillity. But after I first learned from father what he and mother intended to do with their modifications of us, when I was about eight or nine years old, I searched my mind and soul for evidence of this stronger empathy with my fellow humans. And I couldn't find it! In fact, without knowing why, I felt quite indifferent and unsympathetic to what he called the plight of humanity. This left me terrified and anxious for a long time, and I never told either father or any of my sisters about this. I thought that, if I told him, he would conclude that his experiment on me had failed, and he would reject me as being defective.

"I first started ruminating on this when I did some research on autism, to find out what was going on with Moira and Themis. I read that high-functioning autistics, who are more self-aware of their conditions than classical autistics, report an absence of empathy and emotion toward other humans, but, at least sometimes, a heightened empathy toward other animals. In one famous case of a high-functioning autistic, she told of a feeling of being able to sense the anxieties in farm animals that were being led to slaughter. This case gave me the first clue in my thinking about what empathy means, and about the possibility that it might be 'displaced,' so to speak, at least in us. Then I confirmed my impressions through extensive talks with many of my sisters, who reported similar feelings.

"Later I came to believe that I understood what had happened to us. The engineering our parents carried out didn't have the result they intended, but it did have a tangential effect. What I'm getting at is that we *did* feel, quite intensely inside ourselves, an unusually powerful empathy, except that this feeling was oriented toward our primate cousins, not toward other humans! In other words, in us the sense of empathy had undergone a truly radical displacement. At first this struck me as being so odd, but after I thought about it awhile, it seemed less so. Something like the sense of empathy is itself an unusual trait, isn't it? We don't doubt for an instant that it actually exists inside us because we *can* feel it. Yet it's still a mystery how such a powerful and intensely meaningful feeling could spring up out of the neurological wiring patterns in our brain tissue!

"So our parents had engineered our sense of empathy

without fully understanding it. Perhaps it will be a long time, if ever, before scientists figure out what such a trait really is, but our parents believed they could not wait. And I think they did get a result; just not the one they intended. My guess about what happened to us is this: Only a very slight alteration in the neurological wiring structures in that part of the brain where the sense of empathy arises could cause us to see our relationship to non-human creatures in a radically different way.

"Let me put it this way. I believe myself to be as different from humans as Neanderthals were, in their own way, of course. Not superior, mind you, not like humans when they think about themselves in relation to all other animals. How can I explain this? Sometimes, in my darker moments, I feel like an alien species deposited here from a far-off planet. But then I awake and know that I am arisen from this earth. So, when I ask myself how I *feel*, deep down inside, about the welfare of humans, my answer is that I feel exactly the same as I do about the welfare of other living things, especially mammals, since they are the larger class in the phylum to which I belong."

"I remember you once said that you felt cold or indifferent to human concerns, mother. Is that the bottom line? You just can't find it in yourself to care about what happens to them? Are they like androids to you, the manufactured creatures in Philip K. Dick's story, the one that was made into the movie *Blade Runner*? You remember, those androids were designed by their inventor to lack all empathy, even toward their own kind, as well as toward the humans they resemble in terms of outward appearance.

"Are you like Deckard and the other android hunters, mother? Would you be more content if, somehow, humans were all wiped off the face of the earth? I'm not saying you would do this yourself, but let's suppose an infectious disease broke out among them, so virulent it destroyed everyone because it was a virus or bacterium engineered by terrorists and didn't obey the normal rules of nature's game. Would you care if this happened?"

"I've read *Do Androids Dream of Electric Sheep?* Marco. Don't you remember, toward the end of the story, Deckard appears to be developing feelings of empathy toward the androids. The author leaves this tantalizing idea hanging in the air. Anyway, I see what you're getting at, so let me be as clear as I can. I don't wish to contemplate the extinction of humans, and I certainly don't intend to be the cause of it. In a nutshell, I only want two things: To allow my kind to become established and flourish on our beloved earth; and to see that all extent living things have some fair portion of this wonderful planet assigned to them, some room in which each can accompany us for its allotted time on its way to extinction, which is our common fate."

"But it's the first objective that makes you worry so, correct? You think that if humans ever find out what you're up to, they'll make short work of your kind, down to the last remnant."

"Indeed, Marco, that's what I dread. And without a doubt, sooner or later they will find out."

"And you think you're at greatest risk from the humans who wield the latest in scientific and technological innovations, right? Especially their ever-expanding array of clever weapons of mass destruction. You expect them to use these weapons on your little band once they figure things out. So you're hoping that their economies and industrial technologies will gradually crumble under the twin pressures of religious fundamentalism and environmental catastrophe. You're hoping that their scientific establishment will disintegrate along with the rest, until modern technology itself grinds to a halt and they're left with just a few relatively harmless bits and pieces of machinery and weapons, something like what's portrayed in those wonderful *Mad Max* films."

"Please, don't use the word 'hoping' here. I don't hope for any such outcomes, really I don't. It's just that when I look at what humans do—and have always done to each other, the 'other' who's perceived as being different—what should I expect when it comes to my kind? Their exterminating bent certainly predated the arrival of modern technologies, but those technologies make the threat so much more awesome."

"Fair enough. You're willing to live and let live, but you think the others may not be so charitable. So how do you enforce these rules? I'm pretty sure I know the answer. You're betting that their scientific capacity will decay, while you, on the other hand, will keep modern science advancing, at least a small part of it, especially molecular biology, in your little hideaway under the mountain. Then you'll use your advanced technology against them if they do threaten to wipe you out. However, as long as they leave you alone, in your allotted space, you won't interfere in their own affairs. Am I right?"

"That pretty much says it all. What I do hope for is that things turn out just as you said. I don't want a showdown with humans, staged somewhere in the American deserts at high noon, even if we did wind up living in what used to be called 'the Wild West.' If industrial society disintegrates, as I expect it will, human populations will shrink again entirely of their own accord, perhaps drastically so, and more space will open up on earth for all the rest of us. That's what I pray for."

"Do you pray then?" I asked, smiling. "That gives me an idea. Let's take a break and listen to one of our favorite pieces, Bach's cantata *Ich habe genug*."

"Oh, Marco, what a splendid idea," she replied, getting up to find the recording she loved best on the computer in her study. As the aria *Schlummert ein* began, tears rolled slowly down her cheeks:

Fall asleep, let your weary eyes
Close softly and blissfully!
World, I shall not remain here,
For I own no part of you
That could be good for my soul.
Here I pile up only sorrow,
But there will I finally find
Sweet joy and peace, quiet rest.

This was not in response to her silent thoughts, I suspected, but to the almost unbearable beauty of the words and music. Both of us sat silently for many minutes after the work ended.

§   §   §

"Let's go back to where we started in this chat, mother. You'll be keeping alive and intact that precious instrument of modern humans, their natural sciences. You think there's a chance you may end up being the sole repository for science, its guardian and keeper, if you will. But I don't believe you want to keep this science just to use its power against them if they threaten you, as if it were nothing but a weapon.

"Because if this were the case, and if humans declined to the point where they couldn't ever pose a threat to you in the future, you could throw away the legacy of science since you wouldn't need it anymore. So I'm guessing it means much more to you than that. You think you're somehow destined for the role of science's keeper, don't you? That's why you told some of your sisters recently about your vision, where one day your kind would earn the right to call itself *Homo scientificus*. Still, that is one of the parts I just don't understand."

"Well, if you don't, it's because I haven't explained it

clearly, or even attempted to. So I'll try to do so now, since, as you said a while ago, you'll have lots of time for idle thinking during your space voyage, and when you return you can point out all the flaws in my reasoning you uncovered along the way."

"Good. As I recall during that conversation with your father back in Provo, you said something bizarre, something like, 'your science is simultaneously preserved and canceled in my being.' What on earth could you possibly have meant?"

"Now, Marco, I remember nagging you once, a long time ago, that you ought to spend a little time learning the language of philosophy. But you ignored me, so I'll have to give you a short course right here and now. By the way, your quotation was accurate, so at least I know your memory is in fine shape. In that remark I was using a notion in German philosophy called transcendence—the German word is *Aufhebung*—and I think if I recall the actual example I was talking about that evening, it's not all that difficult to grasp. Do you remember in which context this idea cropped up during my conversation with Franklin?"

"Yes, I do. You were arguing that you were an authentic product of modern science, and that this fact was part of your very being. In other words, science isn't just an idea or a concept for you; it represents literally *who* you are. This aspect was quite straightforward I thought when I heard it back then."

"Good! I confess that what I was saying got a little muddled thereafter, and so I'm happy to have the chance now to express the rest more clearly. You see, what I meant at the outset was that I—or more generally my kind—stand in an *essentially* different relation to science than did my father and his peers. All of them had what I call an external relationship to the body of knowledge that they were using. For them it was an instrument—a very powerful and clever instrument, to be sure—of their collective will.

"Their objective was to use this instrument to cajole nature into producing some type of being that did not then exist, or more importantly, might never come into existence except for this exercise of their conscious will. Sometimes they used to say that their science enabled them to master nature, in the sense of compelling nature to do their bidding. In their hands, as I said, their science existed as a kind of tool, just like a measuring rod, albeit much more sophisticated.

"If you think about a measuring rod, you can see what I mean in saying that it is 'external' to the people who are using it. They pick it up, do something with it, put it down again, someone else may pick it up and use it, and all the while it subsists outside them, that is, as something external to them. In this sense the instrument is inert or passive, except when the user wills it into action and it yields the results she wants for herself."

"But they created the tool, too, didn't they? It wasn't external then; it was first the idea of a tool that was held in the inventor's mind and later realized when a craftsman built the instrument, which thereafter could be put to use."

"Well stated, Marco. But once created it takes on a kind of life of its own, do you see? This stems from the fact that, unlike other animals, humans erect an immense house of artifacts to dwell in that becomes the common property of their species. So someone else can come along, pick up the measuring rod that the inventor conceived in order to, say, build a better dwelling, and kill him with it. The tool represents a kind of enlarged mastery over the environment in that people can create useful and deadly things more readily with it, but collectively their relationship to the tool itself is not mastered. So, when you add up all the uses to which the new tool is put, are you better or worse off, on the whole? Well, the point is that you can't even pose the question because there it is, it now exists, and you have to do the best you can in terms of the consequences."

"So your measuring rod is a metaphor for all the technologies that came into being as a result of the modern natural sciences?"

"Yes. That's pretty much the story—until we came along! What happens over the course of modern history is that those instruments gave people access to greatly enlarged powers, more than earlier times ever imagined could be possible. Yet the basic story remains the same. Like the measuring rod, the totality of modern science exists externally with respect to the working scientists who are busily creating new things, such as new life forms, with the powers it has granted them.

"The existence of increasingly powerful instruments for the understanding of nature changes the situation. No individual scientist, or even all of them collectively, controls the armory of clever instruments we refer to as modern science. Anyone who has learned how to use this science can pick up some of the tools and apply them to whatever objectives she wishes. But in this way the existence of the toolbox inevitably contributes to a trajectory of events where things spin out of control, as it were. As I see it, some of the tools are now applied to purposes that would horrify the tool's creators, those great scientific pioneers who were, almost to a person, motivated exclusively by the dream of promoting the good of humanity."

"That reminds me of a story along those lines—Goethe's tale of the sorcerer's apprentice. If I remember correctly, it became widely known to modern audiences through Paul Dukas's famous orchestral work of that name, and especially through Walt Disney's 1938 cartoon film *Fantasia*, where Mickey Mouse plays the apprentice. I think I remember how it goes. The wizard's young apprentice is assigned to do all the routine chores around the lab. Once when his master is away he tries out some of the wizard's spells, ordering a broom to fetch water from the well. Alas, the apprentice doesn't remember the command for 'stop,' and the broom merrily continues hauling buckets of water until the lab itself is awash and the apprentice is drowning. The sorcerer arrives back in the nick of time to restore order."

"Yes, I love that story, too."

"So, by analogy, science is the broom and scientists are the apprentice. Good Lord, mother, then you must be the wizard!"

She burst out laughing. "You've found me out, Marco!"

"Well, I see the point, at least in the abstract—science, as an instrument of great power, needs a wise master who can direct it toward good ends and away from bad ones. But how exactly were you infiltrated into this role?"

"It's a reflection of the effort I made to come to terms with my own existence on earth. I am an entity whose being—body and soul, as they used to say—is the output or result of the science that created me. But more to the point, I *understand* myself as this result. In other words, unlike the other products of this science—the endless series of chemical, mechanical, electrical and biological innovations—I'm conscious of being an outcome of the process that constructed me. But that's just the beginning step, not the end.

"Like other conscious beings, I strive to *be myself,* authentically, that is, to be true to myself. A better, although more complicated, expression of this idea is to say that I strive to *become what I am.* This is the philosopher's notion, Marco, that a conscious being cannot just let the course of natural development carry her along, so to speak, as if she were floating down a river, happy to meander with its currents wherever it takes her. Rather, as a self-conscious being, she must strive to grasp the uniqueness of her being and direct her life toward the full realization of her potential.

"And her potential is what was bestowed upon her in the act of genesis, which in my case was the design and execution of my parents' scientific protocol for engineering my brain. Realizing her potential means *appropriating* that act of genesis, or taking it and making it her own. Now do you see how I stand in a completely different relation to science than the scientist does?"

"Let me see if I'm following you. You said earlier that the scientist has a largely external relation to his instrument because most of the time he's applying it to some practical objective that exists independently of the rational content of science itself. Let's say he wants to insert a new trait into the genome of a plant to make it more nutritious for those who will consume it, and to do this he follows the recipe in his molecular biology textbook. Or, let's suppose he's part of a terrorist group and wants to genetically modify some pathogen so as to wreak havoc on his enemies. Neither of these specific objectives is inherent in his science. He conceives of his particular objective, whatever it may be, and then he looks in his toolbox and finds some bits and pieces of scientific knowledge lying there; he picks up what he requires for the task at hand and sets to work."

"Yes, Marco, and it's completely different for me, because I *know* myself to be such a product. I'm a unique type of product, to be sure, one who thinks and is conscious of myself. This science is not a tool for me, nor is it external to me; rather, it's my own interiority, my *being-as-such*. The scientific project willed me into existence, and this project is what I must appropriate in order to become who I am. You know, this is not so different from what is meant by the believer who says that she has learned to accept God as her creator and Jesus Christ as her savior. When I say that I must appropriate this science that created me, I mean that I must accept it as *my* creator. It lives in me. And that is why I will—indeed, why I must—strive to preserve it."

"Just a minute, mother. Before you go on, explain something to me. You are one of thousands, or maybe tens of thousands by now, of examples of what you call the products of science, in the sense that, like you, they were engineered genetically in some fashion or other. So I come back to a question I posed at the beginning: Why are you so special?"

"Because I've forced myself to undergo the arduous process of becoming who I am, which is the same thing as saying that I've reflected on the process of my genesis. I accept science as the essence of my very being here on earth. I hasten to add, this acceptance results from a rational process of reflection, one that I willed myself to undergo; it's not as if my genes dictated it to me! That's the part I haven't gotten to yet, so indulge me just a bit longer, please.

"I might have come into existence as a specific type of hominin entity purely as a product of natural evolution. The same kind of random reshuffling that goes on all the time inside hominin genomes might have brought me into being someday, spontaneously, just like the process whereby *Homo sapiens* suddenly emerged and survived amidst the various extent species in the *Homo* genus, possibly as recently as 150,000 years ago. No scientific intervention was necessary for any of that to occur: Something just happened one fine day to our ancestors' *FOXP2* gene and other genetic sequences.

"However, I didn't 'just happen.' I'm here on earth now because a scientific project willed me to exist—a purely arbitrary will, I might add. I recognize this will as completely undisciplined in the sense that some other intention might have guided the process of my creation if my parents had had different objectives from the ones they actually held—if, for example, they had wanted to create a being to help them rule the world.

"How shall I put this? Because of who I am, I'm compelled to try to put an end to the arbitrariness of the will that brought me into being. These humans seek to master and control nature in its entirety, while their own will is utterly without self-control and runs amok in the world, creating monstrosities one after another. It's intolerable to me to think that I am the result of a project that might have yielded a race of half-human demons if my scientist-parents had had those objectives instead. This is why I'm special, Marco. I understand—and thus appropriate for myself—this science, not as a tool to be picked up and used for any purpose whatsoever, but simply as my act of genesis. As such I have to try to prevent it from being further defiled."

"Are you saying that science rightfully belongs to you, and not to the humans who devised it over the course of four centuries? Because it was used to create you? I still don't see how you arrive at that conclusion, even starting from your own premises."

She paused before replying, then said, "Look at the situation as if we were both members of an alien race who had stopped here briefly to refuel our spacecraft. We observe this species that sees itself as masters of the earth, even though when we look around we notice instead a great deal of chaos in human affairs. We listen in as they pray in their churches and discover the reason for this bizarre state of affairs: Although in their own minds they are highly rational creatures, most of them refuse to accept the obvious explanation for the fact they exist at all, namely, that a random series of DNA mutations occurred once upon a time in the hominin line to which they belong. Rather, most of them insist they are the sons and daughters of a disembodied, extraterrestrial deity who has no DNA at all!

"Now we aliens look around some more and catch sight of the yuccans, hiding out in their mountain fastness in southwestern Nevada. They're afraid to show themselves and request admission to the larger societies in the vicinity because they've acutely aware that humans created them, and therefore they *know* they're not God's children. In fact, their mere existence proves that the prevailing myth of creation is just that—a fable. But they've also seen enough evidence of the human propensity for undertaking campaigns of genocide and mayhem against unbelievers, and they're smart enough to want to avoid being next in line."

"Indeed, I remember well that part of your remarks to your father. You asserted that you'd like to execute a takeover of the scientific enterprise because you're desperately afraid of what new weapons or new engineered organisms might be cooked up in their labs and thrown against you. Whenever I recalled later that part of your conversation, I was always reminded of the great battle scenes in the second and third books of *Lord of the Rings*."

"My fear remains and grows with each passing year because the threat to us is real and ominous. But I've also had time since then to mull over in my mind what I said on that occasion, and I've come to regard it as too negative, or at least too one-sided. Now I've realized that there's a positive aspect as well, a specific sense in which this negativity is overcome and transcended in my kind.

"Looked at from this positive angle, their modern science has a meaning for my kind that it can never have for humans. For it is *only* through this modern science—not earlier versions, not the Greek science of Western civilization, nor that of ancient China or medieval Islam—that I can know who I really am at the core of my being. And I am, in a nutshell, the random output of the evolution of species and of DNA's infinite recombinatory power.

"Do you see how what I'm saying goes to the very essence of who I am? For the first time in the long march of natural evolution on this earth—a journey that has consumed 3.5 billion years so far—a form of awareness arose in one species that held that process in its gaze, figured out how it works, and *told the truth* about it! It is we yuccans who accept this truth and all its implications as defining who we are. Most humans don't accept this truth; they much prefer their creationist myth. Fine, let them have it. That's why I think we, and not they, are the rightful heirs of this truth-telling science of nature—the one form of knowledge that brought our genesis to light."

"So what you're saying is you need this science in a fundamental way, and humans don't. That's why you need to preserve it and keep it alive, so to speak."

"It's only because of this science that I know both *who* I really am as well as *how* my kind arose out of the bowels of this earth, just like all the rest of nature's creations. This science also tells me that we earth-creatures—all of us together, from the first single-celled organisms emerging out of the primordial soup in the young planet's oceans, down to the present day—have an allotted time. There's about half-a-billion years left before our sun's long death agony begins and all life on earth enters the road to final extinction. That's just the luck of the draw, isn't it? But my science tells me this earth is all we have."

"Well, if you need your science so much, why do you always talk about canceling it?"

"What's canceled is not this science itself, but the particular form it assumed for humans, namely, as an instrument for what they referred to as their mastery over nature. Their fondest hope was that science would make them lords of the earth, able to dictate terms of surrender to all other creatures and to rearrange everything to suit their own interests. They want to control the fate of all other living things, pointing some down the path to their doom, keeping others alive—at least temporarily—to offer comforts or entertainments for the masters, but all the while making it crystal clear to the others that they continue to exist only upon the sufferance of the planet's one ruling species.

"This is a false way of apprehending what modern science means for the simple reason that among humans, there is no commonly held conception of what their interests are. Instead they're continuously at loggerheads with each other, competing for advantage, each faction using the powers of science to advance their particular goals. So there is control imposed on all the others, but precious little exercise of self-control among themselves.

"To put the point differently, what I refer to as the false representation of science is the mindset that sees science essentially as an instrument of power over nature. And the falsehood itself lies in its misrepresentation of the relationship between the instrument—science—and those who wield it—humans. This image they have in their minds makes sense only if humans regard themselves as god-like beings who are both external to nature and superior over it, rather than as creatures who are products of natural forces like all others.

"Most people on earth refuse to turn around the marvelous instrument they wield against other beings and shine its penetrating light back toward themselves, because they can't stand to gaze upon the different image that would be displayed before their very eyes if they did so—the one that shows them clearly to be natural beings, not gods or even the children of gods.

"We, on the other hand, aren't afraid to look through this lens, and when we do, the truth appears: Science is the means by which we comprehend who we are—a minor player among a cast of billions in a drama extending both backwards and forwards over eons. Humans defile this unique and profoundly important instrument—modern science—when they represent it as a means for seizing control of this theatrical production and dictating the final outcome.

"What science really grants us of lasting value is insight;

the power it's thought to bestow is largely illusory. Recreate in your mind for a moment the colossal destructive power of the old multiple, independently targeted warheads sitting atop a single ICBM. Now remember the balance of terror strategy, for there was not one huge set of these weapons, but two. The world was just plain lucky to escape what was called the 'unthinkable' prospect of catastrophic nuclear warfare, wasn't it? Had it not been so fortunate, the alleged power of industrial societies would have vanished in an instant into the radioactive dust clouds encircling the globe. So what kind of enduring mastery over nature do humans *really* possess?"

"I think I follow your line of argument, mother, but I'm also looking for the bottom line, at the practical level, of what this would mean if it were ever played out in the real world. So let me take a stab at it: The difference between you and humans is you're not actually going to *use* this science. I don't mean to be sarcastic, but let me push back a bit.

"When you say that it's your mission to preserve science, you must mean that you're going to mummify it and turn it into a museum exhibit. Then you'll take the children of each new generation of your kind to look at the exhibit and listen to some speeches about what an interesting and important artifact it is. In a way this story will be the founder's myth of your kind, and the children's visits the equivalent of Sunday school classes. The truth is, you don't intend to keep it alive, do you?"

"Impressive, Marco, that's very much to the point. And while I grant you that my words might have such implications, that's not at all what I meant. For a body of thought, preservation cannot mean mummification. But keeping it alive doesn't mean we must obsessively push it forward to its limits, as fast as we can, as humans have done recently, enslaving it to feed an insatiable industrial machine that rolls its innovations out the door as fast as they come off the laboratory bench, as if the whole enterprise would wither and die if it stopped to rest for even just an instant.

"Consider this analogy. The ancient Greeks opened up the sphere of philosophical reasoning twenty five hundred years ago in a sudden burst of intellectual glory. Then the world changed and their works were largely forgotten or destroyed, only to reappear again in medieval times, first among the Arabs and later among the Christian Schoolmen, before being fully revived in the Renaissance.

"In the modern world, down to our own time, these ancient works remain vibrant, even exhilarating. Every generation of philosophers returns to them and becomes nourished and refreshed, ready to engage anew in wrestling with the most important concepts of all—justice, equity, truth, right conduct. No one who holds the respect of her peers would dream of suggesting that these works are obsolete and unworthy of our attention. This is how it will be for us, as keepers and guardians of modern science.

"Obviously we can't recreate the immense nexus of science, technology, innovation, and industrial application that existed until recently. Nor do we want to. We'll continue to remain engaged with the basic sciences, especially with the theoretical aspects of chemistry, physics, biology, and so on; and we'll always remain in the forefront of research and development for applications of molecular biology, because we must defend ourselves against the threat of bioweapons. Once we're secure, however, we might let this science rest a while as we concentrate on other things, fully intending to return to it later."

"So if you're not going down the human path, and using science and technology to impose your will on everything else in creation, what will you actually do instead—that is, if somehow your human cousins allow you to carry out what you call your great idea?"

"We must find our ecological niche, one that's comfortable enough for us to flourish in, but also leaves enough room for other living things to prosper as well. For millions of years our hominin ancestors evolved in a collection of relatively small patches of land along the Rift Valley on the African continent. So when I think about what might be appropriate for us, here in the southwestern deserts of the New World, I imagine something along those lines.

"Remember what I told you once, Marco: If we can hang on there in that very dry land long enough, maybe for ten or fifteen thousand years, the climate will eventually get a lot nicer. When the next ice age descends on the northern hemisphere, as it almost certainly will, our part of the world will get plenty of rainfall once again, as the geological record indicates."

"Yes, but will they really leave you alone? You've conceded that sooner or later, humans will figure out what you're up to. I tend to agree that when they do, there'll be trouble. Not at first, of course. First they'll just find it all quite hilarious— "What *chutzpah* she has," some will say—and regard you as a crackpot, something on the order of the millennial cults, the folks who gather periodically on a mountaintop waiting for God's plan for the end of the world to unfold.

"Then, when your claim about being a different hominin species begins to sink in among the more sophisticated types, their attitude quickly will change. They'll work out a strategy to test you first, to see if you're actually serious and not just a nut case, and when they discover that you are indeed quite serious, and, moreover, that you intend to carry out your non-interbreeding rules, things will get ugly. I think it's inevitable that events will unfold along these lines."

She fell silent and some minutes passed before she spoke again. "No one has ever forecast this scenario, as far as I know. I doubt humans ever expected to have to deal on equal terms with another reasoning species. Oh, I know, there are plenty of science-fiction stories about intelligent life forms visiting from other planets, with bodies unlike ours, or the scenario in *Planet of the Apes*. There's lots of entertainment value in those tales, but nothing more. We'll throw off their calculations because we look just like normal people. So I agree with you; when our claim becomes known it'll be greeted at first with laughter, and then with astonishment and wonder, before it turns to murderous rage. Unfortunately, that progression from laughter to rage is inevitable."

"I believe you're right about that. They won't tolerate your wish to reserve a part of the planet for yourself and keep them out, no matter how small a portion you say you'll be content with. Again, it all comes back to the monotheistic religions. They believe to the depths of their being that God gave them the earth as their patrimony and delegated to them the right to rule over all other creatures—until the day when the Four Horsemen ride forth to propel this drama to its bloody conclusion. Mark my word; when they find out about you, they'll label you as the Antichrist, the denier of God's provenance. So this rage will run its inevitable course to a final battle—at Armageddon, I think the place is called."

Again she lapsed into thought for a few moments. "That reminds me of another story. I know you've read and admired Mary Shelley's novel, *Frankenstein*, Marco. Dr. Frankenstein's creation wanted desperately to be accepted as a human being—clearly, in addition to the flesh out of which he was constructed, he had received the normal human sense of empathy and fellow-feeling. There's such pathos in what happens to him because he yearns so hungrily for recognition of his humanity. Shelley portrays him as innocent and naïve, but his friendly overtures to normal humans are cruelly rebuffed at every turn, and instead he is greeted with revulsion, horror, and rage. He quickly loses his innocence. So he turns to his second-best option, asking Dr. Frankenstein to create a mate of his own kind, and in return he promises that the two of them will quit the continent of Europe and never interact with humans again. But his maker refuses and the story plays out to its miserable ending. I'm so saddened whenever I think of it.

"As I read it, the core theme in Mary Shelley's great tragedy is about the sense of empathy—the creature's desperate need to find an empathetic response from people whom he assumes are his own kind. He then chooses a second-best option and decides to establish a new race of hominins, but his plan is thwarted by his maker. Do you see the weird parallel with my own biography? Of course, my father's science was much more powerful than Dr. Frankenstein's, so at first it seemed that he would succeed where his predecessor had failed.

"But there is an underlying similarity between the two scientists. Both Franklin and his predecessor failed to understand the full implications of what they had set out to do, namely to engineer into existence a being capable of self-consciousness! A being who would have her own mind and will, and who would therefore demand to have a say in the determination of her own fate. Unlike the poor creature in Mary Shelley's story, however, I think I've been given a slightly better chance of pulling it off."

"Why is that?"

"Let me back up again before addressing your question. Because we sisters were designed as natural beings by an act of another's conscious will, I was obsessed with the religious story of creation as a way of understanding us, who we are, why we came to be engineered by our parents, and what it all meant for our lives and the way we should lead them. Like Frankenstein's monster, I thought at first I must get this explanation from my creator—my father. Like that poor creature in Mary Shelley's story, I also then came to the conclusion that I must make my father understand what I was going through, in my mind, and to convince him to accept my side of the story, so to speak. I wanted to get him to complete his work *by accepting me as I was*, not as he had designed me to be in his own mind, prior to my coming into being and consciousness.

"I thought I had to explain myself to him and get him to see the real story, which was not about the so-called 'program' he and our mother had invented with their friends, but rather about who and what we—as the embodiment of another's dream—were in and for ourselves, to use a philosophical expression again. Where I got stuck, where I was really bogged down for years, was in believing that for the sake of my own salvation I had to get inside my creator's mind because it seemed to me that was where the answers lay—in his intentions and expectations. I admit I was influenced by his eminence as a scientist and, later, by the extraordinary care he exercised in re-engineering the Second Generation. It took me far too long to see that this was a dead end."

"That reminds me of how Mary Shelley's story concludes, mother. Do you remember that awful scene close to the end, when the creature is found by the ship's captain, standing over the corpse of Dr. Frankenstein, grief-stricken and in despair? After all the cruel transactions between them, he remains bound emotionally to his creator to the bitter end. I remember the words he speaks: He refers to Frankenstein as 'the select specimen of all that is worthy of love and admiration among men.' What inept words these are when used to describe the man who had denied him the chance to overcome his profound loneliness by having a mate of his own kind! He was in thrall to his master and couldn't break free; Frankenstein's death was simultaneously his own self-inflicted sentence of doom."

"That's precisely where my story diverges from Shelley's, Marco. I came at last to the realization that my sisters and I must wrest our own future path out of our creator's hands. I concluded that it didn't really matter after all what my parents intended. We weren't bound by the terms of whatever bargains they had made, either with themselves or with others. We were capable of setting our own terms. And to do this we had to consign Franklin's *Memorandum* to the rubbish heap and look only inside ourselves to find our destiny."

"You never did succeed in getting Franklin to understand why it was so important to you to figure this out and go your own way, did you?"

"I really have no idea whether I did or not. What I do know for sure is that I spent far too much time and effort obsessing about all this, being fixated on it. Good Lord, when I recall those conversations now, all the many occasions during which I badgered him—poor man!—into sitting and listening to my excursions into the Book of Genesis, which he hated so! Finally the truth dawned on me: We sisters were the story, not him. We had within us the power to redefine the nature of the Faustian bargain he and my mother had made."

"Well, I'm not sure you were entirely wrong in obsessing about the Biblical creation myth, or in making him listen to your exegesis of the Book of Genesis. I still think you made a good case in your arguments about crossing the line—which I heard you articulate on several occasions, including when you were rehearsing them with me."

"I'm glad to hear you say that! What he had done, in effect, was to burn down the ancient edifice, the structure of myth common to all the world's monotheistic religions, that tells of our being brought into the world by God's will, by a purpose and will independent of humankind, one that we all serve. My sisters and I arose from those ashes like the Phoenix, the bird-figure of ancient Greek myth that regenerates itself again and again in its own funeral pyre. We are the new-born ones, fully creatures of this earth, children of a mastery of the biochemistry of that extraordinary molecule, DNA.

"Anyway, that's what I finally figured out, and what I tried to explain to Franklin when I turned the tables on him in our conversations. He had, of course, thought through the possibility that his creations would fail in the mission he had designed for them. But he had not imagined the rest—not the possibility that we of the first generation would rebel against him and set out quite deliberately to undermine the goals that had animated him. I'm sure he never dreamt this would happen, nor that we might actually be in a position to carry out an entirely different mission.

"I have set myself this goal, Marco: I'm going to do whatever I can to have that potent instrument of human ingenuity, modern science, hidden away from them. It's simply far too dangerous for them to be allowed to play around with it any longer. Why? Because these humans have hoisted themselves onto the horns of an insoluble dilemma. They're torn between their unscientific faith in the miracles of religion and their unreligious faith in the miracles of science. They work themselves into a frenzy of self-loathing, because over time the contradiction between the two sides of the dilemma becomes obvious: In the end they'll have to choose, and I'm convinced that when the time comes, they'll opt for religion and abandon science.

"As for me and my kind, we need their science of nature because it defines who we are. I intend to possess it and nourish it and keep it alive forever. It's mine; I'm its rightful owner, because I accept the truth it tells, namely, that through nature's works my kind came into being on this earth. Too much innocent blood was spilled in bringing modern science into existence in the first place, centuries ago, to take the chance of losing it again, and it's entirely possible that it could be lost forever. To ensure this doesn't happen I have to hide it from humans. I honestly believe they'll be much happier without it, but I don't care over-much whether or not this is the case. At bottom, I'm afraid of the kinds of things they may do with it, and so I have to protect myself."

"At the risk of having you think me very stupid, I confess you still lose me here. I do follow you up to the point where you oppose religion and science. But when you say that you *must* hide it away from humans because they are too careless with it, I still can't see how you arrive at such a conclusion."

"I'm always glad when you pull me up short that way. Having to reassemble my thoughts more coherently, in order to try to persuade you to follow me, always helps me to sharpen my own perspective. I'm still groping in the dark-ness myself, I freely admit; these are difficult things to get right. I'll try again. You'll have to suffer with me along the rocky path of my half-formed ideas, but I'll tell you in advance where the path leads: It's the scientific manipula-tion of our minds that threatens to bring the whole enter-prise crashing down upon their heads. This is why their science must be hidden away for the time being. Now I'll retrace my steps back to the beginning and start over.

"Our launching pad for this journey of ideas is, once again, the program devised by my parents. They had initiated the process of designing us, to be sure, but they couldn't continue to own the result; they were not, as they imagined they would be, capable of continuing to steer that process toward their own preselected ends once we had started to mature. Believing otherwise was their crucial error. They had set out to engineer our subjectivity, not just our neurological wiring and neurotransmitter functions; they were trying to manipulate our sense of self—something no one else has ever attempted before, as far as I know. But precisely *because* they had succeeded in their ambition, as I believe they did, they could not predetermine the final end-point toward which such a process tends. Are you with me so far?"

"Yes, I think so. Because our sense of purposes—goal-directed activity—originates in our own subjectivity. And, as I remember from some earlier chats between us on this subject, what is called our sense of self is a complex and many-sided phenomenon."

"Right. Many people regard thinking as a kind of pure, bloodless activity, as if it were analogous to the processing of inputs that computer programs perform. But nothing could be further from the truth. Our thinking and subjectivity is embedded in a rich, bubbling, chemical stew of *organic* modulations. What really goes on inside us is this: First, deep down, there is my awareness of being alive, in particular, of being alive *in a body*. In ordinary language we refer to this as our 'sixth sense'; scientists call it 'proprioception,' the intuitive and unconscious perception of one's own physical being that orients our bodily mass and movement in space. This is, in part, a result of the fact that my brain is continuously engaged—even when I am asleep—in monitoring and regulating the state of both itself and the rest of my body through nerve impulses and chemical markers such as hormone levels. Our internal state signals to us through a variety of indicators, such as skin temperature and the normal rhythm of our heartbeat, that all is well within. So, the first level of thinking is: 'I am alive.'"

"I can remember the rest," I interjected. "Second, there is the process of thinking about something in particular, which gives me, say, a solution to a problem: What is the best route to my destination? Third, there is my awareness that I am thinking about something, a kind of second-order monitoring of my thinking: I am aware that I am the one who is doing this thinking about a problem. And fourth, perhaps most importantly, there is the *feeling* that is created in me about what I am thinking: Why is it important for me to arrive at my destination? What kind of reception awaits me there? Depending on what's involved, I could have an intense feeling of either joy or foreboding, for example. All of these four aspects of what we mean by the process of thinking recur together, spontaneously and simultaneously."

"Excellent, Marco! This is the point I want to emphasize now: We are not indifferent—indeed, we can't be—to what we are thinking about. Even when we make a conscious effort to suspend the emotion that is otherwise always present, our minds can override the attempt. By way of contrast, when a computer processes inputs using a specific program, we don't imagine that such processing gives rise to any feelings about what is happening inside the machine. Of course, software designers have played around here, and some time ago they added a sense of feeling to various states that occur in information processing, which the computer can now report on. But all they've accomplished is to mimic mechanically what our brain does naturally. It's clever, to be sure, but hardly original. The true original here is Mother Nature.

"And now I can better explain why it's important to me to be clear about this. We can think about the whole process of our subjectivity—we can step back and analyze its components, as I have just done for you—thus creating yet another layer or level. I am still the one who is doing this thinking, as if I were standing outside myself and looking in, but I am aware that, in truth, this 'I' also is inside, reckoning with itself, so to speak."

"OK, let's say we've covered the first leg of the journey. My question is, where are you going with this, Hera? And when will we get there?"

"Where I am headed is toward that point there, still in the distance, that you can now glimpse: To reflect on the fact that the brain—our organ of knowing about both the world and ourselves—is special, different from all other bodily organs. And, therefore, that our knowing about the brain—

which is the brain's own activity, as portrayed in the picture drawn by the neurosciences about this organ—must be special, too.

"How is the brain special among all our bodily organs, you might ask? Because it is the only one whose physical structure is differentiated according to how it evolved over time. In other words, it recapitulates the record of its own incredibly long history as an organ of the body in vertebrates and mammals. Most remarkably, it preserves its differentiation, that is, its division into sub-components, while also maintaining its overall unity of function.

"The brain is an integrated set of functionally specific parts that preserves its evolutionary history, beginning with the ancient spinal cord, and proceeding through vertebrate, early mammalian, and late-mammalian stages. In the old vertebrate brain there developed, eons ago, various primitive parts atop the spinal cord that we still have: hindbrain and midbrain (together called the brain stem) and the early forebrain. Much of the so-called autonomic or automatic control systems, such as breathing and heart rate, are located here. Later still came the cerebellum, diencephalon, and cerebral hemispheres, now dividing the brain into two halves joined by a bridge, the *corpus callosum*. Thereafter came the cerebral cortex, subdivided into four lobes, then its extension, the neocortex (unique to mammals), and finally, in the primates, including us, the further extension of the neocortex—the prefrontal cortex.

"What is truly astonishing is that all these separate parts are clearly identifiable in the organ we all carry around with us inside our skull today! It's *all* still there! And not just in we primates, of course—all other birds and mammals, being relatively late in the evolutionary chain, also conserve the most ancient of these structures."

"What you just said prompted another set of reflections for me, Hera. Every member of the genus *Homo* carries around in his or her brain—our thinking organ—the living, pulsing proof of our evolutionary heritage. And not only what we might call this general proof. More specifically, what we are talking about is a *sequential* development, one that happened over time and in quite specific stages. The unique portion of this development that we share only with our primate relatives is at least one reason for your obsession with the great apes."

"Indeed it is, Marco. Once *Homo* emerged out of this evolutionary process, we find that humans possess the highest ratio of brain weight to body weight of any species on earth. But remember, too, that although it is differentiated in both function and evolutionary history, the human brain achieves its unity by strongly interconnecting its parts with multiple, overlapping feedback loops.

"Try to visualize what I'm talking about as the 'House of the Brain,' Marco. There are five structural levels: a subbasement, the brain stem; a basement, the diencephalon and cerebellum; a first story, the cerebral hemispheres; a second story, the neocortex; and an attic, the prefrontal cortex.

"Imagine further that all five levels are interconnected by a large number of internal staircases—as they are, in fact, through the brain's network of nerve fibers. Most remarkably, despite its functional differentiation, our brain appears to achieve its unity without having a single area that acts uniquely as a controller. There are, to be sure, powerful processes in the prefrontal cortex that can achieve a high degree of what's called cognitive control, allowing us to focus intently on a single objective. But these processes can be overridden, for example, by a conditioned-fear response originating in the amygdala, so its control is not authoritative under all circumstances.

"I think that the brain is a perfect illustration of a parallel processing entity. Various processes, going on simultaneously within the organism, actually compete with each other under a set of rules that determines which one will prevail under specific circumstances. Its distributed unity is the outcome of an integrated set of internal feedback loops, which are continuously processing both internal and external sensory information. Our brain is, in the end, the result of adaptation to the environment. In other words, the less-successful prototypes for the organ that evolved eventually died out over time.

"But back to my analogy. It's not just a house, it's a haunted house! The philosopher Nietzsche called us 'hybrids of plants and ghosts.' Phantoms and spirits of all kinds flit about the interior. They are the products of our brain's primary mode of activity—namely, working with visual imagery. The images that float in our brains are the products of an innately combined process—thinking/feeling; this is why we react so strongly to them on an emotional level."

"I remember you said a few moments ago that we are never indifferent to the contents of our mind."

"That's right. All the brain's various parts contribute their share to the assortment of ghosts that populate it. The evolutionarily older parts of the brain tend to make their main contributions during sleep and dreaming, when cognitive control has been suspended temporarily."

"Sort of like vapors rising from the lower structures into the uppermost story?"

"If you like. But the activity of those older parts never entirely ceases. For example, the strongly wired connections between the prefrontal cortex—the newest part of the brain—and the amygdala—one of the older parts—ensure that this cannot happen. So, even when we are fully awake and under the influence of the cognitive control operated by the prefrontal cortex, we are being subconsciously influenced by the brain's deep structures. This happens, for example, when we are processing images of faces—smiling or angry faces—and stereotypical images, which originate in those older structures.

"In my analogy of the house of the brain, its activity, including thinking, is pictured as being implanted firmly in the flesh, in the sphere of materiality. I'm referring to aspects of chemistry and physiology—blood, tissue, electrical discharges, chemical neurotransmitters. This rootedness has two aspects. The mind-brain is grounded both in its body, represented by the sub-basement, and in its evolutionary pathway, represented by the basement. Both the sub-basement and the basement are literally and figuratively sunk into the earth. Together they *incorporate* us within both the invariant or necessary structures of nature—physics and chemistry—that humans share with inorganic life, and the accidental or contingent structures—biological evolution—that we share with organic life.

"If you are wondering why I'm burdening you with this excursus into neuroanatomy, the simple reason is that this picture of our thinking process is fundamental to my sense of self. We reflect all-too-rarely on our deep, deep grounding in the earth. We should do so, and in so doing we should say: 'I *am* the earth, I am *from* the earth and will return to it; I *am* the lizard, the corn-plant, the whale, the tree, the wolf and its prey, the eagle in flight; I *am* my simian cousin, sister ape. All—the earth itself and these creatures—are in me and with me; I am *nothing* without them.' This is the song of the earth, Marco. This is what the poet-composer Mahler sang to us.

"Now the ghosts inside scream at us: 'No! No! It cannot be thus! You *think*, and *therefore* you are. No other creature thinks, therefore you are unique, special. Thus you must have been *made*—designed—uniquely by a Being who thinks absolutely, who is pure thought, unsullied by matter. This Being is your God. You must acknowledge It—it cannot have gender, being immaterial—as the author of your existence.

Otherwise you shall surely be cast into Hell—which is for you the *thought* of eternal, everlasting torment and hopelessness.' This is the song of the soul, and among humans it drowns out utterly the song of the earth.

"We have arrived at our journey's destination at last. Here I imagine myself, in the guise of a neuroscientist, standing outside the house of the brain, looking in at its various parts and its marvelous inner workings, watching the cascading neurotransmitters causing the synapses to fire, generating images, thoughts, actions. I look through the lens of my fMRI apparatus—my functional magnetic resonance imaging machine. I watch in full three-dimensional glory as the signals scurry back and forth among the brain's many parts, up and down, side-to-side, back and forth across the *corpus callosum,* the wired bridge between the right and left hemispheres. And now I ask you, '*Who* is this entity, the one who is alertly watching and recording all this activity?'

"'Why,' you say, 'it is a brain, curiously enough, watching what it assumes is something identical to itself, so that it knows itself at the same instant as it observes the other. And the observer's brain can verify this assumption by becoming a subject in the experiment, causing itself to be inserted into the mechanism, recording the signals, and examining the record later.' So far, so good. Now the watching brain says, 'Perhaps I could do some renovations to a few of the rooms, some redecorating of the interiors. Maybe, just maybe, I could also build some additions to the structure, a new deck, perhaps, to get a better view of the scenery outside, or one or more entirely new rooms, furnishing them to my liking, even adding a new staircase leading to the basement.'

"Then I say, 'If you do this—as my father did—are you entirely sure you will continue to know *who* it is that now lives and thinks inside this refurbished structure, who it is now looking back out at you? This new being will be, to all external appearances, just like it is supposed to be—a normal human being, just like you. But inside itself, as it comes to know itself, who and what will it be? If it happens to think and know itself to be different from you in some important way, will it enlighten you with this information? Or, being apprised of your strong convictions about your uniqueness and special place on earth, will it opine that the wiser, more prudent course is rather to stay silent, to take its own counsel, and to make its own plans in secret? And if it does so, what might its plans turn out to be?'

"At long last, Marco, here's the point! The experimenter's grave error is to use the knowing of his mind—in the form of his science of brain functions—as a tool to be employed on the knowing brain itself, *as if* it were an external thing. This is the religious impulse at work yet again—to represent the mind as external to nature and thus as a thing-in-itself that can be manipulated like every other thing found in the environment.

"But in reality we cannot *ever* be outside the mind. There is no outside in this sense, since all the materials it works with—even sensory inputs from the external environment—are elaborately processed by this brain and its mind. In truth the experimenting scientist is standing on the upper floor in the house of the brain, trying to pull up the foundations from where he stands. The result we might expect—more precisely, one possible outcome—is to watch helplessly as the entire edifice collapses around his ears.

"This is why I need to take that science away from them for a while. Before I set about making renovations to the house of the brain, I think I should understand a bit better how it fits together, and where the bearing walls are. I should also deal with the ghosts, too, because they are rather distracting—especially the devils. I need to know—before I start tinkering with the support beams and rebuilding the staircases—how and why the evolutionary architecture was put together in just the way it was.

"Above all, I need to reflect, long and hard, about what it means to assume that we can carry out a renovation project on the organ that carries within it the very idea of renovation. You know how messy such projects can be. What if in the course of carrying out such a project we misplace or damage the guiding idea, or accidentally just throw it into the trash? What if, having built a spectacular new recreation room, we walk inside once it's finished, and lo and behold, there's a new staircase? We remember that it didn't exist before we started and definitely wasn't included in the architectural drawings for the renovations. Somehow, it just appeared of its own accord. And when we peer down its steps, delighted at this unexpected bonus, we are confronted by an uprushing bevy of ghosts, of such terrifying mien that we lose our balance and tumble down into the basement and remain there, trembling with fear, unable to muster the courage to ever come up again."

I didn't reply—because my own brain had become seriously overloaded! Hera lapsed into silence for several minutes. Then she said, "Now, that's enough. I simply can't dwell on these gruesome images a moment longer. Let's talk about what life will be like inside your spaceship as you journey to Mars. But first, let me play for you a couple of the wonderful Haydn piano sonatas I've been practicing lately."

04 NOVEMBER 2054, HERA'S JOURNAL

In a few days Marco will be arriving from Vandenberg on one of his last visits before the Mars expedition crew enters the month-long lockup prior to departure. Then, as I understand it, a shuttle rocket will take them to the International Space Station, from which two nuclear-powered spaceships—towing 'freighters' full of supplies behind them—will depart for the Mars mission. I'm so afraid I'll never see him again that I can hardly function! But I must conceal my fears, I know that. I'd never forgive myself if I asked him not to go, because if he acceded, things would never be the same between us. He'd always resent me, even if he tried not to, so I must let him go.

I have to keep in mind what Phil keeps saying about this mission having been planned for decades, down to the last detail. The idea of a permanent human colony on Mars may not be feasible if those who are eventually sent aren't able to stand the thought of staying there forever. But it's unlikely, he says, that any disasters will befall this exploratory group there. In any case, the task for Marco's contingent is only to set up the infrastructure for a permanent settlement, possibly to be occupied at some later date, and then return to earth. Marco's already filled me in, many times, about the kind of technologies and installations they're taking with them. I'm trying to get a full picture in my mind about the spaceship and the journey itself, so that I can imagine what it'll be like for him.

§   §   §

(*Marco's Journal, 04 November*) Disaster has struck! Phil is in hospital fighting for his life. Hera's gone there to sit by his bedside. His second-in-command, General Gary Hone, called me in to the base since I'm Phil's executive assistant and thus the only one who knows what he was supposed to be doing today. In return he told me what happened.

"Tension has been building steadily for the past year because of the drug trafficking issue. Apparently the so-called Chumash Warriors were no longer just good customers of the dealers outside our perimeter. They had begun to act as bankers and warehousemen for the entire coastal drug operations from San Diego to San Francisco. They've been using fast boats as the primary means of transport because there were no airports available to them, and our Navy has more important things to worry about. Also, our stretch of coastline happens to be fairly rugged and deserted, and so it afforded good cover for their base of operations. Because of the awesome size of the bankroll these guys can bring to anybody's table, they were moving fast and becoming statewide drug kingpins. They were already talking about extending their operations as far as the coastlines of Canada and Mexico. Phil and I had warned the members repeatedly what was going on and that it had to stop. It didn't stop; instead, it was escalating.

"So Phil decided to teach them a lesson and disrupt the market share growth scenarios in their business plan a bit. We put an AWACS reconnaissance aircraft out over the coastal waters. Then we waited until signs indicated that a big shipment was being prepared for delivery out of the warehouses. When the convoy of boats set out that night a few weeks ago, the recon plane radioed the base and we sent some fighters up. We let them have it with a few rocket volleys. There wasn't much of anything left to fish out of the water, not even enough body parts from all the guys on board to fill one decent coffin. The planes returned to base and nobody was the wiser.

"Nobody, that is, until one of the fighter pilots went club-hopping the next night and got loaded; it's possible his drinks were spiked—unfortunately a common occurrence in those clubs. He apparently regaled the denizens there with the tale of the disappearing boats. There were guys within hearing range whose buddies were on those boats. They didn't confront the pilot, but they knew who must have given the orders.

"Last night Phil was invited to dinner at the compound of one of the richest members, who also happens to be a 'reformed' drug lord. He's now a director, and I'm sure his purpose in having Phil over was to sweet-talk him into going easier on the kids, as he calls them. Those kids thought they were rid of Phil as the boss around here after he was trans-ferred to Nellis, but once he was back in an even more powerful position, they got restive. Phil was dropped off by his adjutant who then returned to base, awaiting the call to pick him up again after the evening's festivities. We can only surmise the rest of what happened at the house.

"My guess is that somebody on the household staff work-ing for the family's eldest son, who—we just now found out—is the main banker for the drug ring within the Chumash Warriors, lured Phil into one of the rooms on a pretext. Somehow he was drugged, taken out a side entrance, and driven to the Cat-House Club, one of the entertainment spots run by the Warriors. The son then undoubtedly fabricated a story for his dad as to why Phil had left soon after arriving. I'm pretty sure they counted on having their fun with him, then polishing him off and dump-ing his body in the ocean before any of his people started looking for him in the gang's haunts. But the combination of their doped-up state and the fun they were having probably made them lose track of time.

"We didn't find Phil until nearly four hours later. When his adjutant hadn't received a call to pick him up by 11pm, he phoned the house, only to be told by the father that Phil had returned to the base shortly after he had arrived. After the adjutant set the guy straight, the father remembered his son's story, put two and two together, and panicked. He told the adjutant to send teams of Ziegler's security force to all the clubs immediately.

"I was with the group who found him at the Cat-House Club. He had clearly been fed an amazing combination of psychoactive drugs. We found out later that he had been stripped naked and tied to the back of the white Brahman bull that wanders through the rooms all night, where every kind of sexual perversion you can imagine occurs simultaneously. They took one of Phil's signed notices about the illegality of the drug trade and pinned it to the flesh on his back.

"Then, at some point, according to the witnesses we interviewed—the few who could remember anything at all—Phil was taken off the bull and made to crawl around on the floor with a heavy cross on his back while being whipped. When we found him, the louts who were in charge of the night's entertainment had just finished nailing his palms to the arms of the cross. They were going to crucify him, literally. I'm afraid we didn't behave very professionally when we stumbled on that scene. We shot the ringleaders where they stood. And we had to take the whole fucking cross with us to the base hospital, because they used spikes through his hands and we couldn't remove them."

I sat down, suddenly unable to breathe. I think I almost fainted.

Hone jumped up and asked, "Are you all right?"

After a moment I answered. "I'm OK. I guess one thing I

don't understand is why he went there alone."

Hone responded, "We all bear some responsibility for that mistake. Obviously, neither Phil nor any of the rest of us had thought hard enough about the kind of folks we were dealing with. I'm ashamed to admit it—we were a bit naïve. These are the kind of people who were powerful enough in their home countries to act with impunity against anyone in government, no matter how senior. We should have anticipated the danger. We should have assumed they would act no differently once they were ensconced on US soil. But we didn't.

"Phil is in intensive care. We think he'll make it, but who knows what his brain will be like when he wakes up? We collected some of the chemical garbage they use in those clubs. There are certain mixtures that are guaranteed to kill you fast. There are others that will just take you to the edge of oblivion. I think what kept Phil alive—so far, that is—is that they didn't want to kill him right away. When we caught them they were trying to revive him, so that he could be awake when they raised the cross. The entertainers wanted to hear some cries of agony before they finished him off."

When he stopped, I told him, "Hera is with him at the hospital. I'm heading there now."

§ § §

(Hera's Journal, 05 November) I can't bear just to sit here and stare at the awful scene in front of me and think about losing him, so I must have something else to occupy my mind. I'm abstracting and summarizing the results of my research on the character and ecology of the North American deserts. Yucca Mountain stands about 85 miles northwest of Las Vegas, located just east of the Amargosa Desert and the northern tip of Death Valley National Park, and on the western edge of the Nellis Air Force Range and the US govern-

ment's Nevada Test Site. Most of the land in the entire surrounding area here, as in the state of Nevada as a whole, is owned by various agencies of the United States government.

This region of southwestern Nevada is situated about midway along a continuous series of great deserts—sequentially from south to north, the Chihuahuan, Sonoran (which includes the Colorado Desert), Mojave, and Great Basin. The Amargosa, Spanish for 'bitter spring,' is the southernmost section of the Great Basin Desert and is adjacent to the Mojave Desert.

These deserts are extremely arid and are also known for wide variation in daily temperatures. In the hottest summer months, temperatures can range anywhere between 60 and 120 degrees Fahrenheit, with the winter months having lows of 15 and highs around 65. Precipitation in the Mojave Desert region is next to nil most of the year, with a year-round total of only a few inches. Vegetation in the area around Yucca Mountain is dominated by shrubs such as sagebrush scrub, creosote bush, shadscale and bursages, and there are also some species of grasses, yucca and wildflowers.

Yucca Mountain forms part of a ridge whose elevations range from three to six thousand feet. It's a section of a large, ancient volcanic field that was created by major eruptions some 12 million years ago, in which thousands of feet of volcanic rocks were overlaid on an older sedimentary basin. The mountain's outer cover consists in several layers of a material known as 'tuff,' which is a hot, pyroclastic substance ejected from active volcanoes that then solidifies into rock. The tuff is referred to as either welded or unwelded, depending on its degree of fragmentation. Beneath the layers of tuff are structures made up of zeolite minerals, which are silicates that occur in volcanic lavas.

The water table at Yucca Mountain is some 1,500 feet below the surrounding valley floor. Although the region around the mountain is generally arid and receives little annual rainfall, there are two separate and significant hydrological zones on either side of it. About 20 miles to the northwest is Oasis Valley, which is at the southern end of a hydrographic area shaped like a rectangle about 200 miles square, reaching northwards to Pahute Mesa.

Oasis Valley has a network of springs, drawing on underground aquifers, that form the headwaters of the ancient Amargosa River, one of two desert rivers in the region (the other is the Mojave). Dry for most of the year and running underground for much of its 200-mile length, the Amargosa River flows fast and deep during the occasional flash floods that are characteristic of desert ecosystems; it meanders south into California and then takes a huge U-shaped bend, heading north to its terminus in Death Valley. Thirty miles directly south of Yucca Mountain is Ash Meadows, a wetland region of springs, seeps, small lakes, and streams sitting at the lower end of Amargosa Valley. Ash Meadows covers 20,000 acres and is a refuge for the many types of birds and small mammals that frequent the area.

The US government's Nevada Test Site is immediately adjacent to Yucca Mountain on the east, across Jackass Flats, while to the southeast is a formation called Busted Butte. To the north, across Beatty Wash, is the Oasis Valley. Directly westwards, 10 miles away, is the little town of Beatty, and then, carrying on in the same direction, are the Bullfrog Hills and Sarcobatus Flat—this wonderful appellation is derived from the name of the plant that is common there, the black greasewood shrub, *Sarcobatus vermiculatus*. Standing on Yucca Mountain and looking southwest toward Bare Mountain, one gazes down on Crater Flat, nestled between the two mountains, where the striking mound called Black Cone, created long ago by volcanic eruptions, rises 4,000 feet from the surrounding floor. Further to the southwest at the Nevada-California boundary is the Amargosa Desert and the Funeral Mountains; little more than 50 miles away in this direction is Death Valley.

The ceiling of the underground nuclear waste storage vault is about 1,000 feet below the crest of Yucca Mountain. A huge network of access and storage tunnels crisscrosses the vault inside the mountain, with external entrances at two portals. Radioactive materials that arrived over many years by rail and road were transferred into nickel-alloy containers, before being shunted by electric locomotives and robots into the permanent storage bays. Titanium drip shields line the roofs of the storage bays to keep moisture seeping through the rock off the containers. The Yucca site was designed specifically for high-level radioactive waste, consisting of spent fuel rods from nuclear reactors, and both solid and liquid plutonium wastes from production of nuclear missile warheads.

In the late 2040s its builders were just about ready to close the doors, turn out the lights, and throw away the key to the vault. That was one of the wind-up options. They didn't think people would try to break in; on the other hand, they also figured it might be worthwhile to ascertain whether anybody was crazy enough to want to become the site's live-in caretakers and maintain the monitoring equipment in good working order. It could prove useful to have a few live bodies sunbathing or gardening in the vicinity, who could helpfully direct the visitors' attention to the warning signs and hand them some terrifying literature if they were really curious.

§ § §

My mind has been wandering during the long hours I've been sitting at Phil's bedside. And so I allowed myself to drift back to the wonderful day we spent on our first flight, the one that took us over Yucca Mountain. Phil had no sooner mentioned his new assignment than I began to wonder if that place could be the foundation's permanent home. What instantly appealed to me, oddly enough, was the time frame that had guided the project's design and construction: At least 10,000, and perhaps as much as 100,000, years into the future, far beyond the life span of human civilization to date!

It seems to me that such a planning horizon is so far outside the human norm as to be almost comic, especially since the vault had to be designed so sturdily on account of the toxicity of the slumbering contents held in its casks. When most human civilizations built for perpetuity in the past, as with the pyramids of ancient Egypt or the cathedrals of medieval Europe, they did so in order to memorialize their deepest spiritual beliefs. But when it came time for modern men to find something to sequester for millennia, their deadliest waste products stood at the top of their list.

No matter. For me, this is just the kind of time frame I had in mind for my very own purposes. My kind will need to see many centuries, perhaps many millennia, pass before it will be able to feel comfortable sharing the earth with its human cousins. During the initial phases of its existence it will have to hide, as craftily as possible, while its numbers increase and its familiarity with surrounding habitats grows. I think I heard Phil say that, when the facility was full and closed, the entire area around it would be plastered with scary signs warning of a cascade of evils awaiting those who foolishly might try to breech its portals. How appropriate! If we could manage to infiltrate ourselves between the facility and the circle of signs, we might be left quite totally alone by our human cousins. Which is, of course, exactly what I have in mind.

§   §   §

(*Marco's Journal, 05-15 November*) I was approaching Phil's hospital room when I saw Hera emerging, leaning on a staff member for support, and one glance at her told me all I needed to know. Her face was mask-like, contorted by sorrow and despair; tears were flowing freely down her cheeks and onto the floor. She glanced up and flew into my arms, holding me with all her strength.

"He's gone, Marco," she sobbed. "Please take me home."

I helped her to her bed and we lay there side by side for hours as the day's light faded into evening. Every so often her whole body began shaking violently and then I held her close until it subsided. During those nightmarish hours, her sisters drifted into the room, one by one, and sat or lay next to her, murmuring words of comfort. Sometime during that night she whispered, "Marco, please put Gluck's *Orpheus and Eurydice* on the music system for me." As the first chords sounded, she explained, "I'm listening for the aria where Love gives Orpheus permission to rescue his beloved from the Underworld:

> *Go and seek Eurydice in her sojourn of death!*
> *If the sweet sound of your lyre and your melodious voice*
> *Should appease the wrath of the tyrants there,*
> *You shall lead her back from that gloomy empire.*

"I, too, would not hesitate for a moment to pass by the fearsome Cerberus, stationed at the portals of Hades, if I were granted such a dispensation. Alas for me, the ancient Greek myths no longer hold sway in the realm of the soul."

And so the first night passed. Another few days elapsed before I could rouse myself and leave Hera's suite; looking back now, I find that I cannot remember anything that may have happened during that time.

Finally I managed to return to the base and check in again with General Hone, who had been named Phil's replacement as head of the Joint Southwestern Air Command. Because Phil's command structure had always been entirely separate from the air force base administration, his staff had been able to keep their fellow officers in the dark about what had really happened. They made up a cock-and-bull story about Phil having suffered a heart attack, and the physicians on duty at the hospital cooperated in spreading this tale for their own reasons. Phil's staff were afraid that if the truth were known, nothing would stop the local commanders from putting their squadrons into the air and bombing the members' compounds to smithereens. And as for reporting 'up the ladder,' since they routinely communicated as little as possible of their activities to Washington headquarters anyway, they saw no reason to vary their practices in this case.

Meanwhile, their security detail has been quietly busy. The base harbor is guarded by an armed detachment and the entire coastline abutting the territory is swarming with patrol boats. No marine traffic enters or exits the area without being boarded and searched. All flights are grounded except for military missions. Guard detachments at all the gates on the fenced perimeter have been doubled. The quarry is boxed in. Only teleportation could help them escape, and that hasn't been invented yet, as far as I know.

One of the senior Chumash Warriors was brought it for questioning. To make him talk, all they had to do was screen a training videotape of a torture session made somewhere in South America many years ago. They got from him the complete list of Warrior membership, and all seventy-five or so were promptly taken into custody.

Hone said, "They're being held in chains below decks on a ship offshore until we decide what to do with them. Their residence permits and all other identifying documents have been confiscated, canceled, and destroyed. The club buildings will be put to the wrecker's ball this afternoon." He paused before adding, "I need you to let me know when Phil's other friends and I can go and see Hera. We know what he meant to her, and we want to express our sympathies. I also need to talk to her about some practicalities."

I told him I would convey his message.

§   §   §

A full week passed before Hera was ready to see anyone other than her sisters and close staff members. Then her mood changed abruptly. She called me into her suite, and when I looked at her I knew that she had temporarily put her grieving into abeyance.

"I need to see Hone at once. For today, just him. I'll be ready to see Phil's friends tomorrow."

I ran off to fetch him.

As soon as Hone arrived and had been allowed to express his condolences, Hera said, "I have to get out of here—I mean, all of us. As soon as possible. I don't feel safe here anymore. Will you help me?"

"I'll do whatever is in my power, whether or not I have proper authority to do it."

Then for the first time in more than a week, she smiled and spoke softly. "Thank you."

"I have a letter for you from Phil. It was found with his personal effects in an envelope marked 'to be opened in the event of my death.' I also have a copy of his will—he appointed me as executor. You are named as his sole heir." He gave her the documents but she remained standing there, holding them.

"I'll look at them later. Now I must tell you what I want to do, with your help. Let's sit down on the veranda."

She restarted the conversation as soon as we were all seated. "Of course, you know about our plan to move to Yucca Mountain." Hone nodded. "Construction has been under way for about a year already, but our facilities are nowhere near finished. I want to set up a temporary encampment in the town of Beatty until our own establishment is ready. I'd like to make the move there almost immediately, leaving just the apes here, along with the professional staff who care for them, and a security detail. That means we'll have to make do for now with a big group of trailers, and I'll need a security fence erected to enclose everything. I'm aware that the living conditions are going to be quite primitive, but it can't be helped. I'll try to have the construction schedule at Yucca accelerated so we can be transferred there sooner than planned."

Hone answered, "I can help to get that done. I'll take Marco back with me to the base, with your permission, and he and I will get started on it right away. We'll have the first progress report ready for you when we return tomorrow with Phil's friends."

She smiled again and shook Hone's hand as we departed.

During the helicopter ride to the base, Hone remarked, "You remember the Chumash Warriors? We stashed the lot of them in chains on one of their finest drug-running ships. Yesterday some unknown folks apparently captained the vessel out beyond the twelve-mile limit before being lifted off by copters. The ship of fools was set adrift, and a few minutes later it disappeared from our radar screens. As for those they left behind at the Colony, military law has been imposed on them, and we're trying to cut out every last bit of the rot that had set in there. Will you relay this to Hera for me when you get back? I want her to know that we took care of things."

"Speaking for myself, I'm delighted, and I only wish I could have taken part in the garbage detail. I will tell Hera, but somehow I don't think it'll make much difference to her."

As it turns out, what did matter to her was what the large group of Phil's friends had to say, beyond expressing their sorrow, when they arrived the next day. Hone and I had come a bit earlier, with the news that a collection of trailers had already been purchased for shipment to Beatty and that a construction crew was on its way to the town, ready to install water and sewage facilities and a secure perimeter fence. Hone reviewed the documents with Hera.

"Your encampment will be ready in two months. And all of this will be paid for by the Colony, as the down payment on a proposed settlement for damages with Phil's estate that, I expect, will total in the hundreds of millions of euros. Since you are his heir, your lawyers will be involved in the negotiations hereafter."

She scanned the papers and replied, "Thank you."

After the larger group had paid its respects, their spokespersons asked for a private meeting with Hera and me. They told us that they were sickened by the whole trajectory of events during the past few years, and that, if she were willing, they would like to take their families to live and work at her Yucca Settlement. She did not have to be reminded that among their ranks are highly skilled technicians in weaponry, communications technologies, transport mechanics, and scientific instrumentation.

After the guests had finished delivering their offer, Hera remained silent. Then she broke down and wept, and after restoring her composure, said simply, "I am overwhelmed. I accept your offer. And once we are settled there one of our priorities will be to create a suitable memorial to the person who has touched all of our lives so deeply."

§ § §

(*Marco's Journal, 11 January 2055*) I had been dreading this meeting, but there was no possibility of avoiding it. I had to say goodbye before entering the crew lockup prior to departure on the shuttle rocket. The timing was awful. To disguise my anxieties I rattled on to Hera about the technical details of the mission. Then I got up to leave.

She rose from her chair but immediately collapsed back into it, her entire body shaking. I rushed over. "Mother, what's wrong. Are you ill?"

She was weeping uncontrollably now, and all I could think of to do was to hold her in my arms until she regained some composure. Finally she blurted out, "I'm so afraid I won't see you again. I don't know what I'll do if you don't come back, Marco. Please don't go! Please, I beg you!"

I relaxed my grip on her and moved across the veranda. I stood there, saying nothing, looking out over the ocean vista now starlit after the moon's decline. Minutes passed but neither of us spoke. Finally she stood up, crossed the room, and took me in her arms.

"No, no, no. I'm so ashamed of my weakness. I've been forcing those words back down my throat for months, every time they threatened to burst out. You see," she smiled at me now, "another half-hour and I would have carried it off. What a shame!

"I've always known you had to make this journey, ever since you sent Phil to break the news. You're as bad as I am, do you know that, Marco? Remember the trip I made to Indonesia to put an end to Klamm's pursuit of us? Well, this is your great solo adventure, away from your family, and I want you to go." We both laughed at the same moment. "Do you believe me?"

"Yes, I do, actually. And now it's time for me to leave. I can't promise I'll write you any letters. But we'll be broad-casting regularly back to earth, both on public and secure channels, through the International Space Station. Try not to worry. Phil's group of friends—now your colleagues—have lots of influence in these parts, and I can't see that you'll run into any serious trouble during the eighteen months or so that I'll be away."

Sub-Compiler's Note: This journal file was sent to me at the base camp on Mars via radio transmission.

15 SEPTEMBER 2055, HERA'S JOURNAL

The Royal Library Collection at Alexandria, the Egyptian city founded by Alexander the Great on the shores of the Mediterranean Sea, was assembled under the reign of the Ptolemies, the last dynasty of the Pharaohs, beginning in the fourth century B.C. The library's huge inventory of 40,000 papyrus rolls—duplicated in its entirety nowhere else in the ancient world—included the most famous works of the age in mathematics, astronomy, geometry, mechanics, and medicine. The library itself was part of the Royal Museum and was surrounded by courts, gardens, and a zoological park. About fifty resident scholars were housed there, supported by the royal family.

According to a legend that originates in one of the Roman writer Seneca's dialogues, the entire library went up in flames in 48 B.C. when Julius Caesar, attacking the naval forces commanded by his fellow Roman general Pompey in Alexandria's harbor, sent fire ships against his foe that drifted to the docks, setting the granaries ablaze in a conflagration that then spread to the palace grounds.

Then during the twentieth century a huge collection of artifacts from the ancient capital of the Ptolemies was found near the harbor of the modern city, buried beneath only twenty-three feet of water and mud. In 2002 UNESCO

opened a spectacular replacement for the ancient library—
the Bibliotheca Alexandrina—but late in the year 2030 it
was sacked and completely destroyed once again.

While preparing the text for my remarks to be delivered
at today's ceremony, I refreshed my memory this morning
about the ancient Royal Library of Alexandria. My Library of
World Science, which I call the Library of Amargosa, is an
admirable successor to its earlier prototype.

Today is the sisters' forty-first birthday. My speech was to
be the inaugural event in our magnificent amphitheater,
only recently completed and dedicated to the memory of
Philip Ziegler, that sits in Crater Flat at the base of Yucca
Mountain. In early morning I stood at the podium looking
out on the sea of bodies arranged on cushions—and shaded
from the sun—in our outdoor meeting area. They were all
garbed in the ceremonial dress we had chosen, a short white
toga, perfect for the desert heat. But it gave me the oddest
feeling of having traveled backwards in time. I imagined
myself to be the peripatetic Aristotle at the School of Athens
in the fourth century B.C., about to address the acolytes in
philosophy.

And what an extraordinary bunch of acolytes our Second
Generation is becoming! Their mental faculties are as good
or better than my sisters' and mine, and they seem less
afflicted with the neurological disorders that have bothered
many of us. They're quick and eager students, as we were,
and even though they've only recently turned nine, they are
mature and introspective beyond their years. They represent
every racial type of humans on earth, thanks to the care my
father and sisters took in selecting their Group of 500. This
also means that there is enough genetic diversity in their
tribe for them to interbreed without the worry of magnifying
inborn defects.

As I surveyed the gathering, another aspect, too, was
striking, namely the unbalanced gender numbers among

them. This is something my sisters and I have been concerned about for some years now. At the time we chose the allocation that was decided upon—three-quarters female and one-quarter male—we already knew that for reasons of safety we'd be living in an unconventional collectivity, not in nuclear family groups. If, when they reach sexual maturity, we were to sort the next generation into small groups, the sex ratios among them would resemble those found among the gorillas. But once their own children started to be born, would we expect the sex ratio of males to females normally appearing in humans—a very slight majority of males—to show up among them? If so, perhaps that generation would revert to a more conventional pattern of family groupings. I'll have to talk to my biology sisters about all this.

I began my address.

ADDRESS TO THE MEMBERS OF THE YUCCA SETTLEMENT
HERA SUJANA-STONE

Before I talk to you about the Charter of the Yucca Settlement, I ask you to call to mind those who are not with us. First, my mother, Ina Sujana, and Franklin Peter Stone, my father, whose dream it was to bring into the world a special group of people who might help save human civilization from descending into chaos. I ask you to rise and dedicate a moment of silence to their memories.

In the places of honor arranged on the podium behind me are the members of the original Band of Sisters who were born in far-off New Guinea in 2014. You know them as your aunts and you treasure their company as I do. We are all here today because the sisters stood together in the face of adversity in order to fulfill our destiny on earth. There is one empty seat, reserved for our sister

Io, who is presently living in Bali, whom we hope will rejoin us before long.

Another empty seat on the podium, on which rests a military cap, marks the place where General Philip Ziegler, my dear partner, would have sat had he not been cruelly ambushed and murdered by his enemies last year. We must never forget him, for without his help it is unlikely that we would be assembling here today, secure in our near-term future. There is one more empty seat, reserved for our beloved Marco, Io's natural son, my adopted son and companion, who at this moment is occupying himself somewhere on the planet Mars. We believe that he will come back to us one day, and for that reason his chair will remain vacant at these ceremonies until he returns to fill it.

Today I have brought you the design for the crest by which your Settlement here, and the Library of Amargosa that is entrusted to your care, will be known to all. The crest shows the profile of the great Carstensz Pyramid, now called Puncak Jaya, the 5,000-meter peak on the island of New Guinea in the shadow of which the First Generation, my sisters and I, were born.

You know that you are special in some respects and that you are this way because you and we were designed thus. Your mental faculties are different from that of the people who call themselves *Homo sapiens,* but not so much that we cannot understand each other. You are unlike them, but not in the way of the Buddha, who is represented with a knot of hair on the top of his head, which is thought to signify the second brain he grew to contain his enlightenment. You differ chiefly in that your sense of placement among all the beings of this earth is not the same as theirs.

The Charter I deliver to you today sets forth the mission that your generation and its successors must carry out. Here are its tenets:

- *To protect this Foundation Settlement, our colony of apes, the staff who assist us, and our Hutterites and their way of life;*
- *To guard the Library of Amargosa and keep secret the access codes to the facility where it is preserved;*
- *To learn the body of knowledge and pass it on to your descendants; and*
- *To establish settlements elsewhere, as you are able to do this.*

Soon all this will be entrusted to you. And if it should turn out, as I suspect it will, that what you have been given for safeguarding will become, in time, the only comprehensive record of modern science remaining anywhere on this earth, then you will have no choice but to take responsibility for determining its fate.

You will become full members of the Assembly upon reaching the age of fifteen. Every generation—beginning with your own—will be divided into seven groups, each of which will share a secret among itself that is not to be revealed to the others. The seven secrets are seven codes. Each code controls access to one of the seven doors in the vaults within the bowels of Yucca Mountain, and behind the set of doors is stored the original version of the complete holdings in our Library of Amargosa.

Our library embraces documentation on all the forms of scientific knowledge, as well as the works of art, crafts and technology we were able to acquire, plus machinery and devices of every kind, and many other artifacts of humankind. You have daily access to this knowledge in our huge videodisc collection and the copies of instrumentation and machinery we have made for our use. However, entrance to the main storage vaults themselves is only possible when your Assembly authorizes the doors to be opened.

The sciences of nature invented by humans over the last few centuries represent a secular instrument of breathtaking scope and deep insight. These sciences, which also bestow on us truly magical powers begetting useful things, describe a domain where no gods reside. As a highly pragmatic species, humans decided to hang onto their ancient faiths as well—as a kind of insurance policy in case science turned out to be wrong. They would have science for their bodies and religion for their souls.

However, you cannot worship two equally demanding and opposed gods without eventually tearing yourselves to pieces. Serious trouble began when science invaded religion's core, when science began to regard God's most precious handiwork— the human creature—as just another chunk of DNA to be improved upon. Once embarked upon this venture, where and why would you stop?

Although humans are an exceptionally cunning as well as super-stitious race, they did not know where to stop. And yet, at the same time, this cunning contained the seeds of their own down-fall because those powers inevitably fell into the hands of reli-gious fundamentalists, among whom there are many trained scientists. These zealous ones rejoiced at the prospect of using all such powers against unbelievers of one kind or another, turning the earth into one vast battleground, a paroxysm of fanaticism and intra-species hatred. Of course, this hatred always wears a disguise, its bearers claiming to be mere blameless innocents doing the bidding of whatever bloodthirsty deity they profess to serve.

When such holy wars raged long ago, in the ancient Near East and Asia or during the Crusades and the Counter-Reformation in the West, the damage done did not last very long, for the earth and its scavengers soon recycled the blood and gore and every-one moved on. But in our own time the zealots began to wield the much-improved weapons of modern science, especially molecular biology, throwing into battle everything a warped and intolerant mind could engineer into the various platforms of life that nature had labored upon. Remember, too, that here we are speaking about an orientation of mind that knows no limit: The very existence of unbelievers anywhere is an affront to the godhead and a rebuke to the faithful who tolerate their presence.

Conjure up in your minds, if you will, this imaginary dialogue. They say to us, "We need our gods. We cannot endure without them." We reply, as we take their science gently from their bloodied hands, "Indeed you do, and you will also be far happier without science's challenge to your faith. You know in your hearts that you need your churches far more than you do your laboratories. We will take care of your science, we will preserve and extend it, because it does not terrify us as it does you." In so doing we redeem the true value in their science, which was never meant to serve the ends of fanaticism. We will restore science to its glory as a pure mode of understanding the physical world.

But modern science cannot understand the inherent limits to its own application. As a self-enclosed system of thought originating in the human mind—which is itself a product of nature—it defines nature, in circular fashion, as that which can be apprehended through science. To understand the limits of science, another type of wisdom is needed, and you will also be its bearers and interpreters. These limits, you have learned, are life and death itself.

We have taught you to listen often to a profound and moving musical composition, Gustav Mahler's *The Song of the Earth*, a cycle of six songs composed in 1908. We asked you to pay particular attention to this line in Mahler's work, which recurs in the first of his series of songs: *"Dunkel ist das Leben, ist der Tod."* In English: *"Dark is our life, dark is death."*

The single line I just quoted occurs three times in the opening song, entitled "The Drinking-Song of Earth's Sorrow," which Mahler wrote for the tenor voice. Now I will give you the full passage in which it appears in the last stanza of that song:

> Look down o'er there!
> In the moonlight, among the graves,
> Crouches a wild and ghostly figure—It's an ape!
> Hear how its howls resound piercingly
> In the sweet fragrance of life!
> Now take the wine! Now is the time, my dear friends!
> Drain the golden goblet to the end!
> Dark is our life, dark is death.

Each of us must interpret the meaning of such enigmatic words for herself and himself. I will tell you what they mean to me and also what I have taken from them, because these sentiments, which are etched so deeply into my mind as to be never far from the threshold of recollection, have shaped the tenets of the Charter I give you today.

First, that passage means to me that life binds us with a heavy and unbreakable chain to nature, and in particular to the wild animality that is symbolized by the figure of the ape. We, too, are primates—specifically, great apes—regardless of how much we worship our superior brains and are tempted to see ourselves as radically different from our closest cousins among created beings. And a great part of your mission in life, as well as that of your descendants, is to secure the future of the great apes on this planet.

You will refuse to accept the lie that humans have told to each other, presuming themselves to be unique in all of creation. The truth is this: We and *Homo sapiens* are an integral part of that late branching of the Hominini tribe that produced two subtribes—one known as pongids (orangutans), and the other,

Hominina, where we and the great apes appear. In differing degrees we have genomes and brains so similar to these apes as to be virtually indistinguishable from theirs. And yet humans wage a campaign of unrelenting terror against them, so that their very survival in the wild is in doubt. Our ape sanctuaries are merely the first step in this mission. Your ultimate aim must be to secure a huge territory for them where they may live undisturbed by us—perhaps even a continent they and other wild species can call their own.

Second, Mahler's words tell me that life's sweetness—the sheer joy of existence—cannot be tasted except in the presence of the looming reality of death, life's constant companion. The joining of life and death in these lines tells me that there is an impenetrable quality to our place in nature, one that resists—and always will resist—our attempts to come to terms with the question as to why we are here on our beloved earth.

But above all these lines say this to me: That no species risen from this earth should seek to shine the light of its thought—whether religious or scientific—all the way down to the bottom of the well of darkness where life and death abide together. This is the same darkness to which the great poet Milton made reference, in the passage where his Adam asks God why He had created him:

> Did I request thee, Maker, from my clay
> To mould me Man, did I solicit thee
> From darkness to promote me?

What did Milton mean in employing the word 'darkness' here? This is my guess: Phrased in the language of modern science, what he is pointing to is the prior evolutionary heritage from which hominins possessing self-consciousness evolved. Thus, in this context, the word 'darkness' refers to the life of animals that have brain activity, as both reptiles and other mammals do, although they are not aware of that activity, as we are.

This darkness represents a limit to our understanding of the meaning of our own existence on earth. It cannot be penetrated by the light of thought. In natural evolution, time and succession are everything: One cannot go backwards, as it were, and ask for an explanation or a rationale for what preceded the first appearance of a species—*Homo sapiens*, the 'thinking species'—having a capacity for self-awareness.

A veil is drawn across the intersection of life and death. Religions have always tried to pierce that veil and to provide an explanation originating outside nature itself, to give life and death a meaning 'beyond biology,' as it were. Religions speak of an immaterial entity, the soul, to be consigned for eternity either to paradisical bliss or unendurable torment; of the vindication of ancient prophecy; and of the demand of the creator-god for an accounting of performance at the end of days. Listen to the words of the Catholic requiem mass:

> *Death and nature are astonished*
> *When all creation rises again*
> *To answer in front of the judge.*

This is not science's nature, however. The universe pictured in the science of nature is cold dust and fierce hot gas and all-consuming black holes. We are alone in this impossibly vast space, bolstering our courage with the meanings we create for ourselves.

This is the primordial void we encounter when we search into the history of nature with our probing conscious minds, back to the beginnings of time in the Big Bang, fourteen billion years ago. We find no evidence of an All-seeing Mind anywhere in its unfathomable reaches. The idea of our sailing alone in a mute and meaningless sea of pure matter and energy can seem absurd, even repellent. But it is part of the truth that our modern science bestows upon us, a truth we are compelled to understand and accept. We need courage to accept the evident fact that our own capacity for thought and self-awareness is a simple accident of evolutionary chance, which arose once, unpredictably, and will disappear again in the same fashion.

I do not fault humans for relying on their religions to shield themselves from the existential horror that this darkness and meaninglessness elicits in them. On the contrary, I believe that *Homo sapiens* is in its essence an innately religious species and more properly should baptize itself *Homo religiosus*. There is no example of a settled human society that did not erect its own distinctive shrine to some set of higher beings. They will always do so; it is a part of their nature at the deepest level of their being. Yet there is a reciprocal calamity in the solution they have chosen, for in seeking to avoid the existential horror to which I referred, their religions have substituted the mundane horrors of mutual slaughter and bitter intolerance.

All too often humans have paid a hideous price for their need of faith. You may appreciate the nature of that price by considering the story of the Hutterites, and appropriately so, for they live among us today and help us with our lives. For what they have experienced since the Brethren was founded in Moravia in 1530 is relevant to why we ourselves are here at Yucca Mountain. Like Mennonites, the Hutterian Brethren are Anabaptists, that is, Protestants who came to believe that infant baptism is wrong. Unlike the Mennonites, they also live in colonies in which all material goods are held in common. They are also pacifists. You might say that these are interesting and worthy beliefs.

However, this was not the way the dominant religious authorities in the sixteenth century responded. For refusing to renounce these doctrines, their founder, Jacob Hutter, was burned at the stake in 1536. Thereafter, the Brethren embarked on an incredible odyssey to escape persecution, which took them from Moravia to Slovakia, thence to Romania and the Ukraine and Russia, and finally to the United States and Canada in the early twentieth century. Here they finally found refuge and safety.

Your Charter obliges you to continue to protect our Hutterian Brethren from assaults by other humans, and to provide them with medical treatment and judicial procedures, but not otherwise to interfere with their lives, especially the religion that they cherish. They have no wish to change their way of life, which has served them well for many centuries now. The agreement I made with the Elders does provide, however, that any of their young who wish to serve among our technical staff may do so, as long as they have the Elders' permission.

Religious terrorism touched the lives of many of Jacob Hutter's contemporaries. I will give you one more story out of those awful times. Gerard Kremer (1512-1594), known to the world as Gerardus Mercator de Rupelmonde, was born in Flanders to humble parents. An uncle sponsored his education and he graduated from the University of Louvain in 1532. A few years later he took training in mathematics from Gemma Frisius and apprenticed to the engraver and instrument maker, Gaspard Van der Heyden. In 1536 the three of them received a commission from the Emperor Charles V to construct a terrestrial globe. Mercator began mapmaking in 1537, and in 1538 he produced his first map using a projection, one in which the name "North America" appeared for the first time anywhere. He had married in 1536 and soon had six children.

In 1554 Mercator was arrested and thrown into a dungeon on a charge of heresy. He had been named as part of a circle of Protestants who held heretical beliefs, including denying the existence of purgatory as well as the physical presence of Christ in the communion host. For these crimes others in the same circle as he were either buried alive or burned at the stake after having been subjected to prolonged torture.

Lack of clear evidence against Mercator caused him to be released after seven months, although in those days even persons who were incarcerated and later deemed innocent had to pay the costs of their imprisonment. He was a lucky man because almost certainly he did secretly hold the same views that cost his friends their lives. Nevertheless he went on to live for another forty years and to be remembered to this day as the inventor of the 'Mercator Projection,' a method of representing the globe on maps that brought about a revolution in maritime navigation.

The fate of these two courageous individuals may stand in your memories as a marker for the crimes committed against larger groups of peaceful and devout believers who were murdered in Europe long ago, such as the Cathars of France in the thirteenth century and the many Jews who fell victim to the Spanish Inquisition's *auto-da-fe*—the appallingly misnamed 'act of faith.' Above all let us not forget those accused of being witches, most of whom were women, who were tortured and burned by the hundreds of thousands under the guise of rooting out religious heresy.

Why have I related these stories to you today? Because you need to know why we are here, in this special and unusual place, and why you may need to stay here for the rest of your lives. The genetic differences from other humans that you carry in your bodies imperils you today in no lesser degree than did Jacob Hutter's stubborn adherence to his faith five centuries ago. You must call upon all the powers made possible in the science and technology entrusted to your care in order to guard yourselves against the fate that befell Hutter and from which Mercator narrowly escaped.

Therefore, you must master that science, develop it further if you can, and put it to use, but not in the same way as other humans would do. You may use it passively and defensively, so to speak, to enhance your own well being and to protect yourselves from threats to your survival. You may also use it to relieve the suffering of yourselves and other creatures. But you may not otherwise utilize it to project your power over other species. Even when you expand your settlements, you must always limit your numbers so as to leave ample room for other species. You must become wise enough to learn how to do this.

Afterward a small group of the youngsters came up to me and asked me to accompany all of the acolytes and sisters on a hiking expedition that would set out at the crack of dawn tomorrow.

§   §   §

(Hera's Journal, 16 September) We set out eastwards from Yucca Mountain, past Fortymile Canyon and the brilliantly multi-colored Calico Hills, rising north of Jackass Flats, and up into the Shoshone Mountains, until we came to a secluded spot where Topopah Spring bubbles gaily to the surface. There stood a small replica of a Greek temple. It was sculpted out of rocks from the local area, left over from the site construction work at Yucca, and hauled to Topopah Spring by mule trains. The temple was built to the proportions of the ancient original—six columns across the short side of the rectangle and fourteen columns along the longer side.

The spokesperson for the children gave a short speech,

concluding, "For all time to come this special place near our Mother Settlement shall be known to our kind as 'The Temple of Hera.'" Then we had a grand picnic.

§   §   §

Athena, Gaia and I stayed behind after the others returned. We were guarded by a small security detail and supplied with provisions for camping out there overnight. That evening we sat beside the temple and watched the stars come out across the desert sky.

"I'm a little ashamed of the false bravado I was exhibiting during my speech today," I remarked abruptly, after we had been sitting quietly for some time. "I didn't want to frighten them, so I stuck to the line that we sisters agreed upon some time ago, and just referred to the fact that we are different from other people ...."

Tina interrupted. "Actually, it was scary enough, after you got done with the references to Hutter, Mercator, and assorted victims of the Inquisition! The point was pretty clear to me, so I assume it was also evident to these bright young kids. In effect, you told them that they're all in hiding in the shadow of their private mountain, and you at least implied that their lives are at risk now and in the future."

"I just couldn't help going down that road. I confess to you that I'm terrified of what will happen when they come looking for us."

Again we sat quietly for awhile and then I turned to face my two sisters. "Our home is almost ready for occupancy. This is where our fate will be sealed, one way or another. If we succeed, we'll be taking separate evolutionary paths from other humans."

"And we *are* different, aren't we?" Athena replied. "Unlike most humans, we're quite comfortable with the idea that we are simply the products of evolutionary chance. We accept the fact that we share a huge proportion of our genome with creatures some people loathe, such as slugs and rats. This idea doesn't bother us."

"Yes," Gaia chimed in. "We do accept the fact of our commonality with much of the rest of life on earth because this, too, is the lesson told by the chemical structure of the DNA molecule: The same sugar-phosphate 'backbone' and the same set of four chemical base-pairs is at work in the genomes of both plants and animals, which in the most recent species classification scheme jointly make up the huge 'superkingdom' called *Eukaryota*. We are the heirs of not just the species of plants and animals still present on earth, of course, but of all that ever arose on this planet. Think of it: This line of inheritance stretches back an incredible 3.5 billion years! It can be tracked across the enormous canvas of prebiotic evolution before it emerges fully in what's called the 'Cambrian explosion,' the great proliferation of animal life that started more than 500 million years ago.

"Frankly, I for one don't care whether or not humans ever come to terms with their genetic inheritance. The fact of the matter is that the true story of creation is told in the book of DNA, not in the ancient holy books of religions. And it includes the two other subgenera of humans— *H. neanderthalensis* and *H. floresiensis*—that coexisted with us in Europe and Asia until quite recently, within the last 30,000 years or so, until both became extinct. I know this story by heart. Here it is:

Superkingdom (Empire): Eukaryota

Kingdom: Animalia
Phylum: Chordata
Class: Mammalia
Order: Primates
Suborder: Anthropoidea
Superfamily: Hominoidea
Family: Hominidae
Subfamily: Homininae

Tribe: Hylobatini

Subtribe: Hylobatina
Genus: Sympbalangus *(siamangs)*
Genus: Hylobates *(gibbons)*

Tribe: Hominini

Subtribe: Pongina, Pongo
(orangutans)

Subtribe: Hominina
Genus: Gorilla
berengei *(mountain gorilla)*
gorilla *(western lowland gorilla)*
graueri *(eastern lowland gorilla)*

Genus: Homo *(Pan)*
paniscus *(bonobo chimpanzee)*
troglodytes *(common chimpanzee)*

Genus: Homo *(Sapiens)*
carstenszi OR scientificus *(us)*
religiosus *(humans)*

"Starting from the bottom of the list I just recited for you, the molecular clock gives us approximate dates for the appearances of the various species on the genetic tree. *Sapiens* and *Pan* had a common ancestor sometime between four and seven million years ago. Both of us had a common ancestor with the gorillas a bit earlier, and further back still there are branches for orangutans, the lesser apes—gibbons and siamangs—and the monkeys. And so on. Remember, our ancestry reaches back into the depths of time in animal evolution.

"It's the 'inside story,' so to speak, the time-dated record kept by nature in successive genomic sequences, that tells the truth: Every member of the genus *Homo* carries around—in *every single one* of the ten trillion cells in her or his body—the living proof of this proposition that we are, quite simply, African apes. This is what the science of molecular genetics means to us: It is our alternative creation myth, if you will."

"You know, Gaia," Athena said, "that reminds me of a wonderful story in a book by an American primatologist I'm just now rereading. Just a second; I have the book with me; I can find the passage quickly." She reached into her backpack and pulled out the book, speaking to us as she searched through its pages. "He did fieldwork in Kenya with baboons for many years, and one day he was talking to two young Masai males just after anaesthetizing a baboon for his research, which he had baptized with the name 'Daniel.' Yes, here it is. I marked the passage:

> Suddenly, I get this giddy desire to shock these guys a little. I continue, 'These baboons really are our relatives. In fact, this baboon is my cousin.' And with that I lean over and give Daniel a loud messy kiss on his big ol' nose.

I get more of a response than I bargained for. The
Masai freak and suddenly, they are waving their
spears real close to my face, like they mean it. One is
yelling, 'He is not your cousin, he is not your cousin!'

"Humans just can't seem to come to terms with what their science of DNA is trying to tell them. If there were an all-powerful psychiatrist in the universe, she'd probably consider them to be in a permanent state of denial about reality."

"Let's not forget *Homo neanderthalensis*, sisters," I added. "Wouldn't it have made a huge difference to how human civilization evolved if humans hadn't hunted them down, to the last man, woman and child? It wasn't that long ago, either; there is Neanderthal DNA that's only about 35,000 years old. What if this species had continued to evolve together with *Homo sapiens* in what is now Europe? Had this occurred, perhaps humans wouldn't have turned out to be so arrogant and domineering on earth. Neanderthal looked much more like African apes than humans do. Maybe humans would have understood their kinship with the apes if Neanderthal had still been around when humans started thinking about these things, when they began to form their civilizations."

"What all this really means, Hera, is that we do believe the story that science tells about our natural history on earth and our close kinship with the apes, whereas most humans don't and never will," Gaia replied. "So we are very different from them in this way. Moreover, we're willing to live by that story, aren't we? What I mean is that we see ourselves as one of nature's many random outcomes. Unlike humans, we don't believe that we're entitled to rule over the rest of nature and to treat it purely as a means for our own ends. All things are ends-in-themselves in our way of thinking. All things also use each other to attain their own ends. But there is no entitlement to dominion anywhere in nature."

"Maybe we believe this and are willing to live by it," I said, "because, after all, we are one of modern science's finest products, aren't we? We *know* that we weren't created by God. We're a bit like Laplace, the famous French physicist, who was queried by Napoleon as to why his *Celestial Mechanics* made no mention of God. Laplace replied, 'Highness, I have no need of that hypothesis.' We were created by science—our father's science. That means we're the rightful owners and users of that science, doesn't it?

"I hope and pray that this viewpoint will become part of our kind's defining culture, so that every future generation accepts it as we do. If our successors indeed do so, they'll be entitled to change the provisional name we've bestowed upon our species. As you already know, I hope that, eventually, we'll be entitled to refer to ourselves not as *Homo carstenszi* but rather as *Homo scientificus.*"

"And is it your expectation," Athena asked, "that there will be a sort of parallel evolution of the two extent species of *Homo, religiosus* and *scientificus,* hereafter? Will the two diverge more and more over time? In the end, will humans give up their science in order to dedicate themselves entirely to their religions, whereas we'll live wholly by science's natural philosophy?"

"Speaking for myself," I answered, "I believe it's entirely possible this could happen. I've watched human societies, the ones that science, technology, and industrialization made wealthy far beyond the dreams of past centuries. This wealth doesn't make them happy. It cannot make them happy because essentially they're religious beings. And if there is one point on which all religions ever adopted by humans agree, it's this: You cannot buy your way into heaven."

Athena interjected. "Remember, only the monotheist's view of the spirit world claims that Spirit created Nature out of nothing. On the other hand, to follow what you called science's natural philosophy does not deny the reality of spirit. Spirit is no more and no less than the disciplined activity of our minds. In our minds, we roam freely across the world of ideas, unbound to matter, passing through the entirely immaterial realms of mathematics, visual images, ideals and the moral order. These are the things that are seen with the mind's eye.

"For thinking beings such as we are, these kinds of hidden things are no less real than is the physical world of nature evident to our senses. *This* spirit world—the world of ideas—exists for us in all its glory and infinite beauty. Traversing our way through this world is the Buddha's path to Enlightenment, one of humanity's ancient dreams. The traveler in that realm seeks understanding of truth and beauty. But she does not seek dominion. That's the difference."

I tried to break in, but Athena held up her hand and said, "Wait a moment, I just want to finish with my train of thought."

"We regard ourselves as purely natural entities, risen from the muck of this earth like all other living things on it. But that doesn't mean we're without all religion, does it? One of the great principles of modern science is the law of the conservation of matter and energy, which says that matter and energy can be neither created nor destroyed. And that means we're made of stuff that is eternally recycled in nature, 'ashes to ashes, dust to dust,' as the Christian burial rite would have it. We're composed of atoms that have appeared before within living forms and will appear again later, after we've finished using them temporarily, so to speak.

"So after our deaths the elements that formed our bodies will eventually re-emerge in the composition of new living forms, perhaps as plants or insects—or even as an ape! This is what has been called 'the transmigration of souls' and 'eternal return,' and it's what Buddhism teaches, as I understand it. All this is perfectly consistent with what the modern science of nature compels us to accept. So I think we may be 'religious' in this sense."

"We have to concede, Tina, that some humans have also sought that path," I noted. "But for most of them this terrain is unsatisfying. Overwhelmingly they have chosen the other path, which requires only obedience to the creator-spirit. I can foresee the time when humans will turn away from science and the world of industrial goods that it brings, so that they may concentrate more fully once more, as they did in the past, on their immortal souls. They will do this, I'm convinced, even though it means regressing back to a premodern, agricultural lifestyle."

"You expect them to surrender their science in order to secure their religion. So shall we inherit that science from them and become its keepers and developers?" Gaia asked.

"Absolutely, yes," I averred. "My objective is to draw a line in the sand between religion and science—in order to protect both. The coming of molecular biology and the science of DNA is the signal for a final rupture between science and monotheistic religion. Each is now a constant danger for the other; in each other's presence they compose an explosive mixture, like the gases hydrogen and oxygen. Both can only survive and endure on the same planet if they carefully avoid one another. This is the meaning of the appearance on earth of our kind and its fate, which we have accepted: To enable this mutual avoidance strategy to succeed."

"Your mention of our new species brings something to mind," Gaia interjected. "There's a huge issue hanging over our heads—the further genetic engineering of our own kind. Our youngsters will be sexually mature in a few years. We must resolve this issue before that time arrives."

I thought for awhile before replying. "Obviously we must consider the matter deeply before deciding what is the right thing to do. We *might* re-engineer the third generation slightly in order to guarantee our reproductive isolation from humans. Doing that doesn't change who or what we are now. All it does is prevent what we are from being diluted by a re-mixing with human genes. In short, we would confirm and conserve our uniqueness in this way.

"But by the same token it would be wrong to alter ourselves again arbitrarily. I regard the experiments on our genomes that our parents performed, as well as the experiments on chimpanzees that they conducted in the course of their scientific studies, as the primal acts of original sin for our species—speaking metaphorically, of course. Our kind will carry their intentional violations of the natural order in its genes until our species becomes extinct. I take the position that there should be no further genetic re-engineering. That's my own position, for now at any rate. The decision will be made by collective consensus of the original sisters."

§   §   §

We remained sitting close together outside the temple in the cool night air and returned our gaze to the worlds above, looking in the direction of the southern sky, where the Red Planet glowed brightly. We heard a wolf howl in the distance under the waning moon, answered by another, and Gaia said, "How quickly they return to the haunts of their forebears." I didn't reply. She knew what was on my mind. "The spaceships leave Mars for the return journey in about six months' time, Hera. Marco will come back safe and sound, I promise you. You will see him again."

Note to the Reader

Go to www.herasaga.com

STUDY GUIDE AND INDEX, including brief explanations of technical terminology, references, and web-links;

MAPS AND PICTURES, containing photographs and web-links illustrating the locations referred to in the text;

IMAGINARY FUTURES, a short essay and bibliography on the tradition of utopian literature in modern Western thought, which begins with Thomas More's *Utopia* (1516), especially the fascination with science and technology in that tradition;

FURTHER READING, a short bibliography dealing with themes in the text;

SCIENTIFIC ARTICLES related to themes in the text.

See also "About *The Herasaga*" at the end of this volume.

🖰 = web link available at www.herasaga.com

ACKNOWLEDGMENTS

During a trip to Nova Scotia in the summer of 2003, my partner, Jeanne Inch, introduced me to her old friends Alex and Rhoda Colville and their daughter, Anne Kitz. Subsequently, the artist gave me permission to use three of his paintings as cover artwork for this trilogy. I am most grateful to Alex Colville for this gracious act, and to Anne Kitz for assisting me with the arrangements for securing the transparencies and permissions from the museums that hold two of these paintings.

In at least some respects, the painting style known as "magic realism" fits well with the minor literary genre of utopian fiction. Both ask their audiences to accept their obvious violations of normal experience as the point of entry into another dimension of existence. More particularly, both seek to achieve their effect on us in the same way, namely, by concealing beneath the work's surreal surface layer an elaborate, precisely drawn architecture—in the painting, an exact geometry of space, and in the fictional work, a methodical dialogue about ideas. The intended effect is, of course, a conjurer's trick, the creation of an illusion. By willingly suspending disbelief, the audience can pass through the work's portal and live for awhile in another dimension of space and time.

The short piece entitled "About the Herasaga," also found in this Back Section, contains an interpretation of the imagery in the three Colville paintings used as cover artwork in this trilogy. No one should regard this brief interpretive exercise as anything else than my own purely idiosyncratic reading of these settings. No claim is made that the painter himself had any such meanings in mind for his creations.

Dr. Don M. Tucker is a professor of psychology at the University of Oregon, and CEO and Chief Scientist of Electrical Geodesics, Inc., a firm based in Eugene, Oregon ♆. This firm supplies high-resolution EEG devices used in brain function research and hosts the Brain Electrophysiology Lab ♆; the website offers links to the many publications by researchers affiliated with the lab. (This field is profiled in the cover photo and lead article in the March 2005 issue of *National Geographic* magazine.) He is the actual author of chapter 5 and of the scientific article linked to www.herasaga.com that forms the basis of that chapter. He also provided advice on the section dealing with the "house of the brain" in chapter 25. His keen enthusiasm for this venture and his willingness to entertain somewhat unusual requests for his assistance is a source of immense satisfaction to me. I also thank Anne Awh of Nashville, Tennessee, who did the three original drawings that appear in chapter 5.

In the course of a pleasant dinner in May 2005 with Patrick and Baiba Morrow of Canmore, Alberta, I received permission to use Pat's photo of the Carstensz Pyramid— taken during his climb to the summit—in the design for the Herasaga logo. Carstensz is one of the famous "seven summits" of mountaineering lore, and Pat's account of his treks up these mountains is told in his book *Beyond Everest* (Camden House, 1986).

Dr. Karen Phillips and Dr. Mike Tyshenko, University of Ottawa, provided expert advice for the sections on reproductive biology and molecular genetics in this volume, for which I am much in their debt. Mike has also given me innumerable briefings on many scientific articles consulted during the writing of this book, and somehow retained his usual cheerful demeanor despite the thankless aspects of this assignment. Neither of them is in any way accountable for the result.

Philip Cercone of Montréal, a dear friend, editor and collaborator during the publication of many of my earlier books, supplied guidance and enthusiastic support to this project from the beginning. Ed Levy of Vancouver, philosopher and entrepreneur, did a detailed and very useful commentary on an early draft. My friend and former student Richard Smith of Bowen Island, BC, provided help with the text as well as with strategies of Internet book marketing. Others who read earlier versions and provided encouragement or suggestions for improvement are Conrad Brunk, Avi Caplan, Kim Curtin, Pat Demers, Taryn Fagerness, Sally Hansen, Holly Mitchell and her parents, Phyllis and Gifford Mitchell, David Ropeik, Marc Saner, Michelle Turner, and Mark L. Winston.

I was a guest in the home of the Vredenburg family of Calgary (Harrie, Jennifer, Jessica, Vanessa, Lauren, and German shepherd Bowen) on many occasions during the years in which this book was written, and I am grateful for the innumerable kindnesses they bestowed. Scarlett Schiaperelli, University of Calgary, provided cheerful and indispensable logistical help for this project throughout its long gestation, expertly producing more than ten complete drafts. I thank also Suzanne Therien, University of Ottawa, for many kinds of administrative assistance during this period. Chad Saunders (Calgary) prepared the "Index and Study Guide" featured on the Herasaga website. Brian Hyde-smith of Winnipeg did the attractive book design and prepared the manuscript for printing; Jenny Gates, also of Winnipeg, provided an expert and painstaking copyediting.

§ § §

Franz Joseph Haydn's oratorio *Die Schöpfung* ("The Creation") was composed between 1796 and 1798. Haydn had delighted in hearing Handel's choral works during a trip to England in the mid-1790s; he was inspired to write *The Creation* after hearing a performance of the *Messiah* ✇. When he was ready to leave England for home, the impresario who had arranged Haydn's own concerts there handed him a libretto entitled "The Creation of the World," which was based on sections of the *Book of Genesis, Psalms,* and Milton's *Paradise Lost.* Haydn brought this English text with him to Vienna, where it was then translated into German, but Haydn actually set the text in both languages. During its first public performance at the Burgtheater in Vienna in March 1799, at the point where the chorus and orchestra together deliver the line "and there was light," the audience rose to its feet with wild applause.

The first performance of Mozart's *Singspiel,* "The Abduction from the Seraglio" *(Die Entführung aus dem Serail),* took place at the Burgtheater in Vienna on July 16, 1782. Mozart is thought to have had a hand in writing the final text of the libretto. The two lines quoted (in my translation) by Hera toward the beginning of chapter 17 occur in the extraordinary Act II duet between Osmin and Blonde that begins *"Ich gehe, doch rate ich dir,"* and in the original German are:

> *O Engländer! Seid ihr nicht Toren*
> *Ihr laßt euern Weibern den Willen!*

Reinbert de Leeuw's recording of *The Early Piano Works* of Erik Satie (1866-1925), referred to in chapter 18, is on Philips CD 462 161-2 ✇.

J. S. Bach's cantata BWV 82 *Ich habe genug* ("I now have enough") was composed for the festival of the Purification of Mary in 1727 and was first performed in Leipzig in that year. The text is by an unknown hand; the English translation of the passage given in chapter 22 is my own. The original German ♫ is as follows:

> *Ach! Möchte mich von meines Leibes Ketten*
> *Der Herr erretten;*
> *Ach! wäre doch mein Abschied hier,*
> *Mit Freuden sagt ich, Welt, zu dir:*
> *Ich habe genug.*

No one who has heard any of the recordings of this work made by the German bass-baritone Dietrich Fischer-Dieskau would be easily satisfied with another rendition, and this is the one (Hannsler CD 94.029, recorded 1983) Hera chooses for herself and Marco in chapter 25; again, the English translation is mine:

> *Schlummert ein, ihr matten Augen*
> *Fallet sanft und selig zu!*
> *Welt, ich bleibe nicht mehr hier*
> *Hab ich doch kein Teil an dir,*
> *Das der Seele könnte taugen.*
> *Hier muß ich das Elend bauen,*
> *Aber dort, dort werd ich schauen*
> *Süßen Friede, stille Ruh.*

Giuseppe Verdi's *Messa da Requiem* ("Requiem Mass") was composed in 1873 in honor of the poet Alessandro Manzoni and first performed in Milan in May 1874. The translation of the Latin text in chapter 23 is from the accompanying notes to the performance directed by Fritz Reiner and featuring the soloists Leontyne Price, Rosalind Elias, Jussi Björling, and Giorgio Tozzi (London CD 444 833-2). The Latin text of the passages quoted is concise and powerful:

Dies irae, dies illa
Solvet saeclum in favilla,
Teste David cum Sibylla.

Quantus tremor est futurus
Quando judex est venturus
Cuncta stricte discussurus.
…

Mors stupebit et natura
Cum resurget creatura
Judicanti responsura.

Judex ergo cum sedebit
Quidquid latet apparebit,
Nil inultum remanebit.

In Vienna's Burgtheater, where in 1782 Mozart's *Abduction from the Seraglio* was first performed, and where Haydn's *The Creation* was presented to the public in 1799, Christoph Willibald von Gluck conducted the première of his opera *Orfeo ed Euridice* (with Italian libretto by Calzabigi) in October 1762. The aria sung by Amor (Cupid) that Hera listens for in Chapter 26 is in Act 1, Scene II; the words of the aria are from the revised French production prepared by Gluck for its first performance in Paris in 1774:

Va trouver Eurydice au séjour de la mort.
Si les doux accents de ta lyre,
Si tes accents mélodieux
Apaisent la fureur des tyrans de ces lieux,
Tu la ramèneras du ténébreux empire.

In the original Italian version, Gluck had written the role of Orfeo for an alto castrato, but he rewrote the French version for high tenor. In the nineteenth century Hector Berlioz reconfigured the role of Orfeo in Gluck's opera once again, this time for a female voice (mezzo-soprano). Today there are recordings in which the role of Amor is also sung by a woman, such as the one conducted by John Eliot Gardiner with Magdalena Kozena as Orphée, Madeline Bender as Eurydice, and Patricia Petibon as Amour (Arthaus Musik DVD 100 062).

Gustav Mahler (1860-1911) composed *Das Lied von der Erde* in 1908, shortly after the death of his eldest daughter and the diagnosis of the heart condition that would contribute to his own untimely death a few years hence. He never heard his immortal work performed, having died a few months before his pupil Bruno Walter conducted its première in Munich in November 1911. An excellent commentary on this piece by Henry-Louis de La Grange is available ✻; La Grange is author of the definitive multi-volume Mahler biography. There is also a lovely picture of the little wooden shack near Toblach ✻, in Austria's South Tyrol, where Mahler worked on his composition during the summer of 1908.

The collection of Chinese poems that are the original source for the text of Mahler's song-cycle date from the eighth century A.D. The original poems are by various authors, but are mostly the work of Li T'ai Po (or Li Bai), whose dates are thought to be A.D. 701-762. They were translated from Chinese first into French, by Marquis d'Hervey St-Denis in 1862 and again by Judith Gautier in 1867. Mahler adapted the German version by Hans Bethge, who had worked with the two French translations, after receiving Bethge's book from a friend as a gift in 1907. When composing *Das Lied von der Erde* during the year 1908, Mahler made his own interesting changes to Bethge's text. The full text in all its variations—the original Chinese, the French translation, Bethge's German version, and the final text that Mahler set to music—may be found online ✻.

"Der Abschied" ("Farewell") is the sixth and last of the pieces in this song-cycle. Mahler, who composed some poetry in his youth, combined two different poems from Bethge's collection for the text of this song, but he himself wrote the words in the short stanza of five lines that brings it to a close. During this final stanza the orchestral accompaniment is hushed, the mood is serene and bittersweet. The German text for the passage quoted at the end of chapter 9 is as follows:

> *Die liebe Erde allüberall*
> *Blüht auf im Lenz und grünt aufs neu!*
> *Allüberall und ewig*
> *Blauen licht die Fernen!*
> *Ewig... Ewig...*

The English translation is my own. In rendering the text I received some useful help from my friend Gernot Böhme of Darmstadt.

Also on the Internet is a good short commentary on this work, as well as an extensive review of some current recordings ✍, by Tony Duggan. "Der Abschied" and two of the earlier songs are almost always performed by the female voice, either mezzo-soprano or contralto, although Mahler had indicated that a baritone could be suitable. (Fischer-Dieskau takes on this role, along with tenor James King and conductor Leonard Bernstein, on Decca CD 466 381 2.) Mahler's *Das Lied* was a signature piece in the career of the distinguished Canadian contralto Maureen Forrester, who sang it under Walter's direction in a live performance in New York in 1960 (unfortunately, there is no currently available CD version sung by her).

The first time that the great English contralto Kathleen Ferrier gave a live performance of this work, under Bruno Walter's direction, she could not sing the last two words in the final song because she was in tears and overcome with emotion. When she apologized to the conductor for what she called her "unprofessionalism," he is reported to have said: "My dear Miss Ferrier, if we were all as professional as you we would all be in tears." At the time when she recorded it with Walter in 1952, now on Decca CD 414 194-2, she already knew that she was dying of breast cancer ᷂.

In the opening piece, entitled "The Drinking-Song of Earth's Sorrow," the tenor soloist has to do battle against the full orchestra. The German text for the stanza referred to in Chapter 24 follows (the translation is mine):

> *Das Firmament blaut ewig und die Erde*
> *Wird lange fest stehen und aufblühn im Lenz.*
> *Du aber, Mensch, wie lang lebst denn du?*
> *Nicht hundert Jahre darfst du dich ergötzen*
> *An all dem morschen Tande dieser Erde!*

For the last stanza, quoted in chapter 27, I have modified the English translation by Emily Ezust ᷂. Mahler's German text is:

> *Seht dort hinaub! Im Mondschein auf den Gräbern*
> *hockt eine wildgespenstische Gestalt—*
> *Ein Aff ist's! Hört ihr, wie sein Heulen hinausgellt*
> *in den süßen Duft des Lebens!*
> *Jetzt nehm den Wein! Jetzt ist es Zeit, Genossen!*
> *Leert eure goldnen Becher zu Grund!*
> *Dunkel ist da Leben, ist der Tod!*

The original Chinese character for the animal referred to in the third line of the stanza is expressed phonetically in English as "yuan." The Chinese original may well have been referring to either gibbons or siamangs, which are classified as lesser apes (*Hylobatidae*) and are—or were—found in

China. The best recent rendition of this song is by the Canadian tenor Ben Heppner, on the recording with conductor Lorin Maazel (RCA Red Seal CD 74321-67957-2).

§   §   §

Some passages from the Bible are cited in the King James version: chapter 4, *Book of Genesis* 1:1-3; chapter 11, *Book of Job* 1:7; chapter 14, *Book of Genesis* 3:2-5 and *Book of Revelation* 14:1; chapter 21, *Psalms* 23. The language of *Book of Zephaniah* 1:18 (chapter 16), *Book of Revelation* 6:1-2 (chapter 18), and *Psalms* 37 (chapter 20) is from the New Revised Standard Version.

For the quotation from John Chadwick's *The Decipherment of Linear B* (Cambridge University Press, 1987), cited in chapter 4, I am indebted to Simon Singh's fascinating volume, *The Code Book* (New York: Doubleday, 1999), page 238. After sketching Hera's dream about the train in Chapter 16, I found in Rohinton Mistry's *A Fine Balance* (Toronto: McClelland & Stewart, 1995), page 164, the account of the trains filled with corpses that Ariadne refers to.

The passage of Milton's poetry quoted in chapters 22 and 27 is from his *Paradise Lost,* Book X, lines 743-5. It forms the epigraph on the title page of Mary Shelley's *Frankenstein: or, the Modern Prometheus,* which was first published in 1818. In Shelley's novel, the being created by Dr. Frankenstein compares himself to Milton's Satan; for a good discussion, see the Preface in Susan Wolfson's edition of *Frankenstein* (New York: Longman, 2002).

Hera's discussion of the bodily basis of the self, found at the end of chapter 25, and the quotation from Nietzsche's *Thus Spake Zarathustra,* are based on Antonio Damasio, *The Feeling of What Happens* (San Diego, CA: Harcourt, Inc., 2000), pp. 143 and 347. In the original German, from section 3 of the Prologue to his *Also Sprach Zarathustra,* Nietzsche's phrase is "Zwitter von Pflanze und von Gespenst."

The species classification scheme alluded to in chapters 25 and 27 is inspired by Jared Diamond's *The Third Chimpanzee* (New York: HarperCollins, 1992) and by John Gribbin and Jeremy Cherfas's *The First Chimpanzee: In Search of Human Origins* (Penguin Science, 2001). Both books propose that humans, gorillas, and chimpanzees should all be grouped together in the genus *Homo*, based on the close similarity of their genomes.

The specific hominoid taxonomy in chapter 27 is adapted from M. Goodman, "The Natural History of the Primates," *American Journal of Human Genetics*, vol. 64 (1999), pp. 31-39. The terminology for the subgenera of *Homo* is adapted from the article by D. E. Wildman *et al.* ☝, "Implications of natural selection in shaping 99.4% nonsynonymous DNA identity between humans and chimpanzees: Enlarging genus *Homo*," *Proceedings of the National Academy of Sciences*, vol. 100, no. 12 (June 10, 2003), pp. 7181-7188. Although Wildman and his co-authors do not include gorillas in the genus *Homo*, they do subdivide the family *Hominidae* more finely than is usually done, grouping both gorillas and humans/chimpanzees in the same "subtribe," slightly distancing both from orangutans (p. 7183): "In terms of observed distances [on the genetic "tree"], humans differ from chimpanzees by 0.9% and each differs from gorillas by 1.0%. Orangutans are slightly more than 2% divergent from each of the African hominids ...."

Other scientists support the idea that humans are a branch of the chimp (or bonobo) clade: Charles A. Lockwood, William H. Kimbel, and John M. Lynch, "Morphometrics and hominoid phylogeny: Support for a chimpanzee–human clade and differentiation among great ape subspecies," *Proceedings of the National Academy of Sciences*, vol. 101, no. 13 (March 30, 2004), pp. 4356-4360 ☝. See also K. Semendeferi, A. Lu, N. Schenker, and H. Damasio,

"Humans and great apes share a large frontal cortex," *Nature Neurosciences,* vol. 5, no. 3 (March 2002), pp. 272-6.

The discovery of *Homo floresiensis* was reported in P. Brown et al., "A new small-bodied hominin from the Late Pleistocene of Flores, Indonesia," *Nature,* vol. 431 (28 October 2004), pp. 1055-1061. See also K. Harvati *et al.,* "Neanderthal taxonomy reconsidered: Implications of 3D primate models of intra- and interspecific differences," *Proceedings of the National Academy of Sciences* ⌘, vol. 101, no. 5 (February 3, 2004), pp. 1147-1152.

Hera's remark about the "famous case of a high-functioning autistic" in chapter 25 can be explored further in the chapter "An Anthropologist on Mars" in Oliver Sacks' book of the same title (New York: Vintage Books, 1996), and in the three volumes by Dr. Temple Grandin, who is the subject of Sacks' study: *Emergence: Labeled Autistic* (with Margaret Scariano, New York: Warner Books, 1996); *Thinking in Pictures* (New York: Vintage Books, 1996); and *Animals in Translation* (with Catherine Johnson, New York: Scribner, 2005). There is also the remarkable novel about a high-functioning autistic child by Mark Haddon, *The Curious Incident of the Dog in the Night-time* (Toronto: Doubleday Canada, 2002).

ABOUT THE HERASAGA

BOOK ONE: *Hera, or Empathy*
BOOK TWO: *The Priesthood of Science*
BOOK THREE: *Hera the Buddha*

Thematic Outline:
The Way of Reflection on mind's relation to nature passes through the moments of submission (religion) and dominion (technology) toward its goal—mind's peace with nature.

Since the beginnings of human civilization 6,000 years ago in the Near East—in Egypt and Mesopotamia—Mind (human thinking) has been at war with Nature in two vastly different but complementary forms, namely, religion and technology. In both of these forms, Nature is nothing in itself, simply a background field of matter and energy onto which human meaning and power is projected and imposed.

Represented systematically, this process develops as follows:

Positing: The religious representation of reality posits Nature passively, not self-originating, as created by Absolute Spirit or God, in which Mind participates derivatively as Soul.

Negation: In order to fulfill itself as technology, Mind posits Nature as the Other to itself, merely "mindless" matter and energy governed by laws, and in this way finally unlocks the secrets of its own self-origins as Nature (that is, as the product of DNA's evolution).

Negation of negation: Mind dissolves Spirit and understands itself as natural, as a product of nature, and thus as limited in time, not infinite or absolute.

Book One. Hera, or Empathy:

The cover artwork, Colville's "Church and Horse" (1964), shows nature in opposition to the religious representation of reality, in which nature is the passive outcome of an act of creation. Here religion is portrayed as a lifeless empty façade (the building) and broken domain (the gate), and is juxtaposed to the fierce energy and determination of the living, riderless animal that moves menacingly toward the standpoint of the viewer, unstoppably away and out.

Book Two. The Priesthood of Science:

The cover artwork, Colville's "Horse and Train" (1954), shows human technology in its head-on confrontation with a vastly more powerful, living nature. The horse, again riderless and uncontrolled, moving away from the viewer, paradoxically towering in size over the train and opposing itself fearlessly to it, sets itself squarely upon the tracks, eschewing the surrounding fields.

Book Three. Hera the Buddha:

The cover artwork, Colville's "Moon and Cow" (1963), shows a much-domesticated animal—which is thus itself both a human creation yet still also living nature—at rest in the night, after a long day of her labors in the service of human needs (but with no human masters now present), facing away from the viewer, at peace with nature.